Praise for Traci Hall and her Scottish mysteries!

MURDER IN A SCOTTISH GARDEN

"Inquisitive and down-to-earth, Paislee makes a charming sleuth in this suspect-packed mystery."
—*Kirkus Reviews*

"In her second Scottish Shire mystery, Hall capably juggles multiple story lines and vividly evokes the Scottish backdrop."
—*Booklist*

MURDER AT A SCOTTISH SOCIAL

"Witty characters match the well-crafted plot. . . . Cozy fans will want to see a lot more of the compassionate Paislee."
—*Publishers Weekly*

"Our heroine solves her mysteries with aplomb against a delightful Scottish background replete with good friends and a loyal dog."
—*Kirkus Reviews*

Books by Traci Hall

MURDER IN A SCOTTISH SHIRE
MURDER IN A SCOTTISH GARDEN
MURDER AT A SCOTTISH SOCIAL
MURDER AT A SCOTTISH WEDDING

And writing as Traci Wilton

MRS. MORRIS AND THE GHOST
MRS. MORRIS AND THE WITCH
MRS. MORRIS AND THE GHOST OF CHRISTMAS PAST
MRS. MORRIS AND THE SORCERESS
MRS. MORRIS AND THE VAMPIRE
MRS. MORRIS AND THE POT OF GOLD

Published by Kensington Publishing Corp.

Murder
at a
Scottish
Wedding

TRACI HALL

Kensington Publishing Corp.
www.kensingtonbooks.com

KENSINGTON BOOKS are published by

Kensington Publishing Corp.
119 West 40th Street
New York, NY 10018

ISBN: 978-1-4967-3925-4 (ebook)

ISBN: 978-1-4967-3924-7

First Kensington Trade Paperback Printing: February 2023

10 9 8 7 6 5 4 3 2 1

Printed in the United States of America

I'd like to dedicate this book to Christopher Hawke, *husband*. We prepped for our own wedding as I wrote this, which made it surreal.
I love you so much and I'm glad that our beach wedding had none of the drama of a murder to solve, but was more of a romance, with a happy-ever-after!

Acknowledgments

I would like to thank my editor, John Scognamiglio. This series would not exist without him giving me a chance.

Thank you, Evan Marshall, best agent ever, hands down.

My mom is my first reader, and a close second is Sheryl McGavin. It takes a team to make a story really shine and I am so grateful to have such dynamic folks around me.

Thank you to the crew at Kensington, from the cover artist to the copy editor. Thank you, thank you!

Chapter 1

A light *ratatat* sounded on the dressing room door in Old Nairn Kirk, and Paislee peered over her shoulder at her best friend to see if she'd heard it, too. Lydia Barron, fifteen minutes away from walking down the aisle to be Mrs. Corbin Smythe, had started her special day with yoga on the beach. Mimosas. *Om.* She had focused on the joy of marrying her soul mate, which would make the nightmare of the past twelve months worthwhile.

All signs of the Zen bride were eradicated as her bonnie bestie shoved tissues and hairpins across the crowded vanity with searing curses. Her muttered oaths were sure to burn the church down around their coiffed ears.

"Should I answer the do—" Paislee began.

"Wait!" Lydia lifted her bridal bouquet in the holder, examined the space around it, and returned it with a *plonk.* The red roses trembled. "I cannae wed Corbin withoot that brooch. Minister Angela placed the box right there." She pointed a slender arm, the silver gown capped at her shoulders, as fragile as a Victorian heroine. Caramel curls framed her perfectly made-up face. "It has tae be here!"

Paislee had searched every inch of the room for the dark

wooden box containing the pin, but it had vanished like a ghost at dawn.

Corbin had chosen the Luckenbooth brooch for Lydia as a betrothal gift from the family coffers, and pandemonium had ensued within the Smythe clan. It seemed the double-heart-shaped pin had a history unknown to him and was supposed to bring bad luck if the bride wasn't the right one for the groom—and Mary, his stepmother, had her doubts that Lydia was on par.

"We'll find it. It has tae be here." Paislee spoke in a calm tone she used to soothe her son, Brody, when he was hurt. She stepped toward the door after a second, more insistent, knock. "Maybe this is news."

"If it's the wedding photographer again, tell him enough already!" Getting hitched hadn't been an easy road for Lydia but she'd managed most of it with grace. She was only human for the few times she'd cracked under pressure. The orbs of Lydia's gray eyes grew wild. "I shoulda eloped with Corbin, and the family be damned."

Paislee remembered the panicked call she'd gotten a year ago from Lydia when Corbin had asked her to elope. Lydia had tried to break the relationship off completely, but Corbin wouldn't have it. He loved her—she loved him. They'd told Lydia's parents, Alistair and Sophie Barron, who'd suggested a wee church wedding so they could celebrate her happy day. Nothing grand necessary, they simply wanted to witness Lydia and Corbin's joy together.

Mary Smythe, Corbin's stepmother, fussed and complained. In the end, it was decided that if Corbin was determined to marry a divorcee, then he would, by God, do it right. They insisted on their family church, Old Nairn Kirk. The historic building had a tall Gothic spire and room for two hundred. The Smythe clan packed the pews.

"It's almost over," Paislee said, her fingers on the doorknob. "What's the worst that can happen now?" She regretted the question immediately.

Lydia wrung her hands. "Mary dislikes me and uses that brooch tae cause trouble. I've heard her spur the girls on. I have tae do this right, and then, and then . . ."

Paislee hated for confident Lydia to be so overcome. She opened the door a crack to see who it was and then widened it with relief. Lydia's father, an average-looking man of fifty-five, smiled worriedly. "Matthew's askin' if we're ready, pet." Alistair peered into the room.

Matthew Dalrymple was Corbin's best man. The other grooms-men were his three brothers. Paislee was Lydia's matron of honor, and her bridesmaids were Corbin's stepsisters, Rosebud and Hy-acinth, and a Smythe cousin. There'd been a drawing among the many girls and Senta had won.

"Did ye find the brooch, Da?"

"Not yet, love. The lasses are askin', discreet as they can."

By lasses, he meant bridesmaids. The guests were already seated but none of the wedding party had yet made it to the altar or things would really be awkward. Paislee's son, Brody, sat with Lydia's mother, and Paislee's grandfather, Angus, on the bride's section.

Paislee was the only one Lydia had chosen for herself, and she wasn't budging from her best friend's side. Alistair, in a tidy kilt of navy blue with black and silver accents, entered the room fully. The silver matched Lydia's silk gown.

Alistair often joked that he and Mrs. Barron were plain Janes blessed with a changeling for a daughter, who was all things beauti-ful and kind. He put his steady hand on Lydia's lower back. "Think tae where ye saw it last."

"Aye. That's a guid idea—retrace me steps." Lydia glanced at Paislee and then her dad. "The bridal party was crammed in here getting all dolled up with the makeup artist."

There'd been six altogether. Paislee gestured to the vanity. "The minister brought in the box with a handwritten note for Lydia, wishing her luck."

"Mary offered tae have the brooch professionally cleaned." Lydia touched the diamond engagement ring on her finger. The couple was going to exchange platinum bands at the altar. "It's agony that Corbin is at odds with his family over me. It's bad enough I'm divorced. I didnae have a title, or family money." She gave an annoyed snort. "Sairy, Da."

"No offense taken here," Alistair said gruffly. "Ye've done quite well for yourself, and your mum and I are that proud."

Harlow Becker entered the room. "Ye find it?" The lass was barely twenty and dating the youngest Smythe brother, Drew. Her fine features and bright blue eyes conveyed a delicate prettiness; her family was old railroad money. She'd been welcomed with open arms, unlike Lydia. She was also a friend of Hyacinth's, who must have enlisted her help in the search.

"No," Lydia said, her voice shaking.

Harlow's gaze took in the messy vanity top before returning to Lydia. "Matthew wants tae know what the holdup is."

"We cannae worry Corbin." Lydia paced the room, arms crossed.

"We had tae tell the boys something"—Harlow shrugged—"so Rosebud said you suffered a case of nerves."

At that, Lydia raised her chin. "I do *not* have nerves. I want tae marry Corbin."

"So, forget the pin," Alistair suggested. "It's not that important."

Lydia whirled toward her father. "He willnae want tae marry *me*, if I didnae have it!"

"He does, too!" Paislee said. It was his stepmother stirring the pot about bad luck.

"*He* wants tae," Lydia conceded, "but it will be World War III if I didnae have the Luckenbooth pin attached tae the Smythe plaid ribbon in my flowers. During the dress rehearsal, Mary strongly hinted that Corbin should replace the brooch with another, but he didnae, out of principle."

Alistair's expression grew concerned. "Is the brooch expensive? The Luckenbooth I gave your mum was silver. We can buy another."

"You're sweet, Da, but this one is gold, and been in the family for generations. Mary feared I would lose it." Lydia groaned. "And now look!"

Harlow snickered—not without sympathy. "Here come Rosebud and Hyacinth," she said. "They dinnae seem hopeful. Senta either."

Alistair stayed in the dressing room as the other bridesmaids filed in. It was a sea of red, blue, and black fabric with Lydia as the silver star of the show. Not white, because it wasn't her first marriage, and Mary had advised another color . . . for Lydia's own good. Paislee had never met a more superstitious woman than Corbin's stepmother.

Lydia had a silver horseshoe, blue thistle, and a sprig of heather to go along with the Luckenbooth pin. She'd agreed not to wear white and signed a prenup that if Corbin and Lydia divorced within five years, she would forfeit any rights to the Smythe fortune. The brooch would be returned to the family.

Lydia hadn't told her parents of the rude treatment, they only wanted for their daughter to be happy, but Paislee knew all the dirty details. Corbin had reminded Lydia often that he'd wanted to elope for a reason. He'd watched the fuss his older brothers had gone through, and that was with brides the family approved.

"The box was next tae your bouquet," Senta said. Her ebony hair was in a loose bun, the soft red gown flattering to her slim figure. "With an ivory ribbon. Right, Hyacinth?"

"Aye. Mum wanted it tae be special, Lydia." Hyacinth's light brown brow arched in a superior manner.

"Neither the box nor the pin is in this room." Paislee stepped between Lydia and Hyacinth, staring the girl backward toward the door. Rosebud tilted her nose with a sniff. Paislee didn't understand their antagonism toward Lydia, but she wouldn't tolerate anything besides rainbows and sunshine until Lydia was wed to her man.

Lydia smoothed the beads on her designer gown. The unique style, and color, was sure to be copied by other summer brides—if, no, *when* they got her down the aisle.

"Let's ask the wedding coordinator if anything's been turned in," Paislee suggested. Perhaps the box had gotten snagged in fabric and flowers when they'd dashed out for photos with Bruce Dundas, the wedding photographer, in the courtyard by a picturesque alder tree.

"I'll go!" Harlow said. "People are gettin' antsy." She hurried out of the room, slamming the door. A row of holders along the wall with the bridesmaids' bouquets—blue thistle, red roses, and the Smythe plaid ribbon—shook. Alistair righted one before it fell.

Paislee's main duty as matron of honor was to make sure Lydia was all right. She rooted through the makeup kit that Lydia had brought from home for anything resembling the antique Luckenbooth pin. She knew it was gold but had personally only laid eyes on it twice before Mary had asked for it back, to be professionally cleaned. Two hearts entwined. A red stone. Ruby that Corbin had chosen for Lydia because it was her birthstone.

The wooden box delivered this afternoon had been heavy, so it didn't make sense for it to be caught up in tulle without noticing. She hated to think someone, like one of Corbin's stepsisters, might have hidden it to create drama but she also wouldn't put it past the spoiled girls. Hyacinth was twenty, and Rosebud nineteen. Their mother behaved as if they were related to the king instead of token nobility. Landing Laird Garrison Smythe, Corbin's dad, had been a feather in her cap and now Mary watched with an eagle eye to ensure her daughters got their fair share.

"Will this work?" Paislee lifted a colorful butterfly pin she'd found among the lipsticks.

Lydia crossed the room and held it to the light, then eyed her bouquet. "No. Mary willnae be fooled."

"Nobody truly believes ye willnae marry Corbin withoot it, do they, love?" Alistair fiddled nervously with a button on his silver vest. The pouch on the front of his kilt, the sporran, was black leather.

"Oh, she cannae," Rosebud said in all seriousness. Her light brown hair had been pulled back in a tight bun, with wisps to fall around her cheeks. "The marriage will be doomed. We didnae want tae tell ye, Lydia, but Mum had her psychic friend cleanse the brooch with sage smoke, then blessed by the minister, tae free it of the curse. I simply cannae believe it's gone!"

"It's a sign from above." Hyacinth glanced at the ceiling and her long braid shifted to the side.

Curse! "I'll tell ye what's a sign." Paislee strode toward Rosebud with indignant anger. "Lydia has jumped through every hoop for your family because of her love for Corbin. *That* is what matters—not some pin!"

Rosebud smirked.

"Here, here," Alistair echoed. "What hoops, pet?"

"It's nothing, Da. Paislee, help me put this butterfly on the ribbon?"

Paislee knelt before the bouquet, her lightweight thistle-blue dress pooling around her legs, and fixed the pin to the ribbon so that just a hint of the enamel wing showed. "There."

"It will have tae do," Senta said. "I dinnae blame you for ignoring their grumbles, Lydia. You're marrying up." She flushed as if she'd just remembered Alistair was still in the room.

The sisters turned on their cousin. "It's terrible luck tae not use the blessed brooch," Rosebud said.

Hyacinth plucked her red rose and blue thistle bouquet from the holder, then handed Rosebud's to her, leaving Senta to reach for her own in a silly snub.

"I dinnae care aboot money or station." Lydia gritted her teeth. "I love Corbin and pray someday we can laugh aboot this, but right now? I dinnae see it."

"Laughter is verra important in a marriage," Alistair agreed. Paislee read his wariness as he tried to navigate the undercurrents in the dressing room.

Paislee peeped into the hall to see the wedding coordinator hustling toward them with Harlow at her side. Eliza Wilbur was from the Caribbean and dressed in bright colors. Today's skirt and blouse were cerulean blue with orange accents.

"What's wrong?" Eliza asked as soon as she was inside the dressing room. "Darling Lydia, what can I do? Your groom is waiting for you and sends his love and encouragement. You have the nerves?" She shook her hands as if to show Lydia how to release negative energy.

"I dinnae have nerves!" Lydia exclaimed. "I also dinnae have the brooch his stepmother gave me."

"Ah!" Eliza raised a finger. She'd picked up enough undertones over the last few months to realize that this was a big deal. She immediately got on her knees to examine beneath the table, then lifted the box of tissues, the flowers, and the little mirror. All places Lydia and Paislee had repeatedly checked.

"Could you please let Corbin know aboot the brooch?" Lydia asked. "Mibbe I should go see him myself." She stepped toward the open door.

"No!" the ladies exclaimed in unison.

"Talk aboot bad luck," Rosebud sniffed. "It's like you're not even *trying*, Lydia."

Paislee glared at the younger lass, who had the intelligence to look away. Lydia had done so much more than just try.

Eliza scanned the dressing room once more but finally nodded. "Yes. I'll tell him what the problem is, but I am quite sure he just wants to marry *you*."

"There's more tae it than that." Lydia explained that they had a different pin as camouflage if Corbin was all right with the ruse. Mary would know once she was close enough. She looked at his stepsisters as she said, "I dinnae believe in curses."

"Curse? Oh, no." Eliza clucked her tongue, then admired the pin on the ribbon. "Today is a beautiful day for your wedding. I'll be right back. Come with me, Harlow. You can alert the guests that we are about to begin."

Paislee clasped Lydia's hand. "You ready, hon?"

"I am." Lydia breathed out. *One, two, three.* "I had tae let him know. I cannae start off my marriage with a lie."

"What he doesnae know cannae hurt him," Senta advised.

"Corbin will not go through with it," Rosebud said. "Mum warned him what would happen if he married you withoot everything just so."

When this was all over, Paislee was tempted to stop by for a one-on-one visit with Mary Smythe. The woman was a menace.

Eliza returned with a folded paper that she slipped to Lydia. Her best friend opened the note with a pent-up breath, then her shoulders relaxed, and she burst out laughing.

Paislee read the note that Lydia handed her. *If you aren't down the aisle in the next five minutes, I'll run off with you. Scandal, curse, whatever. Your call, Lydia. Corbin.*

"The wedding is on!" Lydia exclaimed with bright eyes.

"Wonderful." Eliza hurried out, skirts swinging. "I'll inform the band."

The wedding march sounded, and the bridesmaids left the dressing room to take the arm of the accompanying groomsman. Each man wore a magnificent kilt of red, blue, and black with silver accents. The sporrans were of black leather. The bridesmaids' ribbons on their bouquets matched the kilts. Drew, the baby, escorted Senta. Duncan, the "spare," escorted Rosebud, and Reggie, the heir, hooked arms with Hyacinth.

Paislee watched the others through the partially opened door. "It's beautiful, Lydia." She turned to her friend. The harp melded with the bagpipe and the sound echoed harmoniously around the stones of the old church.

"Really?"

"Aye." For the first time in months, Paislee detected true happiness on Lydia's face. She blinked back tears. "I'd ask if you're sure he's the one, but I can see it."

"He is," Lydia said. "And worth a million evil stepmothers. Remind me of this moment, eh?"

Paislee used her mobile to click a photo of her best friend's wide grin. "Got it!"

She tucked her phone into her wristlet—a purse just big enough for her mobile, credit card, and lip gloss—in the bottom drawer of the vanity, grabbed her bouquet, and stepped past Alistair to the lobby. A June breeze wafted in through the slightly open front doors—a must, or else the building would be too stuffy for the two hundred guests.

Matthew, a blue thistle boutonniere attached to his light gray jacket lapel, held out his arm for Paislee. Joy shone around Corbin from his position near the altar like a halo.

"Ready?" Matthew asked. "Corbin's chuffed. Makes me want tae believe in marital bliss when I see him so in love with Lydia."

"She's ecstatic, too," Paislee assured Corbin's best friend. They'd become allies over the past few months of wedding preparation in getting their pals married.

The door of the restroom next to the dressing room banged open and a young woman with ebony hair charged between Alistair, Paislee, and Matthew. The slightly large nose on her pale face seconded her status as a Smythe cousin, confirmed by the red tartan shawl drooping from her shoulders.

"Excuse me, excuse me," she said, barreling toward the front entrance of the church. The bathroom door slammed shut.

"Are you all right, Felice?" Paislee recognized the young woman from the pre-wedding festivities. She often hung out with Rosebud and Hyacinth, giggling.

"I cannae see!" Felice covered her eyes with her palm, her tone panicked.

"Where are ye off tae?" Matthew released Paislee's arm in alarm and followed the young lady. "The wedding's aboot tae begin."

Felice wrestled the closest door all the way open, crying as if in pain. She exited, tripping on the stone threshold. Matthew tried to grab her elbow, but she flailed and knocked him away.

Alistair joined Paislee with concern. His duty was to his daughter, so he stayed near the dressing room door, but it was clear by his stance that he was torn. His nature was to help.

"What is it?" Lydia asked from the doorway. She held her bouquet before her and glanced from the commotion with Felice, to the altar in the opposite direction, and the guests inside all standing, waiting for the bride.

This was not rainbows and sunshine. "Give me a second!" Paislee hurried toward the church entrance to assist Matthew.

"Felice, stop!" Matthew shouted.

Paislee accidentally jostled Matthew on the stoop. Two dozen steep stairs descended to the cobble street where cars weren't allowed to park. Felice's nose was splotchy, and she blinked rapidly.

"Help me!" Felice whirled her arms and teetered on the top stone step.

Matthew reached for her and snagged her Smythe tartan, but it wasn't enough to stop Felice from tumbling down. She landed at the bottom on her back, her neck at an odd angle. Silent.

"No!" Paislee's stomach knotted.

"What on earth?" Alistair bellowed from the stoop. Lydia, on his heels, stared down at the broken body. Ebony hair spilled to the side. "Go tae the room, love," he said, urging Lydia backward.

Lydia shook her head in disbelief. "No. Impossible."

Matthew pulled his mobile from a pocket in his vest and dialed for emergency services. "Felice Smythe has fallen down the stairs at Old Nairn Kirk. Come around the front."

Paislee dropped her bouquet and climbed down in a rush, slipping on the stone, but catching her balance before hopping over the last two steps to the sidewalk. She leaned next to Felice and took her pulse at her right wrist. Nothing.

She gasped. Something gold glinted in Felice's left hand.

Lydia's missing Luckenbooth brooch.

Chapter 2

Paislee remained on her knees, tempted to retrieve the Luckenbooth brooch from Felice's open hand and return it to Lydia. Entwined hearts, a red stone. She didn't, feeling in her bones that something was wrong and that the police might need to be involved. Nothing could be right about a young woman falling to her death at a wedding.

She stood on shaky legs. Matthew clambered down the stone stairs. "Paislee, is she . . . ?"

Swallowing hard, Paislee didn't answer Matthew as she looked up. She recognized Harry, Corbin's uncle, and more Smythe cousins with ebony hair directly behind Matthew.

"What? Felice!" Harry shoved Matthew aside to kneel by his daughter, only in his shock, he sprawled on his hip as if to gather her into his arms. He stopped, realizing her neck was at an odd angle. His semi-lined face paled of all color. "Oh, God."

"Felice?"

Matthew hauled a tall young man back from grabbing Felice. "Oliver, mate, ye cannae touch her. The paramedics are on the way. Jocelyn, leave your sister be. I'm so sairy."

Poor dears were Felice's siblings. It was too late for an ambulance though the blare of sirens could be heard.

"Is that a Luckenbooth pin?" Jocelyn swiped big tears from her cheeks and her teeth chattered as she hovered by her sister, uncertain. "Wasnae Lydia missin' hers?"

Oliver's nose turned red. "Dinnae be daft. Felice wouldnae have taken it."

Harry smoothed the hair back from Felice's forehead. "What's wrong with her skin?"

The prickled spots around her eyes reminded Paislee of a heat rash. While it was a warm afternoon, it wasn't hot enough for that.

"Don't know." Jocelyn lowered herself to the ground and patted her sister's arm. She sniffed, sad, but also a wee bit put out. "Her and Rosebud were crackin' up. I asked aboot what, and she told me tae mind me own business."

"When was this?" Paislee asked.

Gaze dull with sorrow, Jocelyn said, "Before you all went oot for pictures with the photographer. Felice was jealous of Senta. She wanted tae be a bridesmaid, too."

Harry's chest heaved with emotion as he stared at Felice in disbelief. "What happened tae my sweet lassie?"

Felice and Rosebud, laughing over something. Had Felice swiped Lydia's brooch? Encouraged by Rosebud? A prank, most like, just as Paislee had feared.

Jocelyn reached for the brooch, but Matthew cleared his throat, glancing at Paislee. "You should probably leave it for the police tae sort."

So, he had also sensed more to the story though she wasn't surprised. Matthew was a solicitor in Edinburgh. He and Corbin had met at university and remained friends despite Corbin moving away from law to pursue the tech industry, and work for himself.

"Police?" Oliver dug his fingers in the back of his dark hair.

The police car arrived just ahead of the ambulance and parked in the middle of the street. The EMTs jumped out first and brushed by the family surrounding Felice. "Stand back, please," a medic said.

Paislee edged away and looked up at the people collected in the foyer of the stone church—both doors were now wide open. Lydia waited on the stoop, peering down. Minister Angela descended the stairs, robes billowing around her thin frame, as she murmured a prayer for the deceased.

Paislee raced up the steps to Lydia, who clasped Paislee's hand. "Da went tae check on Mum. What happened?"

"Felice Smythe fell," Paislee whispered. "Her neck is twisted. Lydia—she was holding a gold Luckenbooth pin."

"What?" Lydia scowled but it was fear-based, not angry. "Was it mine?"

"It was gold with a red stone. I can't be sure but what are the chances of yours going missing and her turning up with one not being related somehow?"

"Oh, lordy, lordy." Lydia's lower lip quivered.

Corbin strode toward them, kilt swinging, followed by Garrison. Father and son joined them with curious yet cautious gazes. Corbin noticed Felice sprawled on the street and his body bowed.

"I . . . I was worried something had happened tae you." Corbin slid his arm around Lydia. "Poor Felice."

"Damn it," Garrison blustered. "Did Felice slip?"

Mary arrived with a screech as she brought her hand to her mouth, then pointed her finger at Lydia. Her dyed platinum hair had been styled in a net with a blue thistle tucked above her ear, her plump body stuffed into a too-small Smythe-tartan skirt, topped with a silk blouse. "Rosebud said ye lost the brooch! I warned you aboot the curse."

"There is no bloody curse!" Corbin shouted at his stepmother. "Now is no' the time for your superstitious nonsense."

And yet, his cousin was being hauled away in the ambulance—already dead. Garrison raised a brow at Corbin, then left to join Harry, his brother, his face twisted in grief for the loss of his niece.

"Felice had my brooch," Lydia murmured to Corbin. "Paislee said it was in her palm."

"How could that be?" Corbin demanded. "My cousin had no reason tae steal it."

"I just know what I saw," Paislee said. She wouldn't mention

Rosebud and Felice being in cahoots until she had more information. "Gold. Two hearts entwined. Red stone."

Corbin winced. "It sounds like the one I chose, which was unique, like Lydia. No offense, but I really wish I'd forgone Smythe Luckenbooth tradition and kept the engagement at your diamond and champagne." He kissed Lydia's ring finger. "What a mess."

Lydia leaned into Corbin, ignoring Mary, who glowered at them.

Constable Payne's burly figure had exited the police car, his tablet in hand as he prepared to ask questions. Relief filled Paislee to see his familiar presence. A second female officer, Payne's opposite from her pale skin to trim figure, took pictures. She put on gloves, pulled out a clear plastic bag, and deposited the brooch Felice had held into it. At last, the constable allowed the medics to load Felice's body onto the stretcher.

Harry, Jocelyn, and Oliver crowded the gurney. Jocelyn's chin quivered. "Can I ride with her, Da? Sis shouldnae be alone."

Oliver held his father as Harry's knees buckled. "Aye." He straightened. "We'll meet at the hospital."

The medics loaded the gurney into the back and Jocelyn climbed in behind. The sirens weren't on. There was no need to hurry. Paislee pressed her hand to her knotted stomach. *Poor Felice.*

"I have tae tell the constable about the brooch," Paislee said. "It might be important."

"I'll go with you." Corbin grimaced with pain as his uncle Harry crumpled to the ground. Garrison, Oliver, and Corbin's brothers gathered around him.

Paislee glanced at the church, the stoop and lobby even more crowded, but she didn't see either Brody or Grandpa.

"The wedding is off," Lydia said, her gray eyes stunned. "It has tae be." She viewed Corbin through a veil of tears. "I'm so sairy for your loss, Corbin. The entire clan will be gutted aboot Felice."

Corbin folded Lydia into his arms and caressed her back. "You're right. We should have—"

"Don't you dare say we should have eloped!" Lydia cried, her fist to his chest. She pulled back and exhaled. "I'll go inside tae our family, Paislee. Find me there?" She left them, silver wedding gown trailing behind her.

Paislee's instincts urged her to stay with Lydia, who was hurting no matter the brave face she'd just donned. However, Corbin took Paislee by the elbow and guided her down the stone steps to the cobbled street as the ambulance pulled away.

"And then we heard Felice cry oot that she couldnae see," Oliver said to Constable Payne, "from the lobby. Da was worried that she'd been gone so long in the restroom and might miss the wedding. Jocelyn refused tae go check on her." He shrugged with empathy. "Felice and Rosebud are mean tae her sometimes when they dinnae want her around."

Corbin dragged Paislee next to him.

"Tell me aboot the Luckenbooth pin in Felice's hand," the constable said. Deep laugh lines grooved around his mouth, though he wasn't joking now. He'd told her once that it was better to laugh than cry.

Paislee sighed. "Lydia's went missing sometime after the minister brought it tae the room, and we were out getting wedding photos by the tree." Should she mention what Jocelyn had said about Rosebud and Felice laughing?

"Why would Felice have it?" Constable Payne tipped back the brim of his black hat.

"Mibbe," Oliver suggested, "she found it and was returning it tae Lydia, but then she got confused and fell down the stairs."

And maybe, Paislee thought, Santa would arrive any second on this braw June day with his reindeer and a sleigh filled with elves.

Constable Payne tapped the stylus to his tablet, then phoned the ambulance driver, walking away for privacy.

Paislee made out "missing brooch," but that was all.

"There has tae be a guid reason. Our girl isnae a thief." Harry stared at Corbin. "You've known Felice all yer life. You cousins ran in a pack. Always been family first."

"I'm no' accusing her of anything, Uncle Harry. We'll sort oot what happened tae Felice." Corbin hugged Harry and then Oliver as the gruff Scotsmen allowed several tears to escape.

"Can we go tae the hospital now?" Oliver asked the police officer who was helping Constable Payne. The middle-aged woman's tag read CONSTABLE SARAH MONROE. Red hair was barely visible beneath her shiny black cap.

"Aye. Drive safe," Constable Monroe said. "Speedin' will only put yourselves in harm." The tone was warm, like a mum's might be, as she gave a slight nod.

Harry pulled keys from the sporran on his kilt and grabbed Oliver's upper arm, running around the side of the church to the car park.

"What did you see, Paislee?" Constable Payne asked when he returned.

She told him, ending with, "Felice was scratching at her eyes, and the skin was red and splotchy."

"The coroner will run a toxicology report in case she was on somethin'." The constable glanced around to make sure Felice's immediate family was out of earshot. "You never know these days what kids will do for a kick. Now, what else can you tell me aboot the brooch?"

"It was given tae Lydia today, in a wooden box. Before she could open it, we were called away by the wedding photographer."

"Who is that?" Constable Payne asked.

"Bruce Dundas," Corbin said. "He's been recording special events for our family since I was born."

"Wedding photos by the alder tree in the courtyard are a social media must, according tae Bruce." Paislee wrinkled her nose. "Anyway, I saw the box before we left the dressing room, but I'd honestly forgotten about it when we returned. By the time Lydia remembered the pin, we couldn't find it anywhere."

"Did Felice have the box?" Constable Payne jotted notes with his stylus.

"Not that I saw. She didn't have her purse with her." Paislee rubbed her arms, overcome with a chill despite the blue skies. Life was a precious thing and there were no guarantees. "She came out of the loo, though. Maybe the box is there."

Constable Payne gestured to Constable Monroe. "Head upstairs tae the lavatory, would you?"

"Aye." The officer jerked her chin toward the patrol car. "Might I have a word?"

"Sure." Constable Payne joined her in a whispered huddle.

When they finished, Constable Monroe opened the boot and loaded her arms with supplies, then hurried before them up the stairs. What had they discussed?

Constable Payne, his expression neutral, returned. "While Monroe checks the WC, show me where Felice and her family sat," he said.

They all climbed the stone steps, entering the church where two hundred guests waited for a wedding that wasn't going to happen. Constable Monroe was inside the single-stall bathroom, noisily shifting things around. The dressing room door next to it was closed. Nerves buzzed through Paislee's body.

Constable Payne urged her out of the lobby to the interior of the church. Dozens of long pews filled the space, but she zeroed in on where her family had been sitting.

Brody's eyes lit and he darted away from Grandpa's side to hers. Halfway through the P7 schoolyear he'd shot up six inches and was now all knees and elbows, with thick auburn hair. "Mum!"

"It's all right, love." Paislee squeezed his shoulders as they walked toward Corbin, Matthew, and the constable. Grandpa sidled to the end of the wooden pew, concern in his brown eyes behind the black frames of his glasses. In the last year, he'd grown healthier and filled out his suit jacket and kilt.

The band had stopped playing. Minister Angela floated down the aisle to where they stood. "I put Lydia and her parents in the dressing room with a dram." She exhaled, her brow heavy with sadness. "What now?"

A dram sounded perfect to Paislee, who didn't usually drink. Another death in Nairn was cause for a nip of strong Scotch whisky.

Mary, a few flyaway platinum strands freed of the hair netting, had her arms around her daughters—Rosebud on the right, and Hyacinth on the left—as she butted into the circle. Hyacinth held her bridesmaid's bouquet, and Rosebud her mobile phone. Garrison, broad of shoulder from his work on the family property, stood behind them.

"Corbin, son, what do you want tae do?" Garrison asked.

Corbin put his hands behind his back as he surveyed the milling guests. "I don't know yet. We're discussing what happened with Constable Payne."

"I heard Felice's neck broke." Hyacinth's flowers shook in her grip.

Rosebud's mouth flattened. "*Broke?*"

Constable Payne dipped his head. "We will find oot how this tragedy occurred."

"The steps are slippery after a rain, aye, but the weather's been dry." The minister's tone conveyed anguish at one of her flock dead on the church cobblestones.

"Somethin' was bothering her eyes. Right, Paislee?" Matthew tucked his phone in his vest pocket.

"Aye. Felice said she couldn't see." Paislee studied Rosebud for a reaction of some kind, but the girl was looking at her mobile.

"That doesnae make sense," Hyacinth said. "I mean, it *is* dusty in this old church. Could that be it?"

"Hardly that!" the minister said, offended. "We have several volunteers who clean the church daily."

Paislee recalled her last brush with death. "Could it be an allergy tae something? The candles, or flowers? That would cause red, itchy eyes."

"I'll ask Harry if she had allergies," Corbin said.

"We'll ask the questions," Constable Payne assured the family. "But I'll make a note." He did so on his tablet. "Where was she sitting?"

Matthew pointed to the long wooden pews polished to a shine five rows from the front.

The constable knelt to search under the seats. "Nothin'," he said when he'd straightened again. "How big was the box?"

"About the size that your mobile comes in," Paislee said. "Heavy, dark wood."

"That's not the box I gave her." Mary's plump chin trembled.

"Mary!" Garrison's brow knit. "You didnae give her the brooch today? You said you'd had it cleaned."

"Aye! I picked it up from the jeweler's last week and bought a fine velvet box." Mary's bosom huffed. "Royal blue."

"When did you see it last, ma'am?" Constable Payne asked.

"This morning before church. I put it with the other gifts for the bride's dressing room. I wasnae a member of the bridal party." Mary allowed a heavy pause to show her dissatisfaction. "I packed it with the extra Smythe plaid ribbon and a note for Lydia." She fanned her face. "It's a special day, becoming one of the Smythe clan. I wanted a fresh start for us all."

Laird Garrison Smythe nodded at his second wife with approval.

In other words, Paislee thought, he'd told Mary to shape up. She tried to imagine what it would be like to marry into such an illustrious family—Mary seemed to think it was like winning a gold medal. Lydia didn't care about such things.

"The box was wood," Paislee said with certainty. "Not velvet."

Mary turned to Rosebud, then Hyacinth. "Girls?"

Rosebud shrugged but her cheeks were scarlet. Would she admit to what she and Felice had been joking about? "I dinnae remember."

She was lying! Paislee turned the full force of her mum-stare on the young woman, who ducked her head.

"Me either." Hyacinth batted a tear. "Poor Felice. Caught up by the family curse."

"That brooch was not cursed," the minister said with heat. "I blessed it meself, just as Mary requested."

"Curse?" Garrison spluttered. "What are ye talking aboot, lass?" He glared at his oldest stepdaughter as if she'd lost her mind.

"We know aboot the Luckenbooth curse, Da," Hyacinth said with a whine. "Dinnae yell."

Garrison shifted on his black boot heel to stare at his wife. "I thought I'd misunderstood Corbin on the stoop earlier. Mary, please explain."

Mary drew in a breath, her hand to her heart. "I didnae want tae involve you for this reason, Garrison. You must not deny the paranormal." Oblivious to his narrowed gaze, she continued, "My friend Alexa is a psychic and she told me that more than one Smythe bride has died after accepting a brooch from her betrothed. If the lass isnae suited . . ."

"Corbin's right, Mary. That's pure nonsense." Garrison's skin colored bright red. Paislee wasn't sure if it was embarrassment or anger. "Those pins are guid fortune. They dinnae bring bad luck. I will not hear more of it!"

Mary's mouth gaped but then she bowed her head.

Corbin shifted his attention from his stepmother to his dad. "Felice is dead. How can we help Uncle Harry? That's more important right now than anythin' else."

Reggie, the oldest Smythe brother at thirty-five, said, "I'll drive Da in his car tae Uncle Harry at the hospital. Cynthia and Delilah can go tae the manor in ours and wait for us there."

Paislee turned to see Reggie's wife and daughter in conversation with Duncan's wife, Nell, and their son, Owen.

"I'll spread the word that there's been an accident," the minister said. Truthfully, more than half of the guests were ambling around to find out what had happened. "The wedding is . . . postponed."

A delicate way to say it, Paislee thought.

Duncan and Drew stood on either side of Corbin. "This is shite," Drew announced, an arm loose over Harlow's shoulders. "Let's head home and get pished."

"I could use a drink," Corbin said in a low voice. "We might as well eat the wedding feast, or it will go tae waste."

"I don't know aboot that!" Mary spoke defensively, as if Corbin had stepped on her hostess-toes.

"It's a grand idea, son," Garrison said, speaking over Mary to his boys. "Not a celebration like we'd hoped, but we need tae mourn our kin. Our home is open tae family as it has *always* been in times of joy and sorrow. You're welcome tae join us, Minister Angela, and let our people know."

The minister nodded. "God and family are best at times like these. Again, I'm so sairy for everyone."

"You're not going tae marry Aunt Lydia?" Brody asked Corbin.

"I want tae, aye." Corbin choked up and Duncan patted his shoulder. "It will have tae wait for a better time."

Paislee felt terrible for him and Lydia—a true love match. Brody peered up at her with concern. What was he thinking?

And would he blurt it out like a wee bairn, or wait until they were alone? She breathed a sigh of relief when Brody gave a single nod. He was growing up in more ways than one.

Hyacinth buried her nose in her bridesmaid's bouquet. "Dinnae fash, Corbin. You can choose another Luckenbooth pin, withoot a curse, like Mum suggested."

"For the last time, that brooch was not cursed!" Corbin said.

"Temper, temper," Rosebud chided, staying within the safety of her mother's arm. She appeared so young that Paislee had to be mistaken about her being at all responsible for the missing brooch. Laughing with a cousin wasn't a crime. Felice had taken it, not Rosebud.

"Paislee, will you three join us at the manor, please?" Corbin reached for her hand, his palm damp. "Lydia will need her family around her."

In other words, Corbin was quite aware that his stepfamily was toxic to his bride. Only now, Lydia was back to being *not* a bride and had less protection.

"Let's find Uncle Philip. Have him go tae the hospital for Harry so that we can alert the staff of the change in plans." Garrison stepped toward the lobby, followed by all four of his sons.

Paislee had Scot's blood running through her veins and she believed there was more to this green earth than met the eye. She bowed her head for a quick prayer.

Had Lydia's wedding truly been cursed?

Chapter 3

Paislee needed an excuse to politely avoid the Smythe clan at the manor, but before she could think of one, Lydia had convinced softhearted Grandpa to join her and her parents. Aye, it had been the plan to go for a wedding dinner with gifts and dancing in the barn behind the house, but circumstances had changed. Death paid no mind to future dreams.

"Lydia! We aren't family. We didn't know Felice," Paislee said in a reasonable and logical tone.

"You're *my* family. Just for a wee bit," Lydia pleaded. Her tears had been more than her waterproof mascara had promised, and she had rings of black under her eyes from crying—something she must have done in private with her parents in the dressing room, before approaching Paislee by the back pew.

Paislee looked from Brody to Grandpa, to Lydia, and then Lydia's parents. She was not strong enough to withstand all of those imploring gazes.

"Fine. Fine. But!" She raised her palm. "We won't stay long. Lydia, you still have the tickets tae Heidelberg tomorrow, don't you?" The couple had chosen a deluxe getaway to Germany for two full weeks.

"We cannae go. We arenae married. No wedding. No honeymoon. No beautiful trip tae the German wineries." Lydia crossed her arms and did her best to maintain her composure. "We'll need tae cancel the suite at the hotel, too. What are we going tae do with that enormous wedding cake?"

The wedding had been all about what the Smythes had wanted, mostly Mary, with Lydia conceding left and right. She'd asked for small and intimate. There'd been two hundred guests who had witnessed this tragedy today. She'd wanted chocolate cake but had gone along with vanilla. Five layers of it.

"I'll phone the hotel and let them know." Paislee was happy for a specific task to ease the burden from Lydia. "You'll have tae handle the flights."

Alistair tugged at a button on his vest. She noticed he did that when nervous. "Don't suppose you lovebirds just want tae take off on holiday?"

"Corbin booked the tickets." Lydia's chin quivered. "His cousin is dead. At our wedding! This will just add more fuel tae Mary's gossip aboot the brooch being bad luck."

"I'm sorry, Lyd." Paislee hugged her tight. She hated to consider the possibility that it just might be. When the Smythes got the pin back, it could be melted down to prevent further tragedies.

Lydia's thoughts had gone a different direction as she clasped Paislee's wrist and said, "We'll need tae prove the naysayers wrong."

Paislee didn't like the way that sounded. "How so?"

Leaning forward, Lydia whispered in Paislee's ear, "By finding oot exactly what happened tae Felice. Can you call DI Zeffer?"

"No way!" Paislee stepped back from Lydia, next to Grandpa and Brody, the nerves of her stomach tangled like the cheapest blend of yarn.

She hadn't heard from the DI in months. Amelia Henry, her friend who was also a receptionist at Nairn Police Station, had mentioned over a project on the Thursday night Knit and Sip Paislee hosted at her yarn shop, Cashmere Crush, that Zeffer had left Inspector Macleod in charge more often.

"Well, we have tae get tae the bottom of this, or I might never get married!" Lydia brought her knuckles to her lower lip. Her diamond ring sparkled.

The past twelve months had been focused on Lydia and her wedding, and Brody's last year in primary school. P7 was top of the food chain and her son had a wee bit of a strut. Things between Paislee and the headmaster had cooled and while part of her missed the flutter of attraction, *most* of her realized it was a bad idea for another seven years. Maybe forever.

"Why this Zeffer fellow?" Alistair asked, having overheard Lydia's whisper. "The constable is right there. Or is Paislee friends with the DI?"

"Not friends!" There'd been a stretch of misfortunes when Grandpa had just moved to Nairn after his son Craigh went missing, where Paislee and the DI had joined forces. She'd suggested to her grandfather that he enlist the detective's assistance because she suspected Zeffer knew more than he was letting on, but the old man kept a secret better than a priest in a confessional.

Sophie soothed and clucked around Lydia like a plump hen comforting a chick—only this chick was fully grown. "It will happen, pet. You'll be married soon." Lydia's mother was petite with cherry-red hair. It was possible Lydia had gotten her love for hair dye genetically. Sophie lowered her voice to ask, "When is an appropriate amount of time tae wait after a family member dies?"

"The aristocracy has rules for everything. That too, I bet." Grandpa scratched his freshly trimmed silver beard. "Is tomorrow too soon?" he suggested. "The cake should keep."

"Angus is right, Lydia," Alistair said. "Should we speak with Corbin?" He scanned the inner sanctum of the church where more than half the guests had left after hearing of the tragedy. "He should be with you during this crisis."

"Corbin's with his da and brothers in the lobby. They're all devastated." Lydia bumped her arm to her father's. "He asked if I'd mind riding with you tae the manor?"

Alistair nodded. "We can talk later, then."

Minister Angela patted Lydia on the back. "Lydia! My dear. How are ye holding up?"

Lydia quickly blinked to keep her tears at bay. "Thanks tae you and your whisky, much better. We just arenae sure what tae do next . . ."

Brody's auburn fringe swept to the side of his forehead as he peered up at the minister. "Can Aunt Lydia get married tomorrow? Just tae save the cake," her son said, showing he'd been not only listening but wanted to help.

Grandpa snickered.

"Tomorrow?" The minister turned to Lydia. "I'd be willing tae do the service if that's what you want. All we need are a few witnesses."

Lydia's parents both raised their hands as if in school. "We dinnae return tae Edinburgh until the day after tomorrow," Sophie said. "Tuesday."

"We'd be happy tae!" Alistair agreed.

"Let's slow down so that I can discuss this with Corbin." Lydia shrugged. "I doobt a wedding ceremony is what's on his mind right now."

The minister oozed empathy from her pores. Angela's unlined complexion made it difficult to place her age. Paislee guessed she was in her forties though it could be sinless living. "You were off tae Heidelberg for yer honeymoon?"

"Aye. Corbin will need tae reschedule." Lydia bowed her head. "I havenae been much help tae the man since he proposed."

"Ah, lass. In-laws create an interesting dynamic." Angela gestured to the dressing room off the lobby of the church. "We can stash the flowers and gifts in there for now, if you'd like a quiet ceremony with Corbin this week? Our next wedding is Saturday evening, so it willnae be needed till then."

Lydia's right eye twitched, a clue her best friend was on emotional overload.

Paislee smiled in support. "Let's take a peek." She led the way to the dressing room, and the others followed. Constable Monroe was nowhere in sight, but the bathroom door was closed, a padlock on the knob, then blocked with blue-and-white police tape.

"What's goin' on?" Brody asked.

"Never mind, son." Paislee pushed on the slightly open door to the room that the Barrons had been waiting in moments before and peered inside. "This way, please."

Prettily wrapped gifts were stacked along one wall. Paislee's bouquet, rescued from where she'd dropped it, and Lydia's, were the only two left. "Will they be safe?"

Angela handed her a silver key from a band around her wrist. "This is the only copy."

"That's a terrific solution," Paislee said. It also took the pressure off needing to make an immediate decision. "I'll return after dinner if we decide tae . . ." Skip the wedding altogether? Lydia had poured her heart into this endeavor. She and Corbin loved each other. "Well, whatever we decide." Paislee retrieved her wristlet from the bottom drawer.

"We can help, too," Alistair said.

"We will! Angela, did ye know Felice?" Sophie asked.

"Aye. The Smythe family's been attending this kirk since 1800—not that I was around then," the minister chuckled. "But there are records of a wedding for Nigel Smythe tae Adelia Mac-Duff in 1812."

"That's fascinating!" Grandpa said. He was a history buff and great to have on the team when they played trivia.

"Their fortune began in coal. And unlike a lot of Scots clans, the Smythes have stayed strong—and solvent." Angela laughed and tilted her head. "Could it be genetic?"

"I never got into the DNA craze," Alistair said. "But a fellow I work with has documented his family tree tae the year 1100."

Paislee tidied the vanity while they were talking, part of her still searching for the box though she knew it wasn't there as sure as she knew her name was Paislee Ann Shaw.

Sophie stepped closer to Alistair. "I dinnae understand the mania for it, either. What difference does it make if you're second cousins three times removed? Like Kyra Sedgwick and Kevin Bacon. They discovered the distant-cousin connection because of a television show."

"I saw that," Lydia said. "Kyra's family is from England and related tae the Smythes somehow. It was all Mary could talk aboot for a week. There are so many Smythes around here that the immediate family guest list was well over a hundred people."

"What aboot the cake?" Brody rubbed his tummy.

"I dinnae know aboot the cake," Alistair said. "We can ask the baker how long it's guid for, I s'pose."

"I think the lad is more concerned aboot filling his belly," Grandpa deduced.

"Och!" Lydia picked up the large overnight bag she'd prepared for the hotel that night and dug around inside. "Chocolate biscuits." She handed the packet to Brody. "Thanks for being such a guid sport. You look quite dashing, Brody, in yer kilt." He and Grandpa had worn the same plaid pattern as Alistair.

"Ta!" Brody accepted the snack and opened it, offering the bag around but all the adults said no. Oh, to be so happy from a chocolate biscuit.

Paislee read the time on her mobile. It was half-past four in the afternoon, and the wedding had been scheduled to end at five—then a champagne toast by the alder tree with all the guests, followed by the family, a hundred or more folks, meeting at the manor house for a meal and dancing at the barn to celebrate the nuptials.

Things had gone off the rails and they could only do their best. "Lydia, I'll call the hotel and cancel for tonight," Paislee said. "From the car, if we all want tae get tae the house?" If she was being honest, Smythe Manor was the last place she wanted to be.

"I'll lock up the church and be along shortly," Minister Angela said.

What a sad ending to a hopeful day. Before they departed the dressing room, Paislee asked, "Angela, can you tell us again about the brooch? Mary said she bought a velvet box for it, but the one you brought was wood."

"Aye! The package was by the pulpit sometime after morning services. I didnae see it until I went up tae practice my sermon for the wedding. I saw Lydia's name on the ribbon and delivered it tae the room. I thought it was a gift from Corbin tae his bride." Angela smiled at Lydia, her eyes crinkling at the corner. "The brooch I blessed was in a velvet box, as Mary said earlier."

Paislee tapped her phone. Had the bridesmaids been together the whole time? Oh, she couldn't think about it now. "Let me alert the hotel so they don't prepare your room. I'm sure they have champagne chilled."

Lydia's brave demeanor faltered. "*Lots* of champagne and chocolate-covered strawberries. Corbin told me I'd earned it after all that I've been through, for my love of him, so I have no regrets. Followed by two weeks touring the gorgeous German countryside, sampling delicious white Riesling."

"You can still have your honeymoon." Sophie hugged Lydia's slender side.

"Mibbe later, is all," Alistair said. "Heidelberg isnae going any-where."

"I'd have tae take off work and let my clients know. What a pain in the arse." Lydia sucked in a breath and rounded her eyes at the minister. "Sairy."

"I've heard worse, so not tae worry." It seemed that Minister Angela was not as strict as Father Dixon, where Paislee went to church. "Shall we?"

They all left the dressing room and Paislee locked it, slipping the silver key in her small purse.

Brody wiped a crumb from his mouth and then swiped his hand on the back of his kilt. Paislee made a mental note to spot-check later so it wouldn't stain. She peeked out the front doors. The police car with the constables was gone and there was no hint of a disturbance on the cobblestones. No sign of Felice. She trailed

Grandpa and the others out the back entrance of the church, where the steps weren't as steep, to the car park.

Lydia shouldered her overnight bag, her silver wedding dress sparkling in the June afternoon sun. She was a vision.

By now, Lydia should have been Lydia Smythe.

Her best friend climbed into the back seat of her parents' sedan, but then popped up to blow kisses at Paislee, Grandpa, and Brody. Lydia ducked out of sight and Alistair started the car. Sophie was in the front seat. They had a decal on their bumper that read, I LOVE DOGS ♥.

"I love dogs, too." Brody was observant today, probably because she hadn't let him have his video game in church. "Can we get Wallace and bring him with us?"

Paislee tossed Grandpa the keys to drive so she could call the hotel and cancel Lydia's honeymoon suite. "No, son. You never bring a pup tae another person's home uninvited."

"Why not? Wallace is guid!"

"He's the best, but it's not polite."

Brody buckled up in the back and freed his handheld video game from the center console. "Lame."

She rolled her eyes, since he couldn't see her, and dialed the hotel. The man at the desk was quite rude about the cancellation until Paislee explained the tragic accident that had occurred on the church stairs.

Suddenly, he was all things compassionate. "Will the Smythes want tae reschedule?"

"We don't know yet." If Lydia had her way, she might just elope in Germany with Corbin, and say good riddance to the family.

"If there is anything we can do?"

"We'll be in touch. Ta." Paislee hung up and thought of any other calls she could make on Lydia's behalf to ease the pain of a thwarted wedding.

"Whatchya thinking, lass?" Grandpa peered over his glasses at her when they reached a stoplight.

"How tae help! Mary and Garrison were doing the food, the cake, and the barn dance on their property, so I don't know what else there is, actually, besides the flights." She blew out a breath. "Poor Lydia. This is just so awful. After all that she went through tae make her in-laws like her."

"Mibbe it's for the best now," Grandpa said.

"I just don't see how, Grandpa." Lydia was at the starting line again, or worse.

"Did ye ever hear aboot me and Agnes?"

Paislee was surprised he'd bring up how he'd gotten blitzed the night before his wedding and fathered a child he didn't know about until well over a decade later. Her uncle Craigh was missing from an oil rig and the reason her grandfather had moved in with her. The news had ruined his and Gran's marriage. "Did Gran have doubts? Wait. Did the stag party make you late?"

"Och, I showed up on time, lass. Not even a hangover could keep me from my wedding day." Grandpa straightened the rear-view mirror. "No, I'm talking aboot your gran's Aunt Tillie."

"I never heard this story—what happened?"

"Well, Tillie shared her low opinion of my job as a fisherman. Work was dryin' up and she feared I was gonna starve Agnes or any bairns we might have. I overheard the conversation and thought for sure I'd be oot, but naw, Agnes defended me. I vowed I would *never* let her go hungry. I didnae." Grandpa stepped on the gas as the light changed. "Her career as a teacher gave the extras but I provided for us. She told me later that Tillie had apologized. Anyway. Could be the Smythes just need time."

Paislee patted Grandpa's knee. His love for Gran beamed like a lighthouse, and it hurt that her grandmother had died, unable to forgive him for breaking her heart. Craigh was older than her da had been and that had stung her pride.

"Mibbe," Brody said from the back seat, "if they wait, Aunt Lydia can get married how she likes, with just the people she likes."

Out of the mouths of babes, Paislee thought, perfectly in agreement. However, being a mum meant she had to teach Brody manners. She turned to her son and said primly, "And I'll thank you tae keep your opinions tae yourself, me lad."

Grandpa roared with laughter and destroyed the teaching moment.

Chapter 4

The digital clock on the dash read five exactly when the Shaws arrived at Smythe Manor. Grandpa followed the Barrons' sedan down a long gravel driveway with an expanse of emerald grass on either side of a three-story granite home. The sky couldn't be a brighter blue and white clouds skidded along the peaked slate roof.

"Amazing!" Brody pressed his nose to the rear passenger window. "Will Aunt Lydia live here, too?"

"No." Lydia and Corbin had planned to find something they both loved when they returned from Germany on their honeymoon. He'd sold his flat last month and now mostly stayed with Lydia when he wasn't here in his childhood room. There were over ten bedrooms in the massive home, so it wasn't cramped. Another plan to be put on hold.

"Too bad," Brody said.

A pair of golden Labs raced from around the house to the stone stoop like official ambassadors. The manor had been built around 1850 on the ruins of a stone keep that could be dated to the fourteenth century. Lydia had told her, with the barest hint of an eye roll, that the Smythe clan was a wee bit house proud. It had a stable, a dairy, and a greenhouse for year-round vegetables. The family had been hosting parties for more than a century in the barn behind the kitchen. "It *is* pretty," Paislee conceded.

"It could be a golf course," Grandpa said. "I wonder what Garrison uses on the lawn?" He pulled their SUV next to the Barrons' car before a five-bay timber garage. At least twenty vehicles were parked on the gravel overflow. Granite flower boxes filled with geraniums were on either side of the step to the house where the animals waited, golden bodies wriggling with excitement.

"You should ask him. Our garden could use some sprucing up." The back grassy area behind her home was a twentieth of the size and served a practical purpose: a place for Wallace to chase birds in fruit trees, and a clothesline for her wash. Paislee climbed out, as did Brody, who was drawn to the pups like a magnet. Boys and dogs were a match in heaven, and she didn't call him back as he hurried toward them.

Lydia hooked her slender arm through Paislee's. The capped sleeve of her silver wedding gown shimmered. "This dress is awkward. No mistakin' it for something else."

"You look beautiful," Paislee assured her.

The Barrons clasped hands. "Lydia, my sweet," Sophie said, "there is nothin' tae be done, so lift your chin and be confident in who you are."

Alistair winked at his daughter and then told Paislee, "Our Lydia grew so tall so fast, faster than the other girls, and they used tae tease her somethin' terrible. Sophie had tae remind her that she couldnae change her height, so own it."

Paislee was so used to Lydia's beauty that she'd forgotten the painful years her friend had spent agonizing over clothes and being taller than even the boys, her gray eyes big in her face. Lydia had certainly transformed into a swan. "I'd offer tae change outfits with you, but my knee-length dress would come tae your thighs."

"That would give Mary something tae complain aboot, eh?" Lydia exhaled and squared her shoulders. "I'm fine. Let's do this."

"We are so proud of you," Alistair said. He and Sophie walked toward Brody and the dogs, Grandpa behind them, and she and Lydia brought up the rear.

"Say the word, and we're outta here," Paislee murmured to her best friend. The massive wooden door opened. "I can have a stomach bug in an instant."

"This is for Corbin." Lydia raised her chin and smiled at Paislee. "Thanks for being here with me. It's gonna suck. First order of business will be tae find the whisky."

Paislee laughed.

A butler in dark gray stood on the threshold of the entrance, frowning at the dogs before he looked at the visitors, recognizing Lydia. "M'lady. The family is gathered in the parlor."

The butler didn't remark on the fact that they were all two hours earlier than planned for the wedding feast, or that the nuptials hadn't happened. Did he know about the deceased relative?

"Norbert." Lydia folded her hands before her in the brightly lit foyer. A huge central staircase with a grand chandelier shone down on the marble tiles. Carpet runners in the Smythe tartan protected the floor from shoes and boots.

Paislee's prior experience with a family manor had been the Leery Estate, genteel and run-down. This interior was refurbished, shiny, and simply gorgeous with polished wood and gilt on everything from the picture frames to the light switches. No hiding cracks or water stains here.

"Pure dead brilliant!" Brody said, eyes wide.

The butler's lips twitched in amusement, but he resumed his post and closed the door, keeping the dogs outside. Not a moment later, a knock sounded, and Norbert opened it. "Welcome tae Smythe Manor."

"Hello again," a woman said.

Paislee turned, recognizing Angela's voice. The minister smiled. "May I join you?"

"Of course," Alistair said.

"We're all following Lydia." Sophie chuckled and scanned the impressive foyer, not hiding her admiration.

"This way tae the parlor. I've been here often enough now that

I shouldnae get lost." Lydia stepped to the left. Grandpa and Brody fell in behind her, then the Barrons, and last, Angela and Paislee. "My first time trying tae find the loo I ended up in the maid's closet, and Hyacinth had tae rescue me."

Grandpa snorted. Lydia hadn't shared that story before, and Paislee wondered just how much Lydia had put up with that she'd kept to herself.

Lydia wasn't smiling once she reached the parlor entrance. Double doors were widened to reveal a room the size of Paislee's entire downstairs. Long, dark-brown leather couches with brass trim allowed for large-group seating. Wooden chairs had been brought to fill in any available space. Around eighty folks in wedding-guest attire chatted quietly. A fireplace, unlit, with a massive stone mantel, was in the center wall and family photos were arrayed on every free space. This area was very much used and loved.

A second set of doors had been slid back to connect the parlor to a formal dining room. Paislee peered around Hyacinth and Rosebud, the sisters forehead to forehead as they snickered about something, to the table that had to seat sixty. She would hate to have to do the dishes in this place!

"Will there be food, Mum?" Brody asked in a low voice.

He must be growing again. Cashmere Crush's increased business allowed her to buy what he needed without burdening the credit card if she bought it on sale. Could he wait till next year for new clothes?

Lydia tugged Brody next to her. "Stay with me and we'll find something tae nibble in the dining room tae hold you over."

Angela strode forward in navy-blue slacks, her skinny frame no longer slowed by her minister's robe. "This way, friends. Mary and Garrison are by the cake. Och! How lovely."

The five-tiered confection was so large that it had its own table. Real red roses decorated the edges, next to blue thistles of frosting and red, blue, and black ribbon. "It's too pretty tae eat!" Sophie said.

Lydia folded her hands as she tried to be fair. "It *is* lovely."

They wended through the room and the guests, predominantly wearing some form of the Smythe plaid, to Garrison, Mary, and Corbin.

Corbin's stepmother, her dyed platinum hair again smoothed submissively into the net, craned her neck to address the very tall chef by the buffet table. Silver chafing dishes had already been set out as the staff must have prepared for the wedding meal. He wore a white hat over his iron-gray hair, a white jacket, and checked pants.

"Ma'am, the prime rib is not finished cooking yet. We have the salads ready but not the hot dishes."

"How long must you keep us waiting?" Mary demanded.

"An hour for the hot things." The chef shrugged helplessly at Mary's wrath. "I have a ham."

"Obviously," Mary said as if she were speaking to a simpleton, "that willnae suffice. Bring what you've prepared, and we'll feed the guests buffet style. No sit-down dinner will be necessary. Daily dishware instead of the china."

The chef's spine was ramrod straight. "I have soft rolls tae put oot with the ham. Perhaps sandwiches?"

Mary cringed and backed into the cake table. It wobbled and she brought her palm to her chest. "Oh! And take this away. We willnae be eating it today."

"Yes, ma'am." The chef motioned to another server in all-white, who gathered the porcelain place settings off the formal table.

"It's a disaster." Mary lowered her hand. "I knew when I spilled the salt over my eggs this mornin' that it would be a terrible day."

"Mary, dinnae fash," Garrison said to his nervous wife. "It's important we feed our people during this time of crisis, not how it's bloody well displayed."

"I worked so hard tae make this perfect." Mary sniffed, then pierced Lydia with blazing orbs. "I know you dinnae want tae hear this, Garrison, but—"

"Don't," Garrison warned. He clapped his son on the back and looked down his strong nose to his wife.

Lydia slowed, hesitant to breach their group, but her mother nudged her forward. "Courage, pet," Sophie said.

Corbin shifted and turned, his smile lighting his whole body when his gaze fell on Lydia. "You're here! I was aboot tae leave in search of you. I miss you by my side." His voice broke and he clasped her fingers.

Lydia flowed to him, and Paislee caught her breath at what a striking pair they made. Ebony hair styled to fall over a broad brow, dark brown eyes, and his da's strong nose. Corbin was taller than Lydia, and her friend had told her it made her feel petite. Her bestie had grown her hair to reach the top of her shoulders and dyed it a golden caramel. The silver of her wedding gown brought out the gray in her eyes. Their love formed a rosy aura around them and anybody who denied that was blind.

Mary gave a brittle welcome to Lydia and the Barrons, then Paislee, Grandpa, and Brody. She unbent enough to smile at Angela. "Minister! Thank ye so much for coming."

"Of course!" Angela stood next to Mary. "Lady Mary, you show such grace in this difficult situation."

Mary's cheeks flushed at what Paislee had witnessed to be a stretch of the truth, yet the hostess relaxed at the kind words and turned to the cook. "Chef Patrick, Laird Garrison is correct," she said. "Whatever is simplest tae feed our clan as we mourn the loss of our dear Felice. Slice the ham for sandwiches as you suggested."

Relief flashed over the chef's face as he bobbed his head and returned to the kitchen.

Mary reached for Angela's hand. "We are in need of prayers today. I woke up tae a black cloud this morning, surely an ill omen."

Spilled salt *and* a black cloud? Paislee kept her snarky remark to herself. If she was Lydia, and this was her mother-in-law, why, she might move to Canada.

Garrison gritted his teeth. He was handsome, in his fifties, and smooth-shaven with fading ebony hair. This was Corbin in the future.

His brothers, too, all looked alike. There was Reggie, the heir, Duncan, the spare, Corbin, then Drew, the baby. Corbin joked that he was the expendable Smythe.

His stepsisters, Rosebud and Hyacinth, were light brown–haired, and envious of the boys for being blood heirs to the Smythe estate. Hyacinth conversed with Matthew on a large armchair. Rosebud used her upturned nose and pretty smile to keep Chalmers Whitton close. The couple ambled near the cake. "Chalmers, fetch my shawl, will you?" Rosebud brushed by Lydia without a word of acknowledgment.

Lydia acted like she didn't notice the snub and gestured to Brody. "We were hoping for a snack before dinner. Corbin, can ye sneak us into the kitchen?" She winked at her fiancé.

"Oh, no. You cannae go tae the kitchen. That's the chef's domain and he's busy with food preparation." Mary was not so cold as to ignore a young boy's tummy as she said, "I'll get you a roll, all right, dear? Then you can go play outside with Owen and the dogs until our meal is ready."

"Thank you, ma'am. I like your dogs a lot." Brody looked at Paislee for permission.

Corbin glared at Mary over Brody's head. "I'll take care of it. Come on, me lad. Want tae go through a hidden door tae the kitchen?"

Brody's eyes widened with excitement. "Aye!"

Grandpa darted after them with nimble steps. "Show me, too."

Paislee was left with Mary, Garrison, Angela, Sophie, Alistair, and Lydia. "There's a wee bar next tae the fireplace if I can interest anyone in a whisky?" Garrison said.

They all followed him. Sophie held Paislee back to walk more slowly around the chairs and bent knees of people already seated. "What's going on with Lydia? Mary doesnae like my girl, and that is simply outrageous."

"I don't know why." Paislee saw no reason to deny it since it was obvious. "Her daughters aren't fans, either."

"I dinnae feel right aboot Lydia marryin' into this clan. I had such high hopes for her happiness here, but now I wonder." Sophie sighed with maternal angst Paislee totally understood.

They reached the bar where Garrison poured amber liquid into tumblers and passed them out. It was The Macallan, a higher-end single malt whisky that also produced her less expensive go-to blend, The Famous Grouse. "Sláinte!" Garrison said. Lydia lifted hers to Paislee, then drank.

Paislee sipped the smoky Scotch and let it slide over her tongue. It was a treat to the senses, warming her belly. She surveyed the room, spotting Corbin's brothers with their wives, Cynthia and Nell. They were all attractive, but not beautiful, like Lydia. Brunettes. They'd been nice during the pre-wedding festivities and Paislee hadn't sensed the acrimony of Mary and her daughters. Delilah was Cynthia's mini, attached like a shadow.

Harry wasn't there, nor Jocelyn and Oliver. Philip, Garrison's youngest brother, sat on a couch with a glass that he stared morosely into, then finished. He must not have gone to the hospital. His daughter Sheila, next to him with red-rimmed eyes, got up for a re-fill since Garrison was pouring. Owen, Duncan's son, was outside with the dogs and Brody. Having so many cousins made for auto-matic friendships, attested to by the many photos on the mantel of the brothers and their kin.

The Smythes were one of the wealthiest families in Scotland, yet these pictures of laughter and good times made them seem like regular folks.

"Lydia, which photos have Corbin in them?" Alistair asked.

"This one here—see his smile?" Lydia tapped a silver frame with the four brothers by a horse paddock. "He's aboot Brody's age and quite adorable."

"Look for big groups and Corbin will be toward the end, and the back, because he's so tall," Sheila said. She gave her da's empty glass to her uncle Garrison. "Da would like another, please."

"Aye. Better get some scran in him before he topples into the fireplace." Garrison returned the full tumbler. It seemed he bossed everyone around, not just his boys.

"I'll watch over him." Sheila smiled her thanks.

Paislee had met this particular cousin at Lydia's bridal shower. Sheila had come with Senta, Jocelyn, Felice, and Hyacinth. Rosebud had claimed a migraine, and Mary had stayed home with her. Hyacinth and Jocelyn had spent most of the night drinking wine and snickering behind their hands. Felice, normally Rosebud's companion, had been left out.

Sheila tilted her head in empathy. "You must be crushed, Lydia."

"I am—but I'm sairy for you, too. You and Felice were cousins and grew up together." Lydia cleared her throat. "It hasnae been a grand day, all around."

Understatement of the century.

Corbin returned with Grandpa in tow. The men's cheeks were flushed, and they smelled of malt whisky. They must have stopped for their own libation. She'd never known Grandpa to turn down a dram.

"Corbin!" Sheila patted Corbin on the arm as he claimed a space between Sheila and Lydia. "It's too strange for one of us tae be gone."

He tucked his thumb in the waistband of his kilt, eyelids red-rimmed. "Terrible."

"It's unbelievable," Senta said. She'd changed from her brides-maid's dress to jeans and a top. "We stuck together at school and sports. Nobody ever bullied a Smythe. Didnae matter if we were fightin' amongst ourselves," she chuckled. "Nobody else was allowed tae do so. Remember?"

Corbin puffed his chest. "We look oot for our own."

Lydia squeezed his hand. "I can see it now. The toddlers all dressed in kilts with claymores."

Sheila gave a low laugh. "You know, I think there's a photo like that somewhere around here. Lincoln might know. Or Bruce. He probably shot it. He's got an amazin' gift for capturing special moments. It's the name of his shop."

Harlow, attached at the hip to Drew, joined them. "I always wanted tae be part of the club."

"Now you are, love." Drew dropped a kiss to her forehead.

"You've given her a Luckenbooth?" Senta's eyes sparkled. She'd won the drawing to be Lydia's bridesmaid. Jocelyn had said earlier that Felice had also tried to win the coveted spot. Ten female cousins had entered. Paislee couldn't even imagine so much family! What must Christmas be like?

"I dinnae want tae talk aboot engagements right now." Corbin glared at Senta. "It's a little fresh."

"Sairy!" A hint of pink colored Senta's face.

Lydia released Corbin's hand and sipped from her tumbler, her gaze troubled.

Alistair and Grandpa stepped back to admire the craftsmanship of the leather couches and Paislee wished she could go with them. The circle was too close. Stifling.

Harlow ignored Corbin's statement and said, "The Smythes have a custom, Drew said starting in the eighteenth century, that each family member gets tae choose one of the heirloom brooches for their wedding betrothal. Men and women."

"My heaven," Sophie said. "We're talking a lot of marriages."

"It's a lot of jewelry." Sheila chuckled. "Most of them are silver, though, or iron. Gold gives it more monetary value, but the betrothal is supposed tae be aboot love."

"I dinnae care aboot the gold. I care because Corbin chose it for me." Lydia whirled the inch of liquid left in her tumbler in annoyance.

"Where do ye keep the brooches?" Harlow asked. "Can we see

them, Drew?" She batted her lashes, and it was clear the woman hoped for one herself someday soon.

"Da has them in a treasure chest under lock and key." Drew glanced at his father. Garrison, in conversation with Duncan, didn't see it.

"Enough." Corbin's tone was harsh. "Subject change. Felice is dead, all right?"

And she'd had Lydia's brooch, a family heirloom, in her hand.

Harlow hooked her arm through Drew's and wisely didn't pursue the Luckenbooth brooches.

"Show us the family pictures," Sophie suggested, taking pity on Corbin. "What's your favorite?"

"Along the back wall, toward the left." Corbin's relief was evident in his quick shift away from the small bar area. "Those are the most recent of our generation."

"I hope you have a photographer in the family," Sophie said, only half-joking.

"Bruce Dundas has been around ever since I can remember but he's not related. I think he took Mum and Da's wedding pictures," Drew said. "Our *real* mother."

They moved *en masse* around sofas and chairs to the rear wall. Random inches of wallpaper showed between the frames.

"I love this one of us all." Corbin gestured to a picture that was taken when the Smythes were younger, and the stepsisters weren't in it. A loch shaded by trees, dogs, and horses. A giant boulder was centered and nine kids climbed all over it, wearing wide grins—in the customary kilts, of course.

"I see you, Corbin." Lydia used her long fingernail as a laser pointer. "And Drew. There's Reggie, the oldest, aye? So, this is Duncan. Who are these cousins?"

"That's me!" Sheila said, tapping her smiling face. "Jocelyn, Felice, and Oliver. Senta."

"We were so close it was more like brothers and sisters," Drew said.

"Not quite." Corbin shuffled his feet. "Mum died a few years later. Da married Mary twelve years ago when I was at university, eighteen. I came home for the holidays and suddenly had stepsisters."

"This is my favorite, too," Senta said, curling her biceps to make a muscle. "We were fearless."

Paislee stepped closer for a better view. This photo was on the grass for a picnic by a large red barn. The cousins all sat close to one another, legs and kilts and bare feet overlapping as they laughed. Dogs sprawled in the mix. Golden Labs.

"Are these the same dogs?" Paislee asked. It couldn't be. The picture was over a decade ago.

Corbin shook his head. "No, but they sired the ones we have now."

A commotion down the hall from the front entrance toward the parlor sounded and next thing she knew, the golden Labs were inside, tongues lolling, followed by Brody and Owen. The pups managed to skirt spilling anything by a hair, or knocking over small tables, and arrived under the dining table as if waiting for the chef to bring out the ham.

"Drew!" Mary's voice pitched high to carry over the guests. "I asked you tae keep those beasts outside."

"Sairy." Drew sank out of sight of his stepmother, talking to Owen and Brody. "I guess we better take them back oot. Want tae help? We can pet the horses!"

Brody nodded hard. Anything would be better than being stuck in a house surrounded by adults he didn't know.

"Can we ride them, Uncle Drew?" Owen asked.

Paislee gestured to the empty table. "Food is going tae be served soon."

Brody's face fell.

"True, true," Drew said. "Another time for the horses, then." He whistled. The dogs leapt to attention and carefully maneuvered through the guests toward him.

Garrison joined them, holding his Scotch. "Drew, make yer stepmother happy and put the dogs in the kennels. I dinnae want them tearin' up the grass. I just got it grown back in from the last time."

"C'mon, lads!" Drew escorted the boys and dogs out of the parlor.

"Your lawn is like a golf course, Garrison," Grandpa said.

"The garden is my pride and joy, especially since we got rid of the moles." Garrison rocked back on his heels. "The dogs dig tae find them. We're very self-sufficient on the property here. The secret is getting the right pH balance in the soil . . ."

The pair left the parlor to the hall, and out of sight.

"Your poor grandfather!" Senta giggled. "We've all done our bit listening aboot dirt and rabbits from Uncle Garrison."

"Grandpa might be interested," Paislee said. It was probably more about the excellent Scotch.

"Should we take Lydia tae tour the barn?" Sheila grinned at Corbin. "For old times' sake." She turned to Lydia. "Every grand occasion, be it a graduation or a wedding, we celebrate oot back. I'm surprised you didnae have your engagement party there. It's a Smythe tradition."

Lydia sipped her drink only to find it empty. Her affable expression flickered with alarm.

"Let's go see what's keeping the food." Corbin grabbed Lydia's hand. "We can refresh your whisky and get me one."

Sheila trailed after them, saying to Senta, "I'm starving. Too bad aboot the cake, huh? It looks delicious. Vanilla is my favorite."

Paislee, Alistair, and Sophie remained by the pictures on the back wall. It was the safest place to observe while out of the way.

"I adore people-watching," Sophie said.

"Me too!" Paislee smiled at the woman who had welcomed her into their home until the Barrons had moved to Edinburgh. Homemade treats and simple Scots fare for meals. "What do you think of all this?"

"Oh, I'm content tae be tucked tae the side," Sophie said. "I've never felt more like a third wheel as we have at this wedding. Not that we'd ever say so tae Lydia. We just want her tae be happy, but this is, well, a wee bit much."

Alistair rocked back on his boot heels and put his hands at his waist to watch the throng of Smythes. "I tried a chat with Garrison, tae see what kind of man he was, but unless we were talking aboot farming or gardening, or the Smythe investments, he didnae have much tae say."

"There's more tae the world than this bitty corner," Sophie said wisely. "You think Lydia will be happy?"

Paislee thought best how to answer. "I know she loves Corbin, and that Corbin loves her."

"I pray that's enough," Alistair said. "Can ye imagine all this family around, every holiday, birthday, or special event?" He tapped his nose. "They look alike from their hair tae their noses— see those poor lasses? The men can handle a larger proboscis, but it's not fair tae the ladies."

It was true that Jocelyn, Felice, Senta, and Sheila all had the Smythe nose. Strong.

Rosebud returned with Chalmers on her arm, the two laughing at something as they joined Hyacinth and Matthew, who chatted with Harlow and Drew. The girls were bonnie and didn't have to worry about the Smythe nose.

Paislee smelled fresh bread. The trio turned toward the buffet where Corbin and Lydia assisted the kitchen staff with heavy platters, mounded with cheeses, salads, rolls, and condiments. Chef Patrick himself carried the ham.

"Corbin!" Mary said. "What on earth are ye doing? Chef can do that. It's what we pay him for."

"Sometimes Mum forgets where she is." Hyacinth sounded embarrassed.

"Should I go get the fellows?" Alistair asked. Before they could answer, he strode toward the hall.

"Alistair must be hungry, too," Sophie murmured. "What a day it's been. I hope I was never so sharp as a mother. Was I?"

"No! You were—are kind. Mary cares a lot about being a Smythe, and a Lady—not that it matters." The honorary titles of laird and lady were given for landholders with large estates and homes. They weren't nobles.

"You are a wonderful mother, too, Paislee. I know Agnes would be very proud. I like your grandfather." Sophie smirked, probably remembering how Gran didn't have a nice word about her husband in the later years.

"I do, too. He'd been a surprise but now . . . well." Grandpa was family. "Here they come." Brody led the way into the parlor and immediately gravitated toward the table of food.

"Brody!" She gestured for him to join her while Owen stood with Duncan and Nell.

"Mum, I cannae go another step." Brody sucked in his belly so it was concave beneath his shirt. "I'm famished."

"Wash up first, lad."

Brody raised his palms, which were still damp. So much for drying. "We already did!"

"All right." Paislee tousled his hair and he ducked. "Stay with me." A queue had formed of about fifty people, and they joined the end. Staff arrived with small foldout tables so that folks could eat around the couches. The fancy dining table was for looking at, it seemed, not using.

Lydia brought her parents each a dish of food. "I'm sairy tae have deserted you. Here you are! Why not take that big armchair over there?"

"Thanks, pet," Alistair said. "Will ye join us?"

"Aye. Give me a few minutes." Lydia's gaze shifted to Grandpa with alarm. "Angus, I should have brought you a plate, too!"

"I can wait, dinnae fash." Grandpa was in a mellow mood no doubt in thanks to The Macallan.

Lydia's eyes welled but she blinked quickly. "What a fiasco

and this—this is not the food we'd talked aboot for today. Ham sandwiches! Cold salads. Just another thing gone wrong. The chef isnae even going tae serve the prime rib now. Mary asked him tae save it."

"Are you all right?" Paislee pitched her voice low. "Should we go?"

"No. If we were tae leave I would never hear the end of it. This woman is supposed tae be my mother-in-law, and she resents me. I overheard her talking tae the family historian, Lincoln Ried." Lydia used her chin to point to an armchair in a corner where a lanky, pale, cadaverous figure held court, holding a plate with a roll and ham slices.

"What did she say?" Paislee was familiar with him though they hadn't met yet. Another reason to grab Mary by the hairnet and sit the woman down for a chat on manners.

Lydia's long lashes fluttered. "It wasnae Mary. That's what hurts more. *Lincoln* told her that I dinnae belong here!"

Paislee crossed her arms and tapped her foot, inwardly steaming. What would her gran say about this?

Chapter 5

"Paislee, might I have a word?"

The timber of the voice. The phrase itself. Paislee's skin dotted with gooseflesh, and she lowered her plate of ham to the foldout table she shared with Brody and Grandpa. Surely that couldn't be . . . and yet when she looked up, there *he* was in all his sea-glass-green-eyed glory.

Dark russet hair, a smooth, chiseled jaw, a navy-blue suit appropriate for a somber occasion, as this wedding banquet had turned out to be. Zeffer hadn't been on the guest list, so he must have talked to Constable Payne about Felice. This wouldn't be his case, would it?

"Detective Inspector," she said slowly. He stepped into the room, escorted by Norbert. "What are ye doing here?"

Zeffer's pale skin flushed along the sharp ridge of his cheekbones. "Nairn's been quiet of late, and I do have other responsibilities."

"You haven't been in town." Paislee placed her napkin over what remained of her dinner. Too bad, as she liked ham just fine and the rolls were heavenly—a credit to the chef.

"Keeping tabs on me, are ye, lass?" Zeffer narrowed his gaze at her. Grandpa seemed to shrink backward out of reach.

Paislee sucked in an embarrassed breath. "No, no." She shifted on the hard chair and tried again. "You want tae talk with me, *now*?"

"Aye." The detective allowed a smirk as if he knew he'd won that little skirmish.

They were like oil and water, she and the DI. He'd been new to Nairn at the same time Grandpa had arrived in her life, in fact, delivered by this very officer of the law to Cashmere Crush's door.

Paislee stood and smoothed her hands down the front of her thistle-blue matron of honor gown with red, blue, and black Smythe tartan trim, conscious of Zeffer watching her.

Mary beelined toward them, strands of her platinum hair once again freed of the net to fly at her sides in bleached wisps. "Excuse me? Who are you?"

The DI folded his hands before him. "Detective Inspector Zeffer, ma'am."

Mary relaxed at his introduction. Was she concerned a stranger might crash the buffet dinner? "I'm Lady Mary Smythe." She placed her fingers to a gold chain around her plump bosom. "Are you here aboot our sweet Felice?"

The DI hummed. "Constable Payne is on his way tae interview the folks who found your . . . cousin, was it?"

Slick, how he didn't quite answer the question.

"Not my cousin, but a niece by marriage." Mary eyed him shrewdly. "Family just the same, DI. What have ye discovered?"

Paislee wished the determined woman all the luck in the world getting an answer to that.

Zeffer scanned the room of wedding guests who consoled one another with stories of Felice and said, "Nothing certain as of yet."

"Her neck was broken," Matthew informed him. As a solicitor, and family friend, he had a different demeanor from the others. "But she was crying before she fell down the stairs. Something was wrong."

Zeffer's eye gave the tiniest twitch. "The station is waiting on the coroner's report, which should arrive in the next few days."

The DI liked to have proof of everything. Heaven forbid he made a mistake, Paislee thought. What was he after? He seemed to realize that it would be awkward to pull Paislee away now, for he settled his shoulders.

Rosebud and Chalmers stood next to Mary. Rosebud tilted her upturned nose and said, "Felice's death is Lydia's fault."

Paislee gasped. "It is not!"

"It is," Rosebud insisted, her attitude belligerent. "If she'd returned the brooch and chosen another then none of this would have happened. Mum tried tae tell her."

Paislee turned to where Corbin and Lydia were sitting to share a plate, hip-to-hip on a small leather ottoman. Corbin's complexion went red, and Lydia's waxen. Conversation had stopped so they could all hear what the DI had to say.

"Lydia didnae do anything tae Felice." Matthew's tone was abrupt.

Mary, with a perfectly straight face, said, "Perhaps no' directly. The pin was cursed."

Garrison groaned and clapped his hand to his forehead. He stayed seated at a small table with his plate and his whisky.

Zeffer's jaw clenched at Mary's pronouncement, but he rolled with it. "How so?"

"Corbin chose a Luckenbooth brooch for his betrothed, as is the Smythe Clan way, but this one was cursed," Mary said. "My friend Alexa told me the stories, and Lincoln Reid knows, too."

"Who?" Zeffer asked.

"Alexa isnae here," Mary said. "But Lincoln is."

The cadaverous man, who had been dining with Duncan, Nell, and Owen, put his plate aside and stepped forward. "I'm the family's historian."

You knew a family had been around for hundreds of years if they had their own historian.

Zeffer squared his shoulders. "And you, Mr. Reid, believe the brooch had a curse?"

Now, most Scots were superstitious in some form or fashion—the unicorn was the country's mascot for Pete's sake—but the way Zeffer asked the question, it was clear it wouldn't be wise to say *aye*.

"Mibbe," Lincoln said, discerning that for himself. Old and cunning. "Mibbe not. I only know the stories in our history."

Zeffer was already turning away in dismissal. Mary bestowed a sour expression on the older man for not agreeing wholeheartedly.

Garrison, whisky tumbler in hand, joined his wife, letting everyone know that she had his protection, even if he didn't agree with her theory. "How can we help ye, Detective?" Subtext: Ask your questions and go.

Zeffer wasn't affected. "The brooch. Jocelyn Smythe told the constable that you, Mary, had given it tae Lydia this morning, is that correct?"

Mary blushed a painful crimson. "Oh, no. Not exactly. Well. I had it cleaned for her. And blessed. Is that not so, Minister Angela?"

The minister nodded. "I found the gift on my pulpit, and it had a note for Lydia. It was in a wooden box—"

"But I'd bought a velvet one," Mary interrupted.

"Paislee and I searched the entire dressing room," Lydia said. "I *misplaced* the brooch while we were oot getting pictures with the photographer."

Bruce Dundas lifted his hand. He had fading red hair and freckles that had probably been cute at ten. Mid-fifties? They still lent a youthful air. Trim, he was one of the few men to wear slacks rather than a kilt. "That's me."

"I just dinnae see how it could have been lost," Senta said, echoing Paislee's thoughts. "The door wasnae locked when we left for the photo session. Anybody coulda walked in and helped themselves. I bet it was nicked."

"Senta, you're talking aboot your family, lass," Mary chided.

"Are you suggesting it was stolen?" Zeffer asked. His voice was so cool it gave Paislee chills. "Lydia, who would want tae do that?"

Lydia shrugged rather than rat out Corbin's stepmother and his stepsisters. "Detective, we searched that room high and low. The brooch and the box were both gone."

"You're saying that our sweet cousin Felice stole the brooch?" Hyacinth's big eyes rounded as if Lydia was beyond cruel.

"I never said it was Felice!" Lydia stared at Hyacinth, crossing her arms as if to physically create distance from the younger woman. "You and your sister were supposed tae be searching for it. Did ye bother?"

Rosebud and Chalmers linked arms. "Why should we? *We* didnae lose the brooch."

"Jocelyn said you and Felice were laughing about something before the ceremony. Was it the Luckenbooth pin?" Paislee asked bluntly.

Rosebud and Chalmers wore matching smirks. She didn't care for Rosebud's boyfriend any more than she cared for Rosebud.

"Paislee!" Mary said, clucking her tongue to her teeth. "You're trying tae place blame on my daughter when you should accept the truth. I took great pains tae make that brooch safe for Lydia." Her sigh was so deep it shook the rafters of the old home. "If she'd put it on for the photos, rather than shove it aside, Felice might still be alive."

Bruce, standing next to Sheila, winced. Paislee gasped at the woman's audacity.

"That's a stretch, Mary," Corbin said, cheeks red with anger as he defended his fiancée.

"Agreed!" Drew stayed at Harlow's side. They were an attractive couple, like Lydia and Corbin. All the brothers had chosen beguiling mates in line with their own good looks. The Smythe women were more what one might call handsome.

"Hmm." Zeffer steepled his fingers before him. "The loss of the pin interrupted your wedding?"

"Aye. Mary claimed it would be the worst luck if I were married withoot the bloody brooch," Lydia answered in shaking tones.

Corbin slipped his arm around Lydia's waist. "It's all right, love.

We were going tae say our vows withoot it, and then Felice, well, she fell down the stairs, and broke her poor neck. The wedding was off, it had tae be."

"I see." Zeffer ran his hawklike gaze over everyone in the parlor.

Nobody fessed up, though Chalmers and Rosebud exchanged a furtive glance that made her wary. Corbin's stepsister was nineteen, and Chalmers twenty. They'd met at university and seemed so very young. She'd been a mum at eighteen and hadn't had the luxury of being youthful, so perhaps her judgment was off.

Hyacinth stood close enough to Matthew that their shoulders brushed. "Lydia, you turned your nose at the idea of bad fortune but look at what happened. It's plain tae see that Lydia should have opened the box with the Luckenbooth pin when she got it. She didnae and now she's not getting married."

Matthew stepped away from Hyacinth with a scowl. "I think Felice's death is more important than delayed nuptials."

Lydia pressed her forearm to her waist. "I agree. It's awful."

Corbin swiped his eyes. "We were close as kids. All of us cousins. I cannae believe she's gone. Jocelyn and Oliver must be going through hell." He scanned the room. "I keep waiting for them tae show up."

"Stopped tae see them before coming here," Zeffer said, his tone warming a degree or two. "Harry and his children are with the reverend at the hospital chapel."

The mood turned even more somber, and Lydia buried her head against Corbin's neck. He soothed her, and she, him.

Zeffer tucked his hands into his pockets. Nobody had fessed up to swiping the brooch, so it was time to move on. "Paislee, I'd like you and Angus tae join me for a private word."

Her immediate reaction was to stay in a crowd where she could blend and retreat from Zeffer's pointed questions, but she nodded. She remained unclear if the DI was here about Felice, or to see Paislee. He'd relied on her observations before but that had been a year ago.

Lydia clasped Brody's shoulder as her son stuck to Paislee's side like a static sock. "Stay with me, love," Lydia said.

"But!" Brody's lower lip jutted.

"Seconds on pudding, me lad?" Alistair suggested, leading Brody toward the buffet. The large golden Labs had snuck inside and wagged their bodies by the table. It was just the right distraction for her son.

"For only a minute," Paislee said to Zeffer. Her grandfather stepped after Alistair and Brody, but Paislee nabbed his shirt and pulled him back. "Come on, Grandpa."

"Why us?" Grandpa bristled at being chosen. "We didnae see nothin'."

"I was there," Paislee said, unable to banish Felice from her memory any longer. "Be my moral support." Besides, the DI had asked to see him, too.

"Och." Grandpa's lower lip also jutted out, just like Brody's.

They followed Zeffer, who trailed Norbert to a library with shelves of pale varnished wood filled with books. There was a fireplace, unlit, and soft beige fabric couches. Fresh summer flowers centered the low table between the sofas. It was an inviting room to relax and escape.

Zeffer reluctantly sat down and gestured for them to do so as well. Paislee was well aware that his preferred style was to bark orders and have them fall in line, but whatever he was up to, he realized might take time. The hair on her nape rose in alarm.

Paislee and Grandpa settled on the edge of the sofa opposite the couch. Grandpa's knees poked like hairy doorknobs from his kilt. Zeffer said, "Paislee, did you touch the box?"

"No." Paislee placed her hands in her lap and crossed her ankles, legs bare. "Minister Angela brought it into the dressing room and set it on the vanity table, next tae the flowers and makeup."

"Constable Payne has the box at the station. Wood, not velvet." Zeffer leaned forward, resting his forearms over his knees.

"Did Constable Monroe find it in the bathroom?"

The DI smoothed his strong jaw. Everything about the man was precise and neat. "Aye. Tell me more aboot Felice."

"She stumbled from the loo through the church lobby where I waited with Matthew and Alistair. She passed us by, very disoriented. Crying, and said she couldn't see. I wondered if she'd gotten something in her eye, you know?"

Zeffer waited.

Paislee squirmed and caved, filling in the silence. "Felice was intent on reaching the partially open doors of the church . . . tae let in the flow of air. The place gets so stuffy since it's old with no air-conditioning."

Zeffer circled his hand to mime for her to get on with it.

"She hovered on the front stoop of the church. Matthew tried tae grab her, but he missed." Paislee drew in a steadying breath. "Felice tumbled down the stairs and broke her neck."

Paislee's voice grew thick as emotion clogged her throat. The memory would never leave her, though she knew from experience that the horror would fade with time.

"You saw her face?" Zeffer straightened.

"Her eyes and nose were prickled with red." Paislee glanced from her folded hands to the DI. "I wondered if she had seasonal allergies or had gotten into something tae cause such a reaction. It reminded me of a heat rash."

His jaw clenched and he tapped his knee. "Did you touch the brooch in Felice's hand?"

"No." Her muscles tightened. "I almost did, wondering how Felice had ended up with it, but changed my mind at the last minute."

"You have braw instincts, Paislee Shaw." Zeffer stared at her and Grandpa. "We found residue on the pin. Powdery. White."

"Powder?" Her pulse jumped. "Was it a scented talcum? Mary said she'd had it blessed by the minister, and a psychic."

"No. The toxicologist will confirm the substance, but I've seen it before." Zeffer pursed his mouth. He said nothing. It drove Paislee crazy how well he played his audience.

"What is it?" Grandpa asked after a full minute had passed. "Is it dangerous?"

"Aye." Zeffer gave his knee another tap. "I am quite certain that the results will come back as strychnine."

Grandpa frowned. "Where would someone get that? It's not legal anymore." He shifted and told Paislee, "It used tae be popular for controlling pests, tae achieve a pristine garden."

Paislee thought of the gorgeous entrance to Smythe Manor. "Would it be impossible tae find? Could *someone* have a stash hidden away?"

"Garrison shared that he uses sonar tae keep the moles away. Much more humane." Grandpa turned to the DI, and so did Paislee.

"You're right," Zeffer said. "Strychnine is outlawed as a cruel way tae kill animals. It's deadly tae humans, too."

Paislee didn't feel so good, and she pressed her palm to her tummy. "Felice didn't die of a broken neck?"

"Oh, aye," the DI said. "But she fell down those stairs because she inhaled strychnine from the brooch."

She should have known that there really was only one reason for the DI to be at the manor.

Murder.

Chapter 6

Felice—murdered. The awful thought settled into Paislee's consciousness when another arose: the intended victim had been Lydia, her very best and dearest friend in the world.

Lydia had few allies in the Smythe clan, but murder?

"Grandpa." Air left her lungs in a painful whoosh. "Someone tried tae kill Lydia."

Grandpa stood, his hands in fists at his sides. "Mary, her own mother-in-law-to-be, sent the brooch. Arrest her, DI. You heard her yourself go on and on aboot a curse. Who cast it, do ye think?"

"But it wasn't in the same box." Paislee peered up at the angry older man. His throat flushed crimson and she feared he'd do himself harm if he didn't calm down. She tugged his hand.

"Sit down, Angus," Zeffer said. "It's a guid thing the box was wooden tae contain the poison. Velvet wouldnae have been secure."

Her grandfather slowly sank to the cushion next to her, but his body remained tense.

"The lass must've snatched the box, opened it quick tae retrieve the pin, and closed it again. Else there'd be more folks in the hospital or ill."

"Good point," Paislee said. "She was in the bathroom. Is that why there's a padlock on the bathroom door at the church?"

Zeffer raised his hand. "We won't know for sure until we get the tox tests back, but my experience suggests Felice breathed it in, became disoriented, and fell down the stairs when she tried tae get fresh air."

"Could we have saved her?" Paislee asked. Her heart hammered.

"Doubtful," Zeffer said. "Dinnae beat yourself up. You had no idea what was happening."

She nervously pleated the thistle-blue fabric at her knee. Brody and Grandpa had been three pews over from where Felice sat with her other cousins. Her sister, Jocelyn. Her brother, Oliver. Jocelyn had held the brooch. "Is Jocelyn affected?"

"No," the DI answered. "We've tested her fingers and there was a trace amount, but it came clean with soap and water."

"And Oliver? Her dad, Harry?" Paislee would hate for there to be multiple tragedies this day. She'd witnessed their devastation firsthand.

"All clear." Zeffer pulled an old-school paper tablet from his suit pocket and fanned the pages. "They're aware the brooch is being tested for poison, and now I'm telling you so that you can be on your guard."

She'd realized that something was up for him to share so freely. "I'm not in danger. Lydia is! Someone didn't want Lydia tae marry Corbin."

"That's the easy answer," Zeffer said. "Is it the right one? People are twisted and complicated. You tend tae see them through rose-colored glasses."

"I've changed a wee bit, thank you." Paislee felt like a child standing up to a parent for the first time. "Is Lydia still in harm's way?"

Zeffer shrugged. "What was the intent for the poisoner? Tae cancel the wedding?"

"Lydia should be safe," Grandpa said. "It's over."

"Until they set another date," Paislee countered. "They love each other!"

"Too bad that it would be bad manners tae get married so soon after a death in the family," Grandpa said. "They've put a lot of money into the ceremony and food."

"The Smythes have plenty of blunt. I checked." Zeffer crossed his legs. "The family has invested well. Mibbe that's why Lydia was targeted?"

"Lydia signed a prenup that voided anything coming tae her if they divorced within five years," Paislee said. "She wouldn't get a thing and had tae return the Luckenbooth pin."

"Is that common knowledge?" Zeffer hiked an auburn brow.

Paislee shook her head.

"Lydia deserves better than this, fortune or no," Grandpa stated. He leaned back against the beige cushion on the couch. "Could be a blessin' in disguise, lass."

Zeffer sighed. "Blessings. Curses. I believe in choices and free will, meself. Someone chose tae put strychnine on that brooch and put it in a different box. Perhaps someone else stole it. We can rule oot Felice as the poisoner or else she wouldnae have inhaled it. Whoever did this was savvy enough tae change from a breathable velvet material tae a hard wooden box, keeping the poison contained."

"It's heartless." Paislee rubbed her arms.

"Cunning." Zeffer continued, "They'd have used gloves and a mask. Those things are around everywhere, and nobody would think twice."

"What did Oliver say, and Jocelyn?" Paislee smoothed her dress over her knees. "Their dad?"

"All seem gutted, but the men's clothes will be examined before we clear them. In most cases, the victim knows their perpetrator. Jocelyn has a reason for the trace of poison on her hand, but we're checking her clothes, too. Sibling rivalry is not an uncommon motive for murder."

"You think her family would do such a vile thing?" Grandpa pummeled a side pillow.

"You cannae choose your family, Angus, as you know." Zeffer raised *both* brows at her grandfather.

"What do ye mean by that?" Grandpa's voice hitched.

Zeffer lasered in on him. "I'd like you tae meet me at the station and discuss your missing son. Craigh Shaw, aka Craigh Burnside."

Grandpa stiffened like a board.

Paislee patted his back and came to his defense. "Why, Detective?"

"No," Grandpa said. There was zero room for discussion in that single syllable.

Paislee studied her grandfather's wrinkled features. Seventy-six now, but healthy and strong for a man half his age. He hiked, fished, and walked to Cashmere Crush several times a week where he worked a few hours a day.

He'd been very much against involving the police once he'd filed a complaint with the Dairlee officers only to discover there was no record of the *Mona*, the oil rig Craigh was supposed to be on. He'd told Grandpa that this last job would be dangerous but lucrative.

Then he'd disappeared.

She knew Grandpa worried, yet he was also concerned that by going to the law, he would get Craigh in more trouble rather than help.

It was a tough spot to be in, and nearly impossible to choose. Either way could hurt Craigh, the only child he had left alive.

Zeffer stared at Grandpa, and then her with his narrowed gaze. It was so sharp she feared it would leave a mark. "Grandpa, maybe . . ."

"I said no. Now, anything else, Detective, or can we go?"

"You're stubborn, Angus." Zeffer smacked his palms to his thighs. "There's no need tae consider me the enemy. If not the station, then we can do this here, if you'd like. Right now."

Grandpa removed his glasses and peered at Paislee with pain in his brown eyes. "Not here."

In other words, not in front of Paislee. She bit the inside of her cheek but didn't argue. They had to have a conversation, obviously, since it wasn't the first time Zeffer had hinted he knew something more, but her grandfather refused to take the bait. It seemed Zeffer was done waiting.

"Excuse me a moment." Grandpa stood, and Paislee noticed that he'd left the keys to the Juke on the cushion. "The whisky is runnin' through me."

Had that slip from his kilt pocket been on purpose? Oh yes. Grandpa wanted to leave and fast. Paislee would do her best to get him out of the hot seat. "We'll wait here for you, Grandpa. Do you mind checking on Brody tae see that he's all right?"

"Aye." Grandpa left the library as if his bladder was about to burst.

Zeffer half-rose but then sat back down when he saw that Paislee wasn't going anywhere. His phone dinged a text message and he read it, his mouth hard.

"What?" Paislee asked. "Is the test back already?"

"Inspector Macleod is headed home for his *dinner*, despite the ongoing investigation."

"Even officers of the law need tae eat," Paislee admonished.

"Not when a murderer is on the loose." Zeffer gestured toward the parlor and the dining room. "Could be in that verra room."

"That would be very cold-hearted."

"Planning a murder is cold. You should know that by now."

Zeffer had a point. "Lydia isn't well liked by her future mother-in-law. Someone wanted her dead, but they killed Felice by accident." Paislee fidgeted, eager to see for herself that Lydia was safe.

"You've got fine powers of observation but be careful. Call me." Zeffer took a business card with his mobile number out of his inner suit pocket. "I have a new phone."

She accepted it and put it in her small purse. "What's going on with Craigh?"

Zeffer smirked at her and stretched his leg beneath the low table. "Nice tactic. Almost worked except that I've been doing this job a while. Not gonna slip up like that."

Paislee shrugged. It had been worth a shot. She detected a weary note in his words that didn't match his unlined face. "How long? You don't look older than me."

"You are?"

"Practically thirty!" Paislee had the beginnings of crow's-feet around her eyes. "Turned twenty-nine in November."

"Young mom, but you do a fine job with Brody," he said.

It was like Zeffer knew her biggest fear somehow and the compliment made her smile. "Ta. You?"

"I'm thirty-three. Started with Scotland Yard right oot of secondary. I always wanted tae be a detective."

"Focused. I can see that about you."

Zeffer held her gaze and her stomach twirled. What on earth was that about? Sure, he was attractive, but he was also an extremely cold fish.

Paislee suspected that any woman who dug beneath the ice would be very warm indeed. She fanned her face.

His lips twitched as if he could read her mind.

God, she hoped not. Where was Grandpa? Had he escaped for real, or just made himself scarce? She bowed her head and glanced at the keys.

Zeffer did, too.

He immediately rose and stalked toward her. She snagged the keys.

"Your grandfather cheeked it?"

"He just excused himself. I assume he went tae the loo, after checking on Brody."

"You are very guid, Paislee. Cool as a cucumber." He crossed his arms and stared down at her from his over six-foot height. The fitted blue suit stretched across his broad chest. How would it feel to rest her cheek against it, as Lydia had done with Corbin?

She placed the keys in her wristlet and closed the snap. "Why won't you tell me about Craigh?"

"It's not my place." Zeffer continued to study her.

"Is he alive?" Her belly knotted.

"I cannae tell ye a thing, lass. Convince your grandfather tae see me and ask, so I can tell him."

"But—"

"That is all I can say, and it's more than I should have." Zeffer tugged at the lapels of his suit jacket.

Why did she want to apologize? Something was very wrong with her, all right. Had to be the stressful day.

"Grandpa is worried about him." She met Zeffer's eyes and saw compassion that made her knees weak. It was a good thing she was already sitting down.

"Call me if you find oot more aboot the box, and I can pass it on tae Payne. I assume you're returning tae the lion's den?" Zeffer half-turned toward the parlor.

"Aye. I'm going tae tell Lydia about the powder." She didn't ask but told him. This was a new dynamic in their relationship.

"Keep it on the down-low. Constable Payne will be here in an hour or so tae inform the family and interview them." Zeffer patted his suit pocket. "I know you will. You're not that foolish girl runnin' into a crime scene anymore."

Her body heated from the tips of her toes to her scalp at the second compliment from the aloof DI. "I will. I hope the poisoner is done now that the wedding is over."

"Ach, just when I thought we were on the same page!" Zeffer smacked his palm to his forehead. "Ye don't hope, all right? You take precautions. Ye don't open boxes. Ye don't let Lydia open a box."

Paislee tilted her head, beginning to get a crick in her neck from gawking up at him. "What about their wedding gifts?"

Zeffer sucked in a breath. "Where are those?"

"Guests would have brought them here for the reception, and there are some at the church in the dressing room."

"I'll have Constable Payne commandeer the gifts tae make sure they dinnae have strychnine in them." Zeffer grimaced. "Probably not, but we dinnae know yet the mind of this murderer."

She shivered. "There are a hundred boxes, or more."

Zeffer got on the phone and shot off a text—she imagined orders to poor Inspector Macleod to collect the wedding presents.

"I feel, er, *think* it has tae do with the brooch, DI."

He scowled at her and walked toward the door, making a call. "Payne? You on your way? Bring evidence bags tae collect the wedding gifts. You heard me. Tell the inspector tae get off his arse for Sunday roast and get tae the church and do the same . . ."

Zeffer's voice faded as he reached the hall and walked out of sight. She doubted they'd have any problems picking the lock to the dressing room in the church.

Norbert peered into the room. "All right, miss?"

"Aye." Paislee rose from her seat on the couch. "Did you see where my grandfather went?"

"Oot back. He asked me tae tell you that he'll find another way home."

"Thank you, Norbert." Paislee left the gorgeous library. Smythe Manor was lovely, beyond doubt. She went into the parlor and scanned the room. Brody and Owen were playing with the dogs. Alistair watched from a nearby armchair—close if needed, but not hovering. She liked his style. Zeffer wasn't there.

Neither was her grandfather.

Lydia hurried over to her, Sophie at her side. "What happened? What's going on?"

Paislee didn't want to blurt out the murder attempt on Lydia in front of Lydia's mother, so she kept the tragic and terrifying news to herself. "Did Grandpa come in?"

"No." Lydia studied Paislee and Paislee averted her eyes. "Should I be worried?"

"No!" Paislee chuckled. The sound was awful, and Sophie looked at her with alarm.

"You need tae try harder, lass, if we're supposed tae believe that everything's ducky." Sophie tucked her hand into the pocket of her silk mother-of-the-bride dress.

Alistair joined them. "Where's Angus?"

"That is the million-dollar question," Paislee said evasively. "Oh, thanks for watching over Brody. Those Labs are the same size as the boys."

"Bigger dog, bigger poo," Sophie said with a shrug. "I prefer our little Moxie. She's a shih tzu and staying with our neighbor while we're gone. Home Tuesday. Unless you want us tae stay another day, pet?"

"No, no," Lydia assured her mom. "I wish you wouldnae have gone tae the expense of a hotel. You should have stayed at my condo."

"I'm golfing and the room has a view of the green," Alistair said. "Got your mum tae agree tae drive the cart. It's a treat tae play Nairn, one of the best courses around."

"I know." Lydia sighed.

"Will you stay at Corbin's tonight?" Sophie asked.

"He sold his flat last month. I hope we'll go to my place soon." Lydia gave a discreet yawn. "I'm getting tired."

"Where is Corbin?" Cousins and family talked in small groups. The wedding photographer chatted with Sheila, and Paislee wondered if he had a wee crush from the way he stayed so close. Sheila was an attractive woman, but Bruce had to be at least twenty years older.

Lincoln Reid observed the family from an armchair post, jotting notes into a spiral notebook. What did he think of this tragedy?

He'd told Mary that Lydia didn't belong. Paislee was interested in his perspective.

Rosebud, Chalmers, Matthew, and Hyacinth drank wine by the fireplace. Again, not lit, but the room was warm with bodies—probably sixty people still milled about though some had left now that the food had been served. There would be no wedding cake.

Garrison, Corbin, Drew, Reginald, and Duncan surrounded a small table, the men replicas of one another in different stages of life. Garrison appeared to be giving them all a lecture. Paislee felt bad for them—the wedding of the season a tragic affair. "Lydia, why aren't you with your fiancé, or the other wives?"

Lydia brought her hand to her mouth to cover another yawn. "I hate tae take him from his dad and brothers. Cynthia already left with her and Reggie's daughter, Delilah. I overheard her tell Reggie that he could find his own ride home." She shuddered. "Nell's nice, but I cannae talk anymore aboot horse breeding."

Sophie chuckled. "Do you want tae stay here tonight, with Corbin?"

"God, no." Lydia gasped. "Oh, that makes me sound like an awful wife. Almost wife."

"No, it really doesn't. Hey, can I talk tae you for just a sec? Excuse us," Paislee said, pulling Lydia away from Alistair and Sophie.

"Sure," Sophie said. The Barrons returned to the large armchair, which was just wide enough for them both. Brody and Owen were playing Brody's video game. She nudged Lydia past Lincoln, the notetaker, to the hall, determined to find a loo.

It would be the most private room in the manor.

Norbert appeared right away. "Miss?"

"Restroom?"

He gestured with his arm but didn't escort them. "Down the hall tae the right."

"Thanks." Paislee hurried Lydia to it, went inside, then shut and locked the door of the family guest lavatory. No shower, but a toilet and sink with lavender-scented soap and thick towels.

"What the heck?" Lydia struggled free. "Have you lost your mind, Paislee Ann?"

"I haven't." She stared her best friend in the eyes and whispered, "Listen close, my dear. Someone murdered Felice with strychnine."

Lydia gulped. "That's terrible! What did she ever do tae anyone?"

Her bestie didn't understand. Paislee tried again. "Lydia. They wanted tae kill *you*."

Chapter 7

Lydia blinked gray eyes at her and finally comprehension dawned. "Felice died in my place. Oh my god, ohmygod, ohgod."

"Hush now." Paislee turned the tap water to cold and put Lydia's wrists under the flow. "Take deep breaths."

After a few minutes, Lydia was calm enough that she turned off the water and sank onto the closed toilet seat. "Did DI Zeffer tell you this? Is that what he wanted?"

"Sort of," Paislee hedged. "He also knows about Craigh."

"Who?"

"My missing uncle."

"Oh, *that* Craigh. Sairy." Lydia wore a stunned expression.

"No worries. You've had a shock." Paislee leaned her hip against the sink. "Grandpa took off on foot but left me the keys. Anyway, not a story for right now."

Lydia closed her eyes tight, counted to ten, then opened them. "Not a bad dream. Damn it."

"I'm sorry, love."

"I cannae stay here at the manor. Mary hates me. So do Rosebud and Hyacinth."

"Enough tae poison you?"

"Yeah." Lydia's shoulders slumped. "I don't know. Probably not. I cannae imagine it."

"You can stay at your condo, with Corbin. That should be safe enough. Or you can bunk in with your parents at the hotel."

Lydia crossed her arms over her lap. "Awkward."

"Or you can stay with me. Always welcome."

"Corbin will want tae be with me." Lydia looked up with uncertainty. "Right?"

"Of course he will. Especially once we tell him about the powder on the brooch. The detective has his officers confiscating your wedding gifts tae make sure that they aren't poisoned either."

"Oh my god." Lydia brought her knuckles to her lower lip. "We need tae tell Corbin what happened. His family."

"I agree, but discreetly. Constable Payne is on his way tae talk with them."

"Somebody tried tae kill me. They killed Felice." Lydia attempted to stand but her body trembled.

"Give yourself a few more minutes."

"We cannae tell my parents." Lydia peered up at Paislee. "They'll worry and there's nothing they can do."

"Or we tell them so that they can be on guard, and protect you, if you need it."

"This is outrageous." Lydia stared at Paislee.

"I know."

"Murdered."

Paislee moistened a towel with cool water and put it on Lydia's nape. The updo of her caramel curls remained in place, a testament to the hairdresser and copious amounts of hairspray.

She glimpsed her own image and wasn't surprised to see her hair in flat strands around her face, her makeup smudged slightly, and no sign of lipstick remaining on her pale lips. Not important, though, in the scheme of things. "How does that feel?"

"Better." Lydia patted the towel, then removed it and stood. This time her legs were firm and her balance steady.

Paislee put the cloth near the sink. "What's the plan?"

"I dinnae ken." Lydia sounded lost and uncertain.

So not like her friend! "How about you speak with Corbin, and I tell your parents?"

"Okay." Lydia's pulse fluttered at her throat.

"Then ask Corbin tae stay with you at your place. I don't want you tae be there alone."

"I dinnae *want* tae be there alone." Lydia sniffed and grabbed a tissue from the container on the back of the toilet. "I was supposed to be on my honeymoon. But that's the last time I'll whinge aboot it. Felice died in my place, and you, Paislee, are going tae help me find who did it."

"Zeffer is organizing with Constable Payne and Inspector Macleod." She brushed a wisp of hair from Lydia's cheek.

"I want *you*." Lydia didn't look away from Paislee until Paislee gave a slight nod.

Lydia opened the door and the friends returned to the parlor, where Brody and Owen rested against the dogs, under the table and out of the way. Mary, it seemed, had given up on getting them outside. In fact, where was Corbin's evil stepmother?

Paislee nudged Lydia toward the table with Corbin, his dad, and his brothers. Sophie and Alistair were enjoying cheese and crackers to nibble on, washed down with tea.

She joined the Barrons, pulling up a folding chair next to the wide armchair.

"How's Lydia?" Sophie asked. "I feel redundant here, and I understand better what she must have gone through before the wedding. I've tried tae talk with Mary, but she makes herself scarce when not conversing with her family or friends. Every other word is aboot good luck or bad luck. Suggested a book on aliens and astral planes. The woman's a loon."

Alistair nodded. "I have tae agree. Sophie doesnae make snap judgments, in any case."

The Barrons were kind, salt-of-the-earth types. "Lydia is . . . well." Paislee hadn't ever had to deliver bad news to them, so she wasn't sure how they'd take it.

"Just spit it oot," Alistair said. "We can see ya thinking."

"All right." Paislee swallowed, her throat dry. What she wouldn't give for a cup of tea herself. "Don't repeat what I'm about tae say, all right?"

She needn't have worried. The pair took the news of Felice's death and the attempted murder on Lydia in stride.

"And Lydia cannae stay here where she's not wanted," Sophie said, grasping the situation at once. "She could be in danger this instant." Her gaze flew to where Lydia was in conversation with Corbin.

"I think she and Corbin will both go tae her condo where she's safe."

"All right." Sophie's hand trembled as she scraped crumbs from a cracker to her napkin. "Alistair, should we stay through Wednesday? Edinburgh's not far, but I'd like tae be close."

"Sure, sure," Alistair said. "Whatever you think."

The Barrons ran an insurance business, and Sophie did the accounting. Good, honest people who didn't need a lot of frills. They adored their daughter.

"I'd like tae say our goodbyes," Sophie said. "If we go, we can whisk Lydia with us and away from this nest of vipers."

"Lydia is telling Corbin and Garrison what I just shared with you."

Sophie peered toward the table. "Lydia doesnae look comfortable. Go see what's happenin', Paislee."

She didn't need to be told twice and rushed over. Lydia had her hand on Corbin's shoulder and spoke in hushed tones to the men.

"So," Lydia was finishing up, "we need tae be on guard."

Reggie, the heir, gritted his teeth. "Poison? I cannae believe anybody would do such a thing."

"Believe it, man! Felice is dead!" Drew, the youngest of the brothers, said. Harlow was in conversation with Hyacinth and Rosebud across the room. Matthew kept checking the time on his phone, probably wondering when he could leave.

The clock over the fireplace read seven in the evening. It seemed like days had passed, not two hours.

Duncan exhaled and smacked a palm to the table, making the wine and tumblers of whisky jump. Paislee stood next to Lydia, behind Garrison.

"This is all because of those blasted brooches. The girls"—Duncan gestured toward his stepsisters—"wanted tae have a pick before Corbin and that's when this shite all started. They're spoiled, Da."

"Haud yer wheesht, son. Rosebud and Hyacinth are family. They had a rough start in life and Mary's done her best by them. I willnae hear a bad word."

Corbin faced his father. "They've bad-talked Lydia, my fiancée. Mary created this absurd curse situation. I want you tae ask them if they know anything aboot the brooch and poison; if you willnae, let me!"

Garrison's body turned rigid. "We'll have a family meeting. Tonight." He flicked a glance at Lydia. "Are ye staying at your own place?"

Corbin got up from the table. "No, Da, she's not stayin' by herself when someone tried tae kill her."

Lydia clasped his hand. "I'd hoped you could stay with me."

"If you arenae here, then you willnae be part of the meetin'," Garrison announced. "Philip will be fine after a nap. I'll call in Harry, too."

"He's grieving," Duncan said.

"We make decisions as a family." Garrison didn't budge.

Paislee felt awful for her friend, who was being shown no respect in this situation. The brothers all squirmed at the blatant disregard to Lydia.

"Da," Drew said. "Try and find that heart you claim tae have."

"This is aboot Felice's death." Garrison got up and stood nose to nose with Corbin. "Your cousin. Your *clan*."

Lydia blinked rapidly as Corbin turned to her with concern. "Dinnae fash, I'll stay with Paislee. Let me know if they find poison on any of the other gifts addressed tae me." She yanked free of Corbin.

Corbin pulled Lydia into the dining room for privacy. Paislee remained with the Smythe men and gave them all her mum-glare. Reggie blushed and Drew and Duncan both looked ashamed. Reggie said, "Cynthia and Nell both signed the prenups. They have the brooches we chose for them. Advise Lydia to be patient."

"Were they made tae feel welcome by your family?"

"Aye," Duncan said. "The cousins had parties for them, but this was before Mary."

"Mind yourself," Garrison growled.

Lydia and Corbin returned, Lydia's eyes glittering above a very fragile smile. Her lips were rosy as if she'd been kissed into submission.

Corbin regarded Paislee. "I'll walk oot with you all. I apologize for . . ." He let the sentence draw out.

"It's fine," Paislee said. It wasn't his fault his family was rich, which made Garrison seem entitled. From what she'd seen of Corbin, he was a decent man who did his best. His tech company earned a comfortable living, but would he risk being disinherited by going against his family?

Lydia fluttered her fingers at her future brothers-in-law and ignored Garrison, leading the way across the room to where her parents waited, with Brody. There was no sign of Owen, or the big Labs. It was nice that he'd had someone near his own age to play with. At this stage, money didn't matter to boys just wanting to have fun.

It took ten minutes to make the rounds and say goodbye. It was awkward that there weren't hugs or congratulations, as sadness prevailed. Corbin thanked the Barrons, kissed Lydia, hugged Paislee, punched Brody on the arm, and returned to his kin, with a backward wave at Lydia.

Norbert opened the door for them, and they stepped outside into the evening light. Crickets sounded as they walked across the gravel to their vehicles. Lydia's parents went to their car, with promises to see Lydia the next day. Paislee unlocked the Juke, and she, Lydia, and Brody climbed in, buckling up.

"What a day, huh? I'm ready for some ice cream," Paislee said in a too-cheerful tone. "I think we have a carton of chocolate fudge in the freezer at home."

"Yum!" Brody scooted to the edge of the seat. "What's for dinner?"

"You just had ham!" Paislee drove toward the main road leading home, keeping an eye out for Grandpa.

"I think Aunt Lydia should have pizza," Brody said hopefully.

"She doesn't want pizza, love." Paislee fought a smile and glanced at Lydia, who was doing her level best to keep her act together.

"Pizza sounds fine," Lydia said.

"I have Scotch at home, too," Paislee said to her dearest friend in the world. "Not The Macallan."

"That sounds even better." Lydia sniffed. "Corbin explained that this is how the family operates. He cannae let them down."

Paislee stopped at a red light.

"I told him it was fine, of course." Lydia shrugged. The silver of her wedding gown shone like a star. Though seven at night, the sky was blue.

"Are ye mad at Corbin, Aunt Lydia?" Brody turned on his video game. "He said he still wants tae marry you."

"No." Lydia continued to stare out the window. "I'm sad, that's all."

"Aboot the dead cousin, Felice?"

"Yeah. That's right."

They weren't going to tell Brody that poor Felice had been murdered or that Lydia had been the target. He'd never sleep.

At last, they reached the house. "Home sweet home, be it ever so humble," Paislee said with a laugh. Her house was over a hundred years old without the modernization of Smythe Manor.

"What does that mean, Mum?"

"Just that our house isn't fancy but it's home, and I love it."
Paislee got out of the car, and all three slammed the doors closed at
once.

Wallace barked his welcome from the foyer.

"I love it, too," Brody said.

"Me, three," Lydia agreed. She shouldered her overnight bag
and purse. "Can I borrow some yoga pants and a T-shirt? I'd like
tae get oot of this dress, and I dinnae think my lingerie is appropriate."

"My closet is your closet," Paislee said. "Help yourself." She
unlocked the front door and noticed a light on under Grandpa's
bedroom door.

He was home, thank goodness.

"Lydia, why don't you go upstairs, shower, relax. I'll put the
kettle on and get the whisky out."

Lydia hugged her, somehow keeping the tears that shimmered
in her eyes from falling. She was so strong. What a nightmare.

Brody patted Wallace, who sniffed around his legs at the strange-
dog smell on his boy's socks and shoes.

Paislee put her purse on the foyer table near the front door after
locking it and kicking the iron Scottie doorstopper in place. On her
way to the kitchen, she gave Grandpa's door a tap.

He didn't answer but the light clicked off. No way was he
sleeping. Stubborn was right, she thought, recalling what DI Zeffer
had said about Angus Shaw.

"Wash up, now," she told Brody, as her son headed into the
downstairs bathroom. She cleaned her hands in the kitchen sink.
Her home needed upgraded appliances—oh, someday!—and was
the very definition of humble, but it was hers, thanks to Gran, and
she was appreciative for the roof it provided.

A half hour later, the pizza she'd ordered had been delivered.
Lydia came down to join them, her face fresh-scrubbed without
even a hint of mascara.

"You look twelve!" Paislee chuckled.

"Your cheeks are shiny," Brody said. "We got cheese, and pepperoni. Which one do ye want, Aunt Lydia? You should pick first, since you had the worst day."

Lydia's nose turned red. "I have." She didn't even argue. "I'll take pepperoni, two slices." She accepted the plate from Brody and sat down in the fourth kitchen chair.

"Can I eat in front of the telly?" Brody asked. "I promise not tae spill."

"Be careful," Paislee admonished. "And don't forget it's a school night."

He grimaced but hurried with a loaded plate of pizza to the couch. The television clicked on.

Paislee chose a slice of cheese and put it on a plate, pouring them each a shot of whisky in addition to their mugs of tea.

"Where's Angus?" Lydia asked after a sip of Scotch. The Famous Grouse for Paislee as she didn't spend the big bucks on The Macallan brand.

"Hiding."

Lydia arched a brow, then got up to knock on the door. She spoke through the crack. "If we promise tae keep the conversation away from you know who, will ye join us? There's whisky. I've had a rotten day, and I could use a pick-me-up. You tell the worst jokes."

Oh, Lydia was good.

The door inched open, then widened as her grandpa exited the room. "I cannae deny a lass in need."

He sat at the table. Lydia passed the glass Paislee had poured for her, to him, and got another one ready. The three held their glasses up in a toast.

"What shall we drink tae?" Grandpa asked.

Paislee tried to think of a toast that would encompass the various tragedies that had occurred in less than twelve hours.

Dead family, wedding cancelled, hateful in-laws, and Lydia's life at stake. It had started with such hope. Champagne brunch on the beach, and dreams of her future as Mrs. Corbin Smythe.

Lydia whispered, "Tae finding oot who poisoned my brooch. If anybody can do it, you can, Paislee."

Paislee would do whatever it took to keep her friend safe from harm. How could Lydia consider marrying into that family until the murderer was found?

"Tae true love," Grandpa said. "If Corbin is the one, nothing else matters. I always knew Agnes was my soul mate." Her gran had felt the same, which was why Craigh had been such a bitter betrayal.

"Tae true love," Lydia repeated with teary eyes.

Paislee didn't believe in it for herself, but it was fine for others. "True love!"

The trio drank and smacked their glasses down.

"Sláinte!"

Chapter 8

Paislee awoke to the scent of Lorne sausage and the sizzle of frying eggs. Lydia had spent the night downstairs on the couch, not wanting to keep Paislee awake for what she was certain would be a restless night.

"And she's making breakfast," Paislee said, shoving the knitted comforter aside. She'd planned on getting up early to treat her friend to a home-cooked meal.

She hurried down the stairs, skipping the third and fifth to avoid the creaking out of habit, even though she could hear Brody already in the kitchen.

Wallace raced to greet her as she reached the foyer, his entire body shimmying at having company, and probably a bit of sausage on the sly.

"Morning, boy," she said, patting Wallace on the head. The black Scottish terrier had wiry but soft fur and had been the boon needed in their lives after Gran had died. Six years ago, now. Hard to believe Gran was gone but Paislee still felt her presence each day.

"Mum!" Brody called, devouring a piece of toast with orange marmalade. "Look who's here!"

Her son had known Lydia had spent the night, so that meant someone else. Paislee entered the kitchen. Styled ebony hair, a lean physique in cargo shorts and a T-shirt. Corbin fried the eggs as if quite at home at the old hob. Lydia transferred the sausage draining on a rack to a platter. Grandpa's room was dark so he must be sleeping still.

She smoothed her wayward hair, wishing she'd at least brushed her teeth. "Morning, Corbin."

A beautiful bouquet was on the counter, along with a box of chocolate. Rich mocha, Lydia's first choice, was in a to-go cup from her favorite coffee shop.

"Hello, Paislee." Corbin spread his arm to the side with a sincere expression. "I've come tae apologize for yesterday's fiasco. I should have told them all tae jump in the River Nairn, but, well, it's family."

Lydia kept smiling at Corbin, touching his arm. It was obvious that she'd forgiven him.

"I'm happy tae see you." Paislee meant every word. Corbin made Lydia grin like she'd won estate agent of the year.

Lydia placed the platter of sausage next to a bowl of fresh-cut watermelon in the center of the table, and Corbin brought the eggs.

"I'll get Grandpa. I'm surprised he's not awake already." Paislee knocked but there was no answer. Concerned, she twisted the knob. It was locked.

"He must have earplugs in, he's sleepin' so sound," Lydia decided. Her laugh floated in the air when Corbin kissed her cheek.

Paislee hoped that was the case and that he wasn't avoiding them all. She wouldn't grill him about Craigh until they were alone, so it was safe for him to come out. She slipped a note saying so under his door, then sat at the table.

There was no discussion of the murder, or Felice's death, until Brody went upstairs to get dressed for school.

Once Paislee was sure Brody was out of earshot, she murmured, "Any news?"

Corbin took the lid off his chai tea, his beverage of choice from the shop, and drank. Lydia sipped her mocha, very calm and at ease compared to her manner the prior evening.

Had the pair already discussed this, earlier?

"Uncle Harry, Jocelyn, and Oliver were at the manor last night," Corbin said. "They stayed in the spare bedrooms, too torn up tae go home. Same with Uncle Philip and Sheila."

"Understandably so," Paislee said.

"There was a lot of Scotch consumed last night." Corbin winced and tapped his temple. "It was decided tae have Felice's funeral on Saturday. There was a request that we hold off on the wedding for a while."

Lydia nodded that she already knew and was okay with it, too.

Wallace pawed at the back door, so Paislee got up to let him out. The beautiful June morning showed clear blue skies, the sun warming the flowers in Gran's pots to create a mesmerizing perfume. Her dog chased a squirrel up a chestnut tree and birds chirped from the clothesline.

Paislee kept the door open and returned to the table. Lydia was shoulder to shoulder with Corbin, their chairs tucked close. "When are you thinking? Fall, maybe?"

"Christmas is fine by me." Lydia shuddered. "According tae Mary, June brides are supposed tae be lucky. She'll have tae rethink that particular jewel of wisdom. I dinnae know where she comes up with these stories."

"Da met and married her while I was at university," Corbin said. "I was eighteen, and our mum only gone a year. It came as a shock. Poor Drew was still at home, fourteen years old, tae suddenly have sisters and a new mother-figure."

Paislee found family dynamics very interesting. "How did Drew take it?"

"He signed up for every sport or activity there was tae stay oot of the house," Corbin replied, a smile on his lips.

"Drew is a sweetheart," Lydia said. "I like Harlow, too. You think he's serious aboot her?"

"Aye. But after this fiasco, he's in no hurry tae follow the Smythe tradition and pick a Luckenbooth brooch from the family treasure trove."

"Cannae blame him." Lydia drank from her cup.

"How old were Rosebud and Hyacinth at the time?" Paislee asked.

Corbin scooted back a little from the table. "Hyacinth is oldest, twenty now, so eight? Aye, and Rosebud would have been seven. We had nothing in common, yet Dad expected us tae be a big happy family." He scowled. "Like our mother was never sick."

"What happened tae Mary's first husband?" Paislee stacked the empty plates and half-listened for Brody, still upstairs getting ready for school. "From the righteous way she acted about Lydia's divorce, I'm assuming he must have died somehow."

"You're right aboot that. Cancer. They met at a grieving circle for spouses at the church led by Minister Angela." Corbin shifted on the wooden chair. "Mary was worried aboot her daughters with no father to look oot for them and ours swooped in tae be the hero. He couldnae save our mum, but he could save them."

Lydia patted his knee in commiseration.

Paislee shivered as a breeze tickled her neck. "Were they close with Felice and the other girl cousins?"

Corbin considered this, then shrugged. "I guess so. I mean, we were all friends, a pack, and they werenae treated ill or ostracized. Da would never stand for that."

Rosebud and Hyacinth had whispered together to the point of rudeness whenever they'd come to the same party. Jocelyn had said she'd seen Felice and Rosebud laughing before the wedding.

"Do you think, Corbin, that your stepsisters might be jealous?"

"They have no reason tae be," Corbin said. "Mary ensures everything is equal for the girls."

And yet Duncan had mentioned that this had all started when Rosebud and Hyacinth had seen the brooches and wanted their own.

"Corbin, you don't know this aboot my best friend, but Paislee has a verra curious nature. I've asked her tae help me find who poisoned the brooch." Lydia scooped a curl behind her ear.

"The police are handling it," he said. "Constable Payne confirmed last night that they found the box in the bathroom. Powder was inside. It's being tested right now."

Paislee sipped her tea to calm her tummy. Who would be so cruel?

Lydia finished her mocha. "While the police do that, we will help find who wants me oot of the picture. Now, Minister Angela dropped off the box while we were getting our makeup done. My bridesmaids were all around the vanity table where she placed it."

"Meaning, Rosebud and Hyacinth," Corbin said, his tone sharp. A ding sounded from his pocket.

"And Senta. Paislee." Lydia didn't react to how quickly his defenses rose.

The family was very protective of one another—which was sweet if one was included. "Bruce Dundas, the wedding photographer, showed up as soon as he was done with your groomsmen's photoshoot." Paislee tapped the table.

Corbin pulled his phone from his shorts' pocket and read his text messages. "How did you know the gift was from Mary, since the brooch was in a different box?"

Paislee glanced at Lydia, then Corbin. "The note read, *For Lydia, good luck on your special day.*"

"I recognized Mary's handwriting. I've been the recipient of many to-do—or to-don't—lists. Whoever traded the box used the same ribbon and tag." Lydia nibbled on her lower lip, which probably tasted like chocolate.

"They had tae have made the switch from the velvet box in a ventilated area, probably outside, with gloves and a mask, or they would have chanced inhaling the powder themselves." Were the young women capable of such a thing? They were both educated, and the Internet provided answers to anything you might want to know.

Corbin shuddered and put his phone away. "That's too real, ladies. I dinnae like it, but I cannae deny the truth."

Lydia rested her head on his shoulder. "We have tae discover who is behind this and stop them from trying again."

"The constable said he'd let us know as soon as the tests come back." Corbin's eyes were sad.

"Zeffer is in town and will lend his expertise. He's proven in the past that he's quite smart when it comes tae cracking cases." Paislee hadn't always thought so. Lydia and Corbin snuggled together, and she imagined her leaning on Zeffer in such a way—and immediately banished the image. What was the matter with her?

"Thanks tae you," Lydia teased. "For a while there, Zeffer was very active in our wee shire. The last year has been simpler."

"Planning your wedding was far from simple, Lydia, although the crime element hasn't affected us as much. Inspector Macleod has been around more. I think he's a better fit for our community," Paislee said. "He actually likes people."

They shared a laugh that broke the heavy tension. She and Lydia could discuss the sisters and their motivation later when it wouldn't upset Corbin so much.

Wallace raced in with one of Brody's socks in his mouth that must have fallen off the clothesline and worried it like he was playing tug-of-war with an imaginary friend. She heard her son's bedroom door slam upstairs.

"Will you come tae Felice's funeral?" Corbin asked. "There will be a small lunch afterward, downstairs at the church."

"If you'd like, sure. I'll see if Grandpa wants tae go, too, since Saturday is his day off. Amelia can handle Cashmere Crush, with Elspeth." Paislee gathered the dishes and brought them to the sink. "What are you two doing today while I'm working my fingers tae the bone?"

"Phoning the travel agent," Corbin said with a sigh. "Tae put our honeymoon package on hold. Beautiful Germany will have tae wait."

"You should just go anyway." Paislee started to fill the sink with hot water and a squirt of lemony dish soap. "You deserve a vacation."

"I'll do those, Paislee," Lydia said. "What do you think aboot that, Corbin? Not a bad idea. Take a holiday."

"We cannae even consider it until after Saturday." Corbin shrugged. "Let's discuss it later. See what your parents think. I like them a lot, Lydia."

"I'm glad." Lydia giggled. "Especially since we've invited ourselves to play golf with them."

"I dinnae want tae let you oot of my sight until this is over." Corbin scooched Paislee away from the sink. "Whatever you can do tae help us, I would be indebted."

Brody ran down the stairs, his hand squeaking on the post at the bottom as he swung himself around. "Mum! We're going tae be late!"

She checked the time on the cooker, then the wall clock just to be sure. No way could they make it to Fordythe Primary in ten minutes. "Blast it! It'll be our first tardy this year."

When they arrived at two minutes past nine, Paislee saying many Hail Marys along the way, Hamish McCall himself was standing out front, checking his watch. The headmaster held the blue door of the primary school open for Brody as her son raced in, his palm raised for her to wait in the queue.

She did, the old tension of being called out for bad behavior roiling in her belly like too much coffee. Hamish and she had been friendly last year but that had all come to a halt when he'd been forced to choose school policy over her feelings.

There was no blame toward him for his actions, just acceptance, and this whole year Paislee hadn't been tardy once—her scrawl on the parent handbook had been . . . adamant? Belligerent? Defiant? All of those things.

She rolled down her window and Hamish leaned his elbow on the open ledge. He favored brown suits that matched his brown eyes.

"Not falling into old habits, are you?" His full mouth twitched to show he was joking.

"Can't give me a detention," she replied, not amused.

"You and Brody have both done well. I believe he's up for a student award at the graduation party."

Pride in her son filled her. "I'll be there. He's worked very hard on his end-of-year school project." The class had raised money for a 3D printer in the room, which had been fun but, unfortunately, the plastic filament created waste when these days the catchphrase was green living through natural energy and recycling. Brody and his team had designed several compost bins to recycle, showing the difference between plastic and PLA—polylactic acid—pellets. PLA pellets were biodegradable, and, he hoped to prove, the better choice for the planet.

"There's a prize offered from Zero Waste Scotland. His teacher told me Brody's got a guid chance. He'll be going tae Nairn Academy?"

"Aye."

Hamish searched her face. "I'll miss seeing you, and Brody, when he moves on tae secondary."

He would, huh? Her cheeks heated.

The headmaster would no longer be her and Brody's "boss" as she'd taken to thinking of him. For the life of her, she couldn't summon a clever reply, like, *We won't miss you,* or *We'll miss you like a dog misses a flea.*

She *would* miss him and that was the truth.

Hamish was thirty-four and young to be in charge, which she'd attributed to his insistence on following the rules. He was a stickler for them. They'd gone round and round last year. This year she'd done everything in her power to fly under the radar.

Hamish cleared his throat and backed up a step from the Juke. "See you, then," he said as if he were looking forward to it.

She swallowed, nervous. "Bye, now."

Pulling away from the school, Paislee exited to the street that led to Cashmere Crush. Had that just happened? Had there been a spark?

Paislee had no intention of dating until Brody was in college and probably not even then. She enjoyed her single life and the fact that she had nobody to blame when things went awry but herself. Lydia teased her about being a nun, but it wasn't that. She just couldn't afford to act on things like desire, not when she was in charge of raising her son.

Parking behind the shop, she shook off any lingering ideas of what might happen in the future to focus on the present.

Jerry McFadden, early this morning, waited for her in his truck to deliver her order of yarn. He hopped out and went to the back while she hurried up the four steps to open the door for him.

"Sorry tae be late. Lydia and I got tae blethering," she said.

"No worries here, lass." Jerry brought two boxes of yarn inside and set them on her counter.

She wrote him a check. "How are you?"

"Fine, fine. How was the wedding?"

"Och." Paislee blew out a breath. Of course, folks were going to want to know. What to say? "It was delayed," she said.

Jerry's eyes widened and he pulled on his mustache. "She have a case of cold feet?"

"No!" Why did everyone assume the nerves were Lydia's?

"What, then?"

"There was an accident. A tragedy, really. Felice Smythe, Corbin's cousin, fell down the church stairs and broke her neck."

"That's terrible." Jerry crossed himself. "Maybe a sign tae not get hitched?"

"You sound like Mary Smythe, Corbin's stepmother. She's the most superstitious woman I've ever met." Paislee didn't continue with the rest of the story, and how Lydia had been the victim of attempted murder.

She hadn't had the chance to read the paper yet today since there'd been company. Hopefully, Grandpa would bring it when he arrived for his shift this afternoon.

"For a Scot that's saying something. I grew up with fears of being stolen by fairies if I wasnae minding Mum."

Paislee chuckled. "I know it." A knock sounded on her front door. "You have a good day, Jerry. I've got tae get that."

"You too—my condolences tae Lydia, poor dear."

"I'll tell her." She unlocked the front door, as Jerry went out the back.

"Morning," DI Zeffer said.

She widened the door. "Hiya."

He came in and searched her shop filled with shelves of colored yarn. "Is Angus here?"

"Naw. He'll be in at twelve."

"Paislee, I need tae talk with him." Zeffer exuded arrogance. No, not arrogance. Confidence? "It's urgent."

"You can try him at home."

"I was just there. Lydia knocked on Angus's bedroom door, and he didnae answer."

Wily old man. What was he up to?

"You tell him that if he doesn't talk tae me this bloody day, I *will* tell you everything."

"Oh!" That should get her grandpa chatting like a blue jay. "I'll say those exact words. Want tae save yourself some time and tell me now?" She was about to find out the truth! Suddenly, she wasn't sure she wanted to know.

Blaise O'Connor walked in next, with Mary Beth Mullholland.

Zeffer knew he couldn't hold her up and strode past them with a very curt "Ladies."

"He's cute when he's mad," Blaise said with a speculative gleam in her amber eyes. "I swear he reminds me of someone. One of these days . . ."

Chapter 9

The morning flew by as Paislee knitted with her friends and loyal customers Blaise and Mary Beth. They discussed the cancelled wedding and Felice Smythe, to die so young and tragically. She kept her mouth closed about the attempt on Lydia's life. Customers streamed in and out and she was grateful for her hearty breakfast that kept her engine revved.

At quarter till noon, Blaise folded the wool blanket she was making for her daughter, Suzannah, into her knitting bag. She liked to eat lunch with her husband, Shep, who was the golf pro at Nairn's most prestigious course. "There was just a brief mention in the paper today of Felice's death, but I'll be sure tae send flowers tae the family. Oliver is a client of Shep's."

Mary Beth frowned and lowered her summer project of pink socks for her twin girls, nine this year, and cute as cherubs. "Paislee, you were at the wedding, when Felice fell. I cannae believe I didnae put this together sooner—is that why the detective was here so early?"

Her face heated and she blamed her blushes on the true curse of being a redhead.

"Paislee!" Blaise stared at her. "What do you know aboot Felice's demise? Was it more than just a simple fall?"

The DI had asked her to keep things quiet, but he hadn't forbidden her from saying anything at all. Paislee tried to divert their attention. "Zeffer wants tae talk tae Grandpa, about Craigh." At the moment her shop was empty of customers, but this was summer in Nairn and walk-ins were frequent.

"Is that all?" Mary Beth asked, her sense of something more on high alert.

Paislee lowered her voice to a murmur. "They're investigating Felice's death."

"Oh no," Blaise said. "Why?"

Paislee glanced toward the back door and then the front to make sure they were still alone. "Felice had Lydia's Luckenbooth brooch in her hand, after it had gone missing."

"And you're just now mentioning this?" Blaise huffed an offended breath.

"I shouldn't say anything at all—and you can't! Not even tae Shep, or Arran." Paislee prayed for customers to walk through the door to keep her mouth zipped tight. Mary Beth's husband was a very successful solicitor.

The vein at Mary Beth's throat pulsed in rapid beats. "I cannae believe it. I know the Smythes. Who could want tae do them harm? The family is verra generous with fund-raisers, and well liked by their peers."

Blaise looked at the time and rose. "I have tae go. Please give Lydia my love when you see her. And dinnae think we're done with this subject, Paislee, my sweet."

Mary Beth also stood. She'd quit drinking a year ago and had lost a pants size, she was proud to say. She was an amazing cook, so she'd never be thin, but she was happy, and Arran liked her curves. "I have a meeting with the girls' teacher at Fordythe, or else I'd stay here and badger you aboot it."

"I trust you both, but I can't tell you what I don't know." The Knit and Sip circle Paislee ran on Thursday nights had occasionally chimed in to help her with a knotty problem.

"I was sad tae have missed the wedding, but mibbe I can make the next one," Mary Beth joked.

They'd had a prior engagement so couldn't come. Because the Smythes' immediate family was so large, Lydia's guest list had been small with her few chosen friends that included the Knit and Sip ladies.

Paislee shook her head. "That idea will give her hives!"

"Do they know when they'll reschedule?" Blaise asked as they all walked toward the door. Paislee peered out the frosted front window for her grandfather, due to start his afternoon shift.

"No." Paislee didn't see a single silver hair. "Saturday is Felice's funeral, and that's taken precedence, of course."

"Aye." Mary Beth clucked her tongue to her teeth.

Paislee waved off her friends with a promise to relay hugs to Lydia, and a reminder of their get-together Thursday evening.

At half-past noon, she called the house. No answer. Her grandpa liked to walk to Cashmere Crush, which was a mile from their house.

He was never late.

He hadn't opened his bedroom door this morning for her, or Lydia, or Zeffer.

Her instincts fired up that he needed her, even if he wouldn't admit it. For the first time in a long while, Paislee put a sign on the door that she was gone for lunch and locked the shop.

She raced the Juke home, not sure what she expected to find.

Lydia had left a note on the table, with her thanks. Corbin had signed it, too. She'd left the flowers but would get them later to bring back to her condo. She used her signature *XO Lyd.*

Wallace had been put in the back garden. It was fenced and the pup had protection with the covered porch if it rained. After letting the dog in, giving him fresh water, and making sure he had dry kibble, she tapped on Grandpa's door.

No answer.

Paislee knocked louder. "If you don't open up, I'm going tae take the door down."

A twist sounded of the lock on the knob, and then Grandpa peered out through an inch between the wall and door with weary, bloodshot eyes.

"What's wrong? Are ye ill? I can call the ambulance or take you tae the doctor." Her heart thumped with worry.

"Settle down, now." Grandpa exhaled and patted his face for his glasses, but he hadn't put them on yet. After another loud breath, he said, "I didnae sleep last night. Couldn't. I went for a long drive, following the coast road. Going over every possibility in me mind. I wasnae a guid dad tae Craigh. I could have been better."

Paislee could relate to that fear of not being good enough. No wonder he didn't sleep. "Zeffer dropped in at Cashmere Crush this morning. He was here, too." Since it was obvious that her grandfather was on edge, she didn't mention Zeffer's threat to tell her everything.

"I know." His body quivered. "I'm a coward, lass."

"You're not!"

"Give the DI a ring. I'm ready tae face the worst."

Paislee reached into her pocket and got out her mobile, dialing the new number for the detective. It rang and rang, forcing her to leave a message. "Paislee Shaw here. Please return this call as soon as possible."

Blasted DI had made a point of saying that he needed to talk to her grandpa today and then, when she actually had the old man willing to spill his guts, Zeffer wasn't around.

Her phone rang. "That was fast!" she answered.

"You were expecting me?" Lydia asked. "How sweet."

"Sorry, Lyd."

Grandpa's face paled and she urged him to widen the door and come out. He didn't.

"Way tae hurt a girl's feelings," Lydia chirped over the phone.

"Mum and Da insist you, Grandpa, and Brody join us for dinner tonight at the Lion's Mane. Dad loves the fish and chips there."

Paislee would normally have no qualms to a meal and visit with the Barrons, and she loved fish and chips as much as the next lass, but she sighed. Something was wrong with Grandpa, and she had to find out what. "I'll give a tentative yes."

"What's up?"

"This has tae do with the other matter at our house."

"Craigh?"

"Aye."

"Hmm. You still have tae eat and it's the last time you'll see my parents before they head home tae Edinburgh tomorrow."

"Where are you going to be, my beautiful friend?"

"Corbin and I will stay at my condo."

"Good. I won't worry, then." Paislee smoothed her bangs from her forehead. "I'll do my best tae get us there. What time?"

"Seven. We're going tae invite Garrison and Mary, too."

"Do you think that's wise? Considering one of the Smythes tried tae kill you?"

Lydia's quick, indrawn breath whistled. "If we cannae trust his dad, then I dinnae ken what tae do. I'll be careful. Besides, Corbin doesnae think they'll come."

"Text me! Are you having fun, other than that?"

"Oh aye—Corbin and my da really hit it off. Me and Mum are driving the golf cart with cocktails. My favorite part of the sport."

Paislee laughed. "See you at seven, then." She ended the call.

Grandpa shook his head, on the edge of a full-blown mutiny. "I am not going tae dinner. I need tae find oot what Zeffer knows aboot Craigh." He pinched the bridge of his nose. "How can it possibly be good news?"

"Grandpa!" She'd wondered the same but doubted it after Zeffer's eager demeanor. "If the DI discovered news of Craigh he'd be obligated by law tae tell you, not string you along."

With that slim hope, Grandpa straightened and widened the bedroom door. "Ye think so? God, I hope you're right."

"Get your glasses and I'll make us lunch while we wait for Zeffer."

Color returned to Grandpa's cheeks after a bowl of chicken soup and cheese sarnies, but she still worried he'd pushed himself too far. "Want tae rest this afternoon? I can handle the shop."

"I'll come into work with you, or else I'll lose me mind wondering what tae do next." Grandpa dipped into his room and dressed for the day, his silver-gray hair combed back.

As Paislee drove to Cashmere Crush, Grandpa polished his lenses on his T-shirt. "I need to get my prescription checked."

He'd just gotten new glasses a month ago. "Why is that?"

"Well, last night? I thought I saw Craigh. Wishful thinking, and I drove around Dairlee for hours. Had to be a cruel trick of the light." Grandpa put them on again. "What I wouldnae give tae see Craigh one more time." He turned toward her, his elbow on the armrest. "I just know that Zeffer is going tae tell me my only remaining child is dead."

Her stomach rolled and she wanted to console him, but Paislee didn't have the words. Over the last year, Grandpa had kept Craigh alive in his mind. On the flip side of the coin, he had no proof that Craigh was dead, so maybe that slim hope had been worth hanging on to. To finally face harsh facts would bring anyone to their knees.

They arrived at the shop and both dove into work, treating the subject of Craigh like a patch of poison ivy to be avoided at all costs. Though she could tell Grandpa was ready to rip the bandage off, Zeffer remained MIA.

Chapter 10

That night the three Shaws joined Lydia, Corbin, and her parents at the Lion's Mane pub. The Barrons were very kind, and it was difficult not to compare them to Garrison and Mary. Though invited, the couple had declined, with Mary claiming fatigue. Stress from the curse, Rosebud had told Drew, who had passed the message along to Corbin.

By unspoken agreement, they didn't discuss Felice's death, Craigh, or the attempt on Lydia's life. Paislee knew from experience that these things often took time to sort.

Laughter was the perfect medicine for Corbin and Lydia as they sat next to each other on the booth seat, with no pressure from his family. The old pub was cozy and comfortable, and the fish and chips were truly the best in Nairn.

"Are you sure you dinnae need us tae stay an extra day?" Sophie asked as the meal wound to a close. "It's nice tae see you so happy, Lydia. And Corbin. You bring a smile to our daughter's face."

"Just say the word and your mother and I can be back again." Alistair beamed at the couple, and then Paislee, Brody, and Grandpa. He snagged the check and wouldn't hear of anybody pitching in.

In the car park, Paislee hugged the Barrons goodbye, and So-phie squeezed her close. "You'll watch oot for Lydia? Oh, I know you will. Despite the smiles, I'm so worried for her."

"I'll keep you in the loop," Paislee promised—one mother to another.

"I have Constable Payne's business card and I'm not afraid tae use it!"

It was after nine by the time the Shaws arrived home and that meant getting Brody ready for school the next day.

"Homework?" she asked.

"I did it during class today but tomorrow we need tae work on the compost project after dinner, okay?"

"Sure. I'm curious tae see your results with the plastic bottle."

Brody had a hurried bath and was yawning by the time she tucked him into bed. "Night, love." She kissed his forehead, patted Wallace, and said a prayer for the angels, and Gran, to look after him while he slept.

Paislee went downstairs to speak with Grandpa, but he was al-ready in his room with the lights out. He was either hiding from her, or genuinely exhausted from his previous sleepless night. She understood the fear of not doing enough as a parent and said a prayer for him, too. After folding the laundry, Paislee climbed the stairs to seek her bed, and sleep. She thought she'd be awake with worry but was out before she'd finished counting goats with cash-mere wool.

At noon the next day, Lydia arrived at Cashmere Crush on Grandpa's bootheels. The old man had a smile for her best friend as he held the front door open for her. He'd been quiet at breakfast, taking his mug of tea to the back porch with Wallace. Neither of them had brought up Zeffer. His absence was like a bad joke.

"Thank you, Angus," Lydia said. Her manner was relaxed rather than tense and the change did Paislee's heart good.

"My pleasure, lass." Grandpa shuffled in, hand in his khaki pocket. He removed his lightweight summer tam and flung it across the shop to the counter like a soft wool Frisbee.

"Paislee, I just checked with Angus here, and he's fine if I borrow you for the afternoon."

The wedding was on hold, and Paislee longed for the return of her routine. She had four sweater orders to juggle, all due next month, not to mention Brody's project. "I don't know, Lydia. Can it wait?"

"I've set up a meeting with Lincoln Reid," Lydia said. "I'm a bit nervous."

"The fellow who resembles a walking skeleton," Grandpa said.

The austere historian had sat in his armchair and taken notes, saying to Mary that Lydia didn't belong with the Smythes. Paislee lowered her sweater project to the counter and eyed the time. Someone wanted her bestie dead, and Lincoln might have answers. "I only have a few hours." She could burn the midnight oil to get the sweater orders done.

"I cannae fathom why he told Mary I didnae belong," Lydia said. "But if you're too busy I guess I could go alone . . ."

Not a good idea. Paislee exhaled, then looked at Grandpa. He was all grins for Lydia.

"I'll pick up Brody after school," Grandpa offered. "Take yer time."

"No need." Paislee shook her head. "Brody and Edwyn Maclean have football practice, and then Brody is going tae Edwyn's afterward."

"I've plenty tae keep me busy here." Grandpa pulled a magazine from his pocket. "Got the latest fishing guide."

Normally Elspeth worked Tuesdays, Wednesdays, and Fridays but Paislee had asked her to switch today for Saturday so that Paislee could go to Felice's funeral. Grandpa had Saturdays off. "If the shop gets busy, call me, okay?" Paislee reached for her purse and phone. "Seems I'm free for the afternoon. Where is Corbin?"

"He's with his uncles and his cousins. They're choosing pictures for Felice's funeral on Saturday, tae put together a video tribute. Corbin suggested I might be happier spending the day with you."

Not with his family, who had tried to kill her. "Got it. Your parents left? They were so sweet last night at the pub."

"Yep. Mum missed her little Moxie so much that they were on the road by eight this morning."

"They're such good people, Lydia."

"I am blessed with my family." Her nose wrinkled. "Which makes being with Corbin's clan all the more difficult because I know it doesnae have tae be so toxic."

Grandpa sighed and Paislee knew he was thinking of Craigh. They would get to the bottom of this, this week. If only Zeffer would show up. He was always around when she didn't want him to be, but now?

He'd disappeared as surely as Craigh. Earlier this morning, she'd put in a call to Amelia at the station. Nobody, not even Inspector Macleod, knew where Zeffer was . . . at least not that they would share with Paislee.

She and Lydia bid Grandpa goodbye and walked out the front, where Lydia had parked her Mercedes. Paislee buckled up, wishing she had on something less casual than her denim capris and a short-sleeved knit blouse. Lydia, elegant as always, had on a linen sheath. Did it wrinkle? Of course not.

Lydia expertly pulled into traffic.

"How did you get Lincoln Reid tae see you?" He'd been chummy with Mary. Also Bruce, the wedding photographer. Come to think of it, he'd had a steady stream of visitors while in his armchair with his notebook.

She supposed Lincoln and Bruce both recorded events in different ways, which was obviously important for the family.

"He really didnae want tae, but I had Corbin ask." Lydia adjusted her sunglasses on her slim nose. "And Lincoln might be under the impression that Corbin will be joining me."

Paislee chuckled at the subterfuge. "Should we bring chocolate? Gran believed you should never arrive somewhere empty-handed."

"She was a wise lady." Lydia stopped at a candy store on the way to Lincoln's home and picked up exquisitely crafted chocolates. "Nothing with nuts, in case he doesnae have his teeth," Lydia decided.

"He can always gum the caramel." Paislee placed the shiny black box with a gold ribbon on her lap. "It might sweeten his attitude toward you."

They arrived at an old square building that housed flats and parked in the lot. It appeared almost derelict. "You're sure this is it? I imagined something less . . . decrepit."

"Yep. These were built around 1875 but had a facelift after a fire. This is prime real estate," her bestie said. Since Lydia worked for a premier estate agency, she was in the position to know. "Each suite in here goes for half a million pounds easy."

It didn't look expensive, but perhaps that was part of the draw. People with blunt didn't need to flaunt it.

"Is he an investor, like the Smythes?" Paislee asked, getting out of the Mercedes.

"I asked Corbin how Lincoln fit in the picture. Seems that Lincoln Reid had married one of the Smythe cousins decades ago, so he's considered family. She's gone now, and Lincoln lives here alone."

That put a different spin on the man for Paislee. "I'm glad we're bringing him chocolate."

"Why?"

"What if he's lonely?"

Lydia raised her hand to stop Paislee from going any further. "You've already adopted one grandfather; you dinnae need another."

"Very funny."

Lydia pressed the button outside the building and Lincoln let them in with an answering buzz. Inside, the lobby was dark and stuffy without a single window. There was no reception desk or security. Paislee shivered.

"I prefer modern," Lydia said. "Tae industrial. It's so cold!"

For once, Paislee agreed. They took the elevator to the fifth floor. "It smells like cabbage and potatoes," she murmured. "With a hint of air freshener."

Lydia laughed. "Right you are." She stopped before a door marked REID and knocked.

"Coming," a wavery voice answered. The knob twisted, and the door was pulled back.

The flat had been exquisitely decorated at one point in the last fifty years. Maroon, hunter green, dark wood. Sconces on the wall flickered. Either the place was haunted, or the bulbs needed to be changed.

"Hello, Lincoln." Lydia offered him the gold-ribboned box of chocolate.

Lincoln accepted it, looked at Paislee, who was not Corbin, and seemed like he might shut them out in the hall.

Paislee stepped over the threshold with a friendly smile. "What a lovely home! I hope you don't mind me joining Lydia today. Corbin had a family emergency. We met Sunday, at the manor?"

To act so forward was out of character for Paislee, but this was for Lydia, who wanted to be part of this clan someday.

"Oh, yes. Your son was playing with Owen and the dogs. You can tell a lot aboot a person's character from how they interact with animals." Lincoln gestured for them to come in. "He's a guid boy. I put on water for tea."

"Ta," Paislee said.

Lydia patted Paislee's shoulder.

"I'm diabetic, so I'll pass on the chocolate." Lincoln placed the box on a side table in the long hall. "My maid will enjoy it."

The runner was thick and luxurious, even if dated. To the left was a sitting room with chairs and a sofa. A low table, a fireplace with family photos on the mantel, and shelves of books. The hall was thin and crowded with paintings in gilt and silver frames. To the very end of the corridor, and the right, sounded a shrieking kettle.

"Do you mind?" Paislee asked as she hurried by the slower man.

"No, dear."

She reached the bright, cheery kitchen and turned off the gas burner on the hob. Steam rose from the kettle's spout. Fresh green plants trailed from pots on the windowsill to the ceiling. They teemed with verdant health. "Lincoln, you have a green thumb!"

Lincoln, followed by Lydia, shuffled into the kitchen. "It brings me joy tae keep the plants alive. Some of the cuttings from this English ivy are from when my sweet Florene was alive."

"I have the opposite talent," Paislee said, owning her lack of skill. "May I fix the tea?"

Lincoln had clear canisters of dried leaves on the counter, and another of sugar. She didn't recognize the white powdery substance in one of the jars closest to the water pitcher for the plants.

"I like a dark Pekoe steamed for five minutes, then it's ready," he said.

Paislee poured the water into the ceramic teapot and Lincoln set the timer shaped like an egg. "I'm sorry about your wife, Florene. How long ago was that?"

"It's been twenty years next month and I miss her every day." His rheumy eyes misted. "I talk tae her, in here. I think the plants like it."

"I've heard that before," Lydia said. "Music and conversation help plants thrive."

"Between my brown thumb and your singing, Lyd, we best stay away from the ivy," Paislee teased. Lincoln chortled.

"I've got the tea cart set up in the parlor," Lincoln said. "With scones."

"Do you bake, too?" Lydia asked.

"No. I order from the corner market every week." He tapped the landline with a gnarled finger. "I know me limitations."

They all laughed politely. What was in the canister? It wasn't marked with a label. She reached for it. "Sugar? Powdered creamer?"

Lincoln snatched it from her. "It's me special blend of plant food. It would make you sick."

Paislee glanced at Lydia, who stilled like a mouse when the lights flashed on. Before she could ask what was in it, the timer sounded.

Her heart pounded hard.

Lincoln returned the canister and washed his hands in the kitchen sink. "There we are. Paislee, will you bring it for us? We'll follow."

She gathered the pot and water on a tray, but there was no chance to further study the powder. It made sense with his lovely plants that he'd have special food for them.

The trio traversed to the parlor, where Lincoln had a fancy service displayed, as he'd been expecting Corbin. And if for some reason Lincoln was the killer, it was doubtful he'd be after Corbin, so Paislee felt relatively safe in consuming the refreshments.

Once seated, Paislee poured rich dark tea into the cups and handed them around.

"Why are ye here, Lydia?" Lincoln asked abruptly. This question proved that though the man was ancient as dirt he was mentally on his game.

"Why did you tell Mary that I dinnae belong in the family?" Lydia countered.

"It's nothing personal, Lydia. A divorced woman?" Lincoln clucked his tongue to his teeth. "A career is one thing, but the Smythes believe in forever. The Barrons come from nothing."

"They are Scots through and through." That truth gave Lydia confidence and she sipped, eyeing the room. "What does a family historian do?"

"It's not an actual job," Lincoln chuckled. "A hobby withoot pay. Before the DNA websites were so popular, Florene and I kept track by hand." He raised his teacup toward the bookshelves away from the small window. "All of those are records we gathered."

Paislee turned to peek over her shoulder. There had to be at least a hundred volumes marked SMYTHE on the spine.

"When I die, Oliver will take over. He and Jocelyn agreed tae share the duty. He was resistant at first, but I'm not going tae live forever. I just turned eighty-five."

"That's wonderful," Lydia said, sitting on the edge of her plush armchair. "What is your secret?"

He dipped a scone in his teacup as if to soften it before taking a bite. The man looked like he was a hundred and Lydia was being kind. The dim orangish light did him no favors.

"Purpose," he said, after nibbling the corner with large yellow teeth. "The Smythe history has given me something bigger tae accomplish. After my Florene passed it was difficult to carry on, but I could feel her spirit. Alexa told me that Florene is often here."

"Alexa?" Lydia asked.

Paislee did her best not to check the corners for shadows, but she understood what he meant. Sometimes she felt Gran's love around her, too.

"Alexa Selkirk is the Nairn librarian." Lincoln swallowed tea to down the last of his scone. "A dear friend of Mary's."

Paislee immediately pictured the old brick building that smelled like mothballs, books, and dust cleaner. It was a bright space where she and Brody used to go for storytime when he'd been a toddler. "I love the library!"

Lincoln placed the teacup in its saucer. "Alexa is also a witch."

Lydia snorted tea and coughed. Paislee set her cup on the low table, jumped up, and patted Lydia's back.

"All right?"

"Aye." Lydia's eyes watered as she took in a shaky breath.

Lincoln was quite pleased with himself about that reaction. "It's true. Alexa can see auras and divine the future. Withoot a doubt she is psychic. She's the one who told Mary that your Luckenbooth brooch was cursed."

Paislee sat back down and studied Lincoln. "You didn't tell her?"

"No, no. My scribbles are verified findings—nothing as fanciful as that." Lincoln shook his head.

"You like Mary?" Paislee set her cup in the saucer.

"Her naivety amuses me," Lincoln said. "She's very interested in the family history and offered tae continue the project when I'm gone, but I'd already chosen Oliver. He's a blood relative. Not like Mary or her stepdaughters."

Paislee heard the censure. "But you also married into the Smythe family. That's a wee bit hypocritical of you."

Lydia sipped her tea and watched them over the rim of porcelain.

With a heavy exhale, Lincoln explained, "Florene and I were cousins. I didnae carry the Smythe name, but we had the same blood in our veins."

"Is that legal?" Lydia asked.

"Aye." Lincoln straightened proudly. "In Scotland, it's legal for first cousins tae wed. Back in the day, there werenae a lot of options for marriage tae keep the bloodlines strong, which is why it started."

Paislee took a drink of her tea. It was delicious. The scones, too. She was trying very hard to not be creeped out by cousins getting married. "Is it common now?"

Lincoln waved a scone, dripping crumbs into the plush area rug. "It was common enough as Florene and I discovered, unraveling the Smythe past. There was no evidence of children having defects like the doctors scare you aboot. It wasnae a factor for us as we'd already decided to dedicate ourselves tae documenting Smythe Clan history and didnae want bairns. We loved each other so, so much."

His gaze lowered and his hand trembled.

Paislee got up to pat his arm. "It's a fine legacy. I'm sure that Oliver and Jocelyn will do you proud."

"Felice was not interested," Lincoln said. "It's a shame she lost her life, so young."

"Do you believe the brooch was cursed?" Lydia asked. "You're an educated man."

"I have an open mind. Would you like tae see the records?" Lincoln struggled to his feet. He shuffled to the bookshelves and took down a tome. SMYTHE was printed on the spine, and beneath that the years 1875 through 1900.

Lincoln handed it to Lydia—she and Paislee had followed him to the shelves, Paislee prepared to catch the old man if he tipped over.

"I've marked the page, there," Lincoln said.

Lydia opened the book and gasped. "That's a sketch of my brooch. The one Corbin chose for me."

"As is the family tradition," he said. "Each Smythe can pick from the vault for a Luckenbooth pin or buy a new one. The Smythes are healthy, wealthy, and wise—their bloodline strong. You know the clan has records dating back tae the eleventh century?"

"Are the Luckenbooth brooches that old, too?" Paislee asked.

"No, no. It is believed the name comes from the Luckenbooths of Edinburgh, a row of shops that sold such trinkets. Luckenbooth is the Scots word for a lockable work stall. Heart-shaped pins can be traced tae medieval times, but this"—he tapped the book—"is from the seventeenth century."

They returned to their seats and Lydia showed Paislee the page with a gold brooch, two hearts entwined. A ruby was in the center and a thistle crown over the top.

"It's beautiful," Paislee said. Some of the other choices had been iron or silver. Lydia and Minister Angela had told her that the Smythes' wealth had originally come from coal and investments.

The family was very lucky indeed to have kept and grown their fortune.

"Mary mentioned Corbin chose that one because it was expensive and he wanted tae impress you," Lincoln drawled. "Gold instead of silver. A gemstone."

"I like it because he picked it for me," Lydia said indignantly. "Or I did. I dinnae ken that I want it anymore. Will that make Mary like me better?"

Lincoln snickered at Lydia's show of spunk. "Mary is afraid of doing something wrong. All she wants is tae protect her family."

"She doesnae consider me family," Lydia declared. "She must mean her daughters and Garrison. She's not a warm woman."

"Read the story of the brooch." Lincoln sipped the dregs of his tea. Paislee poured more into his cup. The porcelain was high quality.

"Jamie Smythe proposed tae Magda Huntsman in 1877. His family didnae approve." Lydia scanned with her finger as a marker. "They ran away tae Gretna Green. How romantic! I dinnae blame them one bit, considering the headache I've gone through."

"Keep reading," Lincoln intoned.

"So," Lydia said as she shifted the book on her lap, "the couple got married and returned tae the homestead. The manor that we know today?"

"Aye. It was built in 1845."

After a few seconds of reading to herself, Lydia lowered the book with a huff. "Jamie's mother died from a broken heart that her own son would go against the family wishes. Magda was a known healer in the Highlands. What's wrong with that?"

Lincoln waved his hand. "Continue, aloud please, so that Paislee can hear, too."

Lydia cleared her throat and donned a storyteller's cadence, "'And so Magda, once ensconced in the family home, showed no remorse for her mother-in-law's death, though the servants blamed her for it. It was rumored she was a dark witch. On their first anniversary, Magda jumped from the barn window tae her death, the Luckenbooth brooch attached tae her Smythe tartan.'"

"The Luckenbooth pins are for good fortune," Paislee said, echoing Garrison's words. "Tae keep away the evil eye, not attract it."

"There have tae be other stories," Lydia said.

Lincoln stood on shaky legs. "You are welcome tae read through the history. Most of the brooches are returned tae the family safe at the manor when the owner of them passes. Mary was very interested in them, not having such history herself. She mentioned putting them in a museum, but Garrison and the other brothers wouldnae have it. I hear her daughters liked them, too." He stepped to the door. "Take your time. I'll put on more water for tea."

Paislee watched him leave the room with trepidation. Lydia, pale as a ghost, said, "My marriage is doomed."

"Let me remind you, my dear friend, that you *do not* believe in curses."

At five that evening, Paislee had to pull a fascinated Lydia away from a mound of Smythe books stacked on the low table and the floor by the chairs in Lincoln's parlor. Grandpa had texted an alert that Zeffer would be at the Shaw house around six and she hoped they'd get answers regarding her uncle Craigh at last.

"You're amazing, Lincoln," Paislee said. "You've been a huge help." Thanks to him they had a list of happy Luckenbooth stories, too, though he'd said Mary hadn't been interested in those. Just the tragedies for her.

"It was my pleasure. And I apologize, Lydia, if I was not as welcoming as I could have been."

"Ta," Lydia said. "I love Corbin."

"I can see that, lass." Lincoln kissed Lydia's hand. "It's obvious that you will be a wonderful addition tae our clan. I'll tell Mary so."

Chapter 11

Paislee chuckled and dialed Grandpa at the shop while Lydia drove away from Lincoln's flat. The windows were rolled down on the red sportscar to enjoy the summer day. Brody had called from Edwyn's house, saying that all was well, and they were eating burgers with chips.

"Where are ye, lass?" Grandpa said. "I'm locking up and headed home. Going tae get some Chinese takeaway."

"On my way tae the house, then. Order me some lo mein?"

"Already done. We need tae eat before Zeffer arrives and ruins me appetite."

Paislee blew out a breath. "See you in fifteen!"

"Do we have time tae go tae the library?" Lydia asked, her mind so preoccupied with the brooches that she wasn't listening to Paislee.

Paislee checked the clock on the dashboard. "Hours used tae be nine tae five. I think we've missed them. Can you drop me at the house?"

"Sure. Tomorrow, then."

"All right." Lydia was singularly focused. Well, if someone was trying to kill her, she had good reason. "As soon as Grandpa comes in at noon. Elspeth will be there, too."

"I have a list of questions for Alexa," Lydia said. She put on her sunglasses against the bright evening. "Do I dare trust Mary Smythe?"

"I don't think the librarian can answer that," Paislee teased, to lighten the mood. "Or maybe she can, if she's psychic."

"Not amusing," Lydia said.

"Fine, fine. It was interesting tae hear Lincoln's take on Mary being this scared fish out of water, and not the bossy superstitious woman who's given you hell for the last year."

"I need tae talk with Mary, too, withoot Corbin there. Tomorrow, Paislee. I cannae believe how you got Lincoln tae warm up when he didnae want tae."

"We had tea, that's all."

"You arenae judgy. You listen, and people like that."

"I'm just myself."

"What aboot that ivy, huh? Special plant food that would make us sick." Lydia snorted.

"I kinda wish I'd asked for a sample."

"Killer plant food?" Lydia kept her attention on the road, one hand on the wheel. "I hate being suspicious of everyone. It was interesting how folks have been eloping tae Gretna Green for hundreds of years. If I'd known a year ago what I know now, I would have been one of them." She glanced at Paislee. "Mibbe Felice would still be alive."

"You can't think that." Paislee covered Lydia's free hand on the console with her own. "There's no looking back."

"I know." Lydia pulled free and tucked a curl behind her ear. The caramel colors suited her tanned skin tone. "I was trying so hard tae make Mary happy, and Corbin, and Garrison, that I was bloody miserable."

Paislee lifted her chin, her own hair tousled by the breeze. "Lesson learned? Be true tae yourself. If Corbin doesn't understand that, then . . ."

Lydia snickered. "We need tae shove Mary from the barn, in as tragic a death as Magda?"

Laughter burst from her mouth. "Uh. Not what I was thinking." Her bestie didn't need any more guilt added to the pile.

"Garrison loves her," Lydia said. "Lincoln considers her family. The woman must have qualities I dinnae see since I'm not in her circle."

"You're right," Paislee said. "There has to be a reason for her intense dislike of you. What does she do in her spare time?"

"I dinnae ken. Mary doesnae have a job outside the manor. Hyacinth and Rosebud both think their mother walks on water."

Paislee sighed. "Hyacinth said that Mary made weekly meals and sent them tae her college dorm so that Hyacinth had comforts from home during her first year away. Rosebud wasn't as nervous, being the second child."

"That's sweet. Or overbearing. I cannae decide." Lydia arrived at Paislee's. Grandpa was already there, the Juke parked in the carport.

"See you tomorrow," Paislee said, climbing out of the car.

"Best of luck with the DI—no, scratch that. I'm tired of luck! I hope that Zeffer has positive news. Angus deserves tae know aboot Craigh, either way." Lydia beeped once before backing up.

If Craigh was dead, she meant. Paislee agreed and waved. "Bye!"

Lydia sped down the block and out of sight. The couple planned on staying at Lydia's condo on the beach, just the two of them, for some much-needed bonding time.

Paislee went inside and breathed in the scent of soy sauce and Asian spices. Wallace greeted her at the door. It was strange but she could feel right away that Brody wasn't there. Maternal connection? More like the lack of noise. She didn't know how one boy could be so loud.

"Hey, pup." Paislee walked down the hall to the kitchen. "Grandpa."

Her grandfather had the radio on and was humming to pop music. He whirled, napkins in hand. "You just scared ten years off me life!"

"Grandpa, don't say that." She rolled her eyes. "Lincoln Reid is eighty-five years old and still a vibrant man."

"He's on death's door, ye mean. How did the meeting go?"

"Great. He's got records on the Smythes from before this manor was built over the older stones of the keep. Lydia's brooch was originally made for Magda Huntsman. The mother didn't want her tae marry their son."

"Sounds familiar." Grandpa whipped off the top of the containers of takeout and gestured Paislee to a seat. "Tea?"

"No, thanks." She sat and reached for a white box. "My teeth are floating I've had so much already."

Grandpa chuckled and dug into his noodles with wooden chopsticks. "I ordered orange chicken for Brody, if he's hungry later. The boy's aboot tae hit a growth spurt the way he's been eating lately."

"Dr. Whyte says he's healthy." She felt no small amount of pride and congratulated herself on daily servings of veggies—no easy task. "Not sure I ever told you, but he predicted Brody will be six feet tall!"

"Same height as me, and your da. Craigh, too."

It wasn't often that it was just the two of them at home. Brody was usually buzzing around, these days with Edwyn, or she and Grandpa were at the yarn shop working.

"What time will Zeffer be here?"

Grandpa grimaced. "Six."

"And how did that come about, him getting an invitation?"

He took another large spoonful of noodles, coated in sesame seeds. "Let me enjoy me meal."

Paislee shook her head and swirled pasta around her chopsticks. She wasn't great at using them, but it was fun to try.

At last, Grandpa had eaten enough that he ventured an explanation. "Zeffer stopped by the shop. I think he was surprised you werenae there. He was called oot of town yesterday after he spoke tae you, or he would have returned your message sooner."

"And?"

"Well, there were customers. I didnae want to hear aboot my son's death in front of strangers, so I suggested here, when I knew you'd be home."

"Okay." It was nice that he hadn't tried to shut her out for once.

"I just don't trust the man," Grandpa continued. "Too cool if you know what I mean."

Zeffer was very cool. She touched her lower lip and then cleared her throat. "How would you like tae handle things? Should we be on the couch, or here at the table?"

"The kitchen is fine." Grandpa got up and poured them each a dram of Scotch. "Just . . . follow my lead with the DI."

Paislee clicked glasses with Grandpa and drank. The whisky calmed her nerves.

No matter what happened this evening, Zeffer would change their lives. If it was news of Craigh's death, then Grandpa could move on with his own life.

She couldn't imagine it would be anything else. It was the manner in which Craigh had died that had her worried for her grandfather. What kind of man had her uncle been? She didn't think highly of someone who would deplete the bank accounts without an explanation. The whys were a whirlwind.

A knock sounded at six on the dot, just as they were clearing the dishes. Oh, to have a new kitchen one day. In her dreams, she had stainless-steel appliances with a dishwasher that wasn't her, Brody, or Grandpa.

Grandpa answered the door and brought the DI to the round kitchen table. Wallace sniffed around his Italian leather shoes and gave a woof. Zeffer wasn't a stranger in the house, but he wasn't exactly a friend.

Paislee mirrored the dog's confusion. "Tea?" She put the kettle on for something to do.

"Sure." Zeffer sat. "How are you both?"

"On pins and needles," Paislee said. That was no lie. She'd been waiting for answers so long and now it seemed like she didn't want to know. No wonder Grandpa was so skittish.

Grandpa topped off his Scotch. "Can I pour ye a dram, DI?"

Zeffer held up his hand. "No. I'm on the clock. Angus, aboot Craigh . . ."

Grandpa tossed back the whisky and his eyes watered. He slammed the glass to the table. "He's dead."

Zeffer pulled out an envelope from his inner pocket that had been folded in half. *Craigh Shaw* was written along the top of it. "We're not sure."

Paislee gritted her teeth and stayed seated. It was all she could do to not grab the envelope with her uncle's name. Would she tear it up and set it to flame, or read it? She didn't know. Her stomach was tight, and her pulse sped.

"What kind of answer is that?" Paislee leaned toward Zeffer but glanced at her grandfather in concern. Grandpa was pale. He'd been expecting a different response, as had she. A definite yes, dead, not . . . not sure. Only Zeffer.

"What are ye saying?" Grandpa's voice was deep and rumbly.

"Can I just start from the bloody beginning?" Zeffer tapped the envelope with a forceful index finger. "I've asked you tae talk with me, Angus Shaw, and you refused. People with secrets steer clear of the police. Guilty ones. Have you seen your son?"

"Not since Craigh left for the *Mona*, an oil rig that apparently doesn't exist." Grandpa tugged at his beard, then smoothed his mustache.

"What do you know about it?" Paislee lifted Wallace to her lap. The pup was just the comfort she wanted as he snuggled close. Her gaze returned over and over to the envelope.

Zeffer's jaw was hard as granite. "Craigh Declan Burnside Shaw worked undercover for Scotland Yard."

She straightened in shock. Not dead. Not a criminal. An undercover agent? Her thoughts twisted faster than a tornado.

"Eh?" Grandpa reached for his whisky and groaned that the tumbler was empty.

Zeffer watched Grandpa with his eagle eye, discerning for cracks or giveaways of what her grandfather might know. "Worked . . . past tense," Paislee said.

Zeffer scowled at the ceiling before zeroing his glare at them. "Craigh was arrested two years ago for theft of oil rig parts. Rigs in the North Sea are difficult tae reach, so extra parts are stored on the platform tae keep equipment operating smoothly. If you dinnae have the part, it halts business. That delay equals *millions* in lost revenue for Scotland."

Grandpa's jaw tightened. His son had gone from hero to criminal in an instant. In her mind, Paislee heard Grandpa say *haud yer wheesht* regarding the storage unit where her uncle's things were kept. Would the boxes be filled with stolen parts?

"In a plea bargain, Craigh agreed tae avoid jail and work for Scotland Yard, tae catch the leader in an industrial 3D printing scam, involving parts for the oil rigs." Zeffer tilted his head. "Clean energy is the way of the future, and the Norwegians are shining examples of what a country can do with black gold."

Oil. It was true, Paislee thought, that the rigs in the North Sea were a blight on Scotland's ocean but a necessary evil until the government implemented a better solution. It was awful that she had to choose between heat and electricity over clean water.

Grandpa said not a word under Zeffer's scrutiny. Paislee couldn't begin to wrap her head around the crime. Aye, she knew what a 3D printer was . . . Brody and the P7 class had sold candy bars as a fund-raiser to buy a small one for the rooms to share. The kids had turned PLA filament into figurines they'd first drawn and then transferred to a software program. It really was the future.

"Craigh was in contact with us until last week." Zeffer placed his palm on the envelope. "We believe he was caught gathering information. I've been traveling up and down this entire isle tae find word of him, but he's gone underground—hiding, or . . ."

Dead.

"Craigh was alive?" Grandpa's body trembled in shock, his vocal cords wavering in disbelief. "You knew all this time?"

"I was here in Nairn tae watch you. Tae see if Craigh could be trusted." Zeffer's posture on the chair was loose, but that was a façade. She saw the slight twitch at his eyelid. "He didnae try tae contact you that I could tell. You paid your landlady tae forward any mail tae the storage unit in Dairlee rather than go through the post office. You kept the boxes there and didnae bring them tae Paislee's. It was clear that you suspected something was wrong—or you were guilty, too. I didnae know which one."

Sick, Paislee held Wallace in one arm and got up to retrieve the whisky, pouring Grandpa a shot, then setting the bottle on the table. She sat down again.

"Ta." Grandpa sipped the amber liquid, staring at the center of the table. "I didnae catch on right away. Not until our bank account was closed. He'd told me that this job would be dangerous, but enough tae set us up for the rest of our lives."

"You didnae question him?" Zeffer's lip curled.

"Craigh's a grown man, Detective. We werenae close." He swirled the Scotch. "I didnae discover I had a son until he was grown—Craigh blamed me. Thought I owed him."

Zeffer pleated a corner of the envelope. "You're not responsible for choices he made as an adult."

Paislee cuddled Wallace and scratched under the pup's chin. She widened her eyes at her grandfather, acknowledging his pain. Yet, they had to tell the DI about the boxes in the storage unit. The ones marked PRIVATE that Grandpa hadn't opened.

"Craigh's alive." Grandpa's words rang with hope. "He has tae be! It would be too cruel after all this time."

"I hope so," Zeffer said, his tone dry. "He has answers. My da worked on the oil rigs in the heyday of the oil boom in Aberdeen. He died in an accident with a faulty part when I was a babe. I've made it my mission tae keep the rigs safe. This is very personal tae me, do you understand, Angus?"

Grandpa clasped the tumbler. "Aye."

Paislee swallowed nervously. Dare she tell Zeffer? Grandpa wouldn't forgive her.

"Now. I will ask ye again." Zeffer didn't move or do anything that outwardly appeared more threatening, but Paislee got chills along her skin when he asked, "Have you heard from Craigh?"

Grandpa met the DI's gaze. "Not a peep."

Paislee squirmed on her chair, then got up and let Wallace outside in the back garden. She took a centering breath to gather her scrambled wits. The pleasant evening held a sea-salt breeze. Birds chirped. Her uncle was involved in a crime, and Grandpa knew about boxes marked PRIVATE in the storage unit. He thought he'd seen his son . . . what if it wasn't a figment of his imagination?

It was wrong to keep it secret. She could feel Gran around her and knew her grandmother would believe the same.

But Grandpa was her family now, and she had to give him a chance to handle things how he needed to do.

He'd been left to suffer for more than a year, believing his son had left him, by choice or death. She returned to the table and sank down. "DI, would you have told Grandpa that Craigh was alive and working undercover if he hadn't disappeared?"

"It was not my place," Zeffer said coolly. "There are department rules one must follow."

Blasted rules! Paislee embraced her inner rebel. "Grandpa deserves the truth from you—showing up here, with us expecting a notice of Craigh's death, only tae have you *not sure.*"

Zeffer winced. "Our plan was tae extract Craigh by December. Set him up with a new name, a new life."

"With me?" Grandpa asked.

"That would be up tae Craigh."

Paislee detested the way Zeffer distanced himself, as if they had no emotional stake in this news. She thought sourly of Hamish, very similar to the detective in this way. "What happens now?"

"We're searching for Craigh. If he's alive, we need tae find him before he's killed. Another of our undercover informants washed up on shore yesterday, which is why I was away. We'll take Craigh into custody, for his own good, until we discover what happened."

"So, if you find him, he'll still go tae jail?" Paislee asked.

"It depends on why he stopped communicating," Zeffer said. "When he was arrested for stealing parts, it wasnae his first offense."

"Craigh had a tough life," Grandpa said. His body drooped with exhaustion.

Her grandfather was stuck in the same position. If Grandpa gave up Craigh's boxes to the police, with who knew what was inside, his son might go to prison, after he'd just had confirmation Craigh was alive.

On the other hand, maybe the things in the storage unit could help find her uncle before the crooks did.

"Are you in on this, Angus?" Zeffer asked.

"No!"

Suddenly, Wallace raced to the back door, barking. Her heart thudded in alarm until she recognized her son's laugh at the front step.

Paislee got up to let him in, and hugged him to her side, waving to Bennett, Edwyn's dad, who had dropped him off in their new Jeep.

"Mum!" Brody sniffed the air. "You had Chinese withoot me?"

Grandpa had let Wallace in, and the pup raced around the kitchen like his tail was on fire. Zeffer had said once that he'd never had a dog growing up. His dad had been on the rigs and died from an accident with a faulty part. It was sad and explained why he'd been determined to make detective so young.

"Grandpa ordered you orange chicken, but didn't you just eat burgers?"

"Yeah. Hey, DI Zeffer. What are you doing here?" Brody scraped back his auburn fringe, freckles on his nose. "Who else died, Mum?"

"Nobody!" Paislee plopped her hand on her hip.

Zeffer sighed and shot to his feet. "On that note, I'll be going. If you think of anything that might help us locate Craigh, please call me. No matter the hour."

"We will," Paislee said by rote. Not sure if it was true. "Brody, the detective's visit isn't about Felice but Craigh."

"My missing great-uncle." Brody was already moving on to the fridge and the carton of Chinese food with his name on it. "Thanks, Grandpa. Yum."

Grandpa stayed with Brody, so Paislee walked Zeffer to the door and the front step. She closed the door behind her and waited with him on the small stoop. Their bodies were inches apart and she backed up until she hit the wood frame.

"What's going on with Felice Smythe? It's not right that Lydia should fear for her life."

"Constable Payne is waiting for the official autopsy results, as well as the tests on the powder. These things dinnae happen overnight, especially when foul play is suspected. Has Lydia had any more scares?"

"No."

"Guid. Mibbe the motive was tae stop the wedding." Zeffer glanced at his blue SUV.

"I hope so." She cleared her throat and gestured with her thumb over her shoulder. "Is Craigh dangerous?"

Zeffer descended the two steps with grace. "His rap sheet was petty theft kind of stuff. Nothing violent."

A small blessing she'd take. "Do you think he's alive?"

"I *need* him tae be alive," Zeffer said. "You want tae protect your grandfather, and I understand that. He wants tae protect his son. But there is the law for a reason. Craigh broke it. More than once."

She swallowed over the lump in her throat. "I'm sorry about your dad."

His eyes lost the glacial glint to allow compassion. "Yours, too. I did a background check on you when I first moved here."

"On me?" Paislee pressed her fingers to her chest, feeling vulnerable.

"I had tae see what kind of person you are. And then tae have dead bodies pile up . . ." He shrugged.

"'Pile up' might be a wee bit strong." Paislee frowned at him as he tapped the top of the SUV, anxious to go catch criminals.

"You know what I mean. But you're a guid person; so was your granny. Your grandpa did his best tae take on a son that had a grudge against the world. Not his fault—but he cannae protect him from the law. Ye ken?"

Paislee nodded, her chest tight. "We'll be in touch." As soon as she convinced Grandpa to let Zeffer know about the private boxes in the storage unit.

"Haven't we said that tae each other before?" His sea-glass-green eyes hinted at laughter, and she smiled sadly.

"Aye. This time I mean it."

The door opened behind her and Brody said, "Mum! Oh, sairy. I thought you were alone." He came around to stand next to her. Wallace sat by his feet and stared up at Zeffer.

"What is it, hon?"

"My end-of-year project, remember? We have tae get supplies from the hardware store."

Zeffer climbed into his car, raised his hand, backed out, and drove off. Wallace barked and Brody grinned. "You owe me one, Mum."

"I suppose I do." Paislee crossed her arms and frowned down at him as she thought of the two wooden containers he'd made to compost PLA scrap material from the 3D printer. PLA was partially made of cornstarch and so biodegradable and much better for the environment than regular plastic. Future technology still had its problems, and this generation didn't want to add to the landfills. His teacher thought it was special enough to submit to Zero Waste Scotland, which was running a contest for innovative ideas. "Wait. They're behind the shed."

"It's not a lie," Brody said, seeing her expression. "I decided I wanted tae paint them blue."

Paislee lowered her arms with a laugh. No doubt her grandfather was already locked in his room, and they couldn't discuss Craigh in front of Brody anyway. "I'll be glad of the distraction. Let me get my keys!"

Chapter 12

Wednesday morning, Paislee was still picking blue paint from beneath her fingernails, and she'd showered twice. Brody was in excellent spirits as he counted down the days until he was no longer a kid in P7.

"If I win the prize money, Mum, I want tae buy a new bike. And get my own phone. Can I do that?"

Paislee winced, not on the same page. University? New bike? "Let's discuss it later." She pulled up in front of Fordythe where Hamish greeted the kids. He waved at her. She blushed and waved back. Ugh. "See you later, love!"

As she drove to Cashmere Crush, she texted Lydia to make sure they were still on for that afternoon to visit Alexa at the library, as well as Mary, but there was no answer. Over toast and tea, Grandpa had claimed a migraine, saying he might not be at work today. She'd told him to rest, of course, but she knew he just didn't want to talk to her about Craigh and the storage unit.

DI was as cunning as a fox and it wouldn't surprise him, Grandpa had said, if he was being set up somehow. Zeffer *was* cunning, but she didn't see her grandfather as part of a sting. Would Grandpa listen to reason? No.

Elspeth Booth arrived for her afternoon shift at twelve thirty.

Things in Nairn were bustling during the tourist season and over the last year Cashmere Crush had seen steady growth in customers. Seventy-one, tall, slender, and with a knack for needlepoint, Elspeth filled in during the busy times three afternoons a week.

Susan, Elspeth's blind sister, answered phones three days a week at the med lab that Margot managed. Margot was also dating their landlord, Shawn Marcus, who had to be happy as all of the shops were flourishing. In fact, the corner shop closest to the water on this block had just been leased and would no longer be a tea shoppe, but an ice cream parlor. Brody couldn't wait, though Paislee missed Theadora Barr's raspberry scones.

It was a juggle, and there were lots of nights Paislee worked on inventory long after Brody and Grandpa were in bed, but she wouldn't have it any other way.

The Earl of Cawdor wanted to bring Nairn back to its Victorian glory days—some folks, like Lydia, were all for expansion while others (her) were afraid that things might get too big and fancy. New was not always better.

"I'll check in tae see how crazy it is before I pick up Brody," she told Elspeth. "Grandpa is fighting a headache so if he doesn't show, just give me a call and I can cancel with Lydia."

"I'll be fine. I've got my needlepoint pillow tae work on between customers." Two women browsed the rows of colorful yarn packed onto the shelves and Elspeth nodded at them to let Paislee know she'd seen them. "Since Lydia's not in Germany for her honeymoon, will she be joining us for Knit and Sip tomorrow night?"

Not much of a consolation prize, but the ladies would be a boon for Lydia's flagging confidence. "I'll ask her."

"Poor love."

"I know, I know. That's why I'm spending the afternoon with her." One of the customers admired the bright yellow yarn and took a skein down to touch the softness. "Lincoln Reid was very helpful yesterday."

"Oh, I know Lincoln! His wife was a dear. A professor at university and very intellectual." Elspeth sounded like she approved of the couple. Would she have judged them for being cousins? Legal or not, marrying so close a blood relation was still considered slightly scandalous.

The woman decided that the yarn was to her liking and gathered six rolls, bringing them toward the counter.

Elspeth moved away from Paislee and smiled at the lady. "Good afternoon!"

"Call me on my mobile if you need anything," Paislee whispered—but Elspeth was already assisting their customer. She left out the back and drove to Lydia's condo, knowing the shop was in good hands.

Lydia waited outside her building. It was twenty floors high with balconies overlooking the ocean and very upscale. There was a security guard in the lobby, though no gate to enter the property. Paislee caught the taillights of the Mercedes as Corbin drove off, and pulled in alongside the curb.

"I'm glad you could drive today." Lydia climbed into the Juke. "Corbin's car is in the shop for maintenance because we thought we'd be gone."

Corbin owned a high-end SUV with all the bells and whistles. "Happy tae be of assistance."

"Say your prayers that he can rebook our honeymoon at the travel agency as soon as possible. I just want oot of Nairn for a while. Small problems in the bigger picture, eh?" As in, Felice would never go on holiday. Lydia touched Paislee's upper arm. "How's Angus?"

Paislee quickly brought Lydia up to speed on the Craigh situation. "So, you know, my half uncle is a criminal. Maybe on the run, or maybe dead."

She didn't tell her bestie about the boxes in the storage unit, keeping Grandpa's secret for another day or two. That was all! He had to do the right thing. Could she condemn him if he didn't?

Probably not. Paislee would make a terrible judge, and thanked heaven that knitting kept a roof over their heads.

"Let's drop in on Mary first, then the library."

Paislee nodded. "What did Corbin think about us visiting Mary without him?"

"Oh, that we're mental."

Laughing, Paislee said, "He might be right. He wasn't mad, though?"

"No." Lydia buckled her seatbelt. "He's a sweetheart and offered tae come with us, but that would ruin our angle, so I told him no, thanks."

"Yesterday we had an agenda for what we wanted from Lincoln." Paislee left the landscaped property to the main road. "What's our strategy today?"

"Tae sweet-talk Mary into lowering her guard and find oot if she had something tae do with the poison on the brooch. She doesnae like me and has made no bones aboot it."

Lydia had a point, but Paislee said, "I still think killing her future daughter-in-law is a bit over the top."

"We'll see, won't we?" Lydia slid on her sunglasses. "Then, the library."

Within no time, Paislee slowed to follow the long driveway leading to Smythe Manor. She parked in the same gravel area to the right of the house as before.

"I cannae believe how nervous I am." Lydia showed Paislee her quivering hand. "We should have brought her chocolates or something tae sweeten her up, like we did with Lincoln."

Paislee and Lydia exited the SUV and she thought to what she might have stashed in the back of the car. She opened the hatch. A cleat, a football, and a dog leash. "Sorry, Lyd. Not even part of a project."

The pair trudged across the gravel to the stoop. The dogs could be heard barking in the back of the property, probably in their kennels by the barn.

Lydia gave a sharp rap on the door and Norbert let them in. The butler could give lessons in decorum as no hint of familiarity graced his expression.

"Is Mary in?" Lydia asked.

"I will see if *Lady* Mary is receiving guests. One moment." Norbert strode down the hall, very correct in posture as he left them in the foyer.

"She can always turn us away. Oh, hell. I didnae think of that." Lydia's shoulders drooped.

Norbert walked toward them without cracking a smile, his arms at his sides. "Lady Mary will see you in the green drawing room."

Paislee bit her lip to stifle a laugh. The butler *and* the lady were a bit much. "Thank you," she said.

"This way." After following him for what was beginning to feel like forever, Norbert slid back a pocket door to reveal a room in hunter greens with oxford red and ivory accents. Paintings of hunting scenes—deer and dogs, and men with guns—adorned the walls. It spoke of masculine opulence. She'd thought that Mary would want pinks and lavenders.

"Lady Mary, your guests." Norbert melted backward and out of sight.

Mary lifted her head from a book she was reading. Her posture was perfect, just like the butler's.

When Paislee was involved in a book, she slouched on the couch with crisps and tea, Wallace at her feet. The big golden Labs were out of sight. She recalled what Lincoln had said about Mary not being confident in her role.

"We're sairy tae bother you," Lydia began.

Mary put the book aside after carefully marking her space with a gold bookmark that had a Scottish thistle charm attached. A highly varnished low table held a bouquet of dried flowers. A

Smythe tartan blanket was draped over the couch. "Come in. What can I do for you?"

Her tone was indifferent, as if she hadn't just been planning a wedding with Lydia over the last year, which Paislee found odd.

Lydia perched on the edge of a dark green chair, and Paislee sat on one of oxblood fabric. "How are you?" Lydia asked.

"I'm fine." Mary's platinum brow rose.

Her best friend fidgeted with her purse and set it at her feet. Mary said nothing else.

"We visited with Lincoln Reid yesterday," Paislee said, breaking the awkward silence.

"You did?" Mary's voice rose and she glanced at her book.

"He shared his passion for the Smythe history." Lydia crossed her ankles. "The story of the brooch, from Magda and Jamie Smythe."

Mary blinked and smiled politely. "It's a sad tale, and hopefully over now. Felice's funeral will be Saturday. Surely you can see, Lydia, that marrying Corbin is a terrible idea. I'm *glad* Lincoln showed you the book. Magda was the wrong bride for Jamie and look what happened!"

Paislee didn't care for the fanatical gleam in Mary's eye. "We're glad, too. It's just a story with no mention of a curse. Even so, you had the brooch blessed by Minister Angela."

"Obviously the curse was stronger." Mary peeked at the book waiting for her and then at them.

Paislee read the title, *Astrological Signs and Your Fortune*. It was a Nairn library book. "You follow astrology?"

"Of course," Mary said. "I've had my friend Alexa do my astrological chart, and also for the girls. That's how I knew tae guide Hyacinth toward the literary arts, though Rosebud has more interest in science."

"I dinnae believe in that stuff," Lydia said.

"You should. You're a Leo, a lion, passionate and full of fire.

Corbin is a Scorpio—jealous and with a temper. It's a terrifying combination." Mary shuddered.

"Corbin doesnae have a temper, Mary," Lydia said calmly. "I agree that horoscopes can be fun tae read but tae make decisions on generalities isn't right. We have personal choices."

"I'm also a Scorpio," Paislee said. "I don't have a jealous streak and I don't think I've ever been in a fight." Her gran had been a peace-loving influence.

"When's your birthday?" Mary focused on Paislee.

"November sixth."

"There are many wonderful qualities aboot a Scorpio," Mary said. "Just not when partnered with a Leo."

"Lydia and I have been best friends since primary without a single hitch. I think that she and Corbin will be fine."

Mary smoothed the Smythe plaid blanket on the couch. "Garrison is a Libra and I'm an Aquarius. Very compatible on many levels—I had Alexa do a chart for him, too, tae be sure. It matters, for forever."

"Is this the same Alexa who told you about the cursed brooch?" Paislee asked.

"Aye, she is verra, verra wise. This isnae her first life on this planet."

"Does Garrison believe in fortune, ill or fair?" Lydia asked. "Corbin wasnae raised that way, he said."

"It isnae a matter of belief. Bad things are in the world. Magda's ghost haunts this manor, especially my drawing room. This room is the safest. There are fairies. The evil eye. Illness." Mary tugged a gold chain from beneath her blouse. On it was a gold cross, a thistle, a Greek all-seeing eye in cobalt blue, and a locket. "Warren, my first husband, gave this tae me. He understood my fears."

Mary was afraid of a lot. Warren had died of cancer, leaving her to raise two girls without money. Garrison (and his fortune) had saved her. Probably worth the occasional ghost sighting in the manor.

Paislee leaned toward Mary with an open expression. "If Corbin had chosen a different brooch, would you have been more welcoming tae Lydia? A plain silver pin with no gem wouldn't take away from your girls' choices. Was it the monetary value of the betrothal pin that had you up in arms?"

Mary touched the gold charms and evaded the question. "Alexa and Lincoln both know the past verra well. If we learn from our mistakes, we can thrive in the future."

"I think," Paislee said, "that Lydia's independence frightens you. She doesn't care about the Smythe fortune. Are you worried she might teach Rosebud or Hyacinth tae walk their own path? I noticed at dinner that the other wives all seemed tae fall in line."

Lydia sucked in a breath.

"That's . . . absurd," Mary said. Her eyes flickered and Paislee knew she was right. At least part of this for Mary was about keeping the Smythe money in the family vault and her daughters under her thumb. "My concern is for Corbin. A divorced woman has a higher chance of another divorce. It's statistics."

"Lydia had ample reason tae get rid of her lousy ex-husband, not that it's your business." Paislee wouldn't explain that he'd been a cheat and worse. "It's not your place tae judge her. Corbin loves Lydia and that should be enough for you. Did you receive a pin from Garrison?"

"I think it's time for you tae leave." Mary stayed seated.

She'd take that as a no. Paislee rose and motioned for Lydia to come along. She thought back to how Rosebud and Hyacinth had giggled rudely together at the rehearsal dinner. During any of the festivities, Rosebud had Chalmers at her beck and call. Rosebud had been laughing with Felice. Mary wouldn't put her daughters in danger by poisoning the brooch. What might Rosebud do, to gain favor for Mary?

Lydia grabbed her purse in jerky movements. "I never saw the brooch before Corbin gave it tae me. I didnae ask for it! He chose it because it is my birthstone, not for any other reason. I dinnae need your family's money."

"The Smythe fortune is enormous, Lydia, built from centuries of investments and caretakers with *integrity*, such as Garrison." Mary straightened, nothing flighty in her manner now. "Your family has no history. You bring nothing tae the table. Though my first husband had little money left toward the end, he was related tae the queen. My daughters will marry verra well."

Paislee suddenly felt sorry for Hyacinth and Rosebud for their mother to have such archaic expectations.

"I am proud of my family," Lydia said, her confidence returning.

"Go." Mary stood and brought the book to her chest, covering her heart.

Paislee reached the doorway. Lydia remained by the couch and stared at her almost-mother-in-law across the low table. "If you poisoned the brooch, Mary, I bet you're feeling terrible guilt. Felice wasnae meant tae die."

"If you dinnae leave now, I will call the police." Mary remained rooted to the floor.

"I'm tempted tae let you," Lydia said, "and you can explain tae Constable Payne how protective you are of the Smythe fortune for your daughters, who arenae blood no matter how much you display the tartan."

Mary grasped the book. "How dare you! You deserve tae be cursed!"

"Lydia, love, let's go." Paislee waved her best friend away from the crazy woman. They could call the officer from the safety of the car.

After a tense moment, Lydia joined her, her head high as she left the green chamber. Norbert escorted them out of the manor.

"Oh, my word, she hates me," Lydia said. "There is nothing I can do tae change that. And you know what? It's verra freeing."

"Mary is scared of you, and cornered animals bite. I don't trust her—but she didn't do it. She loves her girls too much tae risk their lives with poison." Paislee got in the Juke at the same time as Lydia, starting the engine.

"You're right," Lydia said with a sigh. "Now what?"

Maybe it was her Scorpio temper flaring to life, but Paislee wasn't ready to give in yet. She had time before picking up Brody for school, and Grandpa had texted that he was better and at the shop with Elspeth. "You call the constable and let him know how the visit went. I'm driving us tae the Nairn library tae meet Alexa Selkirk. If she's as powerful as Lincoln and Mary think, she might already know we're coming."

Chapter 13

Paislee drove from Smythe Manor in the rural outskirts of the Highlands to Nairn Library, in the center of town. Lydia had to leave a message for Constable Payne, and they spent fifteen minutes going over Mary's behavior. Crazy lady but she adored her daughters. No way would she put their lives at risk.

She scored a choice parking spot a block away and was grateful for the walk on this sunny day to clear her head of negativity. They reached the library, and Paislee stopped to admire the colorful display window of bright paper butterflies reading books.

"Cute," Lydia said.

"I remember bringing Brody here for story hour when he was just a wean."

A young woman in her early twenties with blue hair and a flower-print sundress opened the door. "Come on in before ye melt in the heat. I'm Shana." Shana made a show of looking behind Paislee. "Not here for the toddler book bug session?"

"It's been years and now my book bug is finishing P7." Paislee had to pause and catch her breath at how fast time had flown. And then it would be university . . . and then what?

Lydia patted Paislee's shoulder.

They went inside and Shana shut the door behind them, urging them past the shorter shelves and beanbag chairs for the kids.

"We'd like tae speak with Alexa Selkirk," Lydia said. "Is she in?"

"She's sorting books in the back. Follow me!" Shana's dress flew behind her she walked so fast.

The smell of paper brought back the joy of reading with Brody in the library. It had been a terrific place to play and introduce him to the world of stories. Before video games.

"Alexa, you have visitors!" Shana announced when she reached the end of connected rooms partitioned by shelves and half walls. Inviting nooks with cozy chairs tempted readers to sit awhile.

Alexa peered up from a stack of books in a plastic carton. Welcome turned to confusion, and then acknowledgment as she appeared to place them in her mind. No psychic hint they were coming. Maybe, Paislee thought, it was on the fritz. "Afternoon, ladies. How can I help you?"

Lydia stepped forward to shake Alexa's hand. "Nice tae see you again. Were you at the manor on Sunday?"

"Briefly. I dinnae think we've formally met. I was at the wedding . . . the groom's side. I've known Mary and the girls a long time."

Alexa had a youthful face with gray hair in a messy topknot, makeup meant to accentuate the eyes and mouth. Not garish, but bright. Her earrings were miniature dream catchers and she had stacks of crystal bracelets on each wrist. Her outfit was denim overalls with colorful patches and lots of pockets. Her reading glasses were on a beaded neck chain, and she wore yellow high tops with glittering laces. The woman exuded the promise of adventure.

"Almost everyone was on the groom's side." Lydia's laugh was brittle. "This is Paislee Shaw, my matron of honor, and best friend. She owns Cashmere Crush."

"The yarn shop on Market? I often pass by. One of these days I'm going tae pop in and see how it feels." Alexa set the book down on the stack to be returned to the shelves and waved her hand around by Paislee. "You have guid energy. Loved. You have a guardian angel." She laughed. "We all do, but I sense you know this one verra well."

Paislee couldn't help but smile with the eccentric woman. "Gran, maybe. I lost her six years ago."

"I sense masculine energy, too. Your da?" Alexa chuckled. "As you may have guessed, our loved ones are never really gone. We have books on the subject if you're interested." She regarded Lydia closely, her mouth twisted. "My mother died two years ago—we still dinnae get on, even in the afterlife."

Paislee turned to Lydia. Would the librarian offer her opinion on what energy her best friend had?

Lydia didn't wait for pleasantries but got to the point of their visit. "We were speaking with Mary Smythe, and she mentioned you told her aboot my Luckenbooth brooch being cursed."

Alexa flinched.

"We also talked tae Lincoln Reid yesterday," Paislee said, in a softer tone. "He was kind enough tae show us his documentation linking Jamie and Magda's story with Lydia's betrothal pin."

"Oh?" Alexa's eyes, big and brown, narrowed. "You've been busy!"

"There is no mention of a curse in the documents Lincoln collected," Lydia said.

Alexa shrugged, noncommittal.

"Mary is supposed tae be my mother-in-law and she hates me. If you gave her a story aboot a curse on my betrothal pin, then mibbe you can find one that shows her how tae lift it." Lydia gazed at Alexa with hope.

"Hate is a verra strong word, dear." Alexa patted Lydia's arm but immediately drew back as if burned.

"What is it?" Lydia bumped into a shelf, accidentally rocking it.

"Oh, nothing."

It was obvious the woman lied. She might be just as quirky as Mary. Quirkier, even. Paislee cleared her throat to draw the librarian's attention. "Lydia and Corbin love each other. Isn't that all that should matter?"

"Well . . ." Alexa gestured for them to follow her into the very back of the library. She unlocked a door from one of the many keys in her pocket. "This is where we keep the really old books. It's where I discovered the tale of the Witch's Heart."

Goose bumps at the words rose on Paislee's arms. "The Witch's Heart?"

"Aye. The brooch that Corbin chose for Lydia. It had a dark history long before poor Felice died." Alexa flicked on the light, but it remained dim.

"Do you need a new bulb?" Lydia peered at the ceiling light fixture.

"No, dear. This is low wattage on purpose tae protect the delicate volumes. Some of these go back tae the sixteen hundreds, but most are from the nineteenth century."

Alexa located the tome among the stuffed shelves right away, then gestured for them to sit at a long rectangular wooden table with benches on either side.

Paislee's nape tingled in excitement to hear the story. Lydia's gray eyes brightened. They took the right side, and Alexa the left, the book proudly center stage.

The binding was cracked, and the ivory pages stained with age. It seemed to have power of its own, but surely that had to be Paislee's imagination.

"This is a journal from the cook, a man called Bart. Some of the words are difficult tae make oot, but I'll try my best. It's just a snippet among the recipes, as if he hadnae wanted this tae be commonly known." Alexa reverently turned a page and read, " 'In this year of 1877, the Smythe Clan suffered multiple tragedies when Jamie Smythe and his new wife, Magda, returned from Gretna Green, wed against the wishes of his parents. The lady's maid said Magda hadn't wanted marriage, though she held Jamie in high esteem. Magda allowed herself tae be persuaded because she was with child. Jamie commissioned the most expensive Luckenbooth of gold tae protect against fairies and the evil eye. The lady's maid swore me tae secrecy and said that Magda was no healer but a witch, practicing the dark arts. Jamie's mother died of suspicious circumstances after eating'—" Alexa paused. "I think it says 'soup, made by Magda. Magda's babe died in childbirth. Jamie was badly injured after falling from his horse.'" Alexa turned a page. "'I've talked tae the villagers, and they want tae hang Magda for her crimes. Her maid showed me how the Luckenbooth brooch had a tail that now swerved tae the right, proof of her being a witch. Magda took her own life before their first anniversary, leaping tae her death. Guid fortune was restored tae the clan thereafter. Bart.'" Alexa looked up with a nod.

"So, what? I'm supposed tae die tae restore guid fortune?" Lydia's lip lifted in disbelief. "Mary is verra superstitious so if you told her this, no wonder—"

Paislee kicked Lydia lightly beneath the table. Nobody was supposed to know that Felice had been *killed*.

Lydia pursed her lips. "No wonder Mary hates me," she finished. "Why do you think this refers tae the same brooch Corbin gave me?"

"It matches the description written here. Made of gold, when most were silver or iron. Entwined hearts. A crown of thistle."

That did sound like the same one. Almost. "Except for the red stone," Paislee said.

Lydia smacked her palm to the table. "This isnae proof that the brooches are the same. Please convince your friend Mary tae let the idea of a curse go. Corbin and I *will* get married," she said.

After a dramatic inhale, Alexa drew back. "Mary's had aspirations tae be the best for as long as I've known her. She doesnae think you're right for Corbin, or the Smythe Clan."

"It's not her choice," Paislee said. What was the matter with these people?

"You're right. I told her so—no matter how much you want tae save someone from making a mistake, it is their journey. Now that Corbin's wedding is off, she should be focused on Rosebud. There's trouble ahead for her and that young man she was with, Chalmers. Mary willnae approve of his bloodline, either."

"He's not titled or a landowner?" Lydia asked with some righteous snark.

"I do not believe it's serious, but he dotes on the lass. I observed them getting pictures on Sunday before . . . well, Chalmers looked deep into her eyes, but Rosebud averted her gaze. I see a broken heart in their future. His."

"Why do you both believe in the paranormal?" Lydia made it clear that she did not with a dismissive finger flutter. "Mary said that she feels Magda's ghost. You told Lincoln his wife's spirit is around him."

Alexa closed the book. "We grew up that way, I guess. Told tae put oot biscuits at night so the fairies wouldnae steal us from our wee beds. The brooch you're betrothed with is supposed to provide good luck, also for your weans. You pin it to the baby's blanket to keep the fairies away. You should do the same for yours."

"We're not sure we want children." Lydia shifted on the hard wooden bench.

Alexa put on her glasses and peered across the book to Lydia. "Does Mary know that?"

Lydia shrugged without comment.

"Mary might consider that you wouldnae be doing your duty by Corbin, or the family."

"There are a lot of other cousins picking up the Smythe slack if we choose not tae procreate," Lydia said with heat.

"Healthy stock," Alexa said. "Why not be a mistress, then?"

Paislee noticed the parallels the librarian was drawing between Lydia and Magda in the story, leading things her way.

Lydia rested her forearm on the table. "You're talking like it isnae the twenty-first century."

"I suppose I am old-fashioned." Alexa gently caressed the cover of the old book. "You want progress and growth."

"Of course! What aboot you?" Lydia asked.

"No." Alexa's brown eyes glittered with something Paislee couldn't identify. "You're a modern woman. You make your own money and earn a brilliant wage. You dinnae need tae marry. Isnae that so?"

"You got that right." Lydia jutted her chin. "Corbin and I choose tae wed because we love each other."

Alexa's mouth pursed as if that remained to be seen. Pulling a deck of cards from her pocket, the librarian shuffled them. "I read tarot. Let me tell your future, if you dare."

Lydia scowled. "I know what my future holds."

"Then what harm can it do?" Alexa shuffled.

Paislee wanted to drag Lydia away from the woman who had taken on a sinister air. She didn't need to be psychic to understand the shift in energy.

Lydia wasn't the kind to back down and didn't now. "Go ahead, then. Read your cards. You'll see that Corbin and I are a love match."

"A love match is fine, aye, but you dinnae need tae be legal for that." With a last riffle of the cards, Alexa laid out three, facedown. "Past, present, future."

"Paislee, sweet, take pictures, would you? Tae show Corbin. We can prove tae Mary once and for all that we are destined."

Lydia's bravado would also allow them to make sure Alexa wasn't lying about what each card meant.

Alexa's shoulders stiffened, but she flipped the card that represented Lydia's past. "The Empress. This is all aboot money. Luxury and glory. You demand tae be the best."

"That's true." Lydia watched Alexa closely. "I'm verra guid at my job. I willnae apologize for it."

"Nor should you," Paislee said. She opened her notes app to include what Alexa said as well, to go over later.

"This is the present. The Lovers, reversed. A broken engagement." Alexa shook her head with a smirk at Lydia. "I told you, the cards dinnae lie."

"The meaning tae these cards is subjective." Lydia's hand formed a fist on her knee, that Paislee saw, but Alexa didn't. Her friend was worried.

Alexa tapped the third card. Her eyes closed as if she concentrated very hard to hear something that Lydia and Paislee didn't—or couldn't. "I have a message from the angels. The spirits."

Lydia rolled her eyes, her nostrils flared. "Is it Felice? Can she tell us who killed her?"

Alexa's eyes snapped open. "She was killed?"

Paislee sighed, really wishing that Lydia wouldn't have said that.

"You tell me." Lydia waited, not giving an inch.

Alexa's breath grew shaky, and she waved her hand over the cards before finally flipping the one to represent the future. "The Magician, also reversed. This means betrayal and uncertainty."

Lydia stared at Alexa hard. "We make our own choices."

"This card makes sense for you, Lydia, because of Felice. You were betrayed. Don't doubt Corbin's love over it." Paislee glowered at Alexa. "I'm not sure if this is talent, or a trick you should charge for at carnivals."

Alexa gathered the cards and put them back in her pocket. "It's a talent. A curse."

"You bandy that word around a lot," Lydia said. "Your friend Mary eats it up. Tell me, do you read tarot cards for her, in addition tae her astrological charts?"

"Of course, not that it's any of your business."

"What was the message you heard?" Paislee asked, glancing around the room. No spooks or ghosties that she could see.

Alexa tossed her dream-catcher earrings. "It was a warning of caution that I thought I understood, but I was wrong. It was actually tae do with whatever happened tae Felice." She clasped Lydia's hand. "It was meant for you."

Lydia yanked free. "Dinnae touch me."

"It was, and innocent Felice got caught." Alexa sighed. "If you insist on marrying Corbin Smythe, it just might kill you."

Lydia watched Alexa from hooded eyes. "Mary, you mean."

"No! She's afraid of her own shadow. Lydia, you are a flash in the pan," Alexa said. "Corbin needs a woman with substance. One who doesnae care aboot profit over all else."

Paislee got up from the bench before she let her Scorpio temper free and punched the librarian in the nose. "Let's go, Lydia."

"Hang on a sec." Lydia studied the librarian across the table, squinting slightly. "Alexa, do I know you from somewhere, besides the wedding, or here today?"

Alexa rose and put the old tome back on the shelf, then opened the door for them. "Come back any time. I'd be happy tae do another reading for you. I suggest cleansing your energy with sage. Your condo, too."

"How do you know where I live?"

"Naturally, someone like you would reside in the lap of luxury."

Paislee tugged Lydia's hand. "We're leaving."

Alexa settled her glasses on her nose, staying in the safety of the back room.

"That woman!" Lydia exclaimed in the hall.

"Wait tae vent until we are outside."

Fuming, the best friends took deep breaths of air and strode to the bandstand with a view of the Firth. Paislee handed Lydia her bottled water as they perched on the steps.

"I dinnae ken what tae do," Lydia said. "She did not like me. Mary doesnae like me. Lincoln doesnae think I'm guid enough for Corbin."

"Lincoln changed his mind once he got tae know you. You are more than enough for anybody. You are the best thing tae happen tae Corbin because he is surrounded by crazy people." She took a drink when Lydia was done.

"I shouldnae have said that aboot Felice." Lydia glanced at Paislee. "I'm sairy."

"It happened." Paislee screwed on the cap. "For all we know, Alexa already knew. Maybe she did it with her supernatural powers. She's spooky."

Lydia wasn't swayed by Paislee's attempt at humor. "Felice was killed by strychnine powder. I should have been the one tae die."

"No! Nobody should have been in danger at your wedding, Lydia."

"Alexa really didnae like that I made my own money. Is it that generation of ladies? I dinnae understand. What a waste of time."

"It wasn't, though," Paislee said, lifting her face to the sun. "Your brooch might not be the same one as in the story. Who knows how much of that was real? The cook got it from the lady's maid, who was probably trying tae cover her own position in the house. I prefer Lincoln's facts."

Lydia sighed. "Me too."

"Also, I'm curious about Alexa. She encouraged Mary tae believe the brooch is cursed. Why? Mary wouldn't harm her daughters. What if Mary's true concern was that you weren't the right bride for Corbin?"

Lydia sighed, then reached for Paislee's water. "Screw this. Let's get wine at the harbor."

Paislee read the time on her phone. Almost three. "Can't. Have tae pick up Brody. Want tae come tae the house? Grandpa and Elspeth can manage Cashmere Crush."

"No. Thanks, though." Lydia stood. "I'm rotten company. Do you mind dropping me off at my too-luxurious and empress-like condo? I can bake some sugar cookies before Corbin gets home."

Paislee laughed. "Your wish is my command."

"I never want tae hear the word *wish* again!"

Chapter 14

Thursday, Paislee called Elspeth in to work a few hours that afternoon even though it was her day off. She felt forced to employ desperate measures to get her grandfather to talk. He'd dozed his way through dinner at the table last night and went to bed before Brody, without offering his opinion on the compost project. He always had an opinion.

Grandpa ambled in at noon, growly as you please. Dark rings the size of duffel bags shadowed his eyes, proof that he wasn't sleeping. How long could he go on without getting sick? She wasn't a fool and had noticed the mileage on the Juke had gone up while she was in bed, with the gas tank full. Last night she'd heard him leave around midnight and imagined that Grandpa was out searching the streets for Craigh. If he would talk to her then they could work together!

"Hiya," she said.

"Hey." He slid the soles of his sneakers across the polished cement of her floor until he reached the back counter where she was working on a sweater for her inventory.

"How was the walk?"

"Fine." Grandpa grabbed a fishing guide from the stack on the shelf where he kept them along with Brody's comics and Lydia's fashion magazines.

Elspeth entered in the back, startling her grandfather from his slouch.

"Oh! I didnae know you'd be here today," he said, giving Elspeth a smile he hadn't bothered to share with Paislee.

The two were sweet to each other and it was nice to see— though Grandpa claimed he'd only, and always, love his Agnes.

"Hello, Angus. Hi, Paislee! I've brought my needlepoint pillowcase." Elspeth scooted by Angus to the register counter. "I might just finish tonight at Knit and Sip." The woman lifted it from her bag to show Paislee the progress.

Only a few rows to go and the stitches neat. She'd started last week. "That's impressive, Elspeth."

"Ta." Elspeth set her project next to the register. "Where are you off tae, then?"

"Lunch."

"You're leaving?" Grandpa groused.

"So are you." Paislee sighed at his reluctance. There was a reason she'd wanted a witness so that he didn't just flat-out refuse. Having done some homework on Craigh, she planned to kidnap Grandpa and drive to Dairlee. "I thought it would be nice tae have a meal together."

His silver-gray brow rose in suspicion. "The pub?"

She shrugged and lowered her voice. "I had some questions about the old kirk that I could use your assistance on."

Grandpa tossed the fishing magazine down and rubbed his hands together. He'd helped her before, so it was an excuse he believed. "Constable Payne hasnae been in contact?" He scoffed. "Taking a page oot of Zeffer's book."

Amelia often reminded her that things in real life took time. Patience was key. Not her specialty, to be honest. Paislee and Grandpa said goodbye to Elspeth and got into the Juke. Paislee drove toward the Old Nairn Kirk where Lydia was supposed to have been married.

Where Felice had died.

Lydia almost murdered. And kept going.

"Hey," Grandpa said, half-turning in his seat.

"I found a nice chowder shop in Dairlee," Paislee said. "Maybe you know it. Captain Red's?"

"I've been before." Grandpa crossed his arms in the passenger seat like a surly teen with wrinkles. "Why there?"

"I thought we could drive around Dairlee, maybe go tae the storage unit." That had to be what he'd been doing on his own. "Look for Craigh."

"Why would we do that?"

Though they weren't certain of Craigh's fate at the moment, Paislee had heard the relief in Grandpa's voice that Craigh *had been* alive. She wanted to help him find her uncle. "You know his old haunts. His mates. Did he have a girlfriend?" She glanced at her grandfather. "You know him better than Zeffer. If we find Craigh first, we can convince him tae turn himself in. He'd be alive that way, even if in jail."

"No."

"I'm tired of hearing that one word from you, Grandpa. We're family. I didn't tell the DI about the boxes in the storage unit, did I?"

He shook his head.

"Zeffer knows you have something in there but not what. It's wrong tae keep it secret. Do you have any clue what's inside the boxes?"

Grandpa's chin jutted.

"I think we can agree that if Craigh is alive, he'll want his things, Grandpa. He's been out of contact with Scotland Yard for almost a week. Does Craigh know where you and Gran used tae live in Nairn? That you have a granddaughter?"

Grandpa shrugged. He gave away his worry with a jiggle of his knee.

"What if those men come after Craigh, and find you?" She tightened her grip on the wheel. "We need tae keep you safe. Please, show the DI what's in the unit."

"No, lass. Not until I know Craigh is alive, or dead."

"I'll help you look today." She showed him a picture she'd found online of Craigh Shaw from fifteen years ago and printed out. He and her da resembled each other around the eyes. The nose. "Is this him?"

"Where'd ye get that?" He studied the photo of Craigh in alarm.

"Craigh was on some dating sites." He'd been handsome enough that ladies shouldn't have been a problem. "Did he have a girlfriend?"

"Nothing steady." Grandpa stared out his passenger side window, the picture loose in his grasp.

"Where did he like tae spend his free time?"

"The pub."

Just like every other single Scots male. "Which one was his favorite?"

"I dinnae want *you* in danger," Grandpa said. "I've already been looking around the old neighborhood. He can fish and survive off the land if necessary. Just because Zeffer cannae find him, well . . ."

"He's going tae want tae get inside the storage unit for those boxes, if he's alive."

"You're right." Grandpa's voice broke.

"Okay." Her heart ached for his sorrow. "Chowder first, and then we search?"

"I'm not hungry, lass." Grandpa tugged on his beard.

"Did you eat breakfast?"

He tossed the photo to the console. "Tea was plenty."

"I always feel a little more clearheaded after a bite. Also, the chowder place has an outdoor seating area with a view of the storage unit."

Grandpa bowed his head. "Fine. But he won't be a dunderhead and walk aboot in the light of day, will he?"

"I hope so. No offense, but Craigh doesn't seem too bright if he's stiffing Scotland Yard. Grandpa, I know you've spent the last two nights looking for him. You haven't found him, though, right? Let's try tae work together."

At last, he nodded. She put the photo in the side pocket of her hobo bag.

They parked on the street near the restaurant and got a table for two outside. She pulled out her folded printed photo of her uncle. He had a charming smirk as if to warn the viewer he wasn't to be taken too seriously.

"Put that away!" Grandpa said. "What if the wrong person sees it? We want everyone tae believe he's on the rig."

"That makes asking around a wee bit difficult." She refolded the image.

A waiter rushed out with two menus and some waters. He was in his forties and smiled when he saw Angus.

"Angus! How are you, man? It's been ages. No offense, but I thought you were pushing up daisies."

Grandpa leaned back with a snort. "Not yet anyway."

"And who is this beauty with you?"

"My granddaughter, Paislee. Paislee, Tod."

She could see that Grandpa didn't want to give too much information. As if the waiter might get tortured for information by an oil rig criminal mastermind.

"Nice tae meet you," she said.

"We'll take two cups of chowder. Some bread. An ale for me. Lass?"

"Tea is fine."

"Got it! And how is Craigh doing these days? I sure miss his bad karaoke. Only guy I know who sings worse than me," Tod said with a chuckle.

"Havenae heard from him in a while," Grandpa hedged.

"Och, that's normal on the rigs. I'll be back." Tod took off with large strides, checking on the other three tables before going in.

"He's nice."

"He's nosy," Grandpa countered.

They each had a view of the storage unit. Before Paislee could think of a way to get her grandfather to open up, Tod returned with their steaming bowls and Paislee's stomach growled. "Ladies first." He put it before her. A hunk of crusty bread and butter was on the side dish.

Her mouth watered and she picked up her spoon.

A police car drove by, and into the storage facility. "Grandpa, look!"

Tod gave Grandpa his chowder. "Do ye have a unit there?" he asked casually. "Place was robbed in the middle of the night. I have a flat across the street and sirens blasted. Ruined me beauty sleep." He batted his lashes like a pinup model.

"I do," Grandpa said, his eyes alert. "Did they catch the thieves?"

"Dunno. Manager told me there's a pic of a single bloke hopping the fence on a CCTV cam. Hope none of your stuff was taken."

Tod turned away to another table calling for him.

Paislee was about to suggest they go over there after lunch, but Grandpa was already crossing the street.

She stood. Wait? Go? "Argh!" Putting her spoon down without enjoying a single delicious bite, Paislee followed her grandfather.

As she entered the lobby, Grandpa slipped cash to the manager and asked to see the footage. The fellow put the money in his pocket and walked from the computer, video on, as if not noticing that she and Grandpa were by the counter.

A tall figure in a knit cap and gloves leaped the fence. It was impossible to tell who it was—but Grandpa knew.

His relief was palpable, and he braced his body against the counter. "Let's go check oot the unit."

He was so happy that his son was alive that he forgot he didn't want to share anything with her. Paislee didn't remind him.

They arrived on foot to the unit and Grandpa unlocked it. It was the same, boxes marked PRIVATE. Had Craigh gotten inside?

Grandpa's joy had been replaced by fear for his son. "He's on the run. Oh, Paislee. What do I do now?" His body trembled and his mood returned to surly.

"Zeffer will see the camera footage, too, if he hasn't already," Paislee said. "We need a plan. We are *good* at this, Grandpa, but you have tae trust me."

He scowled.

"Can we at least get our lunch? We can't dine and dash, or just order and dash, on Tod. He knows you."

"Fine." Grandpa raised his palm to her. "But I dinnae want tae talk aboot it."

They walked back across the street to where Tod had bagged up their chowders to-go. "Looked like you were in a hurry," he said. "Everything all right? Was your unit okay?"

"Aye, thank you." Paislee paid for their lunch and gave Tod a generous tip. She and Grandpa rode back to Cashmere Crush in silence.

"Drop me at the house, eh?"

Paislee did, praying for a way to get past his Scot's pride. She parked beneath the carport. "Take your chowder."

He shook his head. "Give it tae Brody. I dinnae feel guid. He should stay with you tonight at the shop."

Her grandfather's face was waxy and pale. "All right. He's got the video games there. You rest."

He nodded and climbed out, going into the house.

She returned to the shop where Elspeth was happily helping two women find just the right colors for a blanket.

Brody wasn't thrilled about spending the evening at Cashmere Crush, but he enjoyed the chowder. He did his homework, like he used to do before Grandpa came into their lives. "What's Grandpa doing anyway?" her son asked.

"Resting. He's had a hard day."

Brody frowned at her but thank heaven didn't ask questions. "Okay."

Paislee and Elspeth set up the chairs for Knit and Sip. Lydia was the first to arrive, carrying a container that smelled savory and delicious. Between Brody's project and worry over Grandpa, she hadn't had a chance to speak with Lydia since the tarot reading with Alexa.

"A baked cheese puff with ham? Lydia, this might be my new favorite," Elspeth said. She poured a glass of white wine for herself, one for Lydia, and one for Paislee.

"You say that every week!" Lydia's cheeks pinkened with pleasure.

"I mean it, too." Elspeth sipped and laughed. "How are you, darling? Hanging in there?"

"Aye." Lydia didn't look at Paislee and she found that odd. "What choice do we have, eh?"

"True."

Mary Beth entered, and Blaise, then Amelia. This was their core group of knitters. Some would come and go, but these were her friends as well as customers.

All gave Lydia hugs, and commiseration. Mary Beth added a box of dark chocolate–covered macadamia nuts that Lydia opened to share.

Amelia watched Lydia with guarded eyes. "I was talking with Constable Payne earlier. He's not so tight-lipped as the DI, and Inspector Macleod is very chill, too."

"You were? About . . . ?" Paislee drawled out.

"Felice Smythe's death—in a roundabout way, as we were talking aboot Lydia's wedding that didnae happen and why."

Lydia placed a cheese knife next to her dish. "Constable Payne is a nice man. He returned my call yesterday, Paislee. Told me tae be patient while the officers collect data. I meant tae phone you, but Corbin and I were comatose on the couch watching movies last night. Not getting married is exhausting."

Paislee reached for her sweater project. "All the stress, no doubt."

"Aye." Amelia looked around the shop. Brody had headphones and they were the only ones inside. "This needs tae be in the circle."

"Okay." They all scooched their chairs in. "What did the constable say?" Paislee asked. They'd blown it yesterday telling Alexa and she hoped it didn't come back to bite them.

"It's been confirmed that Felice inhaled the strychnine, which was old and not verra potent. It irritated her eyes, she became disoriented and fell down the stairs. Broke her neck."

The women, except for Lydia and Paislee, gasped.

"Accidental death?" Mary Beth asked.

"No. Murder," Amelia said. "The box has strychnine in it, which is proof that Lydia's life was in danger."

Paislee smoothed the beige yarn on her lap. "Does Payne have a suspect?"

The ladies sipped their beverages, waiting for more.

Amelia didn't disappoint. "Inspector Macleod is going tae request a search warrant for Smythe Manor. Lady Mary Smythe was questioned at the station and acted verra strangely."

Lydia put her fingers to her throat. "She doesnae like me."

"Impossible," Elspeth said. "She should count herself fortunate tae have a daughter-in-law like you."

"Mary wouldn't be the poisoner," Paislee said with certainty. "Not if her daughters were at risk."

Blaise sipped her wine, not bothering to pretend to knit when there was juicy gossip to be heard.

"Constable Payne agrees with you aboot that," Amelia said. "But he thinks Mary knows something more."

"She's into astrology and tarot readings," Lydia said. "Thinks the manor is haunted. Her good friend is Alexa Selkirk at the library."

"I know Alexa. She seems nice but kooky." Mary Beth drank her fizzy water. "The twins adore her storytime hour. They say she tells the best spooky stories."

"I can attest tae that," Lydia said. She didn't elaborate.

"Did Corbin talk tae the travel agent?" Blaise asked. "Last Paislee told us was that he was going tae reschedule your trip."

"He did." Lydia sipped her wine. "We're traveling tae Germany Tuesday, but only for a week since we've both lost time at work already. Corbin has projects lined up that he cannae put off."

"It will be lovely," Mary Beth said.

"I think so. I'm ready tae steal away." Lydia swirled the white liquid in her wineglass. Paislee sensed her best friend was avoiding looking at her. "But, of course, we need tae be here for Felice's funeral."

"I sure hope they catch the killer by then," Blaise said.

"Me too!" Lydia sipped and exhaled—her shoulder to Paislee.

Paislee set her yarn to the side and stood, her hand to her stomach. "Lydia, what's wrong?"

At last, Lydia met Paislee's gaze. "It's just, well . . . Corbin and I had an awful row."

"Why?" Chills erupted on her skin.

"You know he borrowed my Mercedes yesterday since his car was in the shop, but he didnae mention he'd had an accident coming back from the travel agent until this morning, and we got into a terrible fight over it." A tear slipped from Lydia's eye.

"He's okay?" Paislee asked in alarm. "The car?"

Lydia nodded. "He had a wee bruise on his forehead that he hid with his bangs. I wouldnae have known at all except that Bruce Dundas left a message on my landline, making sure Corbin was fine."

"What happened?" Blaise asked.

"A flat tire sent him into the ditch. Corbin was madder at Bruce for letting the cat oot of the bag than sairy for keeping it secret."

"I still don't understand," Paislee said.

"Thank heaven that Bruce happened tae be driving tae Smythe Manor—we have tae decide what tae do with the wedding photos—and passed him by. That road twists and turns! They changed the tire." Lydia drained her wine like a shot of fine whisky. "I wish we could fly tae Germany today!"

Paislee could read Lydia like a knitting pattern. Her best friend feared the flat tire might have been more than an accident.

Chapter 15

Paislee was on her third mug of strong tea the next day at Cashmere Crush, having not slept well the night before. Lydia had featured in her dreams, saved by the wedding photographer, and it was no surprise when her bestie arrived in person at half-past ten, her own eyes shadowed.

"I'd say guid morning, but it's not been grand," Lydia announced, dramatically dropping her designer handbag on the counter by the register. "Why lie?"

"Any more accidents?" Paislee's pulse skipped as she studied Lydia head to toe for injuries. The sleeveless sundress paired with flat sandals were in charcoal and matched her eyes. Not a blemish to be found.

"No, no. But planning a funeral for someone so young is terrible. We stayed at the manor last night in Corbin's room. I was given the cold shoulder by Garrison for not being there until after our Knit and Sip. I dinnae care. I needed my friends."

"Corbin was upset with you?" Paislee picked up her hat project she was doing with circular needles.

"No, he understands and didnae mind waiting until I was ready, since we're sharing my car."

"Then the rest of them don't matter."

"That's what he says, too." Lydia sighed. "I love him. I look forward tae when we're in our fifties, and this is a faded memory."

Paislee glanced at Lydia. "How was Mary?"

"She'd gone tae bed with a headache, Garrison said. Hyacinth blamed you and I stopping by uninvited for upsetting her mother. Rosebud glared while going through pictures of Felice and the cousins. Chalmers was there, supporting Rosebud. Since Alexa pointed it oot, I see how he does everything for her. I feel sairy for the lad."

"You could warn him," Paislee said.

"The way he acts toward me? No, thanks." Lydia sighed. "Oliver and Jocelyn were there, and Uncle Harry. So many tears. Uncle Philip. There's an Uncle Peter on Corbin's mother's side who has three daughters that are all quite bonnie, and there were lots of jokes about kissing cousins. Drew had a crush on one, and Corbin got verra shy aboot it. I didnae press. I think it's cute."

"There is something to be said for being an only child. Besides, I had you."

"Exactly! Besties forever." Lydia peered into Paislee's tea mug, which was down to an inch of cool liquid. "I should've brought coffee."

"We have cans of fizzy water in the back," she said. "Help yourself."

Lydia groaned but retrieved a can of lemon water, and cracked the tab. "There's no caffeine so this is tae keep hydrated, that's all."

"Still important! What are the Smythes up tae today?"

"Finalizing at the church for Felice tomorrow. Service is at eleven with a celebration-of-life buffet in the dining hall downstairs afterward." Her mouth twisted. "Cannae imagine wanting tae eat, but I guess it's what you do. You're coming?"

"Yes. Grandpa, too. Brody is spending the night with Edwyn tonight and they've got a football game scheduled for tomorrow."

"Look at you with free time on your hands," Lydia teased.

"Free time for a funeral," Paislee said. "Not my idea of how I want tae spend the day."

"Fair. All of this planning over the last year has made me mental—but it was all tae be worth it in the end."

"It's a raw deal, Lydia." Paislee set aside her project and gently squeezed her best friend's hand.

"Yeah." Lydia tore off a piece of receipt paper and turned it over for the blank side. Paislee watched as loops and whirls became a heart, then two, entwined. "Does this look like my Luckenbooth brooch?" She turned the paper so that Paislee could see.

Paislee had only seen it twice. "Close. The thistle crown is bigger and more ornate." She'd thought it lovely until hearing the story of the Witch's Heart. Felice's death had tainted it, too.

"It didnae swirl tae the right," Lydia said with certainty. "I wish I had a photo of Jamie and Magda's wedding, tae see her brooch."

"You could ask Corbin if they have a photo album from back then. They definitely had photography." Paislee sipped her cool tea. "Oh! I wonder if Gretna Green would have the record, and a picture, too?"

"You're brilliant." Lydia tapped the pen to the paper, then stood, staring down at the drawing. "I'm an idiot."

"What?"

"I need tae see the brooch Felice held. I mean, I never actually saw that it was my pin in that box, you know? I just assumed."

Nerves skittered up her spine. "You're right. I know it was gold, like yours, with a red stone, like yours. I didn't examine it closely. We should ask Constable Payne."

"I'll jog tae the station right now." Lydia folded the paper. "I've got tae burn off some of this energy."

"Want me tae go with you?" Paislee could chat with Zeffer if the DI was there.

Just then a single woman walked in. "What a pretty shop!"

Lydia smiled and stepped backward toward the front door. "You stay here. I willnae be a moment."

Paislee helped the woman, who was new to Nairn. "I'm Sorcha. I'm a nurse, with two cats, a dog, and an ex-husband. I knit and like tae hike."

"Any kids?"

"No, no. I mean, I dinnae mind them, for other people." Her nose scrunched. "I prefer tae spend my free time traveling."

"Well, welcome tae Nairn. We have a Thursday social group here called Knit and Sip that you might enjoy. We have appetizers and drinks—tea tae whisky, your choice."

Her eyes lit. "That sounds wonderful."

Paislee sold her bright blue yarn and a pattern book for an infinity scarf. She tucked in the business card with the shop's phone number and email address. "I hope you join us next Thursday."

"I'll be here—you can count on it."

Lydia returned right after Sorcha left. "Well, it's good that I brought the constable my awful sketch because he was sure interested in the brooch design. He said he should've asked if I knew for sure if it was the same pin, and actually thanked me for coming in. Maybe he should be running the station." Lydia huffed. "Your Zeffer wasnae there. I asked Amelia."

"What next?"

"The constable said he'd call."

"If he does, it will be a miracle."

The door opened again, and this time it was Corbin and his cousins, Jocelyn, Sheila, and Oliver. Paislee welcomed them to the store and showed them around.

"Sweet shop," Sheila said, admiring a cashmere scarf.

"We were at the church and just walked and walked. Corbin mentioned Lydia would be here. It's so sad," Jocelyn said. "We made a nice video tribute of my sister's life." She put her fist to her mouth.

Oliver patted her back. Sheila handed her cousin a tissue.

"We . . ." Corbin's voice came out scratchy, but he cleared his throat and tried again. "We were hoping tae snag you, Lydia, for lunch. The harbor has a great view of the water, and we could all use a little peace right now. Can you come, Paislee?"

"No. Sorry. It's just me until Grandpa arrives." She could see that Lydia didn't really want to go either, yet her bestie had no choice but to join the grieving family.

"Thanks for being my sounding board on that marketing concept," Lydia said. Code for *Don't tell them about the possibility of a different brooch.*

Gotcha. "Anytime." Paislee walked with them to the door.

"See you tomorrow," Lydia said.

"I'll be there. Call if I can do anything."

Everyone said sniffly goodbyes, and Paislee waved from the sidewalk as they headed toward the park.

Customers kept her busy for the next hour. Grandpa didn't show up at noon, but she figured he was just late.

By one, she still hadn't heard from him. Customers were a steady stream right up until three p.m. She didn't have to go get Brody since he was staying with Edwyn, but she still locked up the shop to go home.

What if something had happened to her grandfather? He'd been so stressed and worried over his missing son. She'd tried to give him space. She'd never forgive herself for waiting if he had a stroke or worse.

When she arrived, half expecting to find him sprawled on the floor, she gave his closed bedroom door a knock.

"Who is it?"

"Who do you think it would be?" She blew out a breath. "Paislee."

"Are ye alone?"

Shivers of apprehension tickled her spine, and she lowered her hand to the knob. "Aye. Brody is sleeping over at Edwyn's."

The lock on the door clicked and she waited for him to open it.

He did and she peered into the space. Grandpa's bed, unmade. His clothes dirty and his hair disheveled. He preferred a tidy room.

Alive, anyway. Next, her gaze went to the far wall. Boxes from the storage unit were piled along one side. It had been a small unit, and only four had remained once Grandpa had brought his things here. All that had been left were Craigh's.

He'd kept them there when Craigh first disappeared. He'd had no money to pay rent, but he never missed a payment on the storage facility in Dairlee.

"What is all this?"

"I had tae see what was inside."

"So, you spent the morning unloading it?"

"Last night," he said in a gruff voice. "I took the Juke. Craigh is the man who leaped over the fence. He's alive still."

"Without telling Zeffer?" She heard her voice hitch and exhaled. "You should have waited. I would have helped you."

"And that would make you an accomplice." Grandpa rubbed the tip of his nose with the back of his hand. "Zeffer already suspects me. I dinnae know what tae make of what's inside. Not what I thought, tae be sure."

The packing boxes marked PRIVATE were stiff cardboard and reached her waist.

A small knife rested on one of the tops and she could see where Grandpa had carefully cut through the tape. His shoulders bowed. She'd never seen him so defeated. "What is it?" She feared the worst.

What kind of things might a criminal keep?

Grandpa read the alarm clock on his nightstand that blinked half-past three, then turned to her in confusion. "Why are you here instead of the shop? Lord help me, Paislee, I don't know what tae do."

"I worried when you didn't show. Or answer your mobile, or the house phone." Paislee had created a compromise for her grandfather to share the mobile when out with Brody so that Brody didn't have his own at eleven. It would be different now that her son entered secondary.

"I slept most of the morning, after being up all night. Then I must've been so involved I didnae hear the phones."

"Oh, Grandpa. You look exhausted."

Grandpa laughed low but there was no mirth in it. "There's a reason the boxes were heavier than I remembered. Last night when I was loadin' them in the back of the SUV, I told myself that I was an old man with a bad memory."

His jaw tightened.

She reached for his shoulder. "I didn't hear you leave."

"I waited until I was sure you were asleep . . . I didnae know what I was going tae do, until I did it." Grandpa slowly parted the top of the box. "I hate tae involve you, Paislee."

Inside were parts. Metal. Lots of metallic straw, like paper from a shredding machine, or plastic grass for Easter baskets. "Is that an engine?"

"I'm not sure. It might be parts of a drill. I never worked on a rig." Grandpa moved aside the straw it was packed in.

"Zeffer said Craigh had gotten caught stealing parts from the rig. Are these what he'd stolen before?"

Paislee moved to the second box and lifted the lid. More metal parts. The material had a unique sheen to it. She ran her finger over the edge. It was very smooth. "I don't understand why he'd keep them."

"Resale?" Grandpa shuffled like he was a hundred years old and took the top off a slightly smaller box. This one was filled with Craigh's clothes. Things that actually belonged in a storage unit.

Until he removed the clothes, stacking them carefully to the side.

Paislee peered into the box. A silver flash drive the size of her pointer finger sat on top of white crew socks.

"It was inside the sock," Grandpa said. "I'm scared of what might be on it." He sank back against the bed he hadn't bothered to make.

"Did you touch it?"

Grandpa shook his head.

Inspired to keep Grandpa out of jail, Paislee used one of the socks like a glove to gingerly lift the device so she wouldn't smudge any prints if there were any on it. "We can try tae read it here, on the computer."

"I dunno . . ."

"Come on." Answers would be on this drive. She led the way through the kitchen to the desktop computer in the living room. It took forever to warm up. Wallace scratched at the back door, so she let the pup in. By the time she'd filled his bowl with fresh water, the computer was on. She donned a pair of cleaning gloves.

"Wait!" Grandpa said. "What happens if it explodes?"

Paislee sat before the computer. "You've been watching too many thriller movies." She placed the flash drive into the slot. Circles and squares filled the screen like an archaic language. "I don't understand."

"Looks Greek tae me," Grandpa said. "Take it oot. Just in case. What if it puts a virus or something on the computer?"

At that, she did remove the device. Paislee wasn't made of money that she could get a new computer if this one broke. She turned to him, her heart breaking at the pain on his face. "Should we call Zeffer? I think it's obvious that the stolen parts are related tae Craigh's prior offense. It might not pertain at all tae what's going on now."

Grandpa nodded and leaned against the couch, arms crossed. His wrinkles sagged as if he had no energy left. She put the flash drive in a plastic baggie.

Paislee dialed and had to leave a message. She texted Zeffer, then spoke with Amelia at the station. "Only thing we haven't tried is a Batman signal," she told Grandpa. She paced the hall, Wallace at her heels. "We have no choice but tae wait for the infuriating man. In the meantime, we can put everything back the way you found it tae show Zeffer."

As she repacked the metal pieces, she noticed that there were no hard edges. She hefted one on her palm. It didn't feel like metal. "What do you think it is?"

Grandpa shook his head. "The shapes are odd, like you'd need a special order for it tae fit. Could be made tae spec?"

"Even the ones that are broken are smooth."

They left the bedroom for the kitchen, Paislee swiping grime from her hands. "We need a plan tae help Craigh get on the DI's good side."

Grandpa switched on the kettle. "Doot he has one. He has rules tae follow. Huh."

Paislee brought out a can of chili from the pantry and opened it, pouring the contents into a pot for the hob. She hoped that if she just made it, he'd eat it without thinking too hard. "Do you think the flash drive is related tae the parts? We can try tae read it on the laptop at the shop."

"Not worth the chance if it has a virus." Grandpa scratched his beard.

Paislee checked out the computer in the living room. "This one is fine, just old. Maybe too old tae read the program."

"Might be, what do you call it? Engraved? Och. Encrypted."

Paislee rummaged in the pantry for some hard rolls. "Lydia has a guy who does stuff like this for a living." She brought everything to the kitchen table. Two bowls, two mugs, two spoons.

Grandpa stirred the chili. "A hacker. I was a mite concerned aboot what was in those boxes. I'm glad it was parts, and not . . ."

She tilted her head.

". . . drugs," Grandpa whispered, eyeing the ceiling as if Gran might strike him down.

Paislee laughed. "What about money? That would be brilliant."

"Not if I didnae know where it came from." Grandpa ladled chili for each of them and she brought the tea to the table as well.

"Out, boy," she called to Wallace, opening the back door to the garden. The dog hurried as if he had urgent business involving birds in the trees. "It's such a beautiful day."

They sat and ate in harmony that she'd never have imagined a year ago. Grandpa finished the whole bowl and two rolls, which made her feel better. Now if he would just be willing to sleep a bit, she wouldn't worry so much.

"Want me tae call Lydia, about the flash drive?" She cleared the dishes. Her stomach knotted when she thought about what information it might hold. Secrets, if Craigh had been hiding it in a sock.

Grandpa scooped crumbs from the tablecloth and tossed them in the bin. "Aye. No word from the DI?"

Paislee showed Grandpa her phone. "Nope. Oh, look." There was a text from Lydia saying that they were at the bandstand listening to music and having drinks. She and Grandpa were invited. "Wanna go?"

"If we have tae stay in this house, I'll go crazy. I feel utterly helpless."

"We can try the flash drive at Cashmere Crush, too. I'd feel silly if this was gobbledygook just because the computer is old. Is there anything else you can think of tae find Craigh?"

"Lass, I've driven for hours and checked his favorite places. He hasnae been there—the only proof he's alive as of two nights ago is his figure leaping over the fence at the storage unit."

It was only six on a Friday night and there were hours of daylight left. This would give her a chance to see how the cousins were acting around Lydia, and maybe ask some questions in a relaxed setting—like, who else disliked Lydia, and why? "Let's bring Wallace and go downtown."

Grandpa reached for Wallace's lead by the back door. "Nice idea." He frowned. "What are we really going tae do?"

"Am I that obvious?"

"Our minds are in sync, Paislee, if you think we should focus on Lydia's problem since we cannae fix mine."

She quickly filled him in on how Lydia and Corbin were arguing, stress caused by the attempt on Lydia's life. "We have tae keep her safe until she gets on that plane tae Germany, and the killer is found."

"Deal."

Ten minutes later, Paislee, Grandpa, and Wallace were at Cashmere Crush. She used the plastic bag to keep her fingerprints from being on the flash drive and plugged it in. The North Shore Oil logo showed in the corner. It was one of the oil giants, so she was familiar with the name. Numbers and symbols showed but they weren't discernable to Paislee. "Sorry, Grandpa." Her skin felt electric, and she knew this was important. Hopefully, Lydia could help.

"No worries, lass. We had tae try."

Paislee locked the shop up again and she, Grandpa, and Wallace walked the few blocks to the bandstand. Wallace pranced before them, head high. The evening was magical in its beauty. Lydia and Corbin sat with the cousins on a plaid blanket. In addition to the younger generation that had stopped in at her shop, Rosebud, Hyacinth, and Chalmers were there.

Lydia made room for Paislee, Grandpa, and Wallace on the corner. Wallace made immediate friends with Jocelyn and Oliver, soaking up the attention.

Rascal.

She sank to her knees, nodding to Corbin and Sheila. Grandpa gestured to a kiosk where a vendor sold beer and wine. "Want somethin', Paislee?"

"Sure. A light beer would be great. Thanks, Grandpa."

Lydia sipped something clear and bubbly.

"Champagne?" Maybe her friend was celebrating with good news from the constable.

"I wish." Her nose scrunched. "This is club soda. The fish and chips on the harbor did not agree with me."

Corbin rubbed her shoulder in commiseration. "It has nothing at all tae do with the amount of aioli on the chips . . . not at all."

Paislee grinned. "You do like your sauce."

Lydia grew green around the gills and raised her palm. "All right, all right. Enough teasing."

"Why don't you go home tae rest?" Paislee asked.

Corbin rolled his eyes. "Lydia doesnae want tae be a bother. If she goes, then I'd go, and this is time tae be spent with family—her words."

Jocelyn patted Wallace, tears glimmering at her lids. "In memory of Felice."

Grandpa returned and handed Paislee her drink in a clear plastic cup. Sheila lifted her bottle of beer and said, "Tae Felice!"

"Tae Felice." Paislee sipped. The breeze from the Firth, the warm evening sun, the blanket with friends and family made her miss Brody. Life was short and he'd be grown before long. As if feeling her sadness, Wallace snuggled next to her.

She surveyed the throng of locals by the stage as the band took a fifteen-minute break. James Young was there with his daughter, Nora, and Grandpa wandered over to chat with the leather shop owner who had a place next to Cashmere Crush.

"Those two were probably wild back in the day," Lydia observed with a slow smile.

"Aye."

"Any news aboot Craigh?"

None that she could share. "I actually need a favor regarding a flash—"

Chalmers and Rosebud argued over something on her phone, and Chalmers grabbed it away from her. "You owe me!" They were all sitting cross-legged, two blankets overlapped.

"Give it back," Hyacinth said to Chalmers, using her big-sister voice.

"Rosebud owes me a kiss," Chalmers insisted. He'd had a few beers already, Paislee guessed.

Sheila and Jocelyn got up, wandering toward the water. Sheila put her arm around her cousin. The young ladies were of similar build, with long ebony waves. Oliver and Corbin conversed over musical artists.

"You are such an idiot," Hyacinth said to Chalmers, grabbing the phone herself and handing it to her sister.

"Thanks." Rosebud powered the device off.

"What are you afraid of, Rosebud?" Chalmers sneered. Paislee noticed the sheath for a dagger in his Doc Marten boot, his legs skinny in black denim, his T-shirt tight to his thin frame.

"Not you," she said. Rosebud stretched sensuously on her elbow. "What happened tae the band? This was *such* a lame idea. There is nothing tae do in this stupid little town."

Corbin leaned across Lydia. "Are you girls both home from university for the summer?"

"Yeah." Hyacinth crossed her arms in a pout. "I'll have my degree next year, and Rosebud will be done the year after that. We want tae move tae France, drink wine, and write poetry."

"Talk aboot lame," Chalmers said.

"You are." Rosebud lifted her chin.

"You don't want tae stay in Scotland?" Paislee asked. This was probably not a Mary-approved plan.

"God, no," Hyacinth said, her mouth downturned. She was a pretty girl with a spoiled attitude that might not serve her well in life, even with the Smythe money behind her. "This is boring. Worse than boring."

Mary had perhaps gone overboard in protecting them from hurt. The sisters also had crystals and charms for their jewelry. They dressed in black, but she wasn't sure if it was in mourning for Felice or fashionable affectation.

"Mum wants us tae marry well and stay at the manor until we croak but we cannae do that. It's stifling. Dogs and horses are gross. Dirty. They smell." Rosebud sniffed and plugged her nose.

Paislee gave a half smile and turned her attention from the sisters to the crowd of people enjoying the summer evening in Nairn beneath the blue sky. She didn't find it the least bit boring.

Her grandfather and James were still conversing, James clapping Grandpa on the shoulder as he told a joke.

Craigh and Grandpa had lived about twenty minutes away from Nairn in Dairlee on the coast. If Craigh was still alive, would he try to find Grandpa now that Grandpa had the boxes?

Maybe it was for the best that Brody was with Edwyn tonight. Where the heck was Zeffer? The parts in the boxes didn't seem dangerous.

As she scanned the fringes of the crowd, her gaze was drawn to someone watching Sheila and Jocelyn, arms wrapped around each other's waists as they took solace in the gray-blue Firth. She squinted and recognized Bruce, the wedding photographer. She relaxed her guard. He was always on the outskirts looking in because it was his job. Thank heaven he'd been there to help Corbin the other day after Lydia's flat tire.

Paislee brought her attention back to the beer kiosk where a tall, thin man in a red baseball cap neared her grandfather, who was unaware. The figure reminded her of her da. Her entire body lit with apprehension.

"Grandpa!"

The man, possibly the uncle she'd never met, made a point of marking her with a hard gaze, then bolted into the throng.

"Paislee?" Lydia got up with Paislee but then her knees buckled. Paislee helped Lydia back to the blanket.

"Are you okay?" Paislee asked.

"I'm fine!" Lydia waved her back. "Just got up too fast. What happened?"

All the Smythe gazes were on Paislee. Grandpa jogged over, his tam in his hands. "Paislee?"

"I thought you were about tae get hit . . . by a ball." Paislee hoped that nobody would notice there wasn't one.

For the rest of the night, she kept looking for Craigh. No sign of him, and zero word from Zeffer. Corbin dragged Lydia home at seven. Her friend looked awful, so Paislee didn't bother her asking about the flash drive.

"See you tomorrow," Lydia said, giving Paislee a hug. Her friend's skin was clammy.

"Bye, hon."

Paislee and Grandpa left at ten once the band was done playing. She and Wallace had joined James and his daughter after Corbin and Lydia went home. Fear for how Grandpa would react meant she kept the possible Craigh sighting to herself. Just like she didn't say it out loud, but it was a terrible coincidence that her best friend suffered a stomach upset the day before Felice's funeral. Or was it?

Chapter 16

Paislee and Grandpa walked to Old Nairn Kirk Saturday morning, leaving Cashmere Crush with Amelia.

"I'm not sure I'll forgive you aboot Craigh. You should've told me," Grandpa growled.

"Tae forgive is divine. Maybe you could pray about it?" She'd confessed over breakfast that she *might* have seen Craigh around the bandstand last night.

"Dinnae be sassy."

"You actually slept. And I'm not sure it was him." Paislee was pretty sure, though. Her intuition screamed aye. Zeffer had texted at midnight that he would call today. She'd messaged him back that she'd thought she'd seen Craigh around the park but couldn't be certain. Zeffer hadn't answered. Thoughts were not proof.

Paislee had slept lightly, Wallace at the foot of her bed as he did when Brody was at Edwyn's. Would Craigh show up, demanding Grandpa back? Was Lydia feeling better, away from Corbin's cousins?

Grandpa had chosen slacks today rather than a kilt, and a black suit jacket. There'd been a slight lift to his step at the idea Craigh was alive, even if he was crabby.

They entered the church. Lydia and Corbin were at the front

with family and she and Grandpa chose a pew toward the back. She sent a quick text to Lydia, letting her know they'd arrived. Paislee wanted to watch the guests and see if anybody behaved oddly. Constable Payne was there, and she waved to him.

The officer got up from his spot across the aisle to join her and Grandpa. "Such a sad reason tae be at this old church so soon," he said.

"Aye. Verra sad," Grandpa agreed.

Lydia hurried to the back, head-to-toe in black. Her skin still had a green tinge. After a quick hug hello, Paislee asked, "How are you feeling this morning?"

"I'm fine. I think it was bad fish." Lydia swallowed hard.

Paislee didn't like the way Lydia looked. "Corbin said too much aioli—the mayo can turn easily in the heat."

"He doesnae know what was in my stomach." Lydia placed her hand over her belly.

"You went oot tae eat?" Constable Payne asked. "I thought you were being cautious."

After a sheepish smile, Lydia said, "It was a nice restaurant at the harbor, with the cousins. I've had the fish and chips there many times."

What was different was the company, Paislee thought.

Constable Payne rubbed his upper lip. "And you feel fine now?"

"Aye."

"I'd watch what you eat and who you eat with until we find oot who tried tae kill you a week ago," Constable Payne suggested.

"Oh!" Lydia raised her hand to her lips.

Paislee reached across the constable. "Constable Payne, what if it wasn't food poisoning?"

Her best friend blinked rapidly. "I dinnae think I'll ever eat again."

The constable patted Lydia's arm. "There is nothing you can do aboot it now, after the fact. Unless you saved the contents?"

"No. I certainly did not." Lydia shivered with distaste.

"We will discover who is behind this. It takes time."

Paislee had heard that more often than she liked to admit. "Constable, what did you find with the search warrant for Mary Smythe?"

He shook his head. Not the time or place, he conveyed without words.

Lydia strangled a tissue in her clasp. "Mary's up in the front pew sobbing like Felice was her daughter rather than a niece—by marriage. That screams guilty tae me. What if she had Felice act on her behalf?"

The constable's brow rose. "There is no evidence that Mary and Felice were close."

"Where is the velvet box?" Paislee asked.

"At this point, probably in the Firth," Grandpa said.

"I happen tae agree." Constable Payne patted the black suit coat he'd put on over his uniform. "You'd be a fool tae hang on tae it, but one never knows. Some killers keep a trophy."

Felice had the brooch in her hand. "What about the pin?" Paislee asked. "Was it Lydia's?"

Constable Payne pursed his lips. "Lydia, you may come in later today tae identify the brooch. But for now, I am here tae pay my respects tae the Smythe family, and Felice. I'm going tae sit somewhere else. Just wanted tae say hello tae Paislee and Angus."

The officer found a quieter spot to sit and survey the mourners. The music started. Minister Angela strode with her head bowed to the pulpit.

Concerned, Paislee asked, "Who was there at the restaurant with you? I'm sorry, Lyd, but you can't trust anyone."

Lydia dabbed the tip of her nose with the tissue. "I have tae trust Corbin, Paislee, or what's the point of love and marriage? Mary was there, and Garrison, everybody in the family had met up for lunch. Rosebud, Hyacinth, Chalmers. The brothers and wives, the kids. It has tae have been bad sauce."

Paislee had no clue where to start since the evidence had been flushed. "What does Corbin think?"

"Corbin's a sweetheart, but I made him go tae his parents' house withoot me. I didnae want him around while I was . . . sick."

Grandpa tugged his beard. "Through sickness and health, lass. That's how the vows go."

"We didnae say them." Lydia sighed. "Anyway, I better get up there. I'll be doing a lot of praying. Poor Felice, and poor me." She strode, head high, to the front pews of the church.

"The constable seemed suspicious of her being ill," Grandpa murmured. "Mayonnaise can turn in the heat, and with her being sick, we might never know if it was on purpose."

"I'm so worried for her, Grandpa."

"Me too, me too."

Minister Angela performed the somber service with quiet dignity, touching on the fleeting beauty of life. Though one might question why an angel was taken too soon, it is God's divine plan. Trust in faith and love. A picture of Felice was at the front of the pulpit area, surrounded by fresh white lilies.

Philip and Garrison embraced their brother Harry between them. The cousins enfolded Jocelyn and Oliver. Mary handed out tissues, her eyes streaming as she comforted her daughters. Had this been a way for Rosebud and Hyacinth to end their boredom? Fantastical and dramatic enough? Only instead of Lydia being buried today, it was their cousin Felice.

Rosebud hung on Chalmers, and Hyacinth collapsed with a tissue to her nose against the pew. Jocelyn and Oliver, Felice's siblings, handled themselves with more decorum. They were old enough to be out of university, which helped with their maturity, Paislee thought, trying to be kind since she was sitting in church.

If there was any place to be nice, it was here.

Yet, someone had put poison on the brooch and given it to Lydia, through Minister Angela. Her head ached. Good and evil weren't simple things.

Lydia was going to identify the brooch today for Constable Payne. Surely there were pictures somewhere in the Smythe house of all the pins. The Smythes were all about their wealth. Investments. Keeping what they had. The Luckenbooth brooches would be insured. Did that require a photo?

She tapped a note to herself in her mobile. Constable Payne had probably already asked, but maybe not.

Chalmers put his arm around Rosebud and patted her shoulder. Why had he wanted Rosebud's phone yesterday? What had he meant that she'd owed him? Could he be speaking about Lydia? Paislee half-listened to the sermon. Lydia and Corbin's wedding had been delayed. Did someone want it to never happen?

Mary brought a large purse to the pew and dug around inside for more tissues that she handed to Hyacinth. That bag was plenty big enough to carry the small wooden box the brooch had been in, as well as the velvet one. A search warrant might be for the house, but what about Mary's handbag? The men's kilts also had pockets big enough for the box.

Paislee recognized quite a few folks at the service. This time instead of happy bright colors there were black dresses and slacks. The men wore kilts and black jackets.

Matthew Dalrymple, Corbin's best man, sat next to Constable Payne. She hadn't seen him come in. The solicitor had been clear-headed in the emergency with Felice.

"And now we say a final prayer for Felice Marie Smythe." Soft Scottish bagpipes played from a dais to the left of the pulpit.

The mournful sound of "Amazing Grace" choked her up. Grandpa handed her a tissue that she hadn't needed until just that moment.

She hadn't known Felice, but death was . . . gone. Paislee believed in Heaven and more to this existence, but it didn't take away the sting of saying goodbye. Unexpected farewells were even harder.

"If you'd like tae join the Smythe family downstairs in the dining hall for a video remembrance of Felice's life, they'd welcome you with a light repast."

She and Grandpa stood. "Should we stay?" Grandpa asked, eyeing the door to the foyer and fresh air. Escape.

"For a few minutes, just tae show our respects."

He shuffled forward a half step. "Times like these the old rituals offer comfort, even for a cynical man like meself."

Lydia brushed by the folks leaving to grab Paislee's hand. "You're staying, right? I need my bestie. Mary just told Corbin that my weak nerves are something that would be passed down tae a child if we had them." She huffed an annoyed breath. "Mary stressed the emphasis on *if*, which means she's talked tae Alexa."

"I'm sorry, Lydia."

Lydia frowned. "They are both gunning for me. Mibbe they're in on it together?"

Schoolgirl friends. Hmm. "When you identify the pin at the station, maybe ask the constable if he's talked with Alexa."

"Guid idea, Paislee. But, love, you're coming with me. I dinnae want tae be alone. Corbin promises that I just need tae hang on till we leave on Tuesday. Beautiful Germany, here we come." Lydia clung to Paislee's arm, her once rosy tones pale with grief and fear.

Her best friend had been ravaged by this whole wedding process. "I'm here for you, however you need me."

Ten minutes and many handshakes later, Corbin reached them in the third-to-last pew as they watched the procession of guests. Most went toward the stairs going to the basement, where there was a kitchen and large square dining area.

His eyes were red-rimmed. "There you are," Corbin said. "Mary told me that you'd left."

"What? Why would I leave? I'm here, waiting for you." Lydia crossed her arms.

"This is a nightmare." Corbin raked his fingers through his hair. The ebony strands fell into place. "Jocelyn hasnae been sleeping, and Mary suggested she try self-hypnosis. Offered tae buy her a pendulum so she could teach herself. The woman is mental."

"That's what I've been trying tae tell you," Lydia said. "What if she messed with my aioli?"

"Lydia, my stepmother did not try tae poison you."

"I've never had a flat tire before. What if someone tampered with it?" Lydia asked, her hand on her hip. "You should have told me the day it happened, but you kept it from me."

"I didnae want you tae worry. The hills are full of potholes and it's not uncommon to lose the cap on the valve of a tire." Corbin rocked back on his heels. "Your car didnae have a scratch."

"Someone put strychnine on my brooch," Lydia said, her teeth gritted. "Felice is dead because of it! I'm not overreacting aboot that, am I?"

The cousins, uncles, and aunts gathered close by. The younger generation watched avidly, Rosebud especially. Bruce was there, next to Drew, Reggie, and Duncan. Their wives herded the kids toward the back and away from the scene.

"Maybe you two should go outside and discuss this," Paislee suggested in a soft voice. "Without an audience."

"Lydia, love, I'm sorry." Corbin took her hand. "The stress is getting tae me, too. Not a week ago we were here tae get married, and now . . ."

Lydia swiped her eyes. "I understand."

"You *should* be understanding," Garrison butted in. "This is a family tragedy."

"Your marriage should wait until next year," Mary suggested, her arm in Garrison's.

Lydia's eyes widened. "Next year?"

Corbin blew out a breath. "We can discuss it later, Lydia. We just want tae do what's best for the family."

Lydia shook off his hand. "I'll tell you what's best for *me*!"

Minister Angela hurried toward them. "Corbin, Lydia. My dears. Why not go into my office tae have a private conversation?" She glowered at the bystanders. "This is aboot Felice right now and honoring *her* life."

A tear rolled down Lydia's cheek. "Fine."

"Ach, stubborn," Mary chided. Garrison led her and the sisters toward the back. "Let that be a lesson tae you," she said, patting Rosebud and Hyacinth. "Marriage is a sacred commitment, and you must choose wisely. Or else."

Lydia squeezed Paislee's fingers, but then followed the minister and Corbin to her office.

"Corbin's got his priorities skewed," Grandpa said, as they stepped toward the stairs.

"I hope he realizes that. Oh, Grandpa." She tugged his elbow so that he stopped to face her. "What if Lydia is making a big mistake marrying Corbin?"

Chapter 17

"Ye can't think that way, lass." Her grandfather hesitated and turned them both toward the carpeted staircase. "Lydia and Corbin love each other, but nobody knows what goes on behind closed doors in a marriage."

Paislee glanced back over her shoulder to Corbin and Lydia, and Minister Angela, as they disappeared down a hallway. Was he thinking of the end of his own marriage?

Grandpa nudged her forward.

"I don't want her tae be hurt."

"Ye cannae stop it. It's life." Grandpa gestured at the funeral photo of Felice as they passed the pulpit to the stairs leading down to the dining hall. "If there is no pain or suffering, there cannae be joy. We have tae know sorrow, tae appreciate happiness."

"Ha!" They reached the lower level and she studied Grandpa's lined face. "When did you get so philosophical?"

"I have me moments." He smoothed his mustache and winked.

The scents of meat pies and brownies lured them forward and Paislee turned to the long buffet line to her right. About seventy people milled around, holding cups of tea or coffee, along with a plate.

She was reminded of the dinner at Smythe Manor. The same

people, but for a different reason. Someone had tried to kill Lydia, and she couldn't forget that. "Should we split up tae scout the room?"

Grandpa led them toward the silver urn with hot water for tea, and another that had coffee inside. "All right. Some tea first, and a bite, tae act natural. What are we looking for?"

"The murderer."

"Easy-peasy." Grandpa poured a cup of tea and handed her one. "Holding a velvet box and a bag of strychnine?"

"If only!" Paislee sipped. It wasn't great but it quenched her dry throat. "Did you notice that Mary's handbag is the size of a suitcase?" She raised her wristlet that had room for only the essentials. "It might be interesting tae see what she has inside."

"And how do ye propose tae do that? Ask nicely?" Grandpa chuckled, amused at his own wit.

"You're right. Bad idea." Paislee located Alexa and Mary, both in black dresses, standing near a round table for six. Alexa had a heart-shaped Luckenbooth brooch attached to her collar. Mary's large purse was slung on a chair.

Rosebud, Chalmers, Hyacinth, and Matthew were clustered by the rolls. Chalmers tossed one in the air, and then another, juggling with the food in an attempt to impress Rosebud. The sisters wore gothic-style dresses like the character Morticia Addams, with silver necklaces and earrings. Matthew was in black slacks and a suit jacket. One man tried too hard and the other appeared aloof. Lincoln Reid sat with Philip and Harry at a table, passing a flask.

Paislee glanced back at the staircase when she heard a noise, hoping to see Lydia and Corbin, but it was Minister Angela with a neutral smile.

"You go talk tae Lincoln Reid. He had a powdery plant food on his counter that he'd said would make us ill if we mistook it for sugar. Lydia was sick yesterday."

"He's old as dirt, Paislee, and I highly doot he's running around with poison in his pocket," Grandpa said.

"Just see who he thinks might be guilty. We couldn't share that Felice had died after someone tried tae kill Lydia."

"One crafty old man tae another." Grandpa wiped his mouth and tossed the napkin into the bin. "What are *you* going tae do?"

"Chat up Alexa, the librarian, about her Luckenbooth brooch. Find out why she's hateful tae Lydia."

Grandpa gave her a determined nod. "Let's meet back at the scones in fifteen minutes. Chances are verra high someone in this room is guilty."

"Yeah." Paislee's stomach knotted. "You're right."

Felice hadn't been the intended victim, which meant the killer remained on the prowl. Were they still after Lydia, or had the murderer been scared straight by the reality of Felice's funeral?

Paislee casually cruised through the cousins and friends of Felice—the uncles, the wives, the bairns—until she reached Alexa and Mary. Alexa had smoothed her messy bun into a chignon and silver hoops had replaced the dream catchers—it was if she'd subdued her personality along with her style for the funeral. Mary's platinum locks didn't dare frizz with so much hairspray.

Alexa saw her first and touched Mary's arm, as if to alert her friend that Paislee was within earshot.

"Hi," Paislee said. She kept her pleasant expression and bobbed her chin at Alexa's Luckenbooth brooch. "Your pin shines across the room. It's very pretty."

"Thank you. My Gareth gave it tae me many moons ago." She held a paper plate with a brownie on it. "Iron is so strong that it wields off the evil eye."

Paislee noted the tail of the heart listed to the right. A witch's heart, according to her lore. Did Alexa truly believe she had magical powers? It was clear that Mary did.

Mary pressed the black silk fabric at her throat, as if to reassure herself the charms were still there, though tucked out of sight.

"Mary, I know Garrison didn't give you a brooch, but surely you have one from your first husband?" Luckenbooths were a Scottish tradition.

Mary's cheeks reddened. Paislee would feel bad about poking the woman's pride if she hadn't been so cruel to Lydia. Why would Alexa encourage her friend to hate Lydia? Surely it was more than not approving of Lydia's financial success.

"Warren Maxwell wasnae one for romantic gestures." Mary glanced across the room to her current husband, who had joined Harry, Philip, Lincoln, and Grandpa. "As for Garrison, I'm sure he thought because ours was a second marriage, it wasnae important."

That might explain some of the jealousy surrounding the Smythe heirlooms. "That had tae be hurtful. You said your daughters will be able tae pick when they get engaged."

"Oh, yes." Mary set her paper cup on the table. "Garrison promised they could choose."

Alexa tilted her head as if trying to find out what Paislee was up to. Librarians were intelligent people. It was possible she had her own agenda regarding Lydia and Corbin's marriage that Paislee hadn't figured out yet. "Did you tell Mary that you read Lydia's tarot cards?"

The librarian didn't bother to deny it. "I did. It was a reassurance for her that Lydia and Corbin are not a good match."

"But that isn't what they said at all. It was about money, and it really bothered you. You mentioned that Lydia seemed tae only care about profit. Why is that?"

"Alexa has every right tae be angry!" Mary said, defending her friend. "Lydia sold her mother's home tae build a parking garage off High Street. Her mum died of sorrow soon after."

Two years ago, Alexa had said at the library. That explained a lot. Had Alexa been angry enough to poison Lydia? She had fanned the story behind the brooch and encouraged Mary's dislike of Lydia.

"That's enough, Mary. Paislee here is fishing for information aboot the killer." Alexa placed her plate on the table, her motions quick, as if she wanted her hands free.

"I dinnae know who is responsible." Mary's gaze ping-ponged between them. "I told that tae Constable Payne!"

Grandpa strolled by the ladies, all standing, and "accidentally" bumped into Mary's chair. He hit her large purse with his hip and it toppled over.

"Oh!" Paislee said, her hand to her mouth. "Grandpa!"

"Och, sorry, ladies," he said. "Didnae mean tae be so clumsy." The large bag had tipped over. Mary's mobile fell out as well as some wadded tissues.

Paislee knelt to scoop things back inside but stopped before actually touching anything. Keys. Lipstick. Comb. A stomach aid to mix with water if one had gas issues. No velvet box.

"I've got it," Mary said, also kneeling. She showed no concern that Paislee might see the contents of her bag as she scooped the mess up and shoved it back in.

Grandpa offered his hand to Mary to assist her up. "Apologies, ma'am."

Paislee straightened and brushed her hands together. "Forgive us. Come on, Grandpa. Let's get some tea."

Alexa mouthed to Mary so Paislee could see, "Rude."

She took Grandpa's arm and the pair ambled toward the rolls, she trying very hard not to dissolve into laughter. "Smooth, Grandpa."

He winked.

Chalmers saw them coming and tried to put the rolls he was juggling back with the others.

"Gross, mate. Toss them in the bin," Matthew said. He read his phone, then glanced toward the stairs as if impatient to see Corbin and Lydia before leaving. Matthew stepped past Paislee and away from the sisters, giving her a slight nod of recognition but not stopping to chat.

Chalmers lobbed the rolls into the trash. Hyacinth trailed after Matthew. The Morticia wannabe had a wee crush on Corbin's best friend. Matthew was oblivious. Young love.

Love was a powerful motivator for many things. Sometimes

passion led to murder. In Alexa's case, she was *passionate* about Lydia's role in the sale of her mum's flat for profit.

Bruce wandered near the food, selecting a scone. A camera hung by a strap around his neck, a tool of the trade. "Hi, Bruce," Paislee said. "It sure was lucky you were there when Corbin had a flat tire."

"Hello, Paislee. Angus," Bruce said. "The valve lost its cap, creating a slow leak. Happens. The luck is how good a driver Corbin is on those winding roads. There wasnae a mark on that beautiful Mercedes."

Rosebud dragged Chalmers by the hand away from Paislee and Bruce. Chalmers tossed a furtive glance back at Paislee. What did they know about it?

Bruce's gaze went to the stairs as Lydia and Corbin finally came down, a relieved smile on his lips. Lydia waved at Paislee and when Paislee turned to ask Bruce more about the incident, he'd slipped away to talk to Lincoln.

Paislee walked toward her friend. Her gray eyes were glistening as if she'd been crying. Corbin had his hand on her lower back.

"I love you, Lydia," Corbin said. "We'll get through it."

Lydia raised her chin as if she wasn't quite sure about that. "Paislee! Just the woman I wanted tae see. And Angus. Let's go identify the brooch."

"Corbin, don't you want tae join us?" Paislee gestured to the stairs and fresh air. An excuse to leave with them.

"No, I need tae stay here. With my family." His jaw clenched. The wound hadn't been healed then but remained tender.

"I'll message you a picture, Corbin." Lydia got to the center of the staircase, turned to the room, and waved a general goodbye.

Paislee and Grandpa had a hard time keeping up with Lydia as she hightailed it out of the church to the street. Once there, Lydia sucked in a deep breath, her hand to her waist like a runner after a marathon.

"You okay?" Paislee touched Lydia's shoulder.

"No. But I will be on Tuesday when I'm on a plane tae Germany. When I'm sitting on the balcony of my hotel room with a glass of wine. Do you know that Germany has a fine selection of wine? People think beer, but no. There is more tae that beautiful countryside than meets the eye." Lydia's steps were manic as she hustled down the sidewalk. Her flat shoes allowed for longer strides.

Paislee and Grandpa were pulled along in her wake. "Lydia, slow down! I found out why Alexa was stirring the pot about you. It seems you sold her mum's house and it's now a parking garage."

Lydia frowned but kept walking. "I thought Alexa looked familiar. Pity that her mum died. She made a tidy profit on the sale and bought a house on the loch in Inverness."

Ten minutes later they reached the Nairn Police Station. It was normally not open on a Saturday. The receptionist's desk was dark, but Constable Payne had been expecting them, so he unlocked the door and ushered them to his office. It was blue and gray with pictures of his family on the shelves behind his desk. A painting of the bandstand was to the left. It was a cozy space and quite unlike DI Zeffer's.

"Zeffer's not here," the constable said when Paislee asked. "Something aboot Dairlee, but he's kinda closed-lipped."

"We know," Grandpa said. He took a chair, as did Lydia and Paislee.

The constable unlocked a drawer in his desk and brought out a clear evidence bag with a gold brooch, of entwined hearts and a red stone. "Is this the Luckenbooth pin that Corbin proposed tae you with?"

"No." Lydia put her hand to her chin, her eyes big and frightened. "It's similar, but not mine. You see the tail of the heart? According tae the librarian—"

"Alexa Selkirk?"

"Aye. She has a grudge against me for selling her mum's house. She told Mary and Lincoln aboot the supposed Smythe curse."

"Go on." Constable Payne rubbed his round chin.

"It's bent tae the right—a sign that this brooch belongs tae a witch."

"That's not real." The constable shook his head. "No more real than faeries."

"Alexa probably believes in those, too," Paislee said.

"I'll question her," Constable Payne said, jotting down her name in his notebook.

"Now what?" Grandpa asked. "Though it's not the right brooch, it was still in a box addressed tae Lydia."

"We cannae make any assumptions. Since this isnae yours, Lydia . . . well." Constable Payne tapped his desk. "I'm at sixes and sevens aboot it."

Lydia took a picture of the pin. "Tae show Corbin. He told me that I was probably just tired, can you believe it? Imagining things."

Paislee patted her best friend on the arm. "Bruce mentioned at the lunch that a lost cap on a valve is very common."

"The wedding photographer?" Constable Payne shifted and his chair creaked.

"Aye," Paislee said. "He happened tae be driving by when Corbin went off the road due tae a flat tire."

"Anything else of interest you'd like tae share?" His tone held a smidge of sarcasm.

"Lincoln Reid has a special plant food in powder form that he warned us would make us sick if we drank it." Paislee felt bad about naming the historian but had to give the constable all the information to sort through. "And Lydia *was* nauseous Friday night."

"Lincoln Reid?" The officer wrote that name down, too. "But he wasnae at the lunch on the pier?"

"No. Corbin would rather believe that than Rosebud," Lydia said.

Constable Payne put the pin back in the drawer and locked it. "Why Rosebud? I've interviewed her and Hyacinth, and they didnae notice anything. I asked specifically what Rosebud and Felice were laughing aboot before Felice died, but she claimed not tae remember."

"Rosebud and Chalmers acted strange today as well as yesterday," Paislee said. "Chalmers told Rosebud he owed her for something. He would do anything for her."

Constable Payne laid his pen down. "That's not proof of anything. Listen, you must leave this tae us. Weddings and funerals are stressful times. People go a wee bit mental."

Lydia rubbed her arms as if chilled. "You should be able tae count on your partner." She glanced at the clock, which read half-past two.

"We're done here." Constable Payne removed his hat and set it on the desk. "We *will* find who killed Felice."

"And my brooch is still missing," Lydia said in a weary voice. "I want the sanctuary of my condo. I'm going tae turn off the lights and the phone tae recoup."

"But check your messages," the constable instructed, "when you wake up. In case we have news."

The trio left the station and walked to Cashmere Crush in silence. Cars and tourists filled the street. The sun shone in a blue sky, but sorrow prevailed.

"The Juke is in the back," Paislee said. "Let me drive you home, Lydia."

"Okay."

"I'll stay at the shop for a while," Grandpa said. "See how Elspeth and Amelia are doing."

After Lydia and Grandpa hugged goodbye, Paislee and Lydia walked around to the back entrance of Cashmere Crush and got in the car.

"Want tae talk?" Paislee asked, starting the engine.

Lydia pinched the bridge of her nose and squeezed her eyes shut. "I really don't. I messaged the picture tae Corbin and he hasnae responded."

Paislee hated that her best friend was so down and there was nothing she could do to fix it. She drove to Lydia's condo and parked before the tall building. "I can come up, if you want."

"No, thanks." Lydia stifled a yawn. "I just want tae sleep. I'm so confused aboot everything, and I know I'll feel better after a nap. You willnae believe the things I'm thinking right now."

Paislee hugged Lydia across the console. "I understand. Text me tae let me know you're okay, or I will use the spare key tae get in and check on you."

Lydia gave her a wan smile. "Dinnae fash."

"I'm going tae worry."

Lydia's chin trembled.

"Are you sure you don't want just a little company? I'll sit on the couch, and you'll never know I'm there."

"I don't need a guardian angel."

It made sense that Paislee had Gran as hers and she didn't take it for granted. Her da, too, maybe. "Fine. Text me a thumbs-up emoji and I won't storm the castle. Every few hours. If you want, I'll bring chocolate ice cream later."

"You are such a mom. And the best friend ever. Go." Lydia got out of the car and disappeared inside the condo without a backward glance.

Lydia's guardian angels, whoever they were, had to be working overtime.

Chapter 18

Saturday night, the Shaw family escorted Lydia Barron to Inverness for a night of fun. There was a showing of the latest adventure film in an outdoor theater. They didn't talk about Corbin, or Craigh, or Zeffer, or Constable Payne.

They ate buttery popcorn, the adults sipped Scotch—just one for Paislee since she was driving—and splurged on fudge bars. They had a blast for the first time in months. Wallace had his fill of popcorn and snoozed the whole thirty-minute ride home.

Lydia raced up to her condo with many thanks and a grin, and Paislee took them to their house, parking under the carport.

A note was stuffed in the door, and she plucked it free. "Zeffer stopped by. He'll try tae call us tomorrow."

Grandpa blew a raspberry, and they all went inside.

Yeah. She felt the same. Why couldn't the man use his blasted phone like a normal person?

The next morning, Sunday Funday, Paislee got a text from Lydia. She and Grandpa were sharing tea and she read the message aloud. "Lydia says thanks for an amazing date night. She wants me tae go with her tae the dragon's den today." She lowered the phone.

"Dragon's den?" Grandpa asked.

"She must mean Smythe Manor." Paislee kept reading. "Oh, tae see the brooches, or pictures of them."

"It was smart thinking they'd be insured and probably photographed," Grandpa said. He slurped strong Brodies tea.

"I wonder if we can identify the brooch that Felice had," Paislee said. She'd set a dish of scones on the table to nibble and broke off a corner. "Lydia will be here at ten, if it's okay with you."

Grandpa helped himself to a full scone. "I'll take Brody fly-fishing, with Wallace, on the river. Lydia needs ye still. It was a week ago today that she was supposed tae have been married."

And the killer not yet caught. "Thank you." She changed the subject before Grandpa could dart from the room and avoid her. "What should we do about Zeffer, and the flash drive?"

"I plan on fishing all day," Grandpa said. "Since you think you saw Craigh Friday night, I'm dragging me feet. What if the contents harm Craigh somehow?"

Paislee covered his hand with hers. "Why is life so messy?"

"Ah, if only I had the answer tae that, I'd be rich." Grandpa finished his scone.

Brody and Wallace zoomed down the stairs and her son showed compassion about her spending the day with Lydia. "Have fun, Mum. I know we will, right, Grandpa?"

"Right."

"Good luck on the river today!" She hated to say good luck because it made her think of Alexa, and Mary, and bad luck. "I hope you catch loads of fish," she amended.

Lydia honked from behind the wheel of her Mercedes and Paislee raced down the steps to the carport and the passenger side. She slid in. "Morning."

"Yes, it is. How are my lovely Shaws? And what's going on with Craigh?"

"The guys are going fishing." Paislee caught Lydia up on the situation without too much detail of the flash drive or boxes of drill parts, focusing more on the fact Craigh was alive, and a possible criminal.

"Not great," Lydia summed up. "And now Zeffer is MIA?"

"His usual. Only this time I think he's actually homing in on the bad guy. Whoever that turns out tae be. Zeffer is persistent. I mean, it's been a year of waiting in Nairn for Grandpa tae come and ask about Craigh." Paislee sighed. "Such patience."

"Are those compliments for the arctic detective?" Lydia glanced at Paislee with a smile.

"No." Paislee turned away to look out the window. The DI was making her feel things she'd rather not.

"You're not a nun, Paislee Ann," Lydia announced.

"Not trying tae be!"

"It's normal tae have attractions tae people."

She placed her hand on her slightly rounded belly. "I very obviously know that."

"Withoot getting knocked up, tae put it crudely. You are beautiful, smart, funny, kind. You are more than a mom."

"I'm a mom first," Paislee insisted. "That's it."

"I never thought that I'd find love again . . . I didn't want tae, and yet Corbin . . ."

"He kissed you and made your toes curl. I remember."

They both laughed.

"Just . . . be open, okay?" Lydia asked.

"No." Paislee wasn't even going to pretend an interest when it had to be very far off her radar. Romance. Ugh. And she wasn't going to point out that at the moment, romance and love were putting her best friend in danger.

They drove out of downtown. Lydia said, "Are you okay if we take the scenic route tae Smythe Manor?"

"Sure."

"I hate that I'm so nervous aboot going tae Corbin's house."

"Does he know we're coming?"

"Aye, I told him I would, since I spent last night with you guys, and didnae answer his calls. But first, I just need the wind in my hair!"

The Highlands were gorgeous hills and valleys that required quick reflexes if one liked speed, as Lydia did—stereo cranked, and windows down. It reminded Paislee of when they were young, and Lydia had gotten her first car. It lifted their moods.

An hour later, they reached the manor. The property was pristine green farmland with a silo and barn in the back, the front perfectly landscaped. Paislee realized with a start that she'd seen this precise image before, in a calendar of Nairn for sale at the tourist gift shops.

They slowed up the driveway.

"There's Corbin's SUV, back from the shop." Lydia parked before the row of garages, next to a truck with a sticker in the rear window that read PROUD TO BE A SMYTHE.

Paislee chuckled.

"Is it wrong tae find the family pride ridiculous?" Lydia asked—after a furtive glance around to make sure they were alone.

"I think they take it a wee bit too far."

Lydia blew out a breath and tromped across the gravel to the stoop.

The dogs sprawled on the top step and greeted them with wagging tails. Norbert answered after Lydia knocked. His brow furrowed the slightest bit to see the dogs in the front yard. Must have escaped the kennels again, Paislee thought. She hid a smile.

"Ms. Barron," Norbert intoned.

It wasn't a good sign if he was back to being uber-formal with someone who was almost a member of the family.

"Is Corbin home?" Lydia sighed. "I saw his car."

"Wait here."

Norbert walked down the hall and left Paislee and Lydia in the foyer. He went into the parlor, and returned, Corbin on his heels. His hair was mussed, and he had shadows under his eyes along with stubble on his jaw.

"Lydia, babe! I asked aboot the photos of the brooches, and you're right." He kissed Lydia's cheek and nodded to Paislee. "Come tae the study. Da found a treasure trove of historical photos that is going tae make Lincoln fall over in shock."

They hurried after Corbin while Norbert went out the front door, presumably to handle the wayward dogs.

"You guys were right that the brooch in Felice's hand wasnae the one that I gave tae Lydia. I should have listened. I'm sorry. I was just caught up in the funeral. It's hit us all verra hard, tae have Felice dead so young." Corbin swiped his hand over his hair, already very tousled as if it wasn't the first time he'd been agitated.

"Oh!" Lydia smiled at Corbin, her cheeks flushed. "Well . . . sairy tae be late."

"You're not! Sheila just got here, too." Corbin paused at the threshold of the room. "Hey, everyone. Say hello tae Paislee and Lydia." Garrison, Mary, Rosebud, Hyacinth, Sheila, Jocelyn, Oliver, Harry, Philip, and the brothers each had a different photo album and they all looked up at the same time with various murmured greetings.

"Check these oot!" Drew gestured to the stacks on the side of the couches.

"How did you find them?" Lydia asked.

"Mary," Garrison said with pride. "I'd forgotten aboot them, but when Corbin was talking over breakfast aboot old photos that might have pictures of the Luckenbooth brooches, Mary vaguely remembered seeing dusty crates in the attic, and here we are."

Paislee glanced at the woman, who beamed with pleasure at her husband's praise. She'd bet that Mary had gone over every nook and cranny of the house when she'd moved in, probably taking inventory.

Corbin handed them each a photo album from the mid–twentieth century. "Great-grandma Smythe put all of these in albums for the family so that we'd have them. It's amazing tae see such a linear history spread oot before us."

"My gran was an angel on earth," Garrison said. "This is her." He raised a photo of a woman in sepia on horseback with the barn behind her. Her gaze was steady, her hair loose around her shoulders. The eyes and brow just the same as the female cousins. Even the nose. His grandmother was stunning and in her element as Lady of Smythe Manor.

"She's beautiful," Paislee said.

Mary shrunk and sipped her tea—whisky wafted from the porcelain cup so no doubt it had been doctored.

Rosebud took the photo from Garrison. "Looks like Sheila and Jocelyn."

"And Felice." Harry brought his knuckles to his lips to stop an outburst.

Philip and Garrison murmured soft, consoling words to their brother. No man should lose his child before him, she recalled her grandfather once saying.

Corbin patted the photo album he'd given Lydia. "Open it. You willnae believe it. Jamie and Magda are in there."

Paislee read the date on the photo. 1867. Jamie and Magda Smythe. Magda's tummy was rounded just a little in her dress. A knit shawl was over her shoulders, a gold pin holding it closed.

"Gretna Green," Lydia said, meeting Corbin's gaze. "This is the brooch—my brooch."

"I know. I picked it for you, love," Corbin said. "Ruby for your birthstone. It meant so much for you tae have that, from me." He cupped Lydia's cheek.

Her best friend melted.

Heck, Paislee melted, too.

The ladies in the Smythe house were made of sterner stuff. Mary murmured something about a curse. Jocelyn cleared her throat after exchanging a look with Sheila. "Lydia, please, if you just return the brooch, then we can help you. Mibbe Matthew can take you on as a client. I cannae bear it that you're here, in this house, when my sister is dead."

Lydia blinked. "Beg pardon?"

"You claim tae have lost the pin, but I dinnae believe you. Where is it? The one Felice held isnae the one dear Mary had cleaned for you." Jocelyn straightened, her expression determined and sad, and angry all at once. "You've created this foul deceit, framing Felice tae cover your tracks."

It was obvious by the stunned expressions on the men's faces that this was the first they'd heard of this possible scenario, where Lydia would be the one to switch the pins and poison Felice.

Sheila patted Jocelyn's back. "Hush, now. You're upset."

"Why?" Paislee demanded, already jumping ahead to defend her best friend. "Lydia has no motive tae switch the pins, or poison Felice."

"Lydia didnae want tae marry Corbin," Hyacinth said in a droll tone. Her nails were painted black; her jeans and boots were black, too. "I heard her in the dressing room. She was stalling for time."

"How could you lie?" Paislee demanded. "She said that your mother wouldn't want her tae marry Corbin without the brooch."

"I know what I heard." Hyacinth shut the photo album. "Right, Rosebud?"

Rosebud immediately nodded. "One hundred percent correct."

"Enough!" Garrison shouted, his forehead flushed beet-red.

Paislee couldn't agree more and hoped he'd control his family once and for all.

Garrison stood and crossed his arms, his gaze hard. "It's obvious that this marriage is not going tae work. I think, son, you should call off the engagement."

Lydia and Paislee whirled on their heels to face Corbin, whose jaw gaped as he stared at his father. "What are you talking aboot, Da? Lydia didnae take the brooch. She has no reason! I gave it tae her."

Mary sat back and surveyed the scene from her armchair, seeming quite pleased.

Harry sobbed into his whisky tumbler, his shoulders quaking with grief. "My daughter is dead. Corbin, your fiancée is responsible."

Paislee flung her arm to her side, almost toppling over a stack of photo albums. "Somebody tried tae kill Lydia, Harry, and it is unfortunate that your daughter stole the brooch. Felice had poison in her eyes and fell down the stairs. That is the bloody truth." Paislee stepped between the Smythes and her best friend.

Lydia's spine was a steel post. Corbin swayed, his palm to his forehead.

Paislee wanted to punch his arm and tell him to grow a pair but refrained. Barely.

"Corbin?" Lydia whispered.

"Lydia." Corbin's voice was ragged. "Maybe we should take a break until things cool down. There is so much sorrow surrounding what should have been a happy day."

Her best friend tugged off the engagement diamond that was worth so much more than the Luckenbooth brooch.

Paislee sucked in a breath.

Rosebud and Hyacinth giggled, wide-eyed. Sheila, Jocelyn, and Oliver all nodded encouragement.

Lydia tossed it at Corbin and the five-carat diamond plunked right in the center of his chest, then plummeted to the floor. "I'm done. This is over."

Drew shoved a photo album from his lap. "Corbin—stop her."

Corbin didn't move. Nobody did.

Paislee hauled her best friend out of Smythe Manor. In shock, Lydia gave Paislee the keys to her Mercedes to drive them home. After ten minutes of awful silence, Paislee glanced at Lydia, who stared out the window. "I'm so sorry, Lydia."

Lydia's body was stiff with hurt. "I did everything his family wanted."

"I know you did." She'd jumped through every blazing hoop and then some. Most women would have told him to take a hike, but Lydia loved him. No way could she accept that behavior.

To be accused of the theft when Lydia had been the target?

Oh!

"We need answers, Lyd. We've got tae find the real killer."

How dare the Smythes throw Lydia to the wolves to protect their own! "You can't be accused of this when you're the victim."

"I detest that word."

"Do you want tae take a drive?" Paislee knew Lydia enjoyed the wind in her hair as she raced along the winding roads of the Highlands.

Lydia shook her head, her fingers entwined together in her lap, her thumb rubbing the spot that used to wear her engagement ring. "Let's go tae the police station and tell Constable Payne this new twist. Then home. I want whisky. A lot of it."

Since it was Sunday, there was nobody at the station. Paislee left a phone message that the Smythe Clan had turned on Lydia like beasts, accusing her of murdering Felice. "We're on our way tae Lydia's condo."

Paislee ended the call and shifted toward Lydia. Her best friend had a wan complexion that tugged at her heart. "I wish you would stay with me."

"I want tae be alone. As I am obviously meant tae be."

"Oh, hon."

They got out and went inside Lydia's secure building, making polite small talk with the receptionist. It was night and day to Lincoln's lobby. The guard had gone home, sick. At last, the elevator arrived, and they went up to the tenth floor, turning left to Lydia's flat. As they rounded the corner, Lydia stopped and brought her palm to her open mouth.

"What is it?" Paislee looked up from her phone and a text from Brody asking when she'd be home.

"Paislee!" Lydia's voice warbled. Paislee, alarmed, noted that the front door was hanging off its hinges.

Her best friend raced inside, and Paislee foolishly chased after her, tugging on her shirt. "Wait!"

What if the intruder was still inside? The sleek furniture had been tossed as if someone was searching for something—like the brooch?

On the kitchen table were pictures of Corbin and Lydia, fighting. Letters had been cut out of a magazine and pasted on one photo. END IT. Another was written in red marker. END IT.

Lydia laughed maniacally. "They got their wish. Is this why I've been targeted?"

Both ladies screamed when Paislee's phone rang. "Hello?"

"Constable Payne here. I tried Lydia's phone but there was no answer. You sounded frightened."

She lowered her shoulders, which had been hiked to the ceiling. "Hurry. There's been a break-in at Lydia's condo."

"Are you both inside? Get oot!"

Paislee grabbed Lydia by the hand and hightailed it ten stories down the stairs to the condo's marble lobby.

Chapter 19

Paislee tucked her arm around Lydia as Constable Payne arrived with the officer from the old kirk, Constable Sarah Monroe.

"The guard was oot sick, eh?" Constable Payne asked Lydia, his tone disbelieving. "Let's head up tae yer flat." He led the way to the elevator while Constable Monroe chose the stairs.

They got off and slowly walked down the hall to Lydia's door. The other officer hadn't arrived yet. Probably climbing and looking for clues took longer than racing in terror down them. Paislee's heart was still hammering.

Constable Payne studied the broken door. "Slipped off the hinges. Easy enough tae do, and since you're in the corner here, doubtful anyone heard."

"I chose it for the ocean view," Lydia said, her eyes round. "We ran in and saw these pictures on the table." She quickly explained about the breakup with Corbin and what had happened at the Smythes. "I didnae lose my own brooch, Constable." Her tone carried hurt.

"I advise you tae get a few things and stay at a hotel or with Paislee for a couple of days while things get sorted." Constable Payne pulled a plastic bag from his vest pocket.

"With me, Lydia, okay? Or else I'll stay with you at the hotel. I don't want you out of my sight."

"Your place is fine. I've disrupted your schedule enough today."

Lydia, Paislee, and the constable went to her room. Nothing was out of order or missing. Lydia packed casual clothes into a leather overnight bag, and then they returned to the kitchen table. Lydia tapped the awful picture of her and Corbin yelling at each other by the alder tree at the church. "Someone is watching me verra closely. This argument happened yesterday after we left the minister's office for some fresh air before returning downstairs."

"Anybody with a mobile can get you on film." Constable Payne shrugged. It was a fact of life. "Don't need fancy cameras."

"Bruce had one on a strap around his neck, but he was downstairs. Mary was with Alexa. Garrison, and the brothers, too. Lincoln. So probably not them."

"Simple tae slip oot of sight for a while." Constable Payne typed notes into his mobile. "If you're ready, I'll walk you tae the car."

After taking pictures of the hinges, Constable Monroe helped put the door back. "The lock is broken, and this isnae secure. You'll need tae hire a professional."

"I'll call the building's maintenance number in the morning," Lydia promised.

"Monroe, I'll be right back. Gonna get the name of the security guard tae make sure his story checks oot. Seems a wee bit fishy tae suddenly get sick right before a break-in."

Constable Payne escorted them back down the elevator to the lobby, and then followed them to the Mercedes. "Where tae?"

"My house for dinner." Paislee raised her mobile. "Brody texted that they caught a few rainbow trout. Plenty for company." On impulse, she asked, "Want tae join us?"

"Nairn's rivers are full of tasty fish, but I best keep working on this case."

"Thank you, Officer," Lydia said. "I've never had a problem with the law and now this past week has been one calamity after another. Makes me wonder if I *am* cursed, like Mary said." She shivered despite the sunshine.

Constable Payne jerked his thumb behind him to the building. "The break-in, and what happened tae Felice, are tangible items we can test and trace. Nothing supernatural. We're gathering proof."

Paislee had heard that before, from Zeffer. Something visible, not a feeling, as Paislee often relied on her intuition. Seeing Lydia with her overnight bag jogged an idea.

"I was thinking, Constable, that women often have handbags large enough tae hold a jewelry box. Did you check the women's purses when you searched the manor?"

"You are relentless," Constable Payne said. "I'm beginning tae understand Zeffer's frustration with you."

Paislee's skin heated. "You know about that?"

Payne rolled his eyes. "The whole station knows. The man is cool as ice unless he's had an interaction with you, and then he slams doors and cabinets."

Lydia arched a brow at Paislee. "Really? That's most interesting."

"No, it's not." She shook her head. "Are you okay tae drive?" Lydia's car was like a dream on wheels, and she wouldn't mind jetting home.

"Huh." Lydia dangled the keys. "I'm just fine. You drive like a granny, Paislee."

"I drive safe, thank you." Paislee turned up her nose.

The officer laughed and returned upstairs to Lydia's flat.

They stopped at the market for treats on the way to Paislee's. Lydia loaded the trolley with crisps, ice cream, chocolate, and shortbread.

"Brody is never going tae sleep tonight if he eats all of that junk. Not a single veggie!" The bags filled the small back seat of the car. "He has school tomorrow and there is no way on God's green earth that I can afford tae be late." She thought of Hamish and his warm brown eyes as he'd waved at her.

"No worries," Lydia said. "We can dole it oot in small doses. How is Hamish, anyway?"

She pushed aside his gaze from her memory. "How would I know?"

"Paislee, you mark my words—life is aboot tae change, my little nun."

"The only change I care about it is Brody going tae secondary, and Craigh being found." She crossed her ankles. "And you. I want you tae be happy."

Lydia pulled into the carport next to Paislee's Juke. "That's a tall order. Let's just get through dinner."

They stood on the front porch. Paislee said, "Maybe we shouldn't tell Brody what happened? He'll worry."

"I agree. I can just be here because, well, I want a sleepover."

"He might believe it, since he and Edwyn have been spending a lot of time at each other's houses." It was worth a try.

Grandpa would know something was wrong, but they could fill him in later. Paislee unlocked and opened the front door, hurrying down the hall to the kitchen.

"Wallace!" Paislee patted the pup on the head as he scrambled by her and Lydia to the round table for four. It had been set with napkins, silverware, cups of water with lemon, and looked very fancy. The scent of dill and cream sauce made her tummy rumble.

When had she eaten last? The corner of the scone this morning?

"This smells amazing," Lydia declared.

"Dinner is ready when you are, ladies." Grandpa noted Lydia's overnight bags. "Brody, why not help your aunt bring her things upstairs, and then we can eat."

"It's torture tae wait," Brody announced, rubbing his belly. "I'm starving, Mum."

Lydia laughed and put the snacks by the pantry, along with her luggage. "We can get this after. I dinnae want tae hold us up."

Five minutes later, after a quick wash, and Grandpa serving, they were all seated around the table.

"What's the occasion?" Lydia asked.

"A good catch on the river," Grandpa said.

"Ah, and here I thought it was all for me." Lydia winked and took another bite of the flaky white fish smothered in sauce.

"We didnae know you were coming." Grandpa arched a brow at Brody, who added, "Or we would have made it extra special."

"Nice save, lad," Paislee said with a chuckle. "Where did ye fish?"

She knew they liked the park by the Leery Estate, so she was surprised, and then alarmed when Brody said, "Dairlee."

She lowered her fork to glare at Grandpa. He tucked into his fish like it might be his last meal.

"Did you run into anybody today?" Paislee glanced from Brody to Grandpa.

"No." Grandpa took another bite.

Well, that was good.

Brody continued, "Nobody even saw us at the storage unit, did they, Grandpa?"

"Nope." Her grandfather broke off a crust of bread to sop the sauce.

"We were like ninjas." Brody had a drink of milk.

They'd gone to the storage unit. Grandpa was probably hoping for a note from Craigh. "Any messages?" Paislee asked her grandfather.

Grandpa devoured the potatoes in cream sauce. There would be no answers until he was ready to talk, so Paislee finished her dinner. But just a teensy bit of the enjoyment was gone.

They'd been to Dairlee, fishing, probably where Craigh knew to find them, in Grandpa's old fishing haunts. Craigh hadn't contacted Grandpa—what did that mean? Did Zeffer have him in custody? Or worse, had the crooked riggers caught him? She'd seen enough movies to know that a snitch who got caught was a dead one. One informant had already washed up on shore.

She sipped her water, counted to ten, then helped herself to another piece of trout. "You're a braw chef, Grandpa."

"Thank you."

"I cleaned the fish, Mum." Brody showed her his fingers, all attached. It was a running joke. She and Grandpa had gone in on a pocketknife for his P7 graduation gift, to be kept in the toolbox and used with supervision. He'd been wanting one for the past year and she knew he'd be surprised.

"Good job!"

"Not a single bone," Lydia said. "Brilliant."

"Ta." Brody beamed happiness. "Grandpa said the flesh of the rainbow trout is white because it mostly eats bugs—cool, eh? Trout in the market is fed fish food, which can turn the meat pink. I want tae be a fisherman when I grow up."

No offense, but Paislee hoped that he'd choose something that paid a wee bit more after university.

"You'll never starve." Grandpa sounded approving.

"I thought you wanted tae be an astronaut?" Lydia said. "Go tae Mars."

"I do." Brody swiped bread through the last bits of creamy goodness on his plate. "Mibbe." He chewed and swallowed.

"It's hard tae pick a career at eleven," Lydia commiserated. "You want tae be happy."

"You want tae pay your bills, too." Paislee also thought happy was important, but Lydia could tell him that. She'd harp on the boring things like a job that paid your rent.

Sunday night was bath night, so after a family game of cards, Brody was sent up to take a bath and get ready for the school week.

"It's still light oot, Mum. I dinnae want tae go tae bed."

"You're just getting ready. Tell you what—I'll let you watch telly in your room for an hour if you hustle."

"Yes!" Brody and Wallace raced up the stairs together. Wallace liked snuggle time with his boy as much as Brody did.

"That gift has been the best negotiating tool in history," Paislee informed Lydia, who'd gotten the TV for Brody over a year ago. She put away the dishes from dinner that had been drying in the rack, then put a load in the combo washer dryer.

"Nothing wrong with bribery." Grandpa went to the pantry

and rooted around past the snacks. "You ladies preparing for the end of the world?"

"No. I didnae realize you were making a gourmet meal for dinner," Lydia said. "Or I wouldnae have bothered."

Grandpa brought the Scotch and the chocolate to the table. "Sweets rarely go amiss around here. Dram?"

"Aye," Lydia said.

Paislee handed them each a tumbler.

Grandpa poured. "All right. Before I answer your questions, Paislee, tell me what's going on."

"I broke it off with Corbin." Lydia's voice thickened with emotion. "He didnae stand up for me against his family. They suggested that I was the one tae steal the brooch and murder Felice."

"Och. No good, that." Grandpa sipped the whisky. They all liked it neat.

Paislee took a small drink and let the flavors warm her belly.

"Right?" Lydia squirmed on the chair. "That's not all—when we got tae my condo, someone had broken in. Tossed the place like something on one of those crime shows."

"Beg pardon?" Grandpa slugged down the whisky and urged them all to do the same to pour a second round.

"I've got work tomorrow," Paislee said. "I'll be sipping this one."

"So responsible." Lydia shot hers back. "I dinnae know what I'm going tae do."

"Call maintenance and get a new door, for starters." Paislee got goose bumps at the violence of leaving the door off the hinges. The red block letters. END IT.

Lydia filled Grandpa in on the details of the pictures, with the threat to end the relationship.

"That had tae be the reason behind the poisoning," Paislee said. "Not a curse at all, as Constable Payne insisted. A real person wants tae stop the wedding."

"And now it's over," Lydia said, her tone final. "I should be safe, once the door is back on my flat."

The trio gave a deep sigh in unison.

"So, Grandpa. Tell me about Dairlee. Why did you go there today? I thought you'd be on the River Nairn."

"I hoped Craigh would find me if I was at my old fishing haunts. He was probably trying tae make contact Friday night, but then not a peep yesterday." He cupped the glass. "It's making me crazy. I need my son tae explain what's in those boxes."

"Boxes?" Lydia asked.

Grandpa nodded at Paislee in acknowledgment that she hadn't ratted out his kid. It was his turn to sip and explain the last few days.

"And now I know why Craigh hasnae gotten in touch. He's been nabbed by the scammers." Grandpa pulled out a folded sheet of copy paper that was very common and could be from their own printing tray. "This was in the storage unit this afternoon. Not this morning, but the second time I checked before we came home." He pushed it across to Paislee.

Paislee eyed it with trepidation. What would it say?

With a gulp, she slowly unfolded the single sheet and read aloud, "'Return the boxes or Craigh dies.'" Her mouth dried. Grandpa and Brody had been watched. Craigh was alive but held captive.

Lydia gasped and reached across the small table to pat Grandpa's wrinkled hand. "Angus!"

"Zeffer needs tae see this," Paislee said, taking her phone from her pocket. It was half-past eight. No messages. "Where is that man?"

Grandpa tapped his glasses against his tumbler. "Can you think of a better plan?"

"There *is* no better plan. Oh, Grandpa." What if it was too late? Just then the water gurgled in the pipes as Brody got out of the tub.

"If we dinnae hear from Zeffer by nine, I'm going tae return the boxes meself." Grandpa pulled the plastic bag with the flash drive in it from his pocket and set it next to his glasses and the whisky.

"You can't do that! You might put yourself in danger, Grandpa." Paislee texted Zeffer to see if he was back from wherever he'd gone. The situation was urgent.

"What is that?" Lydia asked, pointing at the silver device.

"We don't know. It won't work on this desktop or my laptop. We were going tae ask you on Friday for the name of your hacker guy but then things, well, went a little more out of control."

That was putting things mildly. Three dots showed on her mobile, then Zeffer replied: *On my way.*

Paislee sent a quick prayer to Gran that all would be well. "It's a blasted miracle!"

Chapter 20

"Zeffer is on his way," Paislee told Lydia and Grandpa, who each stared at her with mixed emotions. The elusive DI was hard to pin down, with answers or physical presence. She, too, was in shock that things were suddenly happening so fast.

"Here?" Grandpa stood and his chair inched back from the table.

"Now?" Lydia also rose, her hand to her chest.

"Aye. He must have returned from wherever he was, then," Paislee said. Och. She smoothed her hair down. It was thin and tended to fly around her face rather than conform to any particular style.

"Mum?" Brody called down from the top of the second-floor landing. "Can you bring me my game?"

She saw the device on the side table near the sofa with her bag of yarn, and hustled up the stairs with it, to the top landing. "Just for fifteen minutes. I think watching telly is enough of a treat."

"Ah," he said, shuffling his bare feet ahead of her.

Hurrying him into his room, with Wallace to keep him company, she hoped that he wouldn't hear when Zeffer arrived. Brody flopped on the bed, fluffing pillows behind his back. He smelled like shampoo.

Hoping he wouldn't hear wasn't realistic. The dog was a guardian, and Brody had ears like a bat when he wanted to use them.

She needed a plan B. "DI Zeffer is going tae stop by for a visit. He wants tae ask Grandpa a few questions about Craigh."

"Okay," Brody said, flipping his bangs away from his forehead. "I hope Craigh doesnae want Grandpa back."

Her heart ached. She ruffled his hair, something Brody pretended to hate. "I think Grandpa will be in our lives no matter what, now. We didn't really know him before."

"He's guid at fishing."

"That he is." And he'd filled a void in their lives where Gran used to be. Her grandmother must be laughing her butt off up in heaven.

"He loves his son, though. Like you love me."

"You're right." Paislee helped Brody and Wallace get fluffed up on the bed with blankets and pillows. "Mind the time, no more."

"Awright. Mum?" He peered at her from his game. "Is Aunt Lydia going tae marry Corbin?"

How much did he understand about the breakup? "We aren't sure."

"I never want tae fall in love."

Her mothering instincts kicked into gear. This was about more than Lydia, or Grandpa. She perched on the edge of the mattress and patted Wallace. The dog's tongue lolled in delight as she scratched just the right spot.

"Love is a wonderful thing, Brody."

He shrugged, uncertain.

"Does Edwyn have another crush?" she asked in a light tone.

Brody shook his head.

"Do you like someone?"

"No!"

Oh.

That meant he probably did.

"You can talk tae me about it. Or Grandpa."

He glanced at her, then the television screen. "It's just that there's this girl Jenni who sits next tae me, and she passed me a note."

Silly hussy. Paislee kept her expression open. "What did it say?"

"She asked if I liked her." His nose scrunched. "I mean, she's cute, but . . ."

"What did you do?" She kept patting Wallace, needing the dog's calm.

"I didnae answer the note. It was right before school got oot on Friday."

She shifted on the edge of the bed. "What did Edwyn say?"

Brody tightened his grip on the video game. "He thinks Jenni's cute, but he already has three girlfriends—kinda. For the end of the year dance." Brody dared a peek at Paislee. "She wants me tae be her boyfriend."

"Just for the dance?"

"I dinnae ken. I can ask her." Brody was taking this very seriously.

"What do you think you should do?"

Wallace jumped off the bed and barked at the door. That meant Zeffer must be here. The DI could wait a few minutes. Being Brody's mum was the most important thing in the world to her, and right now, he needed her.

Brody saw that she wasn't leaving. He plucked at a loose piece of yarn on his comforter. "I think I like her enough tae dance with her."

She nodded, her heart swelling. "Do you need tae practice the dances?"

"We've been doing some in school," he said. "Nothing crazy."

"That's good."

He smiled at her. "Jenni *is* cute, Mum. She came tae the football game on Saturday with her friends."

"Awesome!" Paislee had known it was just a matter of time before he started liking girls. Edwyn had been ahead of the game, but she'd told Brody that there was plenty of time before he had to worry about that.

And now, here they were. She blinked moisture from her eyes. It wasn't like he was getting married, for Pete's sake.

The years where he would still be her little boy were slipping away fast. She kissed his forehead. "I bet you'll have a lot of fun," she said. "I'm glad you told me about it, Brody."

"Don't make a big deal, okay?"

"I won't."

She left his room and bowed her head. *Oh, Gran. This is just the beginning, isn't it?*

Paislee descended the stairs at a decent clip, worried now that Grandpa and Lydia would have started talking to the DI without her. They had to save Craigh, aye, but not at Grandpa's expense.

Zeffer was seated in Lydia's normal chair, Lydia in Brody's, and Grandpa in his—they were discussing the mundane topic of weather. It was nine and twilight just spreading its violet hues visible through the open back door.

"Paislee," Zeffer said in greeting.

"Hi. Glad you could make it." Paislee propped her hands on her hips. "Where in blazes have you been?"

"Wow!" Zeffer raised his palm, his eyes dancing. "You sound like a fishwife down at the wharf."

"Sorry." She put aside Brody's sweet first crush to focus on Zeffer, Grandpa, Lydia, and the missing Craigh. "Did you show him the letter?"

"No," Grandpa said. "We're just getting settled in for a chat."

"No chatting," Paislee said. They'd wasted so much time that she was ready to burst. "We need tae show Zeffer what you found in the storage unit, Grandpa. Both times."

At this, Zeffer stared at Grandpa. "I apologize for being oot of reach. You realize, Angus, that I've been oot of town, tracking Craigh from Aberdeen. I followed him from the storage unit thanks to the CCTV footage. I'm a better than fair tracker," he said.

Grandpa fussed with his tea mug. "I saw him on the camera as well."

"Did Craigh come here?" Zeffer asked.

"No."

Zeffer turned to Paislee. "You saw him Friday night in Nairn, at the bandstand?"

"I think so. I've never met him, so I can't be sure. He looked like my da, a little."

"And you, Angus?" Zeffer asked.

"When I saw the footage from the break-in at the storage unit, that was the first time I knew for sure that Craigh was still alive." Her grandfather sipped whisky. "Can I get some biscuits for anyone?"

"Grandpa!" Paislee smacked her palms to the table, impatient. "The note!"

"Fine." Grandpa pulled the letter from his pocket and placed it on the table before the DI. "This was in the unit this afternoon, but it wasnae there this morning when I first checked. I had a hunch I should look again, so Brody and I stopped on the way home from fishing in Dairlee. I'd hoped that Craigh would make contact. But it wasnae him. The crooked riggers have Craigh, and say they'll kill him."

Zeffer, red in the face, scanned the letter. "They're bad men, Angus. They'll follow through with their threat. What boxes?"

Angus got up and led Zeffer, with Paislee and Lydia following, to Gran's room.

"The other night, after talking tae you, I feared that the boxes held something really terrible. Drugs. Cash. I didnae know, but I was terrified for Craigh, you understand?"

Zeffer rubbed his smooth chin. "Go on."

"When I moved the boxes into the Juke, I noticed they were heavier than I remembered but attributed it tae the fact that I'm no' a young man anymore."

Zeffer crossed his arms, not saying a word. He wasn't giving Grandpa an inch for not being forthright from the beginning. His blue suit had the slightest crease at the knees.

"I slept the rest of the night, praying that I would wake up with answers, from you, or from Craigh. Nothing. So I, well, I opened them the next morning. I discovered what seem tae be metal drill parts, but I dinnae understand for sure. There is a flash drive but it's all encrypted. We tried tae use the USB on the house computer, and the laptop, but it didnae work."

At this, Zeffer gave Paislee a surprised look. She'd been part of the keeping secrets. She felt terrible. He turned back to Grandpa. "Let me see!"

Grandpa showed him the boxes that they'd repacked just as he'd found it. Metal parts carefully wrapped in metallic straw. Last, the box with Craigh's clothes, and the flash drive in a sock at the bottom—still in the plastic bag. Grandpa must have put it back when Paislee was upstairs.

"Unbelievable." Zeffer sent off a flurry of texts. "I've had men watching the storage unit, and they completely missed you taking these oot in the middle of the night. Heads are gonna roll for that one."

"You've been spying?" Grandpa asked, incredulously.

"I didnae know what was in the storage unit. You werenae telling. Those boxes were bait and they caught a big Norwegian fish. This might be worth trading for, all right—his life for this, if it's what I think it is." Zeffer turned to Paislee and dangled the plastic bag with the drive. "Your idea?"

She nodded, cheeks hot. "What's on it?"

"I cannae tell you." The DI paced the room, his expression angry and annoyed. "I wish you'd been honest from the start, Angus. I hope this doesnae get Craigh killed. These men have billions tae lose, do you understand?" He pocketed the flash drive.

"No. You said Craigh was sent in tae spy for Scotland Yard. Maybe this is proof of what's wrong. You should be treating him like a hero," Grandpa said.

"Are these the same parts from the rig that Craigh stole before? The metal is different somehow."

"No. Damn it, Paislee, you're too observant sometimes." Zeffer's anger dimmed. "We need tae get these boxes back in the storage unit. It will buy Craigh a day or two. We can trap the thieves when they try tae retrieve the evidence."

"Whoa now!" Grandpa said. "I want Craigh safe."

"Don't have time tae create a better diversion." Zeffer hefted one of the boxes. "We'll need something tae make it seem the same weight. Rocks maybe."

"You arenae returning the parts? No way—they'll know something's wrong." Grandpa's face was the color of milk and he seemed on the verge of passing out as he braced his hand against the wall.

"We have some in the back garden you can use," Paislee said. "Bricks around the shed. Grandpa, we need tae save Craigh, and this is how."

Zeffer stacked the metal parts to one side. A knock on the door sounded and two men in black-on-black with three sturdy plastic cartons packed up the drill parts.

"Hey!" Grandpa said, pushing off the wall to stop them.

"Where did they come from?" Paislee asked. "Have you been watching the house, too?"

"Aye." Zeffer stepped between her grandfather and the men. "Angus. Craigh was playing Scotland Yard against the organization. They must have caught him somehow in the act, and he probably turned tae save his own skin. Right now, this is our only chance tae capture them, and free Craigh. As a traitor, they willnae treat him gently. You need tae return the boxes."

Grandpa placed his palm to his chest. "I cannae. I cannae do it."

"Paislee?" Zeffer turned toward her. "You drive. Angus can sit shotgun. I'll be hidden in the hatch."

"But!" Paislee whirled to Lydia. She couldn't just leave Brody.

"I'm fine here with Brody," Lydia said. "Oh, be careful. You have tae go, Paislee. Angus doesnae look well enough tae drive."

Zeffer's team had packed up the real stuff and dismantled the brick fence around the shed, bringing them in to fill the original boxes.

Her skin chilled as she realized Zeffer must be wearing an audio device for the men to know what she'd suggested. "Did your spies see the bad guys? They were watching Grandpa and Brody in Dairlee. What if they followed them home?"

Zeffer paused to look into her eyes. "I'll leave an undercover officer in the neighborhood, just in case."

"Thanks." She clenched her teeth. This was for Grandpa. Paislee stepped toward him, and he slowly raised his gaze.

Sorrow filled his eyes. "I never thought you'd be in danger, lass."

"Aye." Paislee knew that fact in her bones.

"The crooks will be posted around the storage unit tae watch for Angus tae drop off the bins," Zeffer said. "You'll need tae help him, as they're heavy. How did you manage tae load them on your own, Angus?"

Grandpa shrugged. "It wasnae easy, but I was worried what Craigh was into—must've given me strength."

Paislee understood wanting to protect your children. "It's fine. I can help."

"All right." Zeffer nodded. "Stay calm and this will be easy. You just follow my directions. Act natural. Whoever is watching will see a worried father, Angus, and that's what we need them tae focus on. Nothing else."

"Be careful, Paislee. Angus." Lydia followed them down the hall to the door.

"Lock up behind us, Lyd. Maybe shove the table in front of the door?"

Lydia nodded, her eyes wide.

For once, Zeffer didn't mock her.

Grandpa held onto the wall for support as he descended the steps. Zeffer, like a waft of smoke, was already in her SUV and out of sight in the rear passenger seat. He had a knit cap over his auburn hair and black leather gloves on. His suit was a deep navy—almost black. Even in an emergency the man had style.

★ ★ ★

Paislee drove carefully, checking her mirrors, and glancing at Grandpa to see how he was faring. His brow was furrowed, and he'd skipped his tam in the warm summer night.

Tension gripped her shoulders and made her spine rigid. "So what, we just unload the boxes and go?"

Neither man answered.

"Are we supposed tae wait there," she tried again, "for a sign?"

"No," Zeffer instructed. His voice was muffled in the back. "You two are going tae unload the boxes, get in the SUV, and drive oot like it was any other day."

"What aboot Craigh?" Grandpa demanded, keeping his face forward so as not to give Zeffer away. "How will we find him?"

"We will catch the crooks when they collect the boxes from the storage unit. They will lead us tae Craigh."

It felt like Paislee had a lump of lead in her belly. "It's a terrible plan."

"If you two would have shared aboot the boxes sooner, then it wouldnae have been last-minute. You only have yourselves tae blame."

Grandpa put his hand to his mouth, his shoulders shaking—he stared out the passenger window. Streetlights showed the way as night had fallen.

"Rude," Paislee told Zeffer coldly. "It's clear you don't have children. A parent will walk through hell for their bairns."

"Some parents," Zeffer said after a moment. He didn't elaborate.

Twenty minutes later, they'd reached the storage unit in Dairlee. Paislee saw two men on motorcycles pull across the lot.

"Are the motorcycle guys with us?"

Zeffer seemed startled that she'd noticed them. "Aye."

She rolled down the window to punch the code into the security access panel.

"How often do you change the code?" Zeffer asked.

"Never. Craigh knows it and he hasnae been around tae discuss a change," Grandpa drawled.

"Careless if you're trying tae protect your items." Zeffer stayed out of sight.

The gate rolled back. Paislee inched slowly forward, nerves leaving a trail of cold sweat down her back. "Showtime," she said.

"Here we are." Grandpa sat up straight. He peered around. "Dinnae see anybody. Or anything."

Paislee parked in the narrow lane between the rows of storage units. She climbed out, leaving the car running as they wouldn't be long, and opened the hatch. She and Grandpa carried the boxes inside but there wasn't room for them both and the boxes, so she scooted out backward.

She recalled he'd slept in this unit once after first being locked out of his flat for not having the rent. She was grateful every day to Gran for the roof over their heads.

"Hurry," she said, getting the heebie-jeebies. Was someone besides Zeffer's team watching them right now? Waiting to swoop in and get their parts back?

Grandpa made a show of locking it up again, and then climbed into the Juke. "If my son dies over this, I'll never forgive you," he said in angry tones.

"Craigh played a deep game, Angus. He had a chance tae make it right."

"He can explain," Grandpa told the DI without looking back at the officer. "He has tae have a good reason."

Paislee drove out of the unit, searching the side mirrors and the rearview, her body so tense she was ready to snap.

Grandpa's faith was strong that somehow his son would have an explanation for drill parts and a flash drive with encrypted files. For not honoring his word, which her grandfather placed great store in.

Paislee left the storage facility very slowly. She reached the parking lot when suddenly she saw figures in black—not the officers, but huge men with a gold lion against a red patch insignia on their knit caps. They had black masks over their hair and faces and it scared her to pieces. They could have been Vikings of old.

"Who are they, Zeffer?" Her voice wobbled. "They're giants." Zeffer didn't answer and she sensed that he was out of the car. "DI?" She whirled and scanned the dark interior. "He's gone."

"What the hell?" Grandpa asked. He unbuckled his seatbelt and turned around, but the back of the SUV was empty. "That sneaky . . ."

"Calm down! Help me figure out what tae do! Should we wait for him, or keep driving?" Paislee edged away from the facility to the street corner at ten miles an hour.

An explosion sounded behind them and she looked in the rearview to see an orange cloud of fireworks go off.

"Step on it, lass!" Grandpa yelled.

She channeled Lydia and slammed her foot to the gas with a screech of rubber to pavement. Grandpa buckled up.

In fifteen minutes, they were home. She and Grandpa just stared at each other, panting and gasping in the SUV, as they tried to comprehend what on earth had just happened.

Paislee exhaled. "We can't tell them, Lydia or Brody."

"No."

"Do you think Zeffer's dead?"

Grandpa cursed. "If he got my son killed, he'll wish he'd been in that explosion."

Chapter 21

Monday morning, a bleary-eyed Paislee dropped Brody off at school a full fifteen minutes early. Hamish was outside greeting the kids and parents on yet another bonnie blue-skied day. He gestured for her to wait for him.

"Have a good day, Brody!" Paislee ignored the honks and beeps of folks in queue behind her as her son told her goodbye and hustled out to the throng of children.

Hamish arrived at the driver's side. Her window was rolled down for the fresh summer air to clear her mind. Nothing sweeter than a summer morn after a hellish night.

"Is something wrong?" Her brain mulled over any possible hiccup that might prevent Brody from graduating. His end-of-year project was coming along nicely.

Had Grandpa living with them over the last year, and extra help at the shop, allowed her a false sense of security? She wouldn't put it past the headmaster to wait for the last month of school to drop a whopper on her.

Hamish handed her a manila envelope. His deep brown eyes searched hers. "I wanted tae make sure you had tickets for graduation at the art center. New venue this year."

Her body relaxed. "Okay. Is that all? Brody is on track?"

"Aye!"

A double honk sounded as a mom in a van drove around them with a sour look at Paislee. The headmaster stepped back and away from the window. She'd forgotten how much she'd once enjoyed his subtle cologne. She cleared her throat when a mom in a sedan screeched around them with impatience. "I need tae go."

"I'll see you then!" Hamish waved at the other cars in line, bestowing good will on everyone this fine Monday morning.

Exasperated, Paislee tossed the manila envelope to the passenger seat. Lydia called on Bluetooth, and she forgot all about the tickets. "And good morning! Didn't I leave you sleeping just now?"

"Aye," Lydia confirmed. "Angus and I are sharing some toast and eggs. I'm a little put oot, love, that you didnae tell me aboot the storage unit blowing up."

Her tone was as if she was discussing the weather, but Paislee heard hurt underneath the calm words.

Paislee turned on the road toward Cashmere Crush. There was time before she officially opened the yarn shop. Should she drive home and try to soothe Lydia's feelings?

"Grandpa and I didn't want tae worry you."

"Naw, that's not it. I took up the whole evening with my own whingeing and you probably couldnae get a word in."

"Not true! We wanted you tae talk and share. You had a traumatic experience with your flat broken into. Vandalized." *Somebody trying to kill you* went unsaid.

"I've already talked with the maintenance folks, and I'll be getting a new door and lock this afternoon."

Paislee thought of her Monday morning at the shop. Jerry Mc-Fadden wasn't delivering yarn today, and her best friend was still in danger. She could work on the infinity scarf project while she listened. "I'm on my way home."

"What? You cannae do that."

"I can. I'm the boss." She'd also ring Elspeth and see if the woman wanted to work a few hours extra today to cover for Paislee and would shake it off if the answer was no. Family mattered most and hers was in a cluster of epic proportions right now.

"Now you pull that card? Not for yourself," Lydia said, bringing up past incidents.

"Hanging up now! I'm here."

She texted Elspeth from the driveway—keeping it very casual but not an emergency. Tuesday, she had a big yarn order arriving but today, well, she could make room in her schedule.

Lydia opened the front door, calves bare in a knee-length sundress, Wallace racing around her long legs, yipping excitedly at the change of routine. Paislee stuffed the envelope with the tickets to the graduation in her hobo bag, exited the Juke, and climbed the steps to the foyer.

"I've been thinking," Lydia said, as soon as Paislee was inside.

"Yes?" Paislee closed the door.

"Aboot the photos on the table."

"Constable Payne has them, which is too bad. I'd like tae study them, too." Paislee dropped her bag on the small table, then followed Wallace and Lydia to the kitchen.

Grandpa looked up from his toast and tea. "Morning. Again."

She glared at him. He must not have broken the news about Zeffer as gently as they'd discussed last night.

He slurped his tea. "Stop with the death-glare, lass. Lydia's no fool and realized that something had gone wrong—or should I say, more wrong—when we didnae return with Zeffer—and didnae mention why."

"For Brody's sake, Lyd," Paislee explained. "My boy is going tae end up needing therapy for night terrors at this rate."

"He's a strong and resilient kid," Lydia said. "But I understand." She poured Paislee a mug of tea. "Sit down and join us, then."

Grandpa scooted the newspaper off the table. "I feel foolish asking, but have ye heard from the DI?"

"No. I haven't tried tae call him, though. Should I? Just tae see if he's all right?" Paislee was still a touch angry with him for his part in this mess. He blamed them for not being honest, but he'd also held cards close to his chest. Using the boxes in the storage unit as bait.

Paislee pulled her phone from her pocket and texted Zeffer. She didn't want him hurt, even if she was ticked. *You alive?*

No answer.

"Grandpa, sorry for the attitude."

"No need tae apologize. It's been one thing after another. I didnae sleep last night, and from the bags you're carrying under your eyes, you didnae, either."

She didn't take offense since it was the naked truth. Surely the warmth in Hamish's gaze had been a mistake, or worse? Pity. *Ach.*

"You both have me worried," Paislee said. "Grandpa, with Craigh being held hostage, and Lydia, with a killer still on the loose. Makes me want tae rent a caravan, grab you both, Wallace, and Brody, and head tae Wales."

"I'd rather discuss Craigh." Lydia placed her elbows on the table. Her caramel curls framed her face. She was lovely with or without sleep. Bags or no bags. Even when crying, as the photographer had captured in the photos yesterday.

Payne had slammed the nail on the head with his observation that anybody with a decent mobile could capture a picture these days. But what about getting them printed?

"Wales?" Grandpa shook his head. "No thanks."

"Angus just told me the bare bones of what happened. Men in black suits swarming the storage facility. Zeffer disappearing oot of the van." Lydia straightened and tapped the table with slender fingers. "An explosion!"

The ring finger was missing its beautiful engagement diamond. What a nightmare.

"Aye." Paislee looked around the room for her knitting bag. "Does Corbin know about your flat being broken into?"

"No. None of his business anymore, is it?" Lydia snapped,

cheeks pink. She was in defensive mode, and Paislee couldn't blame her. "Spill!"

"We only know the bare bones, Lydia. We heard and saw an explosion behind us and I'm ashamed tae say that we gave Zeffer about thirty seconds before we floored it home." She wrinkled her nose. "Not very brave of us, in hindsight. But we did consider the options."

"I woulda been outta there already!" Lydia declared. "You Shaws are tough."

"Hardly. I'm barely hanging on here." Grandpa jerked his glasses off from his face and dropped the frames on the newspaper.

There was a picture of the pier and happy tourists. An article from the Earl of Cawdor, praising Nairn for its popularity. No mention of Felice's suspicious death—that was over and done a week ago, and not fresh news. The public believed it had been an awful accident. She imagined the earl swiping his hands together. It was his goal to see Nairn as prosperous as it had been in Victorian times. No mention of the explosion at a storage facility in Dairlee, either.

"So, where is Craigh?" Lydia asked.

"I dinnae ken." Grandpa's shoulders bowed. "The note said tae exchange the bins for my son, or they'd kill him. That didnae work oot well, as you know." He choked back a sob. Paislee was reminded of Harry, and his grief over Felice. At least Grandpa still had a slim chance that Craigh was alive. Grandpa's chest heaved as he cried. "He's probably fish food by now."

Paislee got up and gave her grandfather a side hug—awkward, but she didn't care. What could she say? Unless Zeffer's black-suited men had retrieved Craigh before the bomb or whatever went off . . . but they didn't know where Craigh was—did they?

After a few minutes, Grandpa had regained his composure and she sat down again. "Who set the bomb, do you think? Zeffer, or the bad guys at North Sea Oil?"

Grandpa tugged his beard. "I assumed Zeffer and his minions."

"What if it was whoever is crooked at the factory . . . maybe they want tae blow up whatever Craigh had in those boxes tae destroy the evidence."

"And you both," Lydia said. "If you'd been slower, you might have been hurt!"

Grandpa's sorrow turned to anger as he growled, "Or killed."

"They probably don't care about us," Paislee said, patting her grandfather's shoulder. "But if Zeffer hadn't warned us tae hurry, we might have lingered tae wait for a sign about Craigh and been caught in the explosion."

"Did he know because he'd set the bomb, or because of his experience in the field?" Grandpa folded and unfolded the stems of his glasses.

"Terrifying. If they know who you are, Paislee, and where you live, you could be in as much danger as I am. Only worse." Lydia sighed. "I have one lunatic after me; you have an entire secret organization."

"We don't know that!" Paislee said, her pulse skipping. She located her bag of knitting on the sofa and retrieved it. She always had a project nearby to work on, and the clack of the metal needles soothed her. "I didn't see the patrol car around this morning, though Zeffer said it would be undercover." *Clack, clack.* The metal drill bits hadn't sounded the same when she'd bumped them together from their nests of plastic grass, and they'd been a different weight. How many types of metal could there be? She wished she would have kept one of the parts back—no way would Zeffer have agreed to that!

"Grandpa, did you notice the knit caps on the bad guys?"

"No, lass, I was looking for Craigh. What did you see?"

"A golden lion against a red patch. Does that ring any bells?"

"The caravan tae Wales is sounding better and better." Lydia touched the bare spot on her finger again.

"That's verra vague, lass. Any other details?"

She tried to bring the image into focus, but her brain didn't operate like a zoom lens. "What do we know for fact?" Something Paislee had learned from Zeffer was to never assume. "Grandpa, you do a Craigh list, and Lydia, you do a Felice list."

They were each eager to pitch in and Lydia jumped up for scratch paper Paislee kept by the landline while Grandpa got two pens from the jar—also by the phone. The pair sat down and immediately poised their pens over their papers.

"Craigh," Grandpa said, eager to begin. "He was at the storage facility late Wednesday evening. He was caught by the riggers at North Sea Oil he was supposed tae infiltrate for information. The riggers wanted the boxes back in exchange for Craigh's life. Not sure if it happened. Zeffer's team has the drill parts. Craigh was working undercover for Scotland Yard and could be a hero."

Paislee nodded that she'd heard him, not quite agreeing about the hero part. "I saw him around Nairn on Friday night, so he must have been nabbed after that."

Grandpa continued writing. Paislee turned to Lydia, who read down her list. "Felice was killed by poison meant for me. Not ingested, but in her eyes. She fell down the stairs and broke her neck. Mary Smythe claims tae have put the brooch in a velvet box, but the one Angela delivered tae my dressing room that day was wood. The note was the same handwriting as Mary's. Since I didnae open it, I cannae be sure if the pin Corbin had chosen for me was in there, or if the person who changed boxes switched the jewelry then. The one in Felice's grasp was similar tae mine, but not exact." Lydia sipped her tea.

"Where *is* your Luckenbooth brooch?" Paislee mused, the weight of yarn on her lap comforting.

Grandpa looked up from his scrap paper. "In the sea, me lasses, same as the velvet box."

Lydia shook her head. "I don't believe so, Angus. Whoever stole the brooch valued it, I think. My stomach upset when we all ate together at the wharf?"

"Lincoln had plant food on his counter that might have made

you sick. Alexa, Mary, and Oliver are visitors at his house. I also saw a packet of powder antacid in Mary's purse. Or, it might have been bad sauce," Paislee said. "As for the strychnine, Mary wouldn't put her daughters in danger and if you'd opened the box in the dressing room, particles might have gotten free."

"My tire went flat." Lydia scrawled a note. "But we don't know if someone took the cap of the valve off, or if it happened due tae the road conditions." Lydia tucked a curl behind her ear. "I might just be having a case of rotten luck. I don't believe in curses! Is it fair tae say that *someone* didnae want me and Corbin tae wed?"

Grandpa nodded but Paislee wasn't as sure. There were many reasons killers acted. Disgruntled, Paislee let the thoughts come as they would as she knit her scarf and one snagged at the photos of Lydia on the table. Paislee smacked the scarf project to the table with a slosh of tea in her mug. "Lydia. The pictures said 'End It.' They caught you and Corbin arguing inside the church, as well as outside. Someone close tae you took those pictures. Let's make a different list of everyone at the church for the funeral. There weren't that many when compared to your wedding. We can see who was at both."

"Brilliant! I'll group them together," Lydia said. "Harry, Jocelyn, and Oliver. Minus Felice." She cleared her throat. "Garrison, Mary, Rosebud, and Hyacinth. Matthew."

"Chalmers," Paislee said. "He was acting strange and would do anything tae impress Rosebud."

Lydia shivered. "Cocky kid. They're all spoiled in that group."

"Yeah. Mary's fault for her daughters, trying tae make up for their dad dying. Add Bruce—he seemed relieved tae see you and Corbin, after your argument."

"Too bad about the wedding photos. What will happen tae them now?" Sorrow crossed Lydia's face. "Never mind. Corbin's brothers, wives, and kids. Philip, his daughter, Sheila, and her brother. The Smythe fortune provides for them all. Not one of them must work. They can all follow their passion."

"Garrison must be an excellent money manager." Paislee looped yarn around the metal needles. "Lincoln was there, and Alexa. Angela."

"She's the minister!" Grandpa said with alarm. "Surely we have tae believe in some good."

"We're just making a list." Lydia added the minister's name. "I think that's everyone." She sat back and studied the paper. "Two names are popping out at me: Rosebud and Chalmers."

Grandpa set his pen across his paper. "What would Rosebud get from you being poisoned?"

"Kudos from Mary!" Lydia answered. "The brooch?"

"I don't think so . . . Mary believes it tae be cursed." Paislee shifted the weight of yarn on her lap when her phone dinged an alert and checked her messages. Elspeth texted that she would open at eleven. *Thanks.* Paislee sent it off through cyberspace.

"What time is it?" Lydia asked, her focus on the list. She'd folded the scrap paper into two, putting a check by folks at both the wedding and the funeral.

"Quarter till eleven. Grandpa, are you going tae work today? Elspeth is coming in, so you don't have tae, if you'd rather rest."

"Aye. It will keep my mind off my troubles." He drummed his fingers across the page.

"I have at least sixty people who were at both the wedding and the funeral." Lydia scooted back from the table in dismay. "Anything ringing bells for you, Angus?"

Grandpa pinched the bridge of his nose. "My Agnes used tae say that patience was a virtue, but I am bloody well oot of it. You know it's bad when I've been praying tae my dead wife tae help me find my son, the cause of our broken marriage."

Paislee swallowed her surprised response by reaching for her tea.

"Och, you need answers. You deserve answers," Lydia said. "I'm sure Agnes understands. She's an angel in heaven now and knows everything."

Grandpa patted his heart. "She knows the truth, then, and the love I have for her right here. It's never changed."

With a sniff, Paislee eyed the ceiling. It would be a great show of faith for Agnes to deliver Craigh to Grandpa, but her gran had been so hurt on earth by what she felt was his betrayal the night before at his stag party that she'd cut Grandpa from her life with the precision of a heart surgeon.

Nobody was to mention his name and the family learned to leave it alone. To have Craigh here would be against all that her granny had believed.

Paislee sighed. "Gran knows you loved her. She has tae now . . . but that's still a pretty big ask, Grandpa."

"I was going tae say ballsy," Lydia quipped, wiping a tear. "I'd like tae know that true love overcomes all odds tae triumph in the end."

Lydia had to be thinking of Corbin.

"I'd like that, too," Grandpa said. "We vowed forever. And I never strayed a day after."

Paislee and Lydia exchanged a look. Thanks to someone targeting Lydia, she and Corbin had never exchanged those vows.

Chapter 22

Paislee shifted to get comfortable on the wooden chair, her gaze riveted to the wall calendar. She recalled the picture of Smythe Manor for a calendar, taken by Bruce. He'd been the one to snap photos of the Smythe Clan, and he'd taken a lot of wedding photos. He'd worn a camera at the funeral lunch. "You know who might have more information?"

Grandpa tapped his list. "Who? For Craigh, or aboot Felice?"

"This is for Lydia." Paislee put her project in the bag at her side. Lydia folded her arms on the table. "I'm all ears."

"Bruce Dundas. He was there for both events. He's a friend of the family. He got pictures of everyone. What if there is something he inadvertently captured on film?" Paislee stood and stretched her lower back. "It could be nothing tae him, but we might see something in the photos that doesnae belong. It's worth a shot tae ask him, and since Grandpa and Elspeth will both be at the shop, I feel okay going with you."

"Now?" Lydia arched her brow, but then gave a slow nod. "Let's do it. It's probably all digital these days." Relief at being active gave her best friend a lift in mood.

"Do you mind driving? That way Grandpa can have the Juke." Paislee turned to her grandfather. "I don't want you walking tae work, just in case. Please, please be careful." She snapped her fingers. "I'm going tae ask Bennett tae take Brody home with Edwyn this afternoon. No sense him being around this drama."

"Guid idea." Lydia gestured upstairs. "Give me ten minutes."

Paislee topped off their tea mugs.

"I'm tempted tae hang oot in Zeffer's office until he tells us everything," Grandpa said.

"Right? An update of some sort—heck, even a smoke signal tae let us know he's all right." Paislee tidied the table.

"Maybe not that, considering the explosion yesterday. There's no mention of it in the morning paper, and that's got tae be Scotland Yard's doing."

"Power comes in many forms, not just money." She blew the fringe off her forehead. "I wish I'd taken pictures of the metal parts in the box. There was something about them that just didn't sound right. When I was knitting earlier, I noticed the difference but man, Zeffer was so quick tae get them out of here."

"Really?" Grandpa turned strawberry red.

Paislee crossed her arms. "What?" She thought she knew but had to be sure. "Do you have something?"

"A little insurance for Craigh." Grandpa hurried into his room. Paislee stayed right on his heels so he wouldn't shut her out. He opened the top drawer of his bureau and lifted some white T-shirts.

Paislee peered inside and gasped. Inside a metallic shredded nest was a drill part. But what really alarmed her was the flash drive in the plastic bag. "Grandpa!"

"What?" Her grandfather's eyes widened. "Zeffer works for Scotland Yard. Craigh cannae just be forgotten. He only has me tae stand up for him."

"When did you . . . ?"

He shrugged. "The drill part was before I even showed *you* the boxes, just in case you made me turn them in right away. The flash drive? Well, I lifted it from Zeffer's pocket on the way tae the Juke. I had a bad feeling."

Wily! Crafty. "Intuition!"

Grandpa shut the drawer. "Proof."

They heard Lydia's creak on the fifth stair. "Grandpa. I don't know what tae say, but Zeffer is not going tae be happy." The disappointment in the DI's eyes when he realized she'd known about the boxes still stung.

"Leave that tae me. If anything happened tae Craigh, Zeffer owes me." Grandpa urged her out of the bedroom to the hall. "Now, you and Lydia be careful, but I feel sorry for anybody taking you both on," he said in a very lame attempt to lighten the somber mood.

Lydia glided down the stairs to the foyer. The woman looked like she could be on the cover of a magazine with no sign of her previous distress. Her makeup was flawless, along with her hair, which she'd put in a high ponytail. Ruby earrings glittered at her lobes, matching the bloodred sheath. Her ballet flats were gunmetal gray.

"No heels?" Paislee quipped, feeling very underdressed in khakis and a short-sleeved blouse.

"I left them at home. I should be able tae move back in this afternoon. New locks and door, which will make me feel more secure."

"Me too, for you."

Paislee pocketed her phone and set her knitting bag near the sofa. There was no time to compare the metal needles to the drill part, but she would later. After letting Wallace outside, she grabbed her purse and fluttered her fingers at her cunning grandfather. "I'll text tae let you know where we are."

He nodded and disappeared into his room.

Lydia led the way outside to where the Mercedes was parked. She clicked the fob to unlock the doors, and they each slid in. The rich scent of leather never got old.

Her SUV retained the smell of wet dog, beach, and boy.

Lydia started the car. "Where tae?"

Paislee scrolled through her phone's local business directory for wedding photography. It wasn't under Bruce Dundas, which would have been too easy.

"Ah! I think this is it. Sheila told us the name, remember? 'Special Moments, manager B. Dundas.' Go toward the harbor." Paislee rattled off the address.

"I'd like tae see what photos he has. Not that we can use any of the pictures. It was *almost* my wedding day." Lydia placed designer sunglasses on her nose to protect against the glare of sunshine.

"I wonder if Corbin and the family have let people know you've broken up?"

"Mary's probably taken out a billboard ad, which will make it awkward, asking tae see the wedding photos." Lydia's jaw clenched.

"I'll do it," Paislee said.

"Your duties as matron of honor are no longer needed."

"I will always be your best friend. Let me do it!"

"I'm all right. This is tae help find who killed Felice." Lydia glanced at Paislee. "So long as I remember that, I'll be okay."

Paislee patted Lydia's hand.

Lydia pulled before the building along a strip of businesses and parked. "It doesnae look open."

"Photography might be one of those things that is a dying art. As Constable Payne said, everybody has a camera now."

"You have tae grow with the times. Videography, drones. Now that would be brilliant—it would need tae be outdoors, though. I dinnae see Minister Angela agreeing tae a drone inside the kirk."

They each laughed and got out of the sportscar.

"See? Sometimes the old ways are the best." Paislee and Lydia each viewed progress a wee bit differently.

Lydia preferred shiny and new while Paislee liked cozy and comfortable. Yet, she couldn't imagine a better friend despite their differences. What if she'd had parents so kooky that she wouldn't have been allowed to be friends with Lydia because their astrological signs didn't match? It wouldn't surprise Paislee one bit to discover Mary vetted her daughters' mates.

Paislee peered inside the all-glass door of the business. After what happened to Lydia yesterday, it didn't seem very secure.

The building was made of wood and stone. Single story. Perhaps ten shops were along the block, off the main roads. You'd have to know the place was there, but she supposed that family photography wasn't a walk-in kind of business.

"I don't see anybody," she said.

"Hours stated are eleven tae five." Lydia tugged on the handle. "Let's try."

It opened, the bell above the door dinging merrily to announce their presence. Inside the shop was a long counter with four stools and several computer monitors. Must be for viewing the photos.

"Bruce?" Paislee called.

Lydia let the door close behind her with another ring.

The space was half the size of Cashmere Crush. Breathtaking photos of the Firth, the Highlands, and historic places around Nairn hung on the walls. She recognized the photo of Smythe Manor used in the calendar.

"Wow! He's guid." Covering her heart with her open palm, Lydia said, "Not that it matters now."

Other portraits were of the Smythe family. Births. Dances. Graduations. Sheila, Felice, Jocelyn, Oliver, Corbin, Drew, Duncan, and Reggie, about five years ago, were at the pier.

Bruce came out of a back area that was probably an office. Next to that was a door that read DARKROOM. He'd tucked an Oxford into casual jeans, leather loafers on his feet. His smile flickered when he saw them. "Lydia?"

"Aye." Her friend's voice caught, and she cleared her throat.

"Uh." A myriad of expressions crossed Bruce's semi-lined but handsome face—sorrow, to embarrassment, before landing on a professional veneer. As he aged, his freckles had faded along with his hair. "How are you?"

He knew that the relationship was over and if it stung Paislee, she imagined Lydia immersed in pain.

Lydia raised her chin. "I take it you heard aboot Corbin and I?"

"Oh, no." Bruce shook his head, his cheeks flushed. Paislee could commiserate with the redhead blush.

"We'd like tae see the photos you took from the day of the wedding," Paislee said, drawing his attention away from Lydia before he burst into flame.

"I dinnae have anything—I mean, well, after . . ." Bruce glanced at his office, then stepped toward Lydia.

"You don't even have proofs for us tae look at?" Paislee gestured to the monitor. "We're actually not interested in anything formal, though you did take so many. We're hoping for something salvageable as a makeup gift for Corbin, from Lydia."

Paislee didn't know where the words came from, but she went with it, crossing her fingers in her pocket at the tiny lie.

"I don't think so."

"Everything is digital. I have a hard time believing you deleted it all. It doesnae take up space, does it? It would really help me, Bruce." Lydia reached out her hand. He swallowed with a gulp.

Paislee noticed several printers and an open trash can with wadded scraps of paper. A ruler, a paper cutter, a bucket with pens and markers. The scent of chemicals suggested that he did his own developing. "Can you tell us who ordered the wedding photos? Corbin? If so, he won't be happy when he finds out that you wouldn't help Lydia."

Sweat beaded on Bruce's forehead. "I would need tae check my paperwork tae find oot who ordered the prints. I cannae show them tae you, withoot permission."

Bruce was acting way too strange. Of course, he knew who his paying client would be. She ambled toward the closest printer and a metal trash can. A red marker was on the workspace with scissors and tape. Magazines with words cut out. Paislee's nape tingled and she rubbed her arms, turning to Bruce, who watched Lydia. Was the photographer behind the threats?

"Shall I call Corbin right now? You'll make me ruin the surprise," Lydia said with the perfect half pout. Not many people could resist that look.

Bruce was torn between helping Lydia and keeping an eye on Paislee. He was worried.

The door he'd come out of was still open. Paislee stopped just shy of entering what was his office. His desk and laptop were centered on the wall. Pictures of Lydia in her wedding gown were up on the monitor. Lydia by the alder tree in the kirk courtyard. Lydia on the beach, the morning of the wedding.

"These are perfect," Paislee said. "Exactly the kind of thing that we wanted." Lydia joined her, with Bruce trailing.

"You arenae supposed tae see those," he said.

"Why not?" Lydia asked. She also studied the images, but went into the office rather than hover on the threshold.

"They arenae prepped at all or ready for purchase. Normally I would put together a portfolio for you tae choose your favorites from." Bruce brushed by Paislee and Lydia, turning off the computer.

"I'll double what they would pay you," Lydia said, reaching for her wallet. "If I can see the proofs."

"No!" Bruce held up his hand. "I'm sairy, but I need tae talk tae my client."

"Which isnae me." Lydia's nose flared.

"No." He gave another nervous gulp.

Paislee tugged Lydia by the elbow and backed up.

Lydia sighed, realizing she wasn't going to get her way.

"We'll be back," Paislee said. "You've ruined Corbin's surprise." She recalled how Sheila and Bruce had been in deep conversation at the manor house. "I guess we can always call Sheila. She might help us. Or Mary?"

Bruce ushered them through the shop, to the front door, glancing at the trash can. "I'm sairy. I cannae help you." Once they were out on the sidewalk, he even locked it, too.

"Feeling a lot like a pariah right now," Lydia said. "What was his problem?"

"He was probably paid by Garrison and Mary."

"I should've offered tae triple it."

"I don't think it would have mattered. Lydia, he had pictures of you on his monitor. What color was the writing on the photos of you and Corbin arguing?"

"Red."

"He had a printer, with a red marker. Magazines that had stuff cut out. I think we should call Constable Payne."

"Bruce is a photographer." Lydia swallowed with a gulp. "It's his job tae have those things."

"Not for your picture, and only your picture, on his monitor, though." It was creepy. "I don't recall him being there that morning of your wedding tae get those mimosa pictures, do you?"

Lydia shivered. "No."

They got back into the car and Lydia drove to Nairn Police Station. Constable Payne was in and took notes on what they told him about Bruce. The photographer had done nothing wrong.

"Can I see the pictures again, the ones from my condo?" Lydia asked.

"Sure." He showed them the pictures of Corbin and Lydia fighting. The red block letters saying to END IT. Magazine words cut out to spell the same. There were four pictures in total.

Paislee turned the pictures over, hoping for some clue or watermark to link the photo paper to Bruce.

"What are you doing?" Constable Payne asked, taking the photos back and returning them to the evidence bag.

"You must have a way tae trace this printer paper tae where it came from, right? Just saying, Bruce Dundas might be a good place to start. He saw me looking, though, and might destroy evidence."

The officer gritted his teeth but was still more polite than Zeffer when he escorted them out, and just as firm when he told them to let the police handle things.

"Wait! Is Zeffer in?" she asked, before Constable Payne could close the door.

"No. Now, go." He literally shooed them off the step of the station and shut the door.

"Twice in an hour," Lydia said. "I'm going home, Paislee. Gonna take a bubble bath and then bake some double-fudge brownies."

"Lydia!"

"I cannae deal with any more today." Lydia raised her palm as if to physically stop the world from turning.

"I understand." Cashmere Crush was a block away, and it was only noon. "I'll walk, but call me once you are secure in your condo, all right?"

"Sure." Dejected, Lydia climbed into her car and drove off.

Paislee strode to her shop, her thoughts a jumble. It was difficult to be patient and wait for the police to act. What other choice did she have?

She entered the shop and waved to Elspeth, who smiled wide. "Paislee! I wasnae sure you'd be in."

"I wasn't, either. Thanks for opening this morning."

"My pleasure! I'm aboot done with my second pillow cover." Elspeth raised the work of art to show Paislee.

"How lovely!" Paislee admired the bright colors and neat stitches. "You are very gifted, Elspeth." She looked around the shop but didn't see Grandpa. Since it was half-past twelve, he must've decided to stay home.

"Ta." Elspeth lovingly set her project aside. "I sold a fisherman's sweater tae a sweet young lady from America, here with her husband tae visit Nairn."

"Tourists are a great thing."

"How is Lydia?"

Paislee glanced around to make sure they were still alone. "Her flat was broken into yesterday. Someone doesnae want her and Corbin tae be together."

"They should just elope." Elspeth smoothed her sleek silver hair. "Forget the fuss."

Paislee didn't share that Lydia had ended the engagement with Corbin. A part of her really hoped he'd come to his senses and apologize before it was too late.

Grandpa arrived at quarter till one with no explanation of why he'd been late, and the shop was busy all afternoon. It was great for the cash register, but Paislee was mindful that her part-timers were both over seventy.

They closed Cashmere Crush at six, and Paislee and Grandpa drove to pick up Brody from Bennett's house. "I thought Zeffer would be in touch by now," Grandpa said. He rubbed his hand over the back of his neck. "It's like waiting for the ax tae fall."

Paislee reached for her sunglasses on the console and slid them on. "The man has no sense of putting people at ease."

Grandpa peered at her, then out the window. "It's not right, living this way."

She slowed to a stop at a traffic light as it turned red. "What way?"

"Tae put you and Brody in danger." Grandpa wouldn't look at her.

Tingles raced up her spine—he'd been up to something earlier. "That's nonsense!" It wasn't Grandpa's doing, but Craigh's. "It isn't your fault, any of it. You're not responsible for anything that Craigh might do. Even Zeffer said so."

Grandpa shook his head. "I dinnae believe it." He put his hand on the door handle and she got the awful sense that he wanted to bolt into the evening.

"What are you doing?"

"I have tae leave." He started to open the door. "I'm going back tae Dairlee."

"Right now?" She hit the automatic lock button. "From here? Don't be daft."

"In the past year, I've grown tae love you and Brody. Whoever has Craigh might put you in danger. I couldnae live with myself. I went tae my old landlady today tae see if she had our old room tae rent. She didnae, but I'll find one."

"Grandpa—please listen. Our best defense is tae stick together." Her heart beat fast and tears clogged her throat. "If we separate, we aren't as strong. Brody and I need you with us."

He settled back in the seat and bowed his head. Paislee didn't relax until he removed his hand from the door handle. "I just could not . . ."

"Stick with us." Her life with Grandpa hadn't been planned but he'd been an asset in many ways. Just the extra help she'd needed. Paislee didn't want to imagine how empty a hole Grandpa's leaving would be. "I don't want you tae go, Grandpa."

"If me son needs me," he said with a shrug. "I cannae promise."

The light turned green, and she continued toward the Macleans'.

"Fine. Fine." Paislee's nose stung and she exhaled. "We have tae know something soon, right?"

"Aye." Grandpa's voice dropped an octave or two lower and Paislee strained to hear. "The longer it takes, the more I fear it's going tae be bad news."

Paislee agreed but didn't say so as she parked before the small house behind the comic book/arcade Bennett owned. "Here we are. Now, no more talk about taking off on your own, promise?"

After almost a full minute, what felt like forever, Grandpa nodded. "Promise."

Chapter 23

Tuesday morning, Paislee left Grandpa at home to finish fortifying the Shaw house before he joined her for his regular shift at Cashmere Crush. She didn't point out that anybody with explosives could get past the new bolt on the back door. It would bring down morale.

She turned into Fordythe and slowed in queue until she reached the drop-off, where Brody scurried out. "Bye, love!"

"Bye, Mum!" Last night, Brody had documented the progress of his portable PLA compost bins and Paislee was right proud of him. To show the differences between 3D printer material, he'd buried regular plastic in compost bin A, and the PLA scraps in compost bin B. After two months, the PLA was already starting to break down while the plastic bottle hadn't changed. The filament reminded her of the packing material the drill parts had been in.

Hamish waved at her with a friendly smile that confused her until she recalled the tickets he'd given her. They probably needed to be signed or something. She made a mental note to check them when she reached the shop, but when she arrived, Jerry McFadden was already there and waiting outside.

"Hiya, Paislee lass!" Jerry was around forty and friendly, though not flirty, which she liked. He'd been delivering her yarn for years.

"Morning, Jerry. You're in a fine mood." She unlocked the back door and he brought in two cases of yarn that she'd put away between customers.

"It's a braw day. There's nothing tae scowl aboot."

"I agree." Paislee tossed her purse on the bottom shelf below the register.

"And yet, ye had a frown beneath those brows when you pulled up."

"It's Hamish," she said, blaming the headmaster rather than go into full detail of everything wrong just then. Poor Jerry would be at the shop until noon.

"You were an item for a while, right?"

"Wrong! We were never an item."

"He sent you flowers."

"After I was in an accident. It was Ms. Jimenez, the secretary, behind it, I'm sure."

"Your cheeks are red." Jerry chuckled.

"Is that all, Jerry?" Paislee put her hand on her hip. "Or do I need tae start ordering my yarn direct from JoJo's?"

He stepped back, palms raised. "Just teasin', calm down."

She wrote out a check for the total cost of the yarn. "Have a nice day, Jerry."

He left out the back with a whistle as Zeffer strode in the front entrance, blue suit pristine, dark auburn hair perfectly styled. The only sign that anything had been wrong was a deep red mark on his trimmed auburn eyebrow.

Was that a burn?

"Where have you been?" Paislee demanded, coming around the counter to meet him halfway and study him closely for proof of his injury.

Zeffer grinned and it took her breath away. "Well, now I know you care."

She rolled her eyes. "Not bloody likely. We have been worried aboot—"

"Me?"

"No. *Craigh*. You were supposed tae rescue him, and instead, the storage facility exploded. Without a word from you! It's irresponsible and I have half a mind tae complain tae your superior."

"Ah, Paislee. Calm down! Just the back few units."

She didn't care for being told to calm down twice in less than an hour and it fired up her temper. "Grandpa's?"

"Aye. If he fills oot a report, he'll be compensated."

"For what? Drill parts that Craigh probably stole?" She crossed her arms. "I think you can do better than that."

"You *are* in a mood. All right. The bins my team took from your house were full of not just drill parts, but others that an oil rig might need. I mentioned before that if an oil rig shuts down it costs millions in lost revenue that our country cannae afford tae lose. North Sea Oil hired a Norwegian named Erik Larsen tae learn how tae be green, and still profit."

She nodded, aware that the oil industry was a necessary evil and that Norway was a shining star on how to do it right. Except, Zeffer had said he'd caught a Norwegian fish with the storage unit bait. Hmm.

"Even their offshore rigs have solar panels and turbo energy. It's no wonder they're number one for clean living in the bloody world." Zeffer narrowed his eyes at her. "They have an industrial 3D machine aboard."

"On the platform?" Paislee asked. She had rudimentary knowledge thanks to a field trip in secondary school. An oil rig had limited space.

"Aye. The spin for it is that the cost of the machine will pay for itself by creating only those parts that break on-site, withoot storing unneeded parts just in case."

"Industrial-size 3D?" Paislee shook her head. "Brody's class has one for small projects. It's not clean energy by any means. Brody's end-of-year project is on how tae compost PLA filament and avoid overflow at the recycling facilities. Plastic doesn't break down, but there is hope for the PLA filament."

"And here I thought you wouldnae know a thing aboot it." Zeffer scrubbed his jaw, his gaze impressed.

"This is the twenty-first century," Paislee said, annoyed. "Zero Waste Scotland is reaching the younger generation tae make a difference. I believe they can." She tilted her head. "Pure metal hasn't been used successfully, according tae Brody and his teacher anyway. Are you saying that the parts that Craigh stole were made from the industrial 3D machine?"

Zeffer didn't answer but she took that as a yes.

"The material is different. Is that why they needed it back?" A figurative light went off over her head. "The drill parts are packed in filament, not metal. What kind?" She thought of the little nest in Grandpa's T-shirt drawer.

Zeffer raised a finger. "You are verra observant, Paislee. That's something I cannae share with you. Just know, I'm tracking the man behind those faulty parts and I'll put him away for guid."

"Who is it?"

He crossed his arms and pursed his lips.

"You make me so mad sometimes!" Paislee was used to his take-and-not-give way of working. This was about the bigger picture. Craigh. "I saw an insignia that night on one of the men's knit caps. A golden lion against a red patch. Does that mean anything?"

"You saw a golden lion on the knit caps of the men who blew up the storage facility?" Zeffer brought out his smartphone and thumbed through the photos, showing her a close-up of the patch. When she nodded he said, "I could kiss you. This it?"

Paislee ignored the kissing comment. "I think so—it was dark, and we *were* afraid for our lives."

"This is the Norwegian coat of arms."

Her stomach clenched. "They're the bad guys? I thought they were good!"

"Hector Wilson is the Scot in charge of the operation on North Sea Oil. We believe that Erik is using him as a front tae sell these faulty parts, even though Erik is aware they're not strong. From what Craigh discovered, Hector is oblivious tae his partner's schemes. In his quest for that green standard for Scotland, he doesn't micromanage Erik, who is from Norway and has experience. Mistake. You should *never* trust that blindly."

"That's what you meant by catching a Norwegian fish! Where is Craigh?"

"Funny story, that." Zeffer spread his arms.

"Tell!" Paislee barely managed to keep from stomping her foot.

"We had Craigh under surveillance and were ready tae nab him—er, rescue him—when the weasel escaped himself."

"You're just *now* telling us this? It's been two days." Paislee's emotions ran the gamut. "Are we in danger from the Norwegian riggers?"

"I doot it. My undercover patrol hasnae seen any suspicious activity around your place." Zeffer placed his forearm on the counter and leaned in to say, "I followed Angus tae Dairlee yesterday. He wanted tae rent his old flat. Makes him look involved, you see? Not trustworthy."

"He's not, though. Grandpa was just trying tae keep me and Brody safe!" Paislee realized that Grandpa having the flash drive would only make him seem more guilty. Maybe she could convince Grandpa to let her turn it in. She didn't want Zeffer disappointed in her integrity.

"While tryin' tae find his son." Zeffer straightened and shrugged. "We need tae capture Craigh before the Norwegians do. He's slippery, your uncle."

"I've never met him, and we're only partially related."

"Family is family."

Paislee bit her lip at that. "It's a lot of trouble sometimes. Family by choice is better."

"A lot of times more loyal, too." Zeffer looked around. "Where is Angus?"

"He'll be here at noon. Two hours."

"Have him come down tae the station, would ye?"

Paislee hefted the box of yarn to the counter to unpack. "I'll tell him, but that's aboot as much as I can do." Grandpa was stubborn with a capital S.

"How's your friend, Lydia? Married yet?" The DI relaxed against the high-top worktable.

"Single." She brushed her bangs back. "Constable Payne might tell you—she's at home resting after calling the marriage off completely. Her condo was broken into. Threatening photos on the table, telling her tae end it. The wedding photographer had pictures of her."

"That's his job." Zeffer smirked.

"More pictures than necessary." Paislee removed a soft skein. "What if he's a stalker?"

Zeffer raised his singed brow. "Payne's a decent officer. Monroe, too."

"He's been helpful but as close-mouthed as you when it comes tae sharing information."

Eyes narrowed, Zeffer asked, "What do ye want tae know, Paislee Shaw?"

She laughed abruptly. "Who killed Felice? Who was trying tae kill Lydia? It's been over a week. In the past, you've been faster."

"Is that a compliment?" Energy zinged between them like a current.

"Don't get too full of yourself."

Blaise walked into the shop with Mary Beth. "Morning," the ladies said to Zeffer.

"Mornin'." He stepped back from Paislee, and it was only then that she realized how close they'd been.

Her cheeks heated.

Zeffer chuckled. "I'll see what I can find oot for you. Send Angus tae the station, dinnae forget."

He left, taking the air with him, and Paislee had to catch her breath.

"I swear he's familiar." Blaise tapped her nose, her forehead scrunched.

"And what was going on between you, is what I want tae know," Mary Beth said with a low laugh.

"Nothing is going on!"

Lydia walked in next. "I just saw Zeffer and he actually smiled at me. I pinched myself tae make sure I wasnae dreaming."

"Nightmare, more like." Paislee boxed up the rolls of yarn for later since it was clear she was to get no work done at the moment.

"How are you, Lydia?" Blaise took Lydia into a hug.

Mary Beth was next.

Paislee, third for the hugs, had gotten her redhead blushes under control. "I've been worried."

"I called before I went tae sleep! I'm a grown woman, Paislee," Lydia laughed. "I brought brownies."

"I would have felt better if you'd stayed with us again."

"No offense, but thanks tae your criminal uncle it was a fifty-fifty shot over whose house would have been safer. Is Craigh found?"

"Not yet. He escaped. The Norwegians are behind the explosion, and Zeffer is pretty sure Craigh will hide in Dairlee. He's not sure about Grandpa's involvement."

Lydia snapped her fingers. "Norway is the gold standard for how tae run an oil rig properly. That doesnae make sense."

"I can't tell you more than that for now," Paislee said.

The ladies got out their knitting, except for Lydia, who ordered delivery tea and coffee to go with her brownies as they caught up with a good blether.

"So," Lydia said, after they'd discussed the Corbin situation for over an hour, "he called last night tae apologize." She wadded her napkin into her paper cup.

"His family put you through hell," Mary Beth said. "Can you imagine holidays moving forward?"

"He would always pick them over me." Lydia swiped a crumb from the counter and added it to the cup.

"It's no' right," Blaise said. "You deserve tae be his number one. Trust is crucial in a successful marriage."

Lydia brushed her hands together. "I agree. No trust. No wedding."

By the end of the chat session, they all agreed that Lydia'd had a close call.

Paislee smiled at Lydia, who returned it with sorrow in her eyes. Sometimes being around your women friends was the best medicine.

Blaise gave a small yelp after checking her phone. "How can it be almost one already?"

Mary Beth packed up her project, as did Blaise. "Oops. I'll be a wee bit late bringing Arran his lunch. He'll understand."

Paislee walked them out. "Lydia, any word from the constable about the wedding photographer?"

"No. It's probably nothing, and I'll end up lookin' like a fool, again, for being too emotional or reactionary."

"Your home was broken into, so please be careful."

"I will." Shadows haunted Lydia's face. "I could use some of your strength, Paislee, tae keep Corbin at arm's length. I fear that if I meet with him, I'll forget aboot being mad and remember why I fell in love with him."

Paislee sighed. "Remember Felice, dead. His family blaming you. That should annihilate any romantic feelings."

"Fair point." Lydia left with them, and Paislee greeted a walk-in customer.

It was after twelve. Where was Grandpa?

Chapter 24

Paislee's entire body was on high alert, warning her that something was not right. It still took another hour to lock up Cashmere Crush and drive home. A terrible feeling nagged at the nape of her neck.

She stepped on the gas.

Everything seemed okay from the outside of the carport when she arrived. Front door was closed. Yet her intuition, that thing Zeffer mocked her for, screamed something was wrong.

What if Grandpa had a stroke from all his worry over missing Craigh? Sunday night he hadn't even been able to drive. At the image of him sprawled unconscious or worse somewhere in the house, she exited the Juke and raced up the stone steps.

The front door was unlocked, odd, and the table in the foyer tipped over. Wallace wasn't around.

"Grandpa?"

"Get oot, lass!" Her grandfather's voice wobbled.

Where was her dog? Wallace was a fierce protector no matter his short stature. Paislee reached for the iron Scottie doorstopper on the ground and hefted it in her hand.

She heard Wallace growl and then a man yelled, "Back off, mutt!"

Paislee hurried to the hall and the open door of Grandpa's bedroom. Her heart plummeted.

A lanky figure with messy brown hair had Grandpa pinned by the shoulders to the bedroom wall. He was tall, like her da, but while her father had bulk from his work at the harbor, this man had skipped a few meals. There was nothing Da liked more than minced beef and tatties. These men were not the same.

Wallace's teeth were sunk into the man's ankle above a filthy bare foot. Grandpa wore beige khakis and a polo shirt, dressed for his shift at Cashmere Crush. By contrast, the man had on dirty too-small jeans and a grungy T-shirt that didn't quite fit. She imagined it had been taken from someone's clothesline as he'd bolted from capture by the Norwegian riggers.

She presumed but had to be sure. "Uncle Craigh?"

The man peered at her from manic brown eyes. "Not yer kin, hen. Never met ya, dinnae plan on exchangin' Christmas cards."

"Let Grandpa go!" She raised the iron Scottie doorstopper and nodded at her Wallace, who was protecting Grandpa from a bad man—on this there was no doubt.

"Nope." His hands tightened on Grandpa's shoulders. "Not until I get the formula back!"

"What formula?" Paislee's pulse fluttered like a hummingbird's wings. "Where?" All she could think of was a recipe. Gran's shelves in this room were stocked with books. As an English teacher for thirty years, her collection was vast and might contain something to help.

Craigh shook Grandpa. "This daft old buzzard has it somewhere. Willnae tell me where he hid it."

Grandpa's T-shirt drawer held the faulty parts and the flash drive. Should they give Craigh what he wanted so he would go? Paislee lowered the doorstop. "Grandpa?" She scanned Gran's room. Books and photos were knocked off the shelves, ransacked. Vandalized.

Grandpa's face reddened to a terrifying eggplant purple.

Paislee quaked with anger and fear. "You let him go. I've already called the police."

Grandpa and Craigh whirled toward her.

"No!" Craigh released Grandpa. Wallace refused to release Craigh; if anything, the pup tightened his teeth into flesh. Craigh howled.

She raised her iron Scottie and shook it at Craigh.

Craigh leapt toward Paislee, but Wallace slowed the man down by yanking on his bare skin.

Craigh yelped. Grandpa grabbed Gran's giant dictionary and whacked his son across the back of his head.

Craigh collapsed in a heap on the floor between them.

Wallace yipped and surrounded Craigh, strutting at his part in the rescue, his ears and tail lowered.

Grandpa stumbled backward, his hand over his heart.

"Grandpa! Should I call the ambulance?"

"No. No. Just let me catch me breath." His gaze was as pleading as his tone as he said, "You didnae call the police, did you, not really?"

"No." Paislee put the iron Scottie on the floor by her feet and pulled her mobile from her pocket. "But I'm going tae. Zeffer knows you went tae Dairlee yesterday. What on earth happened, Grandpa?"

Craigh, on his back, roused and Wallace sat near his face emitting a low warning growl.

"He followed me. I didnae know. I wouldnae have led him here, Paislee, you know that's true, aye?"

"Aye. Zeffer is concerned you're working with Craigh." She glanced at her uncle on the floor and nodded to the dresser, where Grandpa had hidden the flash drive that must contain the formula. To what? "That isn't going tae help your case any."

"I had tae protect Craigh if something went wrong, and it did!"

It had, in monstrous proportions. "Is he one of the good guys, or one of the bad guys, Grandpa?"

Grandpa sank onto the edge of the bed, sitting with his knees out and his head bowed, fingers in his silver-gray hair. "I don't know."

"It's okay." She patted his shoulder but kept her eye on Wallace and Craigh. Her heart pounded at how close he'd come to her, willing to hurt her. Not a great man.

"I'm sairy, lass."

"It's not your fault. You saved me." Paislee nudged the thick tome Grandpa had used to come to her defense. "Gran loved that dictionary."

Craigh mumbled and his lashes fluttered.

"Grandpa, Brody and I want you tae be here with us. Tae live. This is your home, too. We don't want you tae go with Craigh."

His stubborn jaw set.

Warmth filled the room, the kind of love that Paislee felt when she thought of her grandmother. "I think Gran is okay with everything now. She knows from Heaven. I think she helped you find your son."

"I doubt that verra much." The pages of the dictionary ruffled, and Grandpa straightened, his hand to his chest. "You're sure?"

"Aye." Paislee gave her Grandpa a playful nudge. "If we can believe in the Loch Ness monster, why not angels?"

Grandpa smiled at her.

"What aboot me, then?" Craigh sat up and rubbed his head. "Stop growling, mutt."

Wallace backed up, but kept Craigh within biting distance.

"Craigh, I'm disappointed in yer choices but you're a grown man."

"So, what? You're going tae rat me oot? Zeffer's gonna throw away the key."

"Not if you give him the flash drive, and tell him it was your idea tae turn yourself in," Grandpa said.

"Not goin' tae do that." Craigh's hair was wild with static. "You give me that flash drive. You have no idea how important that is. I risked me life on that rig tae get into Erik's office, past his henchmen."

"What's on it?" Paislee turned toward Craigh.

"Not telling you." His scruffy jaw clenched.

Paislee thought of all that she'd learned about 3D printing

in the past year. "If I tell *you* what's on it, then will you turn your-self in?"

"No way can you know. That's encrypted!"

"Deal, or no?"

"Yeah. If you guess, then I'll turn myself in." Craigh sat up slowly, a sly grin on his face.

Grandpa looked at her with worry.

"The boxes held oil rig parts made of a new material that broke easily, but your Norwegian boss didn't care and was selling them anyway. That flash drive contains the formula for the material."

His words had been the last piece to the puzzle.

Craigh's jaw dropped. "Are you a hacker or somethin'?"

Grandpa stood in front of Paislee. "Honor your deal, son. Take the flash drive and make a bargain for yourself with Zeffer and Scotland Yard. This will give you a chance for a better life."

"And you?" Craigh stood. "I suppose you want tae mooch a new place."

"He's home already," Paislee said, glaring at her uncle.

Craigh swallowed hard as he weighed his options.

"Grandpa never stopped believing in you," she said. "He believed you were alive, and that you'd have a good reason for disappearing."

Craigh glanced at Grandpa, who shifted from bare foot to bare foot. "I obviously couldnae tell you aboot being undercover. For being caught stealing parts in the first place. I just wanted something better."

"Scotland Yard gave you a chance tae make things right," Grandpa said. "And then what happened?"

"I guess I saw an opportunity tae make even more money and I grabbed it. It was my turn tae make a mint. Why not?"

"Stealing's wrong?" Grandpa held out his arms to his sides.

"You dinnae live in the real world, old man."

Paislee didn't like Craigh's tone. "I want tae give you a chance tae do the right thing. Make Grandpa proud of your choices."

"Screw that!" Craigh raised a fist. Wallace bared his teeth and Craigh backed into the shelves.

Grandpa exhaled very loudly. "I'm so very sairy I wasnae there for you. I didnae know aboot you. Once I did, I was part of your life at the detriment of my own. I lost the love of a guid woman." He nodded at the picture of him and Gran at their tenth anniversary.

Paislee's eyes welled.

"Mum said you didnae know. I begged her why she never told you. She said it wasnae right." Craigh tugged his hair, the same way she'd seen her grandfather do. Come to think of it, her da had done so too. Would Brody?

Grandpa spread his arms to the sides. "I dinnae understand."

"Mum said that, well, she knew you were blasted. She tricked you."

Grandpa wheezed in a breath. "Why?"

"Jealous of the woman ye married." Craigh shrugged. "She never thought in a million years she'd get preggers. She married my stepdad, and none was the wiser till she was dying and had tae confess all her damn sins. Tae explain why I got the beatings."

Her grandfather stepped toward Craigh and held out his hand. What the heck?

In his clasp was the flash drive in the plastic bag. "None of that was your fault, son. None of it was your choice."

Paislee's throat grew thick.

Gran's picture on the shelf rattled and she sensed her grandmother in the room more strongly than she'd ever felt before. Forgiveness and love were as tangible as a soft blanket.

Grandpa grabbed Craigh in a hug. "I love you. The choices you've made havenae been guid, but this is your chance tae start again. Turn yourself in, with this as leverage for a new beginning."

Craigh dashed a tear from his cheek and stepped back from his dad. He accepted the flash drive and glared at Paislee.

She had to trust in the love that was in this room. This was

Gran's doing as surely as she was breathing. Paislee crossed her arms and stared at her uncle. "You said you would turn yourself in."

His cheeks flushed in shame as he eyed the door. Even Wallace waited for Craigh to make up his mind.

After what seemed like hours, Craigh said, "Call Zeffer. Tell him I'd like tae make a deal."

She sent the DI a text that they had Craigh at the house, and that he wanted to talk. Just talk—no sirens, no jail. Was that possible?

OMW.

"He's coming. Now what? Why is the formula a secret?"

Craigh laid the bag in his open palm. "Erik Larsen, master of clean energy, is a thief. He stole this formula from his partner in Norway. It's awaiting patent."

"But some of the parts are broken," Paislee said.

"When you make a part at a factory, the shapes of the pieces for drills and pipes can be very odd, which makes it time-consuming. Though Norway has an industrial machine on their platform, that's not feasible for most companies." Craigh leaned back against the wall, not letting go of the flash drive.

"The patent for the material is stolen," Grandpa said.

"From his business partner. Intellectual property rights are near impossible tae prove with the speed of inventions on the free market these days. This material"—Craigh raised the flash drive—"is supposed tae be as close tae natural as you can get. The samples in the boxes are his progression, and he finally got one tae work brilliantly. You understand I could make millions on the black market?"

Grandpa shook his head. "That was your grand plan."

"Sell it tae the highest bidder." Craigh shrugged. "Then take off somewhere tropical and live a life of ease, drinkin' margaritas by the bucket."

"And Grandpa?"

"He's on his feet, isnae he?" Craigh studied the room. Though it was Gran's, Grandpa had his things there, too. "Or he could come."

"He wasn't on his feet." Paislee shook her finger at her uncle, who was damned well old enough to know right from wrong. "You left him with no funds."

"I didnae know that," Craigh said. "Ask Zeffer! I said that part of my cooperation was for someone tae look after me da. I dinnae know who cut off my funds. Could be Scotland Yard, could be the Norwegians. Nobody's going tae admit it, are they? Put the squeeze on me. I knew you wouldnae go hungry, 'cause you're smart that way and can catch fish. Hunt. I didnae know you'd met up with your granddaughter."

"Until . . . ?" Paislee kept her voice harsh, but she softened a little at how he'd done his awkward best for his da.

"I saw you together Friday night at the bandstand. You called oot *Grandpa*."

Zeffer knocked on the front door, but Wallace wouldn't leave his post of guarding Craigh. She checked the time on her phone. Seven minutes had passed.

"Come in!" she called, standing in the threshold of Grandpa's room so she could see the front door.

Zeffer entered, taking in the knocked-over table in the foyer. "You'd better have a guid explanation, Paislee Shaw, or I will toss you in jail right next tae your uncle and your grandfather."

Chapter 25

Paislee's uncle stiffened at the sound of Detective Inspector Zeffer's voice. His body tensed, poised to fly and escape. She lasered her gaze on him, daring him to go back on his word. "You promised."

After a tense few seconds, Craigh nodded at her, then Grandpa. "DI Zeffer!" her uncle called as if he and the detective were mates down at the pub, and him about to buy a round. He passed by Paislee and met the DI in the hall. Zeffer, arms akimbo, wasn't letting Craigh near the front door. How hadn't she noticed how broad Zeffer's shoulders were before now?

"I'll heat the kettle." Paislee stepped around Craigh. "Let's sit down and discuss what's going on."

"Great idea, lass," Grandpa said, following on her heels.

Wallace's attention skipped between Craigh and Zeffer, but he didn't let either man out of sight until the pair shuffled into the kitchen.

Testosterone peppered the air as the men settled around the kitchen table.

"Please sit," Paislee said, "and I'll get the mugs."

It would give her something to do with her hands, and she was glad for that. Zeffer scanned the kitchen, then took a seat where he could block the front entryway in case Craigh made a wrong move. Wallace paced between her feet and the back door, his canine gaze bright with awareness.

Paislee plonked mismatched mugs to the center, then the sugar and a package of store-bought shortbread. She didn't bother with a plate. Napkins, cream. Spoons.

The electric kettle whistled. She brought it to the table on a trivet. Nobody spoke as they waited for her to join them. Why bother with polite chitchat when so much was on the line?

Grandpa poured as she sat. Craigh accepted a sweet with his tea and Paislee could feel Zeffer's frustration like a slap of energy.

At last, Zeffer said, "Explain tae me why I shouldnae call my team and throw you behind bars forever."

Craigh swallowed his shortbread in two big bites. "Dinnae be mad, DI. There's been a misunderstanding is all."

"Is that right?" Zeffer tapped the red singe mark on his auburn brow. "My men were in tae rescue you at the factory in Aberdeen, but you were gone. Why would the Norwegians set off an explosion in Dairlee? Paislee saw the golden lion on their knit caps. Morons—but great for me."

Craigh gulped his tea, knuckles white on the handle of the mug. "Erik Larsen must have had his minions follow me, and I didnae ken."

Her uncle didn't seem that bright of a criminal.

"I'd made off with a few bolts and parts that I was storing in the unit tae show you later, DI. Da had nicked 'em, for what reason I'll never know." Craigh scowled at Angus.

"I feared getting news that you were dead, son. I figured I'd better look in the boxes meself tae see what was so private before handing the lot over tae the detective."

Craigh smirked. "I wish I coulda seen your face when you saw the parts! Probably hoping for cash."

"Why'd you take them, Craigh?" Zeffer asked. His stern tone reminded them this wasn't a picnic or social call.

"Well, DI, things were heating up on the rig once I was almost caught with my hand in the cookie jar, so tae speak. They brought me tae the factory in Aberdeen and roughed me up. Told me they'd already taken care of one weasel and tossed his body in the sea. I didnae think you'd get me oot in time. Had tae have a backup plan."

Zeffer simmered in anger. That meant he wanted something from Craigh—or rather, needed.

It was a crafty thing for Grandpa to have the flash drive and barter for Craigh's life. Paislee wanted Craigh to go far, far away.

Craigh placed his palm over his knee to stop it from shaking.

"So." Zeffer was cool as he smoothed the lapels of his suit jacket. "You didnae cause the explosion at the storage unit, and you didnae double-cross Scotland Yard?"

"No, I didnae blow anything up," Craigh insisted, "but I took advantage of them waiting tae kill me once the boxes were returned. Either way, I was done for. So, I knocked Sven over the head with a rock and cheeked it. Had no shirt, so had tae chore one. Lucky for me summer is late in Nairn and folks are hanging oot their clothes."

"Lucky," Zeffer agreed in a dry tone.

"I didnae deliberately turn into a little punk, but things at the onshore factory were gettin' verra hot. I was protecting me own arse, if you know what I mean."

"You have a braw talent for that, it seems." Zeffer stared at Craigh, who squirmed.

"So. What can I do tae prove my loyalty? I did my part in gathering information for the Yard." Craigh placed the drive to the center of the table and gave it a tap.

Zeffer sucked in a breath that made a whistling noise between his teeth. "I wondered where that had gone." He glanced at Paislee, then Grandpa.

"This is the patent," Craigh said with excitement. His eyes glittered. "This is the program that shows how tae make the material

Erik Larsen stole from his business partner in Norway. I told you I'd get it, DI. That's what got me busted by Larsen's thugs."

Zeffer held out his hand. "I can confiscate the flash drive right now and put you in jail just because you've slipped from surveillance when you are the property of Scotland Yard."

Craigh chuckled, then swallowed his tea. He clanged the mug back to the table. "Well. I have a verra guid memory, and I can tell you the exact layout of the factory. You'll need tae hurry tae catch them before they blow up the place. Larsen's thugs love their explosives, including the industrial machine they've been using with this special material. The parts in the boxes are a progression of faulty parts as Erik tried tae copy his partner's formula."

Zeffer studied Craigh closely. "Did he succeed?"

"I'm not sure what the durability of the material is, and Erik doesnae care." Craigh placed the flash drive in Zeffer's palm. "He wants money."

"Let's go, then. Capturing the machine will seal our investigation tae match the parts and material." Zeffer clasped it, his jaw clenching, then called his team from his mobile as he stayed seated at the table. "I have Craigh Shaw. He's turned himself in—lucky SOB clobbered his guard and ran." Zeffer rolled his eyes. "Yeah, I believe him. It's time tae arrest Erik Larsen at the factory in Aberdeen. I'll be on my way shortly."

Grandpa bowed his head.

Craigh exuded gratitude with an exaggerated bow from the waist. Wallace growled a warning for the man to not make any sudden moves.

Zeffer noticed the bite marks on Craigh's ankle and grinned. "Well done, pup."

Wallace gave Zeffer a cool blink. *No prob, mate*, the dog seemed to say.

Now what would happen? "Wait!" Paislee said. "Will Craigh go into witness protection?"

"*If* the information works oot, and *if* Craigh is being honest, then aye, we will offer a new identity somewhere away from Scotland. Oot of Europe, actually."

All three looked to Grandpa.

"Da? Will you join me on a tropical island somewhere?"

Paislee held her breath. *Please, please say no.*

"Can I think aboot it?"

Everyone, even Zeffer, appeared disappointed by Grandpa's answer.

Her phone rang. It was Fordythe Primary. It was also four in the afternoon. She cursed under her breath and gave the swear jar on the counter a guilty glance, then answered, "Hello!"

"Paislee? It's Hamish McCall."

Alarm spread through her veins, and she rose to her feet. Wallace scooted back. "I'm on my way."

"Don't speed!" Zeffer warned as soon as she hung up.

Paislee made no promises. "Craigh, if I never see you again . . . I wish you well. I'd just as soon you not be here when I return with my son."

Zeffer stood. She could tell he wasn't done but now was not the time. "Your uncle will be in Aberdeen with me. We know aboot the explosives at the factory from our surveillance and they've already been dismantled."

Paislee held out her hand to shake Craigh's, who remained in his chair. "Bye." She turned to Grandpa. "Please stay until we come home, no matter what other decision you make, all right?"

Grandpa cleared his throat. "I wouldnae leave withoot saying goodbye."

Neither of them looked at Craigh. Her chest ached with emotion. Paislee shook Zeffer's hand next, surprising them both. "Thank you. I know you didn't have tae trust me, but I appreciate it."

Zeffer gave a single nod. Abrupt. Cool.

She hurried out before she burst into tears. Why oh why did life have to be so hard?

★ ★ ★

Arriving at Fordythe late, she parked in the lot so that she could make a proper apology. Hamish and Brody kicked a ball between them on the sidewalk.

"I didn't know you played," she said, forcing a lightness she didn't feel.

"I used tae, back in my glory days." Hamish appeared younger to her as he shared with a smile, "I was on the team at university."

"You were?" Brody asked as if suddenly realizing that the headmaster of Fordythe in his boring brown suits might have been a kid once upon a time.

"Aye." Hamish winked and the sight warmed her, reminding her of times when they'd been friends.

Maybe now that Brody would be in secondary, they could be friends again. Or not. She had so much to get settled with Grandpa and Craigh, Lydia. Her best friend had to be just as lost at sea as Paislee.

"I bet you were guid," Brody said.

"I had my moments tae shine." Hamish stopped the ball. "Now, what happened with you tae be late? A sweater order?"

She blushed—not sure what she would be at liberty to say. If Craigh was going to be given a new identity, would he claim this one before he left?

Where would he stay tonight? Och, not Gran's house. No way. That was too much to ask. Paislee could dip into the emergency fund and put him up at a hotel somewhere—yes, that would be best.

Hamish tilted his head to study her. "Everything all right?"

"Fine, fine! Brody, love, let's get going. We need tae stop by the shop." She wasn't in a hurry to return home in case Craigh was still sitting at her kitchen table.

"Didnae you just come from there?" Hamish unbuttoned one of his buttons on his suit jacket. She remembered that he did that when he was nervous.

"No." Paislee sighed. "I can't explain right now."

"Oh." Disappointment clouded Hamish's gaze. "Did you get a chance tae look at the graduation tickets?"

"No. I promise I will." She realized she owed him something of an explanation just to be polite.

Brody blew back his auburn fringe, his foot on the ball.

"Well. My friend Lydia, you probably remember her?"

Hamish nodded.

"She was going tae get married last week, and then she didn't."

"Cold feet?"

"No." She palmed her phone. "A missing Luckenbooth brooch. She was going tae marry Laird Corbin Smythe."

"Oh. They're a well-to-do family in the area. How nice for her."

"They didnae like Aunt Lydia," Brody said, tossing the ball between his own feet since Hamish wasn't playing.

"Seriously?" Hamish frowned.

"No, they didn't." She hated to reprimand Brody for repeating the truth, even if it wasn't kind. "But Corbin and Lydia were in love."

"So why no marriage?" Hamish tucked his hand into his slacks' pocket.

"The brooch was stolen. It's supposed tae be lucky, and an heirloom from the late nineteenth century." Paislee started to feel like she was babbling.

"Oh! That's too bad."

"It was cursed," Brody explained, as if this was totally acceptable. Since Scotland's national mascot was a unicorn, fairies and curses weren't that far off in daily life.

Her face warmed. "Lydia doesn't think so, but one of the cousins fell down the stairs before the ceremony and broke her neck."

Hamish's brows rose in alarm. "That's awful."

"Felice stole the brooch," Brody interjected. "Curse got her. Edwyn says it's karma."

Hamish glanced from Brody to her as if expecting her to straighten the curse situation out. She cleared her throat. "Brody, hon, you know we don't believe in curses."

"So, what happened?" Brody balanced the ball on his toes. "Seems fair tae me."

Paislee wasn't free to say that Lydia had been targeted by poison. "I don't know. Constable Payne is checking into it."

"The police are involved?"

"They are." She gave Hamish a look that suggested he drop it. Maybe even change the subject.

He did, bless him. "We have a special guest coming tae the graduation ceremony. The kids are all trying tae guess who it is. The winner will receive a special prize. It's a celebrity here in Nairn."

"Awesome!"

"No helping," Hamish said with a finger wag. His eyes shone at her.

Whatever he was talking about was probably in that darn envelope he'd given her. Paislee sighed. There were only so many hours in the day.

Her phone dinged a text message. Grandpa, saying the coast was clear.

Should they tell Brody about his great-uncle? She prayed with all her might that Grandpa would stay with them, and let his son go drink margaritas in the sunshine by himself.

"Come on, Brody. Headmaster, thank you. And I do apologize for being late."

"I'd love tae catch up someday. You tell the most interesting stories."

Unfortunately, a lot of the stories were actual events, but no matter.

Brody climbed in and waved goodbye as Paislee drove them toward the main road. "That was ace," he said. "I didnae know the headmaster played football. Can you believe it?"

"No." Hamish often seemed too buttoned up and staid to have fun. She glanced at him as she drove toward Cashmere Crush. "How are things with Jenni?"

Brody's face flamed with color. "Well, Jenni wants tae make sure I know how tae dance. So, we practiced a little at lunch today. Sam teased us, but I dinnae care."

"Good for you!" She wished she could let Sam know to back off. "Who is Edwyn going with?"

"Anna. That girl he liked last year, who can draw?"

"I remember."

"Mum?"

"Yes?" She pulled behind the yarn shop and turned off the Juke. "What is it?"

"Edwyn and Anna kissed." Brody regarded her with big brown eyes full of panic. "What am I supposed tae do?"

Chapter 26

Paislee about swallowed her tongue at the idea of her son kissing. Weren't they too young for that?

Edwyn had been interested last year at ten, and now at eleven, well . . . she cleared her throat and prayed for the right answer. *Keep calm.*

"A kiss, huh?"

Brody nodded. "By the swings."

Surely Hamish had something in his handbook about that! She thought back. "I didn't have my first kiss until I was fourteen or fifteen."

"You didn't?" His whole body sagged with relief.

Paislee chuckled. "People are different, Brody. It's okay tae take your time aboot who you want tae kiss because it's a special thing."

"What aboot holding hands?"

"What are the rules at school?"

"No PDA."

"Ah. So, you have tae sneak tae do it." She wrinkled her nose.

"Yeah."

"So, it's probably not worth it, right?"

He shook his head, but he wasn't a hundred percent on board. He would be twelve soon and then, horrors, thirteen.

Tweens were maturing faster these days, according to Mary Beth, who found it a fascinating subject. She was very protective of her twin girls.

Paislee hoped to keep Brody in the slow lane for as long as she could. It didn't help that his best mate was all about speed.

"What does Jenni think?"

Brody's mouth gaped and then he snapped his jaw closed. "We dinnae talk aboot it!"

She dipped her head to hide a smile. "That's okay. You know, she might be nervous, too. You never want tae press the issue."

"Yeah." He blew out a breath. "Mibbe next year I'll think aboot it."

Thank you, thank you. "Sure. There's no rush."

"Thanks, Mum." He bolted out of the car to the back of the shop.

Paislee followed him inside a little more slowly. This was the most important job she had in the world, and she prayed every day that she wouldn't mess it up.

Her uncle Craigh was an example of not being raised with values and morals. Paislee's heart had broken when she'd heard his story, but at what point did a man become responsible for his own choices? The law said eighteen and that was the world they lived in.

"Elspeth!" She dropped her hobo bag beneath the counter and greeted her employee. "How was it?"

Brody curled up on the chair, his video game in hand, headphones on.

"Fine!" Elspeth looked behind Paislee to the shut door. "Where's Angus?"

"At home. He's not feeling well."

"Oh! I can make him some of my chicken soup. Guaranteed tae kick any germs oot of the body," Elspeth said. "Lots of garlic does the trick."

"That's so thoughtful!" For what ailed Grandpa, soup wouldn't cure. Two customers browsed near the sweaters at the front of the store.

Her phone dinged from the side pocket of her purse and Paislee tugged it free to read a message from Lydia. *Can you come over?*

She replied, *I have Brody with me.*

Can't Angus watch him for a bit?

Grandpa is busy. Are you okay?

I need to show you something.

After six?

Perfect. Thank you. I owe you.

You don't. Love you.

Paislee managed to focus on the shop and customers for the next hour, glad to be busy because every free second, she wondered what Lydia needed, which warred with what Grandpa was doing, until at last she and Elspeth locked the door.

"Thanks for all of your help," Paislee said. "You're such an asset tae the crew."

"My pleasure! Dinnae forget tae let me know if you'd like that pot of soup for Angus." Elspeth blushed. "I mean, for all of you. It's quite tasty."

That was sweet. Elspeth had a wee crush that Grandpa would probably never act on due to his love for Agnes. Despite the years and tragic miscommunication, Agnes remained his great love.

Crushes were harmless things, and she needed to remember that when it came to Brody and his sweetheart.

"I will. See you later."

"Grandpa's sick?" Brody asked, having taken his headphones off to catch the last of the conversation.

Heartsick. "A little. We'll see how he is when we get home." If Grandpa wasn't there, she'd let Brody stay alone with Wallace. Erik Larsen was as good as caught once Zeffer made the arrests, thanks to Craigh. Even if he had been weaselly.

Bottom line? Craigh had turned over the flash drive with the stolen intellectual property formula, and the faulty parts, to shut down the factory run by a greedy Norwegian. Would Grandpa pack up and join Craigh to drink margaritas?

Her stomach knotted.

They were home before she could decide whether or not to tell Brody about it, which was probably for the best.

Paislee twisted the knob. Locked. Using her key, she opened the door. Wallace greeted them with a wagging tail and lolling tongue, exuding happy dog vibes.

No Craigh, or Zeffer. Grandpa came out of his bedroom to the hall.

"How was school, Brody?" Grandpa smiled and headed to the kitchen, as if there hadn't been a scuffle earlier. He'd brushed his hair and changed his clothes.

"Fine. You okay? Mum said you were sick. Elspeth wants tae make you soup."

Grandpa chuckled, his back to them as he switched on the kettle. "I'm fine. Had a headache, which is now gone."

Ha. The headache was six feet tall if she had to guess. "Brody, hon, why don't you run upstairs tae change into play clothes?"

He nodded and raced down the hall, to the foyer, turning sharply to dart up the stairs, two at a time.

"I don't know where he gets that energy," she said. "Grandpa, are you . . ."

"Craigh is going tae cooperate with Zeffer and that makes me verra proud. I'm going tae accept your offer tae stay here. We rub along okay, aye?"

Paislee hugged him tight. "Aye." She blinked back tears and sagged backward. "Aye, we do."

Grandpa gestured toward the stairs. "What did ye tell him?"

"Nothing. I thought we'd discuss how you wanted tae handle it."

"Thanks. I'll think on it. Zeffer will let us say goodbye before they ship Craigh off tae wherever."

"The Bahamas, maybe."

"Mibbe. I like the idea that he will be safe and cared for. And not putting you and Brody in danger."

She squeezed his arm. "You should be proud of yourself, too. You're a good da."

He shook his head at that. "I didnae know aboot him."

"On purpose, from what he said."

"I have some anger in my heart aboot that."

"I don't blame you." Paislee recalled the love in the room earlier. "I don't think Gran does anymore, either."

His eyes filled with wonder as he nodded. "That was something, wasnae it?"

"Yeah."

"Wallace was a hero."

"He was." They both grinned like loons at the dog. Paislee tossed Wallace a piece of shortbread. "Good pup."

"I saw that, Mum!" Brody had put on his scruffiest pair of shorts and a sloppy T-shirt. Avengers.

"Busted." Paislee chuckled. "So, I need tae go tae Lydia's for an hour. Brody, get yourself a snack and watch telly."

"By myself?"

"What am I, chopped liver?" Grandpa patted his chest. "I was going tae make cheese toasties, but if you dinnae want any . . ."

"Yes!" Brody pumped his fist. "Yours are the best."

Grandpa nodded, then asked Paislee, "What's going on with Lydia?"

"I don't know. Lydia says she has tae show me something." Paislee had no clue what it was about. Brody wandered out the back door with Wallace to play fetch. "It must be something tae do with the case. It's been over a week since Felice died."

Grandpa removed his glasses and wiped the lenses with the hem of his shirt before putting them back on. "How's Corbin?"

"Lydia said he apologized but she's not interested in his family drama, even if she does love him."

"That's a lot tae ask," Grandpa conceded.

"Aye."

"Be careful, all right? No buttin' in where you dinnae belong."

"Says you?" Paislee laughed loud at that. "I'll text tae let you know what's going on."

"What were you going tae do if I wasnae here?" He tugged his beard.

"I was going tae let Brody stay home alone." Paislee held his steadfast gaze. "I don't want tae take advantage of you."

"You would never do that, and I know it. We're family." With that, Grandpa opened the fridge to get out the ingredients for cheese toasties.

Her heart couldn't be more full. "See you soon!" She waved to Brody outside and then grabbed her bag for the fifteen-minute drive to Lydia's.

She parked at the condo and went into the lobby. A new security guard in a crisp beige-and-brown uniform gestured for her to sign in. This one was older, and hopefully wiser in his position. The previous guard had been fired for his negligence. "Hi," she said. "I'm a friend of Lydia Barron's."

"Evening. May I see your license?"

"Aye." Paislee handed it over and smiled as he compared her face and signature to the sign-in sheet.

When he was satisfied, he said, "Shame aboot what happened tae Ms. Barron."

"It was. Have you heard anything about who might have done it?"

"The camera lens was disabled so we dinnae have footage, but there's a street camera that might provide answers."

Had the previous guard done that as well as taken a bribe to go home, sick? That was more than negligence, if so—he was part of the crime. "It's hard tae wait."

"We're on our toes here, so I dinnae want you tae worry aboot your friend." The guard returned Paislee's ID. "The manager told me when I started this position that it's not the first time this situation has occurred."

"Is that right?" Paislee pressed the button of the elevator to the tenth floor. "What happened?"

"An ex-husband was stalking his wife. Security caught him trying tae break in and he ended up in jail."

Could that be the case with Lydia? Doubtful, as her cheating ex had remarried. "I hope it works that way for Lydia. I mean, that whoever it is goes tae jail. Soon."

She got into the elevator, with a finger flutter at the guard.

Lydia was waiting for her in the hall as soon as Paislee stepped out to the tenth floor. "Hey! The guard texted me tae let me know." Her cheeks were gaunt, and her eyes the swirling tones of charcoal.

"You look awful." Paislee hadn't thought it was possible for her friend to appear anything but put together.

"I cannae sleep. I bake but cannae eat. I think of Corbin's favorites." Lydia rubbed her arms, and they went to her flat. "We were supposed tae be on a plane tae Germany today."

Lydia slammed the bolt as soon as the door was closed behind them, both brand new, and led the way to the dining table. An empty wine bottle was on the counter, a glass half full. Crackers. Cheese. Cookies, cakes. The messy kitchen screamed chaos.

This was so not Lydia. "Oh, hon!"

"Never mind that." Lydia exuded manic energy. "Check this oot."

Paislee turned her back on the kitchen and the dishes that overflowed the stainless-steel sinks to follow Lydia into the small home office with its grand view of the Firth.

A sleek, black state-of-the-art laptop was open to a wall of digital photos. "Sit."

Paislee perched on the edge of an office chair. "What is it?"

"Bruce's website, with all of the Smythe family photos."

"Aren't those private?"

Lydia cracked her knuckles. "Not when you have friends who

know how tae hack into them. My mate assured me this was a verra low-security site."

"Oh!"

"Bruce has access tae all kinds of chemicals that might be poisonous. We saw his darkroom. He had photos of me on his computer that he didnae want me tae see. On the beach that morning with mimosas? I hadnae invited him tae be there."

"True." Paislee studied the online gallery.

Her stomach grew sick when she saw the array of photos Bruce had of Lydia—Lydia dazzled like a shining diamond. Her smile, her head thrown back in laughter, her with her bridesmaids, the bouquets, the wedding shoot. There were pictures of the guests, and one that caught her attention was of Sheila, Jocelyn, and Felice all watching Corbin and Lydia with jealousy on their faces. That was the kind of emotion that made someone act irrationally. Jocelyn had felt left out that morning of the wedding.

The Smythes were a good-looking clan with brown hair and piercing eyes. They had on their matching plaids—even the girls were in kilts, sitting on the green lawn at Smythe Manor. The barn was in the back.

"There!" Lydia reached over her to scroll down to a series of photos. "Recognize Drew, Reggie, Corbin, and Duncan? With the other cousins? It's a family photo shoot."

"From the wall of fame at Smythe Manor. How old are they all here?"

"Probably between twelve and fifteen," Lydia said.

Paislee shrugged with confusion. "I still don't understand."

"Who is that next tae Corbin?"

A very pretty girl with ebony hair and a soft smile, thirteen, maybe, sat thigh to thigh with Corbin—but they were all scrunched together.

"Jocelyn?" It would make twisted sense.

"I don't think so. See? Jocelyn is next tae Oliver and Felice on the other side of the photo."

"Sheila, then. She's so cute! They all are."

Lydia nodded, the wheels in her mind churning hard enough for Paislee to smell smoke. "I need tae talk tae Bruce. Come with me, Paislee. You've got tae drive. I'm a wreck. I love Corbin so much." She sobbed.

Paislee wrapped her best friend in a careful hug.

Lydia's eyes swam with tears when she pulled back from the embrace. "I think Bruce is the one who broke into my flat. The pictures he has of me are verra up-close. Like, stalker close. But what if Corbin hired Bruce tae get candid wedding pictures and I'm wrong? What if the aioli *was* bad, and the cap on the valve simply lost?"

"Let's call Constable Payne. We have nothing tae lose. Maybe he found out more about the photo paper." Paislee dialed the station—which was closed. "It's after six. You have his mobile?"

"I do." Lydia retrieved her phone and pressed a button. "Dang, no answer." She exhaled with frustration as she left a message. "It's Lydia, Lydia Barron. I'm aboot tae go tae the photography studio tae talk with Bruce. I think he's stalking me!"

It was not a good idea to go to the photography studio, especially if Bruce was dangerous. Paislee recalled the hours, eleven to five, with relief. "Special Moments is closed right now, too."

"Love sucks." Lydia scowled and dropped the phone to the sofa.

"Hey . . . could this have anything tae do with your ex-husband?"

"No. He's happily married with kids." Lydia paced the space between the kitchen and couch. "I thought of that already and had Mum check. He lives in Glasgow."

Paislee snapped her fingers. "Well, what about Corbin's exes?"

"I asked Matthew, then Lincoln. They both said Corbin didnae have any significant loves as he was too busy creating his tech business."

"Lincoln?"

"He's an old dear, calling tae see how I am—the only one of that wretched family." Lydia crossed her arms at her waist. "He had a laugh at us for telling the constable aboot his plant food, but he gladly gave them a sample."

Not the sign of a guilty man.

The phone rang and Lydia answered right away. "Hello?" She put it on speaker so that Paislee could hear.

"Ms. Barron!" Constable Payne's voice boomed across the receiver. "Please *do not* go tae the photoshop! Though the pictures were printed from his place of business, Bruce Dundas has a solid alibi for the day in question."

"Who?" Lydia demanded.

"A client," the officer said, impatience in his tone. "It's been verified. Mr. Dundas didnae break into your flat."

Paislee whispered to Lydia, who repeated, "What about the powder he works with tae develop pictures in his darkroom?"

"Boric acid is not the same as strychnine."

Disappointed, Paislee leaned against Lydia's desk. At least he'd done his due diligence.

"Still used for roach killer among other things, but not what was on the Luckenbooth brooch. Stay home, Ms. Barron. Let me do my job."

Paislee sidled closer to ask, "The new security guard mentioned the camera outside the building?"

"Paislee! Why am I not surprised that you're there, too?"

"Constable, it's been nine days since Felice was killed." Paislee raised her brow at the phone, though he couldn't see it.

"I know." His voice returned to neutral.

"What if someone comes after Lydia again?" Paislee patted Lydia's shoulder.

"Like I said. Stay put."

Lydia stuck out her tongue at the phone and raised her gaze to the ceiling.

"We have a figure on CCTV. We're tracking down personal

information from the license, but that doesnae mean the person is guilty. Paislee, I thought you'd be coolheaded here."

"I am!"

"Keep your best friend with you. Watch telly. Drink wine. Eat chocolate. Butt out of police business." Constable Payne hung up.

Lydia burst into tears.

Paislee hugged Lydia, poured her a glass of wine, and settled her on the sofa with the television showing a baking program. Scrolling through her phone, she saw the picture of Lydia she'd taken right before she was going to walk down the aisle. Joy glowed in every pore. Lydia was marrying the man she loved.

She excused herself to the bathroom.

Once the door was locked, she turned on the faucet and dialed Corbin's mobile number. "Corbin? It's Paislee."

Chapter 27

"Paislee? You have Drew here," Corbin's younger brother answered.

"Oh!" Paislee brought the phone away from her ear to see the number she'd dialed. It was correct. "I was hoping tae reach Corbin."

"Och, I was aboot tae call Lydia tae see if her and Corbin are together."

"No—I'm at her flat. He's not here." Paislee paused. "Is something wrong?"

"Damn it," Drew said, frustration in his tone.

"He's not there?" Alarm tickled her senses.

"No."

"But he left his phone?"

"That's what I keep telling Da. Corbin always has his phone for business. He wouldnae forget it."

Paislee shifted on the uncomfortable toilet seat. "When did you see him last?"

"This morning over breakfast. The cousins were all here trying tae make him feel better since Lydia broke up with him. His heart is crushed." Drew had the nerve to sound accusing.

"You understand why she did it?" Paislee demanded. "You

were there! Your father made it impossible. Corbin should have stuck up for Lydia."

"Oh, he did. I thought him and Da were going tae come tae blows, but Sheila stepped between them. She's always had a way tae calm him down. Corbin, not Da. Mary was useless as usual, making it all aboot her and that stupid brooch."

"Why didn't Corbin do it when Lydia could see it?"

"Oot of respect for our father, that's why."

She sighed.

"Corbin told us all this morning over sausage and eggs that he was going tae convince Lydia tae take him back, no matter what it took."

"He was planning tae come here?" She glanced guiltily at the bathroom door. "Does he know that Lydia's place was broken into, the day of the breakup?"

Drew sucked in a breath. "No! Is she okay?"

"Aye. There were printed-out pictures of Lydia and Corbin fighting at the church, with the words tae end it scrawled in red marker, as well as cut out of a newspaper, inside on her kitchen table."

"That's awful! If Corbin had known that then nothing would have stopped him from keeping Lydia safe by his side. He thought he was protecting her from the rotten egg in our family."

Lydia knocked. "Who are you talking tae, in the loo?"

"Uh, just a sec!" She whispered to Drew, "I didn't want Lydia tae know that I was calling Corbin. Ah—game's up. Hang on. I'm putting you on speaker."

Paislee left the bathroom and Lydia stepped back, her brow arched. "What's going on?"

"I've got Drew on the line. They can't find Corbin."

"What?" Lydia's face turned ashen.

"Hi, Lydia," Drew said. "Corbin's not at the manor, I have his phone."

"Do you trust Bruce Dundas?" Lydia asked.

"Sure. He's the family photographer. He's been taking photos of us all since birth. Why?"

Lydia glared at the mobile in Paislee's palm. "Are he and Sheila an item?"

"No. He could be her grandpa!"

Lydia shook her hands to release her nerves, her back straightening. "That doesnae matter these days. I'm on my way over tae help look for Corbin. What if the attempts on me have been aboot Corbin all along?"

"Felice's death?" Drew asked, to be clear.

"Aye."

Paislee nodded. She had that goose-bumpy feeling that she got when she was on the right track.

"Check his phone calls tae see who he was talking tae last, that might help," Lydia suggested.

"Got it," Drew said.

"Can you get the family together?" Paislee imagined a clan of Smythes stomping the grounds of the property to search for Corbin.

"We're all oot at Uncle Harry's place tae plant a tree for Felice. Today would have been her birthday. Except for Sheila—she stayed behind tae wait for Corbin. I keep thinking they're going tae be here any minute."

"All right—call us when they show up, just so I dinnae worry," Lydia said.

"Same, if he ends up at your place. It's strange that Sheila didnae call."

"Is Bruce with you all?"

"Of course! And Lincoln. Though sad, this event needs to be recorded. So sayeth Laird Garrison Smythe." Drew's tone was self-mocking.

"Why does your da not like me?" Lydia asked.

"He does! He's trying tae appease Mary, aboot that damn brooch." Drew's voice lowered. "I'll tell you a secret, Lydia, and Paislee, that will make the arrogance of the Smythe Clan a wee bit more tolerable. You willnae find this in the biography, either. Lincoln and his wife refused tae put it in their documentary. Oliver might, though."

"That Lincoln and Florene were cousins?" Paislee asked.

"No," Drew said. "That's nothing compared tae this."

She and Lydia stared at each other.

"The grand Smythe fortune—and it is grand, ladies—was built off the first 'laird' Smythe, who was a shyster in the diamond industry. Scammed folks into investing in diamonds that werenae the grade promised. But he was smart, old Seamus Smythe, and got out with piles of cash. The others in the scheme were greedy and that was their downfall in the end."

"Oh . . ." Paislee said.

Lydia's face grew red with anger. "And he acts so much better than everyone else!"

"I know, I know. If we can convince you tae join us again, and give us another chance, it should help, eh?"

"We need tae find Corbin first. And there is no guarantee!" Lydia stomped her foot. "Oh! Oh, all right. Thank you, Drew. Let's keep in touch!" She pressed the off button. "Can you believe it?" Lydia shook Paislee, her movements frantic. "Mental, all of it."

Paislee gestured to the bathroom. "You should brush your teeth, my sweet, so we can go in search of Corbin."

"Where tae begin?" Lydia twisted her hands before her.

"You brush—I have a few ideas. When you're finished, join me at the computer."

Lydia started to turn but then stopped. "I cannae believe you went behind my back tae call Corbin."

"I'm sorry." Paislee squeezed Lydia's fingers. "I did it for you . . ."

Lydia returned the pressure with understanding. "What were you going tae say?"

"I wanted tae know where his guts were that he would let his da walk all over you both like that, and ruin a chance at happiness. You love each other."

"We do! We do." Lydia swiped her cheeks and rushed into the bathroom, slamming the door. She shrieked. "Paislee Ann! What happened tae my face?"

Paislee knew she had about five minutes and hurried to the laptop. She scrolled through the photos taken by Bruce.

She was wrong—Lydia was ready in three minutes, a knit cap over her hair despite it being June. Her teeth were brushed, her cheeks shiny. "What?"

Paislee pointed to the Smythe Manor and the pristine lawn. The rocks where the photos were taken, and the barn behind. "I say we go tae the house. If Corbin is the target of the 'curse,' I bet he's around there somewhere."

"That makes sense. Hurry, Paislee. It's time tae find Corbin and fight *for* us, not walk away."

"That's my girl."

Paislee pushed her comfort zone as she drove fast toward the manor. Who was Corbin close to? Who might want something from the third Smythe brother? Images flitted across her brain. She smacked her palm to the steering wheel. "I know who it is. Someone very, very close to him loves him."

"Rosebud?"

"No."

"Hyacinth? If you think she's been secretly in love with Corbin, just . . . ew."

"No. Think cousin. A kissing cousin." She glanced at Lydia, remembering how Bruce had watched Sheila and Jocelyn. Had he suspected something? Caught something on his camera? "At first I thought it might be Jocelyn, but she was broken up over her sister's death. That's when I remembered how Sheila urged Jocelyn tae accuse you of stealing the brooch yourself. She's covering her tracks."

"Sheila?" Lydia pressed her hand to her stomach, her face pale. Paislee screeched to a gravelly halt before the house. Her best friend seemed doubtful.

"The picture of them that Bruce took—their fingers are touching. Drew said Sheila has always had a way tae calm Corbin down. Sheila had just arrived at the manor before us the day of the breakin! She was jealous because she loves Corbin."

"That's just . . . wrong."

"It's not illegal, and it used tae be quite common. The stigma is a reason tae hide it." It made perfect, twisted sense.

Norbert opened the door with a surprised expression. "Ma'am?"

"Have you seen Corbin?" Lydia raced up the steps to the threshold.

"No. I told that tae Drew and the others already. He's still missing?"

"Aye." Lydia gripped the startled butler by the lapels. "Where is Sheila?"

"She was looking for Corbin oot back." Norbert pulled free of her grasp and brushed his lapels down.

The barn. The scene of every happy Smythe event. Having been in the house before she knew the way to the back door and the rear of the property. "Will you call the police station? Ask for Constable Payne!"

Norbert pulled his mobile from his pocket and dialed even as he followed Paislee and Lydia to the back exit.

Lydia burst ahead of Paislee. The dogs barked manically from the sunroom. Had they been kept out of harm's way, or meant to not interfere? Norbert stayed inside, talking to the police.

Paislee and Lydia rushed outside to a gorgeous landscape of summer trees and paddocks with horses in the distance. The barn was a hundred yards back from the house. A horse neighed from a paddock, the scene calm. Serene.

Paislee halted. What if she was wrong? They'd been wrong about Bruce. And Mary. And Lincoln. Her intuition urged her forward. Experience suggested caution.

Lydia put her finger to her lips to signal for quiet and whispered, "I think he's here."

Paislee turned her ringer off even as she had Zeffer's number on speed dial in the event something went sideways. Did she trust him a wee bit more than Constable Payne? Perhaps.

Lydia gently stepped on the dirt and gravel, trying not to make a sound. Paislee walked on her tiptoes.

They peered into the barn. Dance lights had been strung up as if for a party. Pop music from two decades ago played on a radio, coming from the loft.

There was no sign of Corbin or Sheila on the main floor.

This could all be a big mistake. She heard rustling above.

Paislee led the way up the ladder, her nose twitching from the hay. The loft was sturdy wood planks covered in straw.

"If you just admit that you love me, then this can all go away." A high-pitched voice traveled across the open space.

Paislee peeked over a hay bale to see Sheila in the kilt she'd worn the day of the photo shoot when they'd been teenagers. The white knit top was tight. A heart-shaped Luckenbooth brooch was pinned to a dried thistle above her breast, like a corsage for a home-coming dance.

She texted Zeffer to hurry to Smythe Manor and gave a warning headshake to Lydia. Corbin's hands and ankles were bound, his lips covered with a piece of Smythe tartan. There was a line of blood at his temple and the mounds of straw and dirt made it clear he'd struggled.

Whisky tumblers were half-filled, and a bottle of cheap Scotch was on a hay bale being used as a table.

Lydia ignored Paislee's warning and simply reacted to seeing her lover in harm. "Corbin! Sheila!"

Her best friend bounded by her with only her mobile as a weapon. Paislee glanced around the loft for a pitchfork or something. A shovel at least?

There!

She followed Lydia once she grabbed the handle of a . . . scythe. Oh, she did not want to use this.

Corbin was facing Sheila and didn't see Lydia, but Sheila turned, and showed no alarm at the tableau. If anything, she was annoyed by the interruption.

"Go away, Lydia. I warned you already. Corbin is mine. He gave me this pin." Sheila's ebony hair was a disaster, and she had bits of straw caught in it.

From the brawling with Corbin?

Sheila pulled the Scottish knife from her kilt and brandished it before her. "Take one more step, either of you, and I'll slit his throat and then my own. We will be together forever. Soul mates, right, Corbin?"

Corbin shook his head no so wildly that his body started to slip from the hay bale.

Paislee raised the scythe and stepped around Lydia. "Put it down. What are you doing here?"

"Claiming my love." Sheila's eyes glittered with passionate madness.

"Your actions killed Felice," Paislee said, trying to use reason. "Please put that knife down and let Corbin go. Your family has already been through so much!"

Sheila winced at the mention of Felice. "I didnae mean for my cuz tae get hurt. Lydia was supposed tae heed the warning."

"Lydia might have died."

Sheila waved the dirk and gestured to a forgotten shelf with rat poison and mole poison covered in cobwebs. "The stash of strychnine I found was old and probably not deadly. I wanted tae scare you, Lydia."

"Please, Sheila. Put down the knife," Paislee said. "Felice is dead!"

"She tripped and fell. Stupid Rosebud thought it would be a lark tae steal the brooch and spread the rumor aboot the curse. Felice thought she was helping me." Sheila's voice thickened. There was an open window to their right to unload the hay to the cleared ground below.

Corbin spat out the plaid fabric, but it remained caught on his lip. "Murderer!"

Sheila sucked in a breath and walked behind Corbin. "We can start over in another country, Corbin, just you and me. I used tae dream aboot our wedding." She shifted and brought the knife to his throat. "But I can see that you've changed."

"I hate you for this," Corbin said. "I always will."

"You loved me!" Strands of dark hair straggled down her back. "You told me so!"

"Never in love . . . we were kids!" Corbin struggled against his bonds.

Paislee exchanged a pitchfork in a bale for the scythe. She got behind Corbin while Lydia stepped toward Sheila.

Sheila couldn't watch all three of them, and Paislee gave the woman's calves a sharp poke with the tines.

"Hey!" Sheila whirled.

Lydia kicked out and the dirk in Sheila's clasp went flying. Corbin rolled toward the scythe, and put his bonds over the blade, rubbing back and forth until the fabric around his wrists loosened and he was able to grab the weapon. Paislee held the pitchfork out toward Sheila as the woman ran toward her, but Sheila barely slowed. Paislee shifted so as not to kill her.

Lydia had snatched the dirk and cut Corbin's bonds around his ankles, helping him stand upright.

He kissed Lydia, then lunged for Sheila. The two wrestled, slipping and sliding on the hay.

Corbin had Sheila's arms behind her back. Sirens could be heard coming toward the manor.

Sheila's gaze was full of panic as she realized that she was not going to get away with murder. She was not going to marry Corbin. Her deceptions had all been for nothing.

Paislee glanced out the open barn window as DI Zeffer ran around the house, followed by Constable Payne, to the barn.

"Paislee?" Zeffer shouted.

"Up here!"

Hands grabbed the ladder, and she knew help was on the way. Corbin was safe, and Sheila would go to jail.

It seemed that the Smythe cousin also realized the end result because Sheila broke free and threw herself out the window to the hard-packed dirt below. Paislee gasped and peered out.

Her neck was broken. Just like Felice. Dead from this barn, like Magda, centuries ago.

Just maybe, Paislee believed in a curse.

Chapter 28

Paislee and Lydia waited at the manor as the EMTs checked Corbin and taped the wound at his temple. He was told to rest after giving the constable his statement.

Zeffer had disappeared without a goodbye. That man.

"I'm sairy that it came tae this," Constable Payne said to Lydia, Corbin, and Paislee before the barn door. Norbert watched the backyard from the house, angst for the Smythes on his face. He was family, too. What a complicated word *family* was.

"I didn't put it together until we were on our way here tae search for Corbin, and we called you right away," Paislee said. "I still wasn't sure."

The constable pursed his lips. "You werenae completely wrong about Bruce. He admitted tae following Lydia, and possibly crossing a line. Sheila called him on it the day of the wedding at the manor. Made him look a little harder at how she'd been acting around Corbin."

Paislee remembered their heated conversation. "What did he find?"

"He'd gotten shots of Sheila staring at Corbin like Corbin looks at Lydia. Sheila had been at Special Moments the day before the break-in, printing oot photos. Bruce thinks Sheila set him up for that. The original security guard at Lydia's condo admitted that the person who paid him was a woman, but he never saw her face."

"Sheila!" Paislee said.

"Probably," the constable said. "That's not proof."

"It's over though, now." Lydia staggered into Paislee.

Corbin grasped Lydia's hand. "Stay with me?"

Lydia pulled free. Paislee elbowed her bestie, conveying with an arched brow that they'd come all this way to save the man she loved and now here he was—and so was Lydia. Both of them alive by a hair.

"All right." Lydia caressed Corbin's jaw with gentle fingers. "Just tae talk."

Corbin stared deep into Lydia's eyes. "Thank you, my love."

Constable Payne answered a phone call and ambled away, returning quickly. He touched the rim of his officer's hat. "The velvet box was in Sheila's bedroom at her parents' house. The wooden box was what she'd kept her keepsakes in, and that included the silver Luckenbooth from you, Corbin."

"It was for a school dance. She had no partner and I felt bad for her. Family helps family." His face reddened with embarrassment. "I loved her like a cousin. I wasnae in love with her. We kissed. Once. After a lot of whisky. I thought we were friends."

Lydia patted his back. "It's all right. You didnae know Sheila had feelings for you."

"She'd moved home?" Corbin asked. "I thought she had her own place with her boyfriend."

"Her mother said they'd broken up and was there until she got on her feet again. Sheila spent a lot of time recalling the past, when she was happy. Here at the barn."

"I'm so sairy," Lydia said to Corbin. "You were the target all this time."

"No, Lydia, you were the target," Paislee clarified. "Corbin was the endgame."

"Aye. That sums it up." Constable Payne, finished speaking

with them, walked over to the paramedics as they were ready to leave with Sheila's body.

"I'm off, then." Paislee noted how close the couple stayed, hip to hip. "Lydia, text me, let me know how and where you are? You're always welcome at our place."

"Ta. Drive safe and tell Angus and Brody I love them."

"I will." Paislee smiled as Corbin kept his arm around Lydia to anchor her there. Norbert led her out to where she'd parked, and she left with a nod of goodbye. The natty butler was professional, she'd give him that.

Paislee maneuvered around the police car to the driveway and headed home where Brody and Grandpa waited for her. Cheese toasties had worn off, so they'd ordered pizza. Shaw family heaven.

Saturday morning, it was Paislee's turn to drive the boys to the football game. Since it was also Grandpa's day off, he'd cheer the team on, too. She hoped to meet Brody's crush, equally hoping the romance would fizzle over the summer. Eleven was too young, in her mind!

As she packed snacks, and a portable water bowl for Wallace, she realized she still hadn't looked at the tickets from Hamish for graduation. Who would the special guest be?

She wiped her hands on a dish towel and searched for the envelope in her bag before she forgot again.

Opening the flap, she pulled out graduation tickets. Four. Good. If Lydia wanted to come . . . or Corbin. Never mind—focus!

Special guest: Tilda Swinton. Fabulous. The woman was talented and generous within the community. The kids would love it.

A blue envelope with *Paislee* written in neat penmanship fell to the table. Her heart fluttered and her stomach did a whirl. For some reason Hamish's disappointed brown gaze came to mind.

She gulped and opened the envelope. Inside was a beautiful card with roses on the front. She flipped it open and read, *Can't get you off my mind. Brody will be finished with school in three weeks. I'd like for us to have dinner the second weekend in July. I hope we can start our friendship again. Hamish.*

"Whatchya got?" Grandpa asked.

She squealed and brought the card to her chest. "Nothing!"

It slid from her fingers to the floor. Grandpa picked it up and saw the roses. He winked. "Nothing?"

"That's right." Paislee held out her hand and he put the card in her damp palm.

"You cannae hide behind Brody forever, lass."

"I'm not!"

He hummed and switched on the kettle. "Suit yourself."

She changed the subject. "Any word from Craigh?"

"He called this morning. Zeffer put him up at a hotel with free breakfast. I guess he's leaving today. Wants tae see us."

Though the words were casual she felt the emotion behind them. "Brody, too?"

"Aye. But he'll be in disguise . . . going by the name of Logan McFee."

"Oh!"

"He and the DI thought it best if Brody didnae know that he was Craigh, at least until a few years have passed and we know there is no longer danger from the Norwegian oil riggers. We'll see what happens."

"If you're sure." She would do whatever was needed to keep her son safe, and that meant ignoring the uncle she'd just met.

"They're coming tae the game so Craigh can watch for a while. Is that all right?"

"Of course. Best tae meet him somewhere neutral." *When he's not trying to break in or shake his da around for the flash drive.*

Paislee raced upstairs to put the card from Hamish on her vanity and peeked in the mirror. Her cheeks were pink and her light blue eyes glittered. What should she say to Hamish?

Get on with it, Paislee. You have too much to do to be daydreaming.

★ ★ ★

The Shaws and Edwyn arrived at the ballpark, the boys so excited about the game that there was no talk of girls or the upcoming dance.

Paislee brought out a tub of cheese sticks, crisps, and apples to the sideline, greeting the coach. The young man was in his early twenties, lean, and had a nice balance of work and play without yelling at the kids. Taught good sportsmanship—which she approved of—more than the need for a gold medal.

"If we win this, we're in the championship," he said, nodding his thanks for the snacks. "If we lose, we tie and will have another game."

"Brody is very excited. Edwyn, too!"

The coach nodded at the boys all warming up on the sidelines. "They're both pretty guid players. I hope they continue next year."

"Me too." Busy meant less time to get into trouble.

Paislee and Grandpa started off in their foldout camp chairs on the sidelines, but within ten minutes were up on their feet to cheer their team. Craigh—now Logan—joined them at halftime. Logan's disguise consisted of dyed light brown hair and a scruffy goatee and mustache that had to be pressed on. His shirt was decorated with flamingos, and he wore flip-flops.

"Brody, this is Logan, a friend of Grandpa's."

Brody shook the stranger's hand. "Nice tae meet you." Her son was polite, and that was all she asked for as she compared the tall man who now only faintly resembled her father as he chucked Brody on the arm. His brown eyes were blue with contacts.

Wallace gave the man's ankles a sniff and growled. Two faded teeth marks were a souvenir for Craigh to remember.

He moved away from the pup. Brody now eyed him warily.

"And you," Logan said. "You've got an amazin' left foot."

Brody gave a wary smile. "You think so?"

"Oh, aye. I was watching that run you did, passing tae your mate for a score. Brilliant." The two high-fived.

The coach whistled for them all to get back to the circle.

"Thanks. See ya!" Brody ran off.

"You were watching?" Grandpa asked.

"By the trees in the shade with Zeffer."

She looked back and there the DI was, in his blue suit, lounging like he had not a care in the world.

Paislee lifted her hand.

Logan/Craigh stayed facing forward. "Just in case anybody is watching us, old stick in the mud doesnae want tae be seen with the new me. Zeffer doesnae want it tae be a giveaway, and lead the riggers tae you. Bloke is brilliant. Annoying but brilliant."

She'd learned that in the last year since he'd come to Nairn. Because of Craigh, as it turned out. Now that the Shaws were sorted, would Zeffer move on to solve another crime?

What did she care?

Grandpa nudged her and she focused back on the game as the boys streamed to the field.

"Did you play, as a lad?" Paislee asked. Her da had loved the sport as well.

"At school, aye," Logan/Craigh said. "Not extracurricular."

"You look like my dad, a bit."

Logan/Craigh's face saddened. "Aye. Sorry. He died in a fishing accident?"

Paislee blinked. "He did."

"Hey. Aboot that whole Christmas card thing, mea culpa. If you get a card from Key West with a sloshed snowman, it'll be from me."

Grandpa's lips twitched.

"I gotta go." Logan/Craigh gestured over his shoulder toward where Zeffer waited. "I promised just a few minutes and it's been longer than that. Paislee, you're a guid lass."

She accepted the hug from her uncle and gave him an extra squeeze.

Grandpa hugged him, hard but quick.

"I regret a lot of things, but most of all, that I didnae know you sooner, Da. You're a special man, Angus Shaw."

And then, Logan/Craigh wandered away from the game, as nonchalant as you please. Wallace stared at him until he was out of sight.

She tucked her arm through Grandpa's to make sure he stayed at her side.

"Will I see him again?" he muttered.

"Aye. I think you will. If Logan doesn't come visit us, then we can take a trip tae America. Maybe stop in and see my mum while we're at it." Forgiveness was important in relationships. If Gran had forgiven Angus, she wouldn't have been heartbroken and alone at the end of her days. She'd felt Gran's love around them earlier. She hoped that Lydia would forgive Corbin.

They turned their attention to the game. The boys won, and they celebrated their victory with ice cream—a perfect summer day.

Epilogue

"Mum, are we there yet?" Brody asked for the tenth time.

Paislee read the clock on the dash of the Juke. She drove, Grandpa had shotgun, and Brody and Wallace were in the back. "Three minutes!"

"We cannae be late," Brody said.

They'd left Nairn this morning at nine to be at Gretna Green to surprise Lydia, all set up by Corbin and his baby brother, Drew, at two thirty. The trip was supposed to be around four hours but that wasn't including pit stops to use the restroom. Yes, the male passengers in the car could all use the great outdoors; rustic wasn't Paislee's style.

They'd all dressed in their Sunday best, but nothing too fancy. Corbin would be arriving with Lydia, who believed they were on the train to see the sights before going to Germany to use the tickets as rescheduled (for the third time).

Since they'd reconnected, Corbin had showered Lydia with love, apologies, flowers, and more true love. Lydia had told Paislee that was enough. She didn't want marriage.

Who needed it anymore?

Paislee parked at two thirty on the nose. "We're here!"

Lydia's parents, Sophie and Alistair Barron, were also there. Drew would be the only one attending on his brother's side, and that was only because Corbin required a family witness to prove he meant what he'd said about Lydia coming first.

"Hello!" Grandpa greeted the Barrons. "Here we are again."

"Nice tae see you all," Sophie said. "And Wallace! What a cutie. And that knitted collar is just perfect tae carry the ring. I should have brought my Moxie. Do you think Lydia will want the Luckenbooth pin?"

Paislee shrugged. "Lydia hasn't been excited about marriage. Can't blame her. I'm hoping she'll accept the ring she'd tossed back at Corbin."

"Oh, but Corbin loves her so much!" Sophie wrung her hands.

"And Lydia loves him." Paislee brushed a lock of errant hair down on Brody's forehead. "Take Wallace for a walk, and then bring him back tae get ready."

Brody ducked away and hurried Wallace out of sight to a grassy patch. The red from the Smythe tartan on his leash and harness was quite striking against his black fur. It hadn't taken her long to knit and she'd created a new pattern to sell at Cashmere Crush. Designer dog wear.

Paislee and Alistair each received a text that Corbin and Lydia were five minutes out—to take their positions inside the office of Gretna Green.

Sophie tied the diamond to Wallace's collar. Wallace puffed his furry chest as if he knew he had an important part to play. Brody grinned and opened the door.

Paislee was first inside and saw the historic anvil that folks had been getting married over for hundreds of years. She had no idea what Lydia would say when Corbin proposed. She thought him awfully brave to risk it, actually.

Corbin claimed love made him brave. Or dumb. Either way, *Lydia* was his soul mate.

The car he'd rented from the train station arrived. Drew hopped out from the back seat, in gray denim. Lydia and Corbin each exited from the front seats. The door was partially open.

"Sairy, Lyd," Drew was saying, "but I've never been here.

What if we can find a record from some of the other Smythes? The guid ones," he joked.

"We do have some." Corbin's tone cajoled. "If you go back far enough every tree has a few bad apples."

"Your tree started off bent," Lydia countered, but Paislee could tell she was teasing. "It's fine that we stop. I just dinnae want tae be late tae check into the hotel for tomorrow's flight."

"We willnae!" Corbin assured her.

Drew widened the door to Gretna Green.

Lydia and Corbin, arm in arm, entered. Candles had been lit for romantic atmosphere. Lydia blinked to bring them all into focus as they clustered near the anvil.

Wallace, off his lead, trotted proudly toward Lydia.

"Sit," Brody said. The pup did, as noble as you please.

"What's this?" Lydia stooped to pat Wallace. "Mum? Da?" She sucked in a breath when her fingers caught the ring on Wallace's collar. "Paislee, Brody, and Angus." She whirled to Corbin. "You've brought my family here."

Corbin dropped to one knee and untied the engagement ring she'd thrown the day she'd broken up with him. "I love you, Lydia Barron, with all of my heart."

"No, Corbin," Lydia said, shaking her head.

Paislee's chest ached.

Corbin didn't move but peered at Lydia with love they could all feel. See. And when he spoke, hear. "I love you."

Lydia tugged him up. They fit so perfectly together, like yin and yang. "I dinnae think marriage is a guid idea. Not for us! We don't need it."

"I've brought people to help me plead my case," Corbin said. "Your parents have the kind of marriage I want for us. That I know we can have. One of trust. Sharing. Love."

"It takes work, but you both know that. You've been through tragedy." Alistair folded his hands over his slightly rounded belly. "Now, daughter, I pray you can embrace the joy of a loving union."

Paislee's grandpa cleared his throat and rocked back on his feet. "Tae forgive is divine."

Sophie watched Lydia with hope in her expression.

Paislee's eyes welled. "Take a chance, Lydia. You are well loved, *cherished*, by this man."

Lydia bowed her head and glanced at Drew. "No offense, it's the man's family I object tae."

Drew tilted his head. "We're verra sorry."

"You're the nice one!" Lydia kept her hand on Corbin's arm.

They all chuckled low, but tension was a thick fog in the room. Corbin pleaded with Lydia, his gaze intense. "I promise that I will love you until my dying breath. In fact, I've brought Drew here today tae witness. I dinnae believe in curses but just in case, the brooch has been melted down and the gold donated tae the church. I want tae be with you, Lydia. That's all. I will always choose you first. And if you willnae take my name . . ."

Alistair stepped forward. "I've offered ours."

Lydia's mouth gaped as she stared from her da to Corbin. After a moment of inner deliberation, she tossed her curls and gave them all a dazzling smile. "I accept your proposal, Corbin." She grinned wide. "I'll be content if we both take a hyphen. Barron-Smythe."

They all applauded, and the minister made his presence known. "Are we ready?"

"Aye!" Paislee kissed her best friend's cheek. "Are you okay, for real? I can get us out of here . . . say the word!"

"I know you would." Lydia hugged her close. "You are the sister of my heart. Thank you for not letting me give up on love."

There were all kinds of love, and family. Paislee was blessed to be surrounded by it. A pair of brown eyes clashed with a pair of sea-glass green, but she buried both to be in this moment.

Lydia and Corbin joined hands, and this time, Paislee knew that no matter what came their way, their love would be forever.

Visit our website at
KensingtonBooks.com
to sign up for our newsletters, read
more from your favorite authors, see
books by series, view reading group
guides, and more!

BOOK **CLUB**
BETWEEN **THE** **CHAPTERS**

Become a Part of Our
Between the Chapters Book Club
Community and Join the Conversation

Betweenthechapters.net